To Jaron,

Sunburned
The Solar Flare that Silenced the Internet

By Jake Blake

Jake Blake

Copyright © 2012 Morgan Online Media

All rights reserved.

No part of this book may be reproduced in any form without prior written permission from the publisher.

Published in the United States by Morgan Online Media, P.O. Box 550, Toledo, WA 98591

www.morganonlinemedia.com

First Edition

ISBN 978-0-9858081-2-9

All space photos are courtesy of NASA.
Cover design and illustrations by John Morgan.

For Emily

Author's Note

In early September of 1859, a massive solar storm slammed into the Earth, severely disrupting early electrical and telegraph communication systems. That storm is known as the Carrington Event, named after the English astronomer and observer Richard Christopher Carrington.

"Sunburned" is a science-fiction thriller that imagines an identical solar storm, set in our modern, highly connected and interconnected world. This story bounces around to many locations on and above the Earth, but everything takes place in a linear fashion. Specific descriptions of mathematics, science, physics, astronomy, finance, seamanship and viral communications are as accurate and realistic as possible.

While many of the corporations, buildings and merchandise described in this book exist in our world, the characters and scenarios within are fictitious, and any resemblance to real persons living or dead is purely coincidental.

Neither the author nor publisher received compensation or special favors from any of the corporations mentioned within. Apparent product placements are intended to convey value to the characters and to the reader, and do not constitute an endorsement or disparagement any of this fine merchandise.

Religion also plays a role in this story, as it does in life. Some of the characters rely on the interpretation of ancient texts to explain unfolding events, while others rely solely on their understanding of scientific theories and facts. Many characters combine the two, along with their own personal history and experiences, to develop a worldview that makes sense to them.

In the year 2014, billions of people had virtually unlimited and interactive access to all human knowledge, but most of us took this power for granted. A massive solar flare and coronal mass ejection temporarily severed these connections, and the world was forced to adapt. Enormous amounts of data were lost forever during this blackout, which is why this story took nearly 10 years to write.

Even as I write this introduction, another solar maximum approaches.

Jake Blake
Toledo, Washington, U.S.A.
July 9, 2024

Jake Blake

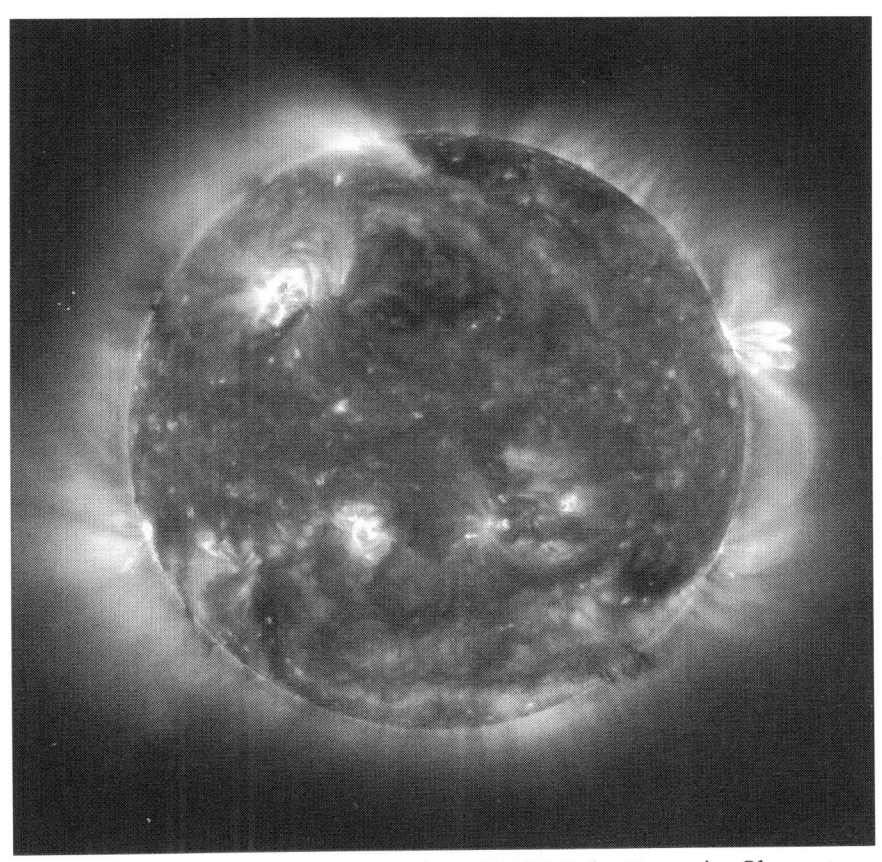

photo: NASA Solar Dynamics Observatory

Part One: Hubris

Chapter 1

NEW YORK CITY - 110 Central Park South, penthouse
In the near future, July 9, 2014, 5:33 a.m.

A narrow beam of light cut through the darkness of the bedroom, resting on the closed eyelid of a sleeping man. The eyeball twitched twice, then opened to reveal a deep, blue iris.

Adam Morgan woke up at dawn with a strange feeling in his stomach. He turned to his left and saw the soft, fluffy brown hair of the woman sleeping next to him, her naked back exposed from beneath the silky white sheets of the king-sized bed. The sunlight was just beginning to fill the bedroom and a ray of light was dancing on the few blonde highlights of the woman's hair.

He started to sit up, but felt a spasm of pain from his stomach. Then the gag reflex.

Adam quickly rolled out of bed and ducked through the bathroom door, heading straight for the toilet. Kneeling on the cold, marble floor in front of the toilet, his whole body heaved for a moment, then purged.

***

At that exact moment, another purge was happening worlds away that would change the lives of everyone on Earth. On the surface of the sun, approximately 150 million kilometers or 93 million miles away, an unusually large coil of magnetic energy erupted, sending a solar flare toward Earth at the speed of light and an enormous coronal mass ejection at speeds approaching 3,000 km/sec. In approximately 14 hours, Earth would experience a severe electro-magnetic storm, the likes of which the planet had not seen in more than 150 years.

***

A cold sweat rushed over Adam's naked, muscular body. Admittedly, he felt a bit better.

He flushed the toilet and looked in the mirror above the marble-covered double sink.

Here before him was the reflection of a 41-year-old white male, handsome in a slightly boyish way, almost entirely bald but for the black stubble on his face, neck and the sides and back of his smooth, well-shaped head. He was of medium height and in pretty good physical shape, but he hadn't seen his personal trainer in a few weeks and wasn't feeling his best.

"Are you alright in there?" asked the woman from the bedroom.

Adam turned from the mirror and stepped into the master bedroom. Hanging on the main wall opposite the bed was a large oil painting of the dreamscape "Temptation of St. Anthony," painted by Salvador Dali in 1946.

"Stomach ache," he said. "I feel nauseous this morning."

As he walked to the bed, Adam almost stepped on a large pile of diamonds sitting on the floor. He picked up one of the diamonds and the rest followed, attached together by a thin wire. He set the glittering diamonds and precious gems in a heap on top of the nightstand.

The woman was gazing up at him from the bed with sleepy, blue eyes. She was young, fair-skinned, extremely fit and quite attractive without makeup. Her lips were pouty and her eyebrows were a thick, dark brown. She smiled, revealing a wide mouth of big, straight teeth.

"Tee many martoonies?" she teased.

"I'll be OK," he said, watching as her leg slowly moved beneath the bedsheets. "I'm sorry I woke you. It's still pretty early. You can go back to sleep if you'd like."

Natasha closed her eyes and smiled, rolling back onto her left side. Adam shook his head slightly and could hardly believe he was married to such a beautiful person. He looked down at his ring finger and admired the simple-looking gold band that he and Natasha each wore.

She's just 25, he thought, *and already on the A-list. I'm a very lucky man.*

He opened the shades to the bedroom window to reveal a sliding glass door and small balcony. As Adam stepped out into the warm, morning air, he thought about their wedding two months earlier. They had been married at a private villa in the Bahamas, surrounded by 200 of their closest friends, family members and business associates. The party had cost a small fortune, of course, but felt like a dream. Even if it was a dream, he wanted to go back.

He stepped into the bathroom and turned on the shower. Everything in the bathroom was either white marble or silver-plated, giving the room a cold, hard feel. As Adam stepped into the rectangular glass box of his shower and began to lather up, he briefly thought about remodeling the bathroom, but then he thought of all the red tape involved. He turned on his waterproof electric razor and shaved his face, neck and the rest of his head. Having washed and rinsed, he turned the shower knob to cold for a few seconds, then off.

Stepping out of the steamy glass box, he grabbed a white cotton bathrobe and strode out of the bathroom. Turning the corner, he walked down the spiral staircase to the lower level, picked up his smartphone resting on a coffee table and stepped outside onto the penthouse terrace. *Another beautiful summer morning,* he thought.

Adam looked northeast at his spectacular view of Central Park. Far below his perch on the 28th floor, he could barely see joggers and dog walkers scurrying about like ants. *A different life,* he thought. The shady green trees of the park swayed in the morning breeze, capped with a clear, blue sky. He punched a few buttons on his smartphone. It was 5:41 a.m., and according to the weather app, it was already a balmy 74 degrees Fahrenheit, or about 23 degrees Celsius. Meteorologists were predicting another record-breaking day. *This would be a good time to get out of the city,* he thought.

Just then, a brilliant flash of white light exploded across the morning sky, coming from the east. The atmosphere was instantly brighter, the colors even more vivid. *Who turned up the lights?* he wondered. *It feels more like 8 a.m.* He checked the time on his smartphone again, using his left hand to shield his eyes from the sun. His smartphone was turned off. *Something's not right*, he thought, as he turned on the small, electronic device.

All at once, car alarms across the city began to honk and blare.

Adam felt another stomach spasm and ran for the bathroom.

Chapter 2

NEW YORK CITY - Sheepshead Bay, Brooklyn, 6 a.m.
TIME TO SOLAR IMPACT: 13 hours, 32 minutes

A shrieking alarm pierced the morning stillness. A rough and calloused hand reached from a nearby bed and slapped the snooze button. The alarm clock was silent again. A few seconds later, another different alarm shrieked from outside the apartment.

"Goddam car alarms," the man grumbled, pulling the red cotton sheets off his sweaty body and sitting at the edge of his bed. The car alarm continued.

Frank Rosario got up and walked to the window of his second-floor apartment. Across the street, a blue hybrid electric car was completely flipping out, flashing its lights and baying its horn like a doomsday alarm. The tone sounded a bit like an ambulance, then changed to a steady, two-toned ringing. It changed once again into a loud blatting, fire-truck noise, before returning to the first tone pattern and repeating the cycle. The sequence of warnings coming from the unoccupied car repeated six or seven times, despite the clear absence of thieves, other nearby vehicles or pedestrians of any kind. Eventually the alarm switched itself off. *Doomsday has been canceled*, he thought. *Another false alarm.*

The wind-up alarm clock on the dresser began shrieking again.

"Yeah, I got it. I'm up," Frank said, turning off the alarm.

Frank squeezed into his tiny bathroom and turned on the hot water for the sink. His reflection revealed a 33-year-old, slightly handsome, dark-skinned face, with tired brown eyes and a brush of gray hair on the sides. He splashed hot water on his face, lathered up some shaving cream from a can and painted on a white shaving-cream beard. He took his disposable razor and made a few quick passes — first with the grain, then perpendicular to — shaving his face and neck quickly and without thinking.

After a minute, the hot water from the sink had steamed up the mirror, obscuring his reflection. He finished shaving from memory, still on auto-pilot. Frank turned off the sink and turned on the shower. Past experience told him the building's hot water supply diminished after about 7 a.m. and was non-existent after 9 a.m. when the beauty parlor downstairs opened. Hot water wasn't as important in the middle of the summer, but his carefully followed daily routines tended to make his days more predictable.

Stepping out of the shower a few minutes later, he turned on the radio and toweled off.

"Gonna be a hot one today, folks," the radio announcer said in a cheery voice. "If you're working indoors, I hope you've got air conditioning today, 'cause it's supposed to hit 110 degrees in the city. If you're out at the beach, be sure to wear plenty of sunblock."

Frank had just toweled himself dry but was already wet with sweat again. He decided to air dry this time and walked about his apartment with his blue towel wrapped around his waist. There was no television or cable, no computer or Internet and no land-line telephone. On the coffee table was the latest issue of *National Geographic*, *Fortune* magazine and several international yachting and sailing magazines including *Cruising World*, *Sailing*, *Sailing World* and *Yachting*.

Frank looked out the window at the beach. The morning sun seemed extra bright, bathing the boats in the marina in a harsh, twittering light. Leaning forward and craning his neck to the right, Frank saw his office, a 41-foot sailing yacht named "Reciprocity," bobbing gently in the bay. *Can't beat the commute*, he thought, as he rubbed sunblock on his neck and shoulders.

Chapter 3

NEW YORK CITY - 110 Central Park South, 6:30 a.m.

Adam was sitting outside on the large terrace flipping through *The Wall Street Journal, The New York Times* and *The Financial Times* newspapers when Natasha came outside with breakfast. She was wearing a tight-fitting, two-piece exercise outfit and carried an espresso cup and saucer in one hand and a small bowl of fresh berries and plain yogurt in the other.

"I brought you some coffee," she said, sitting in the chair next to Adam at the glass-top table and setting the espresso directly in front of him. "Are you feeling any better?"

Adam looked up from his newspapers and admired his young wife. She seemed to look adorable in just about anything, he thought. This morning she was wearing a pink cotton zip-up sweat shirt and matching pink cotton sweat pants with a draw-string waist. The pants had something written on the legs in large, silver letters he couldn't quite make out, and her pedicured feet were bare on the stone tile floor. He was still wearing his bathrobe.

"Thank you for asking. I wish I felt as good as you look," he said with a slight smile, reaching for the espresso. "I saw a strange flash in the sky this morning, and then my phone went off. Your brother had better not be up to any of his old tricks," he said with a wink.

"I'll ask him," Natasha said, flashing him one of her million-dollar smiles before spooning a small bite of raspberries and yogurt into her mouth.

Natasha's brother Aleksandr had nearly ruined their wedding with a practical joke, but the crisis was easily averted due to his quick thinking. *He would have to know about the flash*, Adam thought, looking up at the sky. *Smart Aleks.*

"Do you have a shoot today?" he asked.

"Yes, from 8:30 to noon," she said. "I'm going downstairs to work out for a bit first."

The apartment building at 110 Central Park South was technically a condop, a hybrid of a condominium and a cooperative. He owned the two-story penthouse apartment, but someone else owned the building. This made it complicated to do things like remodel their stark bathroom, but had benefits like a full-time doorman and concierge, a resident manager and a valet. There was also a fitness center, a private Zen garden and a large conference room with a fully equipped Viking catering kitchen.

Technically, Natasha owned the apartment, he recalled. She bought it two months ago as a wedding present for him for a cool $12 million. Getting married also helped her with some immigration and tax issues. Dual citizenship had many perks for jet-setters like the Morgans. Natasha's maiden name was Manakova, but she changed it to Morgan when they married. Not that it mattered, though. The world knew her as simply Natasha.

She finished eating her breakfast, set down her bowl and spoon and reached for a copy of the latest *Vogue* sitting on the table. Natasha was on the magazine's cover wearing a white dress with black polka dots. The photo was a close-up of her face and torso, and a large caption next to it read "FRESH SUMMER STYLE," and a smaller headline read "Natasha's Beauty Secrets."

As she began flipping through the magazine, Natasha recalled that she had been paid about $200 to model for that cover shot and was allowed to keep the dress. Five years ago, when she was just breaking into the New York fashion scene, $200 was a good salary for a few hour's work, but it wasn't really enough to live on anymore. *That's why models are skinny,* she thought, reflecting that every time she made a magazine cover, her public image had risen.

"Are you working all day?" she asked, pausing to read the brief article about herself.

"I should probably make an appearance," Adam said, closing one of the newspapers and picking up another. The front-page headlines screamed "Chinese IPOs Ignite Solar Thirst," "Dems Seek NASA Boost," and "OPEC Says Output Stretched."

"What's the rest of your week look like?" he asked, finishing his espresso.

"After today, zip until the twenty-first," she said with a giggle. She was scrutinizing another photo of herself in an advertisement wearing nothing but a live snake and clutching a faux-snakeskin purse. For a moment, she thought of that particular photo session with the trained boa constrictor named Roberto. *Or was it the trainer who was named Roberto?*

"I'll keep that in mind," he said, getting up and leaning in to give Natasha a quick kiss on the cheek. She turned her head at the last moment and kissed him on the lips. He smiled as he picked up his smartphone from the table. "I'm going to get ready. If I don't see you before I leave, have a great day," he said, before turning and going back inside.

Standing before his full-length mirror in his walk-in closet, Adam put on a light blue and white-striped Canali dress shirt with a spread collar and no pockets. Most of his clothes were high-end, luxury designer brands that average people outside the fashion world would probably not recognize. Underneath, he was wearing charcoal gray Dolce & Gabbana underwear and gray silk socks. He pulled out one of his light gray suits from his wardrobe and inspected the label. Ermenegildo Zegna. *Nice*, he thought, as he slid on the tailored suit pants, put on a pair of blue and gray striped suspenders and slipped on a brown leather belt. He pulled out a pair of brown, leather John Lobb Oxford shoes from a drawer and slipped them on.

"Tie or no tie?" he asked his reflection. Better to be safe, he thought, reaching for a metallic-blue Gucci tie from his rotating tie holder and watching his reflection as he maneuvered the tie into a full Windsor knot. He walked over to his watch case and opened the mahogany lid.

Elegant designer wristwatches are one of my weaknesses, he thought, selecting his Blancpain "Fifty Fathoms" analog sport wristwatch with the blue numerical dial and white gold features. The luxury timepiece was self-winding and would be one of the few watches on earth that would keep accurate time over the next few days. Adam put on his suit jacket, grabbed his smartphone, brown leather billfold, keys and silver and blue Giorgio Armani sunglasses. He paused for a second to take a picture of himself in front of the mirror with his smartphone. A moment later, an app on his smartphone called "Fashion Snob" reported back with a cartoon image of a cat wearing sunglasses. "Hot as fire and cool as ice. Nice duds!"

Adam continued to press buttons on his smartphone as he headed his suite's antique elevator. His smartphone's synchronized calendar listed a full day of events and meetings.

"Good morning, sir," the elevator attendant said as the doors opened.

"Morning," Adam replied automatically as he stepped into the elevator and scanned the morning news on his smartphone, paying no attention to the commercials playing on the elevator's TV screen.

> Chinese IPOs Ignite Solar Thirst
> BEIJING - Chinese authorities have announced the completion of a $15 billion solar array near the city of Zhangjiakou, 200 km northwest of Beijing. The new array is the largest in the world and promises to light a new ...

Adam skipped to another story.

> Judge Postpones Barney Fraud Hearing
> NEW YORK - The New York District Attorney's Office postponed the hearing for accused hedge fund fraudster David Barney, one of Wall Street's elite money managers. Barney, who was released on a $1 million bond this morning, is accused of using inside information to illegally trade and manipulate the markets with his powerful ...

Adam looked up and noticed the elevator wasn't moving.

"Everything O.K.?" he asked. The elevator's small TV screen was switched off.

"I think the power went out," the elevator attendant said, adding "I'm terribly sorry, sir." Just as he was apologizing, the power kicked on and the elevator resumed its descent with a slight jolt. Adam returned his attention to his smartphone's headlines for the rest of the ride.

"Good morning, Mr. Morgan," the doorman said, holding the door open as Adam stepped out of the building and onto the street. A pungent smell of horse manure filled his nostrils as he looked up from his smartphone for the first time since stepping out of the elevator.

A row of horse-pulled carriages lined the opposite side of the street along the southern edge of Central Park, a living relic from Manhattan's earlier days that continued to charm tourists. Adam put on his sunglasses.

"Taxi, please, Hector," Adam said, looking back down at his smartphone. A yellow cab pulled up almost immediately and Hector held open the back door.

"Here you are, sir," Hector said. "Have an excellent day."

"Chrysler Building, please," Adam said to the driver, not looking up from his smartphone.

The driver was wearing a wireless, bluetooth-enabled earpiece that functioned as a phone and was having a long conversation with someone on the other end in a language Adam didn't understand. The dark-skinned, dark-haired driver typed "chrysler building" into the navigator's search feature and it instantly plotted a route. The cab driver was listening to Middle-Eastern music on the radio. Adam considered asking him to turn it off, but the song had a good beat. His smartphone instantly identified the song, artist and album and gave him the option to buy it.

Adam opened a web search engine app on his smartphone and typed in the following:

bright light in sky

The search engine revealed 30 million results. Most were old news stories about meteor showers or rants by UFO conspiracy enthusiasts, but there was one story from the National Oceanic and

Atmospheric Administration's website, www.noaa.gov, that caught his eye.

> <u>Bright light</u> sightings <u>in</u> the <u>sky</u> could be explained by a number of factors, including meteor showers, <u>light</u>ning storms, space weather or the result of a nuclear blast. Unidentified <u>light</u> sources have been attributed to extraterrestrial intelligence, but no ...

Adam quickly ruled out the possibility of a nuclear blast and started a new search, typing in "space weather" in the search function. A moment later, the search engine revealed it had found more than 800 million related articles.

He read the top few articles about solar flares, geomagnetic storms and something called the Carrington Event of 1859, but most of the stories were at least a year or two old, hyping previous solar flare doomsday countdowns that had already turned out to be false prophecies. "Solar Superstorm Could Strike This Week, Leaving Millions Without Power," was rated as the most relevant to his search, but it was written more than a year earlier. Eventually Adam noticed the cab was not moving. He looked up and saw a traffic jam of taxis.

Adam switched from the web search app on his smartphone to a traffic app. Using Google Earth, the GPS locator magnified or zoomed in on a composite satellite photo to his exact position in Manhattan. An overlay traffic map of Fifth Avenue and the surrounding streets depicted the route as red, indicating heavy traffic. Two blocks east on Park Avenue, the traffic was listed as green. Lexington was a straight shot, but the real-time traffic app listed the avenue as orange, indicating moderate traffic.

"Driver, can you take Park Avenue instead?" Adam asked.

"Yes, sir," the driver said, checking the GPS and taking the next left.

A few minutes later, the cab came to a stop in front of Grand Central Terminal at 42nd Street and Lexington Ave. Adam swiped his credit card on the panel behind the passenger seat, left the driver a $10 e-tip and stepped out onto the street a few minutes after 7 a.m.

"Spare change?" asked a ragged, homeless man sitting in a wheelchair on the sidewalk. Adam shrugged as he walked past. *I don't have any change,* he thought. "How about some food?" the elderly man asked as Adam entered the iconic Art Deco building.

Inside, Adam flashed his picture ID to the security guard and waved his smartphone over the mechanical turnstile, which slid open to allow him passage. He strode across the magnificent lobby with its red Moroccan walls and exotic wood detailing, yellow Siena marble floors and enormous ceiling mural titled "Transport and Human Endeavor." The mural, painted by Edward Trumbull and installed in 1930 when the building was completed, was intended to be a celebration of energy and technological progress.

Adam stepped inside the small but elegantly inlaid express elevator that serviced floors 57 to 67, turned around to face the door and pressed the button for floor 65. Another five people squeezed into the elevator after him, pushing him up against the back wall. As they filed in, everyone instinctively turned around to face the door. No one spoke as the elevator began its smooth ascent, and Adam's head bobbed down to look at his smartphone. 7:15 a.m. He felt his stomach drop as the elevator quickly rocketed skyward. A few moments later, the pressure began to build inside his ears. He knew from experience that his ears would pop if he swallowed, but rebalancing his internal pressure mid-ride meant he would have to relieve the pressure again when the elevator reached the top. *Don't swallow,* he thought. He checked the progress on the elevator's display above the door. Floor 40. Forty-one, 42, 43.

The elevator suddenly jolted to a halt with a heavy clunk. Another wave of nausea swept over him again as his stomach heaved once more. He quickly covered his mouth and briefly retched, then swallowed a bit of bitter stomach bile. His ears popped.

Chapter 4

EARTH's ATMOSPHERE - 11:15:00 UTC
On board the International Space Station, altitude: 250 kilometers above the Earth
TIME TO SOLAR IMPACT: 12 hours, 17 minutes

Aleksandr Manakova raised his left arm, looked at his black and silver, B-42 Fortis Cosmonaut Chronograph and noticed that the hour and minute hands were aligned, pointed at his own hand. Three fifteen.

He looked out a nearby window and saw a dark, featureless Earth, surrounded by an infinite expanse of empty space and stars that stretched on forever. *We must be somewhere over the Pacific Ocean right now*, he thought, making notes in his journal using the Cyrillic alphabet. He was using an ordinary pencil that was tethered to the journal with a piece of string.

Time is relative, and no more so than on the International Space Station. The watch was a gift from his father, also a cosmonaut, and was so accurate, it was one of the only timepieces approved by the Russian Federal Space Agency. It was always set to Moscow time and helped him keep a relatively normal schedule. Three fifteen was Aleks' time to use the treadmill.

The three astronauts on board the space station kept similar schedules based on their home countries, but they all referred to Universal Time Coordinated (UTC) when communicating with one another, also known as Greenwich Mean Time, Zulu Time or Space Time.

Having a fixed notion of time was crucial, as the space station orbited the Earth every 90 minutes. Watching 16 sunrises and 16 sunsets every day could play with the mind, but not as much as the zero gravity. If the astronauts and cosmonauts didn't exercise for at least two hours a day, their muscles could atrophy from lack of use.

Aleks finished writing in his journal. He unzipped his one-piece blue flight suit and slipped on a pair of blue sweatpants and a blue sweatshirt bearing the name Pockocmoc, pronounced Roscosmos. The sweatshirt had a large logo of a tilted red triangular shape surrounded by a gray swoosh and looked similar to the Star Trek logo from American television.

As Aleks floated through the maze of rooms and chambers, he observed that the International Space Station resembled a five-bedroom college dormitory inhabited by mechanical engineering and computer design students. Without gravity, any direction could be "up," but most of the pods were decorated to include a floor, walls and a ceiling, with the floor area typically closest to the Earth.

Nearly all the modules on the space station were similarly designed as rounded cylinders on the outside with rectangular interiors. In addition to the storage areas behind the flat walls, nearly every interior surface was covered with storage bins, laptop computers, wires and other equipment, and there were little experiments taking place almost everywhere.

Aleks moved from the Zvezda Service Module through the Zarya Control Module and the Unity Node to the Tranquility, where the exercise machine was located. As he floated past his comrades, he often did a corkscrew spin through the air and said something like "dasvidania."

When he got to the Tranquility, he put on a velcro belt and strapped himself into the American-made COLBERT treadmill. In order to jog in zero gravity, he had to be pulled down to the running surface. There was a little tension and resistance, but not too much. The point was to keep moving his muscles. *Use it or lose it*, he thought as he began jogging.

He looked up at the Tranquility's cupola observatory at the world spinning below.

Aleks switched on the laptop computer attached to the side of the exercise machine and logged on. After reading a couple of work-related e-mails, he received a chat request.

"NATASHA would like to chat," the message read, showing the image of a kitten.

Aleks pressed the "initiate chat" button and the screen filled up with a live video of a stunning young woman in pink sweats jogging on a treadmill. A smaller window showed a live video of himself, taken from the tiny camera at the top of his laptop.

"Hey, big brother," Natasha said in Russian. "What's the weather like up there?"

"Cold and dark," he replied in Russian, adjusting the monitor to better frame his 33-year-old Caucasian face in the video of himself. "Like Russian winter, but much quicker. Here, it will be spring in minutes, not months."

Natasha smiled.

"My Adam says he saw a white light this morning above the park," she said, continuing their conversation in their mother tongue. "Have you seen anything unusual?"

"Nothing is unusual in my life, precisely because it is all unusual. A white light could be many things: an airplane, a cloud, a dove ..."

"He said his phone went off right after the flash," Natasha interrupted.

Aleks studied his sister for a moment. A furrow slowly formed in his brow.

"I will check on this and let you know," he said.

"I am working from eight to noon, but you can message me," she said.

"Thanks. Enjoy your run and knock them dead today, sister," he said. "Goodbye," he added, as the video image of Natasha smiled and waved back across the airwaves. He pressed "end chat" and closed the window. He pulled up a web browser and began looking at satellite images of the sun, delayed by about 15 seconds. There was a large, dark spot on the surface. And another. *Unusual, indeed.*

Aleks kept jogging as his fingers furiously typed out an e-mail to his superiors.

"Code crimson. Notify Mishka of possible extreme solar activity. Request instructions."

He clicked "send" and waited a few seconds for the reply. A single tone indicated he had a new message, which he immediately opened.

"Initiate verification processes. Mishka is being notified. Silence is golden."

Aleks began gathering and recording all relevant data on solar activity, but found he was limited by the information his laptop could access. He would need to manually check the instrument data in the Zarya Control Module, but he still had more than an hour left on the exercise machine. *We all must make sacrifices*, he thought as he logged off the computer and unbuckled himself from the exercise machine.

There were few advantages to being tall on a crowded ship like the space station, but fortunately his flexibility and his championship swimming skills more than made up for the disadvantages of his nearly two meter tall, muscular frame.

As he was preparing to squeeze through the small porthole into the Unity Node, the bright light from the swift sunrise quickly filled the node and cast his shadow against the opposite wall. He noticed his American crew mate was emerging from the attached habitation module.

"Good morning," Aleks said in English to American astronaut Charles "Chuck" Wilson as he floated past.

Chuck was 45 years old, but looked about 35 after he shaved. He was wearing black shorts and a T-shirt bearing the name of his hometown baseball team, the Houston Astros.

"Done with your workout already?" Chuck asked as he rubbed an electric razor over his morning stubble in small, circular motions. His zero-gravity space razor was a prototype that had a little vacuum that collected his trimmings and kept them from floating away.

"Yes, I need to check some equipment," Aleks replied, noticing Wilson's shirt. "How about those Astros?" he asked, changing the subject.

"Aw, man. Did you see last night's game?" Chuck asked. Aleks shook his head as he continued floating toward the Unity

Node. "A heart-breaker. They're playing the Marlins again tonight," Chuck called after him, but realized he wasn't listening. "Lopez could be a hero," he added, mostly to himself.

Americans and their games, Aleks thought as he floated into the Zarya Control Module.

Chuck looked at his reflection in a small mirror and rubbed his hands over his face to make sure he had a clean, smooth shave. He smiled and nodded at his reflection.

As he was turning to leave, he noticed a quotation tacked to the wall next to a circular window that pointed away from Earth. The view out the porthole was of the dark, endless and mostly empty cosmos. The quotation was written in German and translated into English, Russian and Japanese. Next to it was a popular Hubble telescopic image of a deep space nebula.

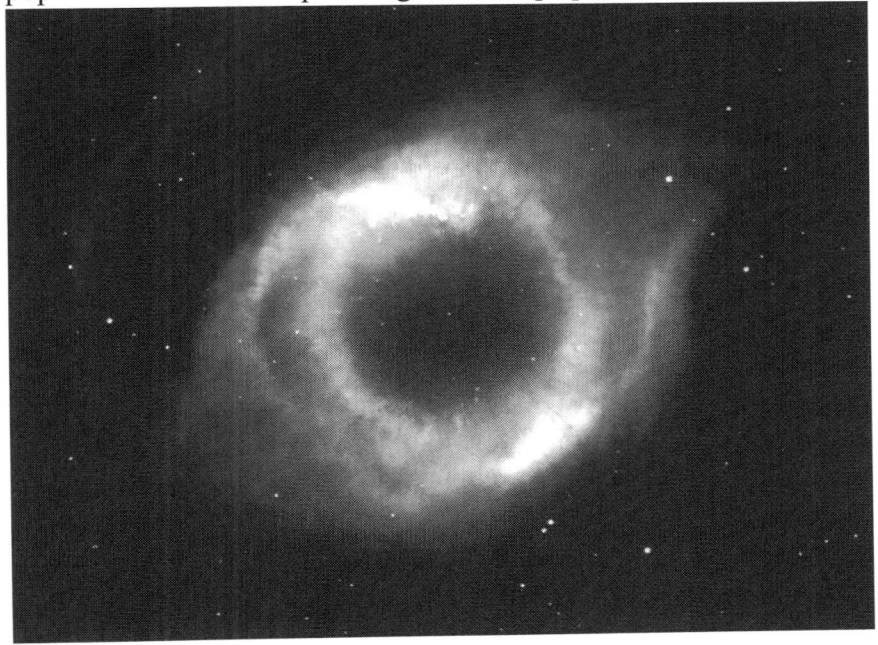

"Whoever fights monsters should see to it
that in the process he does not become a monster.
And if you gaze long enough into an abyss,
the abyss will gaze back into you."
- Friedrich Nietzsche

Chapter 5

NEW YORK CITY - 110 Central Park South, 7:25 a.m.

Back in the basement fitness center, Natasha patted the sweat off her face and chest with a white towel. Her smartphone chirped to announce another incoming video chat, this time from someone named Kitty. She sat down on a giant blue, rubber exercise ball and answered the call.

"Razzle dazzle!" the woman on the video screen cheered. "Look who's Miss Fitness this morning. Another photo shoot, or just restless again?"

"Little bit of both," Natasha said, smiling. "How are you, Kitty? Are we still on for the party this afternoon?"

Kitty, a.k.a. Katherine Johnson, was Natasha's publicist, manager, spokeswoman and personal assistant, as well as one of her closest friends. Kitty had ghost-written the short article in *Vogue* magazine about Natasha's beauty tips and had made sure the article kept a positive tone and listed the names of all the cosmetic companies that Natasha represented.

"I have confirmations from about half of the people on your list," Kitty said. "I invited five major designers and their assistants, a few TV actors and actresses, some public relations people and a bunch of your model friends. We've got the DJ booked and your building's concierge is doing the catering. So I'm fantastic, actually."

"Fabulous," Natasha said. "I think I'll invite some people from today's shoot as well. Any word yet on the new children's hospital wing?"

"Yes, they love the idea," Kitty said. "The director was gushing about you the whole time we talked. You're probably used to that, though."

Sponsoring a children's hospital was one of the major initiatives of Natasha's new charity. In addition to being a noble cause, it was great PR and a substantial tax write-off.

"Are you still playing around with that damned thing? Get off the phone and do some more crunches," nagged Damien, Natasha's personal fitness trainer.

"Two seconds," Natasha said, holding up two fingers. "Sorry Kitty, but I have to go now. Gotta stay fit. See you at the party?"

"Sure, text me," Kitty said. "Wish I had a trainer like yours. Kick some butt!"

"Thanks, bye!" Natasha said, pressing the end call button on her smartphone. "Sorry, Damien. Didn't I already do crunches this morning?"

"We're doing four reps of crunches today, along with butterfly kicks, squats and I was thinking a little shadow boxing at the end to finish up. Gotta keep those chiseled abs chiseled."

"What would I do without you, Damien?" Natasha asked with a sigh, sitting down on the exercise mat as Damien held her feet together.

"Probably talk on the phone 24 hours a day, no doubt. C'mon, it's crunch time," he said as Natasha began her second rep of abdominal exercises.

Chapter 6

NEW YORK CITY - The Chrysler Building, 43rd floor, 7:30 a.m.

Adam looked down at this smartphone. It was still turned on, which was an encouraging sign, although the battery was running low. He dialed 911.

His call was immediately sent to the nearest cellular tower, then bounced at the speed of light to the nearest available emergency dispatcher, located downtown.

"I can't believe this is happening to me," said a 50-year-old white businesswoman standing next to Adam in the crowded express elevator. He couldn't tell in the dim light coming from his smartphone, but she had strawberry blonde hair and was dressed in a black blouse with a black skirt, black stockings and black pumps. "I just knew I should have stayed home today. I should be on vacation right now but they never give me time off. You know, I haven't had a vacation or a day off in six years? Isn't that swell? That's progress for you."

"Nine one one. What is your emergency?" asked the female dispatcher.

"Hi, this is Adam Morgan. I'm stuck in an elevator with about five other people in the Chrysler Building, on about the 43rd floor. We've been stopped here for about fifteen minutes and the lights just went out about a minute ago."

"I was trapped in an elevator about 10 years ago when I was in Tokyo and we were stuck in there for five hours," the businesswoman continued. "It was just horrible."

"Is anyone hurt?" the dispatcher asked.

"It felt like we were in a coffin, dangling above a mine shaft," the businesswoman continued. "I thought we were going to die, but we didn't. We could have died, though, if one of the cables had snapped."

"Excuse me for a moment," Adam said, turning toward the direction of the obnoxious businesswoman. "I'm talking to 911 dispatch. Could you please keep it down?"

"Oh, I'm sorry," the woman said. "I beg your pardon."

"Is anyone hurt?" Adam asked in the dark. There was no response.

"No, we are all fine, but some of the passengers are a little restless," Adam told the dispatcher. "We really appreciate your help."

"I have confirmed your location and I am notifying your building's maintenance and security," the dispatcher said. "We should have you moving in a few minutes. Please tell everyone to stay calm and stay on the line until your emergency is resolved. Thank you for calling 911."

"Thank *you*," Adam said, turning to face the other elevator passengers. "Nine one one is on the way. Everyone try to relax and stay calm."

The obnoxious businesswoman did not say another word. She had recognized Adam when she stepped in the elevator and knew he lived in the penthouse apartment directly above her mother at 110 Central Park South, but she felt it was improper to introduce herself under the current circumstances. Her father had been a tycoon and had left behind an enormous fortune when he died in the form of real estate, jewelry, artwork and a trust fund with a bond ladder that provided her mother with tax-free income in perpetuity. When her mother eventually died, the trust would go to her two surviving children, both unmarried career businesswomen.

Eventually the elevator lights came back on and the elevator resumed its ascent.

Chapter 7

NEW YORK CITY - Sheepshead Bay, Brooklyn, 7:35 a.m.

"Hi Jean, iced coffee with milk and sugar," Frank said as he walked up to the coffee and news kiosk next to his apartment. "And today's Post," he added.

"You got it, Frank," Jean said, scooping a plastic cup full of ice and filling it with cold coffee made the night before. She put in a small scoop of sugar and a splash of milk before snapping on a plastic lid and poking a straw through the top. The straw had a bit of the original paper wrapper still covering the top end.

"Great, thanks a bunch," Frank said, handing her $3 and taking the coffee and a copy of *The New York Post*. He tucked the tabloid newspaper under his arm. As he turned to leave, his cell phone took a picture of the inside of his pocket, making a sound like a muffled sneeze.

"Bless you," Jean said.

"Thanks," Frank said. "That was my camera phone, but thanks again."

"Hey, if you ever want anything besides coffee and a newspaper, just ask," Jean called out as Frank walked to the marina.

Frank's phone took dozens of pictures of his pocket every day, but he had no idea how to turn the camera feature off. He didn't even want a camera on his cell phone, but he couldn't find any that didn't have cameras.

Two local boaters were shooting the breeze with a security guard by the marina entrance.

"Hey Frank, waddya know?" Dave the security guard called out.

"Another hot one today," Frank said, raising his iced coffee in mock salute. "Stay cool, gentlemen," he said as he walked through the gate and down one of the docks to his yacht.

Reciprocity was his boat, even if she wasn't officially. She was a 41-foot Hans Christian ocean sailing yacht, currently owned by some Wall Street trader who liked to entertain guests on the weekends. Frank had been captain for nearly two years now, but the vessel had changed owners three times in those two years. Most of the week she sat in the marina. Frank was paid to be on call, so he spent a lot of time hanging around the boat, cleaning, reading and he even slept in one of the cabins on board. He had put a fresh coat of paint on her last night and had needed to escape from the fumes. All the windows were open but had canvas flaps covering the openings. Frank inspected and admired the vessel from the floating causeway. *Just as I left her,* he thought, setting up the gangplank connecting the causeway to the ship.

The yacht tipped to the starboard side as he stepped aboard, then rebalanced itself. As he climbed inside the main cabin, the smell of fresh paint and linseed oil made him smile. *I love this boat*, he thought as he flopped down onto a white leather sofa and began reading the paper.

"Hedge Huckster Held Over," read the top headline in giant letters that filled most of the front page. The cover photo featured candid shot of a man in handcuffs being escorted by two uniformed police officers. The man had a dress shirt covering his head to hide his identity. Frank flipped the paper over to the sports section on the back and took a sip of his iced coffee. *This is the life*, he thought.

Chapter 8

LONDON - 260 Devonia Rd., Islington, England, 12:40 p.m.

Major Tugnutz peered out a small window and fired his laser-powered sniper rifle at a figure running along a ridge. The words "Major Tugnutz has killed Agent Orange" flashed on the screen as the figure fell over.

Tugnutz ran forward a few meters down a darkened hallway and ducked behind a large packing crate as a wave of laser blasts flew over his head. He switched to a laser assault rifle and reloaded the magazine, giving himself a full clip, before jumping back up and firing at his green, heavily armored opponent. The enemy was nowhere in sight.

"Come out, you green-faced trolley bugger twit," a 16-year-old boy yelled, clicking a few buttons on his next generation Xbox game controller. As the figure reemerged, the boy sent a heavy wave of firepower toward his opponent, accompanied by a glittering arc of empty shells that showered from his automatic rifle. Another opponent fell to the floor with a thud.

"Major Tugnutz has killed Green Baron," flashed on the screen.

Tugnutz ran forward and picked up a floating pink cross and a floating blue assault rifle. The cross restored his health to 100 percent and the rifle gave him an additional 200 rounds of ammunition.

A wicked laugh echoed down the chamber as two additional figures emerged, firing their laser guns in Tug's general direction. He ducked as he sprinted across the floor to the the left wall and hid behind a support pillar. Laser beams whizzed by as Tugnutz braced himself against the pillar and switched to a grenade launcher. When the shooting stopped, he popped around the corner and launched a grenade in the direction of the firing before hiding behind the pillar again.

A large explosion and flash of light erupted from his target, causing the Xbox controller to vibrate. "Major Tugnutz has killed King Charles and Dirty Larry," appeared on the screen.

Tug slipped from behind the pillar and ran forward over a puddle of red liquid where his opponents had stood, leaving behind a trail of bloody footprints. The bodies and blood disappeared after a few moments. Tug reached the doorway at the end of the corridor, opened it and grabbed a waving blue flag.

"Major Tugnutz has captured the blue flag. Game over."

"Blimey, that was a sotter spew fest," Jacob said, setting down the game controller and picking up his smartphone. He had 81 new messages, all of them short texts from friends and Twitter followers.

"luv the new video," said Beckers14. "u shud come to jersey," said JerseyGirl2013. "rad vid, man," said bonerdonor99. "u r cute," said miteybits2000. "u r gay," said devinhatesyou.

Jacob Baker scrolled through a few dozen comments before checking the status of his latest YouTube video, "How to Hypnotize Your Mom," a 60-second video he posted two days ago. The video already had more than 700,000 views, more than 52,000 "likes" and 720 "dislikes".

Jacob pressed a button on his smartphone and looked at his Twitter account. He now had more than 100,000 followers and was following about 50,000 people, most of them young girls his age. The reason his video had had so many hits was due in part to his wide smile, clean complexion and shaggy brown hair, but also because of his rampant networking and marketing on various social media websites. He quickly scanned the tweets from his friends.

"mum sez i spend 2 much time on net so im grounded for a week," said samsamsong.

"b4 ur cut off, check this cool new vid," Jacob typed in reply, leaving a link to his new YouTube video. He continued scrolling through the messages.

"omg ur so funny!!! lol thanks,jake!" samsamsong replied a minute or so later.

Jacob clicked a button and looked back at his YouTube video. 750,000 views, and climbing. His smartphone rang. The caller ID feature said the number was from London.

"Yo, Jacob here. Who this?"

"Jacob Baker?" the caller asked. "This is Bryan Conners from YouTube London. Did you post a video about hypnotizing your mom?"

"Yeah, what about it?"

"We love it!" Bryan said. "We think it's got big potential to go viral and wanted to talk to you about advertising."

"K, I guess," Jacob replied, picking up his Xbox controller and joining a new first-person shooter network game.

"Are you 18?"

"Why?"

"You have to be 18 to have an advertising contract," Bryan said. "If you're not 18, that's OK, but I need to talk to your mom or dad."

Major Tugnutz was riding in the back of a Jeep, firing a chain gun at a lone figure running in front of him. Bullets were flying everywhere and the Xbox controller vibrated again as the player he was chasing dodged his shots and climbed inside an armored helicopter.

"Mum's at work, but it's fine by me," Jacob said.

The armored helicopter lifted off into the sky and turned towards the Jeep.

"May I call your mom at work?" Bryan asked. "It's really important to get this set up soon."

The armored helicopter fired a volley of missiles at the Jeep, instantly destroying it.

The words "Curious George has killed Major Tugnutz," briefly flashed on the screen.

"That's fine with me, mate," Jacob said, pausing his game. He gave the YouTube rep his mom's cell number and ended the call, then texted his mom.

"youtube likes my video an wants to advertise it," he texted. "fine w me. gave him ur #. luv u mom!"

As he resumed the game, Major Tugnutz rematerialized at the starting point. He began running through an airfield junkyard and saw he was being strafed by the armored helicopter gunship he had fired at earlier. His health dropped to about half-full as he ducked inside an empty hangar where a floating blue rocket launcher was waiting. He picked up the weapon.

"It's about to go down, mates," Jacob said with a grin as he switched from his assault rifle to the rocket launcher.

Chapter 9

AFGHANISTAN - Approximately 100 miles west of Kandahar, 3:45 p.m.

Staff Sergeant Timothy Layton checked the news on his smartphone as his three-vehicle caravan sped along a dirt road across hundreds of miles of harsh, unwelcoming terrain. The big international news was the opening of an enormous solar-powered array in China.

They could use a solar power plant out here, Layton thought from the spacious front passenger seat as he stared out the front window. *Afghanistan certainly has a surplus of sun. But that's about all they have.*

Layton and his fellow soldiers were wearing the new "MultiCam" Army Combat Uniform, a fire-proof, bug-proof blend of slate gray, desert sand and pixilated foliage green, specially designed to blend into the Afghan environment. In addition, each man wore a matching camouflage flack vest, kevlar helmet, utility belt and backpack, and they each wore tan-colored combat boots, knee pads and sunglasses. Layton carried a modified M4 carbine assault rifle and a .357 magnum Glock 32 pistol holstered and strapped to his right thigh.

Layton's smartphone chirped to alert him that his convoy of High Mobility Multipurpose Wheeled Vehicles — HMMWV or Humvee for short — was heading into an area tagged as previously hostile, although neither he nor any member of his convoy had personally experienced trouble there. He forwarded the alert to his superior officer traveling in the identical armored Humvee directly in front of him. Layton read a synopsis of the recent history of the village as the convoy turned down a narrow, empty street with two-story buildings on either side.

Suddenly there was a huge fiery explosion directly in front of them. The first Humvee in their convoy burst into a fireball and landed upside down in the middle of the street. It had driven over a hidden improvised explosive device (IED) that had been activated remotely using a pre-paid cell phone that had been purchased with cash.

The 19-year-old driver of Layton's vehicle jammed on the brakes just in time to avoid running into the back of the burning Humvee, but the driver of the vehicle following him was not so quick to react and rear-ended Layton's middle vehicle, pushing it closer to but not touching the burning vehicle. The third vehicle's engine stalled out and wouldn't restart.

The popping sound of small-arms fire began outside and a bullet ricocheted off the windshield, cracking the glass just inches away from Staff Sergeant Layton's face.

"Get us out of here!" he yelled to the driver. U.S. Marine Corporal Terry Linfield put the vehicle in reverse, but found the way blocked by the stalled Humvee.

"We're trapped, Sarge!" the corporal shouted as he tried in vain to maneuver the large vehicle out of the situation. "What do I do?" Another bullet struck the hood of the Humvee, followed by two more shots that struck the right side and one that hit the vehicle's left side. None of the bullets pierced inside, thanks in part to the extra kevlar vests Layton and his men had secured over the side doors and windows. There was no sign of life from the burning vehicle directly ahead, only black smoke.

We're being ambushed, the 32-year-old Layton quickly thought. *The lieutenant was in the first vehicle, and he's gone, which means that now I'm in charge. We're sitting ducks in the middle of this street. We need to find cover.*

"Everybody listen up!" Layton shouted. "We need to take cover and eliminate the hostiles. On my mark, we're all going to exit the vehicle at the same time and take cover in or against those buildings. There may be sniper fire, so don't stop moving until you find cover. Watch out for rooftops and tall buildings. Ready? Three, two, one, GO!"

The four soldiers burst out of the vehicle and ran to find cover. Gunshots rang out and bullets narrowly missed their moving targets. Layton scoped out second-story windows and rooftops for gunmen and saw an Afghan man in civilian clothes firing a Kalashnikov rifle from the rooftop of one of the neighboring buildings on the left side of the street. The man was aiming at the young corporal. Layton trained his M4 carbine on the Afghan gunman and squeezed the trigger. His rifle went off with a loud "pop" and the figure fell over.

A few meters away, on the left side of the street, the corporal aimed his rifle at a rooftop gunman on the right side of the street, out of Layton's line of sight, and neutralized the threat with two shots in quick succession.

"Got him, Sarge!" Linfield said. "There's another shooter in that building down the street, left side, second story, center window."

"Cover me, I'm going to flank him," Layton said. A bullet hit the wall next to his head.

"I got you," Linfield said, popping up from behind his cover and firing several shots at the target's window. As soon as the corporal began firing, Layton jumped up and crossed to the left side of the street, keeping low and out of sight of the gunman.

Layton snuck around to the back side of the primitive structure in an attempt to flank the shooter, but he dared not go inside the bottom story without backup. There was nowhere to take cover and he couldn't get a clear shot without exposing his position, so he grabbed one of his hand grenades, took aim, pulled the pin and pitched the grenade through a small glass side window on the upper floor of the building. The hand grenade landed on a table covered with bombs and bomb-making equipment. A second later, the surprisingly powerful explosion collapsed the roof and the entire second floor, crushing the shooter and sending out a large cloud of smoke and dust. Layton was knocked to the ground by the blast. The shooting stopped.

As Layton stood up and walked back down the street to survey the damage to the remains of his convoy, he thought he heard another series of shots, but quieter, like fireworks. A heavy force slammed into the center of his back, knocking him face-down on the dusty earth. *I've been shot, but I don't think I'm hurt,* he thought. *There's another gunman somewhere.*

Layton remained motionless as though dead, even though it might have been possible to reach his rifle resting a few feet away. He waited for a few moments until he heard several cautious footsteps approaching and listened as they came to a halt beside him. In one lightning-fast, fluid motion, he quickly rolled over and shot his attacker once in the head with his .357 magnum pistol.

His attacker's lifeless body dropped to the ground. Layton stood up to check on his enemy and saw that he had just shot a 16-year-old Afghan boy armed with a Russian assault rifle. A foreign, high-pitch sound began ringing inside Layton's head, indicating the start of a migraine headache. His heart rate and breathing were way up as he scanned for signs of another ambush.

A shrieking wail came from inside the damaged building and a figure dressed head-to-toe in black robes ran out of the first-floor door, headed directly for Layton. He picked up his M4 rifle from the ground and pointed it at the woman, who immediately stopped running. After a second, the woman began screaming again and ran not to Layton but to the boy's body. She collapsed to the ground on her knees and began crying hysterically.

Corporal Linfield ran over to Layton's position with his own rifle raised and scanned the rooftops for danger, then noticed the screaming woman. The remaining soldiers in the convoy had fanned out and were in defensive positions, covering each other.

"Corporal, radio the base and tell them we've been ambushed," Layton said, adjusting his sunglasses, which turned out to be broken. "How's that other Humvee? Is it running?"

"It stalled out during the ambush, but it's running now," the corporal said, dialing the base. "Both remaining Humvees are ready to roll, Sarge."

"Tell the base we lost a vehicle and part of our team, but we're back online and ready to roll out."

He pulled out his canteen and took a drink of water as the corporal radioed in the command. He put his canteen back in his side pouch and checked his smartphone. It was almost 4 o'clock and it was still a scorching 40 degrees Celsius, or about 104 degrees Fahrenheit. He pointed his smartphone at the burning

Humvee and took a picture for his report. He took another picture of the woman in the burka and her dead son.

"Sarge, the base says we're cleared to roll out," Linfield reported. "They want to know if you want to recommend a Predator drone airstrike on the area."

Layton looked back at the body of the boy he had just killed. It had been in self-defense, he reasoned, but a growing sense of sorrow and anguish began to creep over him, momentarily petrifying his mind. His advanced equipment and training had saved his life, but the first Humvee hadn't stood a chance against the homemade roadside bomb.

The dead boy's mother was sitting on the ground with her son's body draped across her legs, wailing hysterically in Pashto. She was waving her hands in the air and shouting to the sky. Layton didn't speak Pashto, but he could tell what she was saying.

"Sarge?" Linfield asked again. "The airstrike?"

The nearby rattle of small arms fire echoed through the air, waking Layton from his temporary stupor.

"OK, boys, saddle up," he said. "We're going back to base. Tell them negative on the drone. There's nothing here but heartbreak."

Chapter 10

NEW YORK CITY - The Chrysler Building, 65th floor, 7:50 a.m.

Adam strolled through the quiet, empty office to one of its sun-lit corners. By nine o'clock, the whole office floor would be buzzing with energy and movement, but before eight, most of the U.S. business world was still waking up. *The early bird gets the worm*, he thought.

As he approached his office, he saw his executive assistant was already at her desk.

"Morning, Karen," Adam said, unlocking the frosted-glass door to his office.

"Good morning, Adam," Karen replied in an educated, slightly upper-class British accent. Her fingers were a blur as she continued typing something important on her computer.

Adam sat down at the large mahogany desk in his corner office. Behind him, the breathtaking view overlooking lower Manhattan was dominated by the shimmering top of the Empire State Building, located eight blocks to the southwest. Farther south, the skyscrapers of the financial district and the newly constructed One World Trade Center, also known as the Freedom Tower, pierced the bright blue morning sky. Looking west to Times Square, he could see the rectangular top and spire of the New York Times Building, exactly the same height as the Chrysler Building, and the even taller and irregularly shaped Bank of America Tower. Adam pressed the large, white button on the intercom sitting on his desk.

"Karen? Could you please bring me some aspirin and water?" Adam asked.

"Right away," the woman's voice replied over the intercom.

Adam swiveled his leather executive chair around to look out the window. *Incredible*, he thought, admiring the view. The Chrysler Building was once the tallest building in the world for 11 months, until the Empire State Building surpassed her by 62 meters in 1931. The singular honor of the world's tallest completed building now belonged to the Burj Khalifa in Dubai, but a new building still under construction in Jeddah, Saudi Arabia, had already surpassed them all.

Karen came in with the water and aspirin. She was wearing a tight-fitting white blouse, a knee-length black skirt, black nylon tights and stylish black heels. She had shiny, red hair that was pulled back into a tightly coiled bun.

"You have a 9 o'clock with H. Walter Donovan," she said, setting down the water bottle on the edge of the desk and dropping two aspirin tablets into Adam's outstretched hand. At 28, Karen was tall, pretty and smart as a whip. She had been Adam's secretary for almost a year and enjoyed her job, though she had yet to take any time off. "You have a number of appointments this afternoon, including an interview with that reporter from the *Journal*."

"Thanks, Karen," Adam said, taking the aspirin with water. "The meeting with Donovan is here, is it not?"

"It is."

"Great, let me know when he arrives," Adam said. "That will be all for now."

As Karen left, Adam pulled out his smartphone and noticed that he had received a new text message from Natasha. "Feeling better?" it asked.

"Got stuck in elevator twice," he texted back. "All is well, tho. Good luck today."

Adam noticed that the battery charge on his smartphone was low. He logged on to his desktop computer and saw that he had more than 200 new e-mails. He was about to plug his smartphone into his computer's USB port to begin charging and synchronizing the device, but he was distracted by a small chime notifying him of a new message from Natasha.

"Sorry to hear that. Today can only get better. Call me this afternoon. Love, N."

Adam pulled up his file on Donovan. Harvey Walter Donovan was the current director of the U.S. Securities and Exchange Commission's Division of Enforcement, as well as one of Adam's former clients and a longtime associate. The two had met about 15 years ago when Adam was working as a junior researcher for the Treasury Department and Donovan was working at the investment banking firm Goldman Sachs.

Adam had uncovered some questionable accounting practices at Goldman and had wisely brought them to Donovan's attention. Donovan was impressed with Adam's resourcefulness and offered him an entry-level job at Goldman, which he accepted. Adam quickly climbed the firm's ranks by helping Goldman's investors make a killing during the dot-com crash at the turn of the century and quietly began amassing his own personal fortune on the side.

From the start, Adam's specialty had been tech stocks. He stood out at Goldman not for his ability to pick which stocks to buy and sell, but *when* and *how* to buy and sell them. Most of his colleagues had devoted their careers to orchestrating corporate take-overs, consolidating and eliminating well-known American brands and insuring against the corporate bankruptcies they had carefully planned. Adam was turned off by this capitalistic creative destruction and left the firm shortly after the stock market crash in 2008, retiring as a multi-millionaire at the age of 35.

Donovan's departure from one of the top spots at Goldman made headlines in 2010 after he received a $60 million "golden parachute" severance package and immediately took a job at the SEC watching over the very people with whom he had been working.

"That's like having the fox guard the henhouse," pundits had criticized. *But that's also what they said when Roosevelt made Joe Kennedy the first SEC chairman*, Adam recalled. *Sometimes you need a fox to outfox the other foxes.*

Sixty million dollars was a huge payoff at any hedge fund or private equity firm, but it paled in comparison to the $6.8 billion in bonuses Goldman Sachs doled out to its top executives at the end of 2008, shortly after Congress approved an historic, $700 billion federal bailout.

Four years after leaving Goldman Sachs, Donovan was still working at the SEC and had built a reputation for being tough on fraud, particularly on retail and institutional mutual funds, but he also had garnered a reputation among some for failing to regulate or oversee hedge funds in any way. That reputation was quickly changing. Adam knew that Donovan was behind the SEC's push to indict hedge fund manager David Barney for insider trading, and his "friendly" visit this morning could have serious consequences for the old friends.

Adam had actually stopped worrying about money for a few years after he got his huge bonus check in 2008, but eventually he realized that having $900 million can only get you so far in life. He was achingly close to becoming a billionaire and decided to just go for it, despite having more money than he could ever hope to spend. In 2011, he started his own hedge fund.

Adam's "Techno Savvy Robot" hedge fund quickly ballooned in size thanks to both his own personal investment and his preternatural ability to bring in average annual returns of 40 percent or more. His fund's major investors included prominent members of Congress, Hollywood film producers, celebrities and other hedge funds, as well as dozens of state and federal pension plans. "Techno Savvy Robot" was based in the Cayman Islands with offices in Manhattan, London and Hong Kong. This organizational structure allowed the fund to operate continually on most of the world's financial exchanges and also meant that Adam was not legally required to disclose his fund's complete trading information to anyone.

As he checked the fund's account balance, Adam briefly held a pencil up to the screen to help him count all the numbers.

At that exact moment, Techno Savvy Robot had $20,326,914,761.88 in assets, putting it among the top 15 hedge funds in the world, almost at par with his old firm. Ironically, Goldman Sachs was also one of his fund's largest investors.

Three years ago when he started his hedge fund, Adam told himself he would get out when the fund reached $10 billion in assets, but it was now double that and continued to pull in obscenely high returns for his investors. After a while, Adam found that the numbers ceased to make sense and took on a life of their own.

He quickly scanned the news on *The New York Times* website.

> Brownouts Slow NYC Commuters, updated 5 mins ago
> NEW YORK - City electrical workers are scrambling to control a wave of partial electrical blackouts sweeping over major urban centers Wednesday morning in New York City. Officials from the mayor's office are telling New Yorkers to turn off any extra air conditioning units and other electrical equipment during the day to help relieve the area's massive demand for electricity ...

> Earthquake Rattles Mecca During Ramadan
> MECCA - An earthquake measuring 5.0 on the Richter scale rattled windows and knocked down a few primitive structures today in the Saudi Arabian coastal town of Jeddah, located on the Red Sea, approximately 73 km from the holy city of Mecca. Saudi officials say the tremors were felt by followers gathered at the Masjid al Haram mosque, but no serious damages were reported. Ramadan festivities continued throughout the ...

> Norway Kindles Annual Festival of Lights
> OSLO, Norway - Spectators here celebrated Norway's third-annual festival of lights, the weeklong celebration of the country's abundant energy surplus. Thousands of ...

Adam did a quick online search for flights to Norway. There were a dozen airlines that had service between New York and Oslo, but most were overnight flights with layovers and none were advertising first-class service. He picked up his phone and dialed an airline's toll-free number.

Chapter 11

MUMBAI, India - 808 Manaji Rajuji Rd., Maharashtra, 5:40 p.m.

Savitr Shashikant wished he could take a smoke break, or a break of any kind.

Sixteen-hour days are much too long, even with overtime, he thought, *but I would rather be in here than outside in the monsoon. Half the city is flooded.* His phone was ringing, but he ignored it for the time being. He looked at his colleagues seated a few feet on either side of him. Both were engaged in conversations with customers on the other side of the world.

Savitr stood up at his desk for a moment and looked out over the vast sea of cubicles packed into the warehouse's call center. The building's large metal roof buzzed loudly from the steady pounding of seasonal rains. The humid atmosphere mixed with the sweat of hundreds of bodies, giving the building a lingering musky odor. There were at least 500 people working the phones at any given time, but they were still flooded with calls nearly 24 hours a day.

Savitr's phone continued ringing. He put on his headset, sat down in his squeaky, wooden chair, and answered the call. The caller ID informed him the call came from New York.

"Steadfast Airlines, this is Steve," he said. "How may I help you?"

"Hi Steve," said a man's voice on the other line. "I'm looking for two first-class tickets from New York City to Oslo, Norway, preferably seated together."

"Thank you for calling, sir. I am happy to help you. First I will need your departure and arrival dates."

"I'd like to leave this afternoon, if that works," the man said.

"Is this a round-trip ticket or one-way?" Savitr asked.

"One way for now," the man said. "I want to catch the Festival of Lights."

"I am sorry, sir, it sounded like you said you want to catch a vestibule flight," Savitr said. "All of our airplanes are vestibules."

"Do ... you ... have ... any ... first-class ... tickets?" the man asked, slowly and carefully enunciating his words.

"Let ... me ... check," Savitr said, mimicking the caller's disdain as he entered the new figures into his computer terminal. "There is a flight that leaves New York's John F. Kennedy airport at 9:30 tonight and arrives in Oslo on Thursday afternoon, with a five-hour layover in London."

"I can see that one," the man said. "Are there any other flights that leave sooner, like maybe a non-stop?"

"You wish to leave sooner?" Savitr asked, entering new information into the search field. "There is a non-stop flight from London to Oslo leaving in 30 minutes. I see there are two first-class seats together for this flight. Would you like me to book this for you, sir?"

"I'm in New York right now," the man said.

"You are trying to get to London tonight?"

"I want to go to Norway tonight."

"I am sorry, did you say 'Norway' or 'no way'?" Savitr asked.

The caller hung up. Savitr took off his headset, stood up at his desk again and stretched his legs. *I need a break*, he thought as his phone began ringing again.

Chapter 12

NEW YORK CITY - 110 Central Park South, 8:15 a.m.

Fresh from a shower and wearing a pink miniskirt, push-up bra and white silk blouse – all by Victoria's Secret – as well as a pink baseball cap, sunglasses and white Converse All Star sneakers, Natasha left her apartment building and walked west along 59th Street towards Columbus Circle, largely unnoticed.

Turning south on 7th Ave., Natasha could see the flashing billboards of the Times Square district from 10 blocks away. As she approached, she chose to ignore all the ads except her own. Several people pointed and stared at her and a man took her picture with his smartphone, but most of the tens of thousands of people scurrying about in the streets seemed to be oblivious to her presence, walking in a hypnotic daze, stunned from all the flashing signs and billboards competing day and night for their attention. This was information overload at its best and worst.

Nearly every square foot of every vertical surface was advertising something, from corporate logos to Broadway shows, restaurants, movies, investment banks and financial service companies, designer clothing, websites, digital cameras and carbonated beverages. News feeds stacked on top of other news feeds announced important and trivial information side by side.

Looking up, Natasha saw a dramatic, three-story photo of herself wearing a diamond-studded fantasy bra and bikini thong, stiletto heels and a pair of enormous, feathered angel wings. Her goddess-sized image wore thick, dark eye liner and her lips were slightly parted to reveal perfect, white teeth. A group of male tourists from Iowa were blocking the sidewalk, staring up at Natasha's billboard with mouths agape. She pushed through the crowd undetected.

"I heard that diamond bra costs $3 million," one of the tourists remarked.

"Does she come with it?" his friend asked. "That might actually be worth it."

Natasha stepped off the street into the lobby of one of the buildings at 8:25 a.m. and approached the receptionist.

"May I help you?" the woman asked, taking a sip from a giant Starbucks coffee cup.

"Hi, I'm here for the Victoria's Secret photo shoot," Natasha said.

"Hair or make-up?"

"Um, model," she said with a grin.

"Oh, gosh! I'm sorry, miss. I didn't recognize you. Please go upstairs to the fifth floor. You can take elevator No. 4."

"I think I might take the stairs, if that's OK."

"Actually, the elevator has been kind of spazzy today," the receptionist said. "The stairs are around the corner on the left."

"Thanks," Natasha said, flashing another smile at the receptionist and heading down the hallway to the stairwell.

When she emerged from the stairwell on the fifth floor, Natasha found herself in a crowded office hallway. She stopped a busy-looking 20-something woman who was swiftly walking by. The woman's uncomfortable high heels loudly clacked against the hardwood floor.

"Excuse me, could you please tell me which way to the make-up room for the Victoria's Secret photo shoot?"

The woman briefly examined Natasha's outfit, starting at her neck and scanning down to her feet, made a subtle sneer at Natasha's comfortable shoes, then brought her gaze back up to meet her eyes. It was clear the woman did not recognize Natasha and said flatly, "Straight ahead, last door on the right," before turning around and quickly bustling off again, followed by the loud, rhythmic clacking noise of her heels against the floor.

Natasha walked down the hallway and found a door marked "Make-Up." She knocked twice and peeked inside.

"Natasha darling! You made it!" cried Eugene, her personal hair and make-up stylist. "Wow, just look at you. You're like a blank canvas. Well, let's get to work, shall we?" he said, spinning around a leather chair propped in front of a large mirror surrounded with bright lights.

"It's hot, hot, hot outside, but in here today it's winter," Eugene continued. "We're going to do hair extensions, big lashes and pouty lips. Hans told me he wanted a 'lioness in winter' look, with lots of fur."

"Are you giving me whiskers?" Natasha asked playfully as she approached the seat.

"Ha! I wish!" Eugene giggled. "You would look great in anything, but today your eye lashes will be your whiskers. We may as well begin there. Have a seat, gorgeous!"

Chapter 13

TOLEDO, Washington - 251 Layton Rd., 5:35 a.m.

A rooster called out through the crisp, morning air, announcing a new day.

Farmer Bob Layton stirred in his bed, reaching over to check his wristwatch on the nightstand. *Too early*, he thought, collapsing back into his feather pillow. Outside, the rooster crowed again, then once more for good measure. *Guess not*, the 68-year-old farmer thought.

Reluctantly, Bob sat up on the edge of his bed. He looked over at Maud, his gray-haired wife, still snoring loudly on her side of the bed. *Might as well let her sleep*, he thought, scratching his white beard. Bob put on his socks, pulled his overalls over his blue boxer shorts and white T-shirt and headed to the bedroom door, grabbing his favorite black and red-checkered flannel shirt hanging from the closet door.

When he reached the kitchen door, he slipped on a pair of leather work boots, grabbed his denim jacket, slipped his well-worn, green John Deere cap over his pale, balding head and stepped outside into the morning air. There was a heavy mist, but it wasn't raining.

The rooster called out again as Bob walked through the wet grass and fog to the chicken coop across the yard. He reached over the chicken fence, pulled a rope string and opened the small, wooden trap door to the chicken coop. Almost immediately, the rooster and about 20 hens jumped through the small doorway and raced down a ramp into the fenced-in pen, running over each other in their search for fresh worms, seed and kitchen scraps.

The chickens came in a variety of colors and breeds. The Cochins had luminescent, white feathers; the Buff Orpingtons were yellow and gold; the Rhode Island Reds had a rich burgundy color; and a few, like the Barred Rocks, were speckled in black and white. By now, all the chickens had grown distinct, bright-red, fleshy combs and wattles, but they didn't have these when Bob and

Maud had first raised them as chicks. Several of them were fearless and friendly, while others cautiously turned their heads sideways and watched Bob with raptor-like eyes.

Bob attached the rope to a nail on the side of the coop, holding the trap door open. He walked a few paces to the dog house and let out Spike, his collie/shepherd mix mutt. Spike smiled at Bob with his tongue out and wagged his tail, but didn't jump.

"Morning, Spike," Bob said, patting his old dog on the head. Bob turned and walked to the barn, Spike following alongside him as the rooster gave another morning call. At the barn, Bob lifted a wooden latch and slid the large barn door open to the left. The smell of horse manure filled his nostrils. Inside, a cow mooed. Bob stomped through the straw lining the floor to the horse corral and used a pitchfork to shovel some fresh hay and alfalfa into the horse area. His two horses were acting restless and jumpy and seemed to ignore the new fodder. The cow mooed again.

"I'm coming, Betsy," Bob said, stomping through the straw to the other side of the barn. As he reached the other wall, he grabbed a metal pail and wooden stool before opening the inner barn door and stepping inside. He walked over to his Jersey dairy cow and calmed her by brushing the light brown hair along her side a few times before setting down the stool and sitting down next to the cow. He placed the bucket underneath Betsy's udders and began to milk with both hands. Hot streams of fresh milk gushed forth in spurts into the metal pail.

Doesn't get any fresher than this, he thought, as the pail began to fill up.

Outside the barn, the rooster crowed again.

Chapter 14

NEW YORK CITY - Sheepshead Bay, Brooklyn, 9 a.m.

Frank began polishing the yacht's teak interior with a clean rag using small, circular motions, occasionally spritzing the surface with linseed oil. Afterwards, he checked the ship's refrigerator. There were two bottles of Heineken light beer, a nearly empty carton of 2 percent milk set to expire that day, a jar of green olives, three kinds of leftover cheeses and some stale baguette. His cell phone rang.

"Hello, this is Frank," he said, answering the phone as he closed the fridge.

"Hey Frank, this is Dave from Marina Security. You have a delivery at the gate marked perishable."

"Thanks, Dave," Frank said. "I'll be right over."

A few minutes later, Frank carried the boxes of cold food and bottles back to the *Reciprocity* and took a quick inventory as he loaded the fridge.

> One package of 50 pre-made sweet potato gaufrettes
> Two dozen fresh quail eggs
> Two boxes of frozen baby lamb lollipops
> One five-pound package of prosciutto cured ham
> Eight kinds of specialty cheese wedges, including camembert, cranberry chevre with cinnamon, Crotonese, gorgonzola, Manchego, pecorino, Piave and ricotta
> Five pounds of frozen ratatouille mix
> One fresh cantaloupe
> A dozen fresh peaches
> One two-pound package of frozen crab-stuffed mushrooms
> Two packages of frozen cigar-shaped spiced duck tenders

"Jesus, who eats this stuff?" Frank said to himself as he put the last of the hors d'oeuvres into the fridge and freezer, filling them completely. He checked the last two boxes. The first had several jars of cranberry black pepper chutney and pomegranate dipping sauce, four small jars of beluga caviar, two cans of macadamia nuts and a jar of maraschino cherries. He stowed the contents in a cupboard and checked the last box. Six bottles of Dom Perignon 2006, one bottle of Hennessy cognac, one bottle of Knob Creek bourbon and one bottle of Johnny Walker Blue Label scotch.

There was also a bottle of a California pinot noir, a bottle of French cabernet sauvignon and a bottle of Italian shiraz. He put the liquor and wine in another cabinet next to a few bottles of gin, vodka and Puerto Rican rum.

This is a party boat all right, he thought. *These people wouldn't last one week on the open sea.*

Frank grabbed one of the bottles of champagne and opened the fridge, searching for any room at all. He traded the champagne for the milk, which he smelled and then drank from the carton.

"Looks like I might need to get some real food," he said, tossing the empty milk carton, leftover cheeses and old baguette in a black plastic trash bag before heading back out the door.

Chapter 15

TOLEDO, Wash. - 251 Layton Rd., 6:15 a.m.

When Bob Layton had finished up milking Betsy the cow, he took the pail of hot milk back to the farmhouse, stopping by the chicken coop to check for eggs. There were 12 fresh, brown eggs sitting in the straw-filled roosts. He gathered the eggs in a wicker basket and walked back to the house, setting the milk pail and egg basket inside on a table by the door.

"Smells good," Bob said, taking in the aroma of the coffee brewing in their French press and giving his wife a quick peck on the cheek.

"Thank you. It's almost ready," Maud said, gathering the milk and eggs. "Oh, and happy birthday!" Maud was wearing a yellow-flowered summer dress that stretched almost to her ankles, covered with a dirty, white kitchen apron. "We're the same age again!"

"Thanks. I'm off to feed the pigs and goats," Bob said, grabbing the full compost jar Maud had set by the door. "Call me when it's ready," he said, heading back outside.

Maud threw a few slices of bacon that she and Bob had brined and smoked themselves into the cast-iron frying pan and began chopping a potato, fresh onions, garlic and bell peppers on a wooden cutting board. All of the ingredients had come from their farm and were free from pesticides. When Maud was done chopping, she poked the sizzling bacon with a metal spatula, tilted the pieces to check their underside, then tossed the vegetables into the hot grease.

Maud took two coffee cups out of a cupboard and filled them with hot coffee. She walked back to the stove and cracked four fresh chicken eggs into the hot grease and vegetables, savoring the aroma as the eggs bubbled and popped in the bacon fat, their yokes a vivid orange.

She walked to the door, stepped outside and briefly rang the triangular metal dinner bell for Bob.

Chapter 16

NEW YORK CITY - 11 Wall Street, 9:30 a.m.
TIME TO SOLAR IMPACT: 10 hours, 2 minutes

The loud, clanging bell announced the start of the day's trading on the New York Stock Exchange. The four cavernous rooms felt impossibly crowded with computer monitors sitting on top of desks, hanging on walls and dangling from metal tubes. Wires and pipes jutted out of every wall and from dozens of places on the ceiling. There were no fewer than 10 American flags hanging in the room and many of the traders wore small American flags on their jackets, but all that red, white and blue patriotism seemed to fade in amongst the clutter.

Computer monitors were stacked one on top of the other, side-by-side, even overlapping other monitors. Scurrying on the floor below, hundreds of men in blue jackets began shouting into phones, at each other and at the computer monitors as the screens flickered to life and millions of numbers began scrolling by almost too quickly to read.

"Give me 10,000 shares of Intel!" "I need GE!" "Apple!" "Microsoft!" "Oracle!" "Boeing!" "China Solar! Who wants China Solar?!" "Buy!" "Sell!" "Buy!"

One balding, white man began crying, clutching the remains of his hair in his fists as he watched the numbers scroll past at breakneck speed. Ten feet away, two other men were laughing and hugging each other as the numbers on their monitors began to climb.

"One hundred thousand! We're rich!" they yelled. "One hundred five! A hundred ten!"

The men continued to dash from one corner of the room to the other, frantically typing on keyboards and shouting into phones, sometimes with a phone in each hand.

"I need more! No, MORE!" "I don't care what it costs! Buy! Buy now!"

Chapter 17

NEW YORK CITY - 1601 Broadway, 5th floor, 9:35 a.m.

With techno pop music thumping loudly in the background, Natasha laid back in a chaise lounge in full supermodel mode, surrounded by about 10 or 15 handlers scurrying about checking the lighting, adjusting the lighting, taking photos and getting her next outfits ready.

Today she was doing a shoot for the Victoria's Secret winter catalog and had already tried on about 50 outfits this morning, with at least another 150 to go. Presently she was wearing a large, puffy, quilted jacket with a gray faux-fur collar, a gray V-neck blouse, black satin miniskirt, faux-fur covered sheepskin boots with four-inch heels and a push-up bra. Her face was heavily made up, her complexion flawless, her hair was long and straight and her wedding ring was absent.

Hans the photographer was shouting over the loud music, barking commands at Natasha and the handlers, switching cameras and constantly taking pictures.

"You're beautiful, darling, but no smiling! You love your clothes. They make you feel warm and sexy. You are a bear or a wolf or a lioness, hungry for fresh meat. Show me your hunger. That's good, honey, but no smiling! OK, let's try one with some shag carpeting. No, not that one, the gray one! That's good. Natasha, can you lift up your legs a little? That's good. I need more lighting on the carpet! No, it's not working. Get the shag carpet out of there. I don't want any carpet! Can we try the boots with all the belts? We did that already? No, the tan boots this time! Somebody get her a different jacket."

As soon as one of the assistants had unbuckled and removed her boots, Natasha stood up, pulled off the miniskirt and immediately slipped into a pair of skinny jeans. She sat down on the chaise lounge and pulled the gray blouse over her head as an assistant crouched at her feet, buckling on a pair of three-inch high heels. Someone else handed her a dark blue, long-sleeved, V-neck shirt, into which she slipped her arms before pulling the fabric over her head. Eugene, her stylist, helped her put on a silver necklace with a small heart-shaped medallion and quickly gave her nose a dab of powder and her hair a subtle correction. In less than 30 seconds, Natasha had completely changed her outfit and still managed to look amazing.

"That's great, let's go stand by the ladder," Hans said, as everyone shuffled 10 feet to the left. "Beautiful, everyone, beautiful. This is really hot. I love the look, Natasha. Can you arch your back a little? Yes, that's really sultry and seductive. Let's try one with the red top, shall we?"

Natasha pulled off the blue top and gave it to one of the assistants, who handed her the exact same style of shirt in red. *Can't decide what to wear? Try on everything,* Natasha thought as she pulled the red shirt over her bra.

Chapter 18

NEW YORK CITY - The Chrysler Building, 65th floor, 9:45 a.m.

Adam's morning meeting with Donovan had gone well. The Securities and Exchange Commission was asking a lot of questions about Adam's "Techno Savvy Robot" fund, questions that Adam was not obligated to answer, thanks to the limited oversight required of hedge funds like his. Their meeting was more of a warning between old friends.

Specifically, the SEC's Division of Risk, Strategy and Financial Innovation – or Risk Fin for short – was becoming increasingly worried that enormous hedge funds like "Robot" were becoming too large and influential to continue to operate unmonitored and unregulated.

The argument went like this: Investors of regular investments like stocks, bonds and mutual funds are your average, run-of-the-mill, working-class people. A large percentage of these investors are looking for simple ways to save for retirement that allow them to benefit from a rising economy, but do not require them to take risky bets that could jeopardize their life savings during a market downturn.

Hedge funds, on the other hand, require a minimum investment of $1 million and are therefore afforded special privileges. Since anyone investing more than $1 million was considered to be a "savvy" investor, one could assume they would be more aware of the risks they took with their money. Hedge funds weren't regulated because their affluent investors didn't "need" the protective oversight of the SEC. Adam didn't have a Series 7 license to sell investment products and never bothered to take the test. He had such a large personal stake in his fund that he didn't "need" a license. People with lots of money know what they're doing.

This logic was quickly undermined by other "special privileges" employed by hedge funds, such as the rampant use of leveraging, high-speed trading and frequent dealings on dark, unmonitored exchanges known as "dark pools." Adam liked to think of dark pools as two ships passing in the night, making trades without knowing each other's identity or greater purpose.

Adam's argument to Donovan was that his "Techno Savvy Robot" was a pure profit generator, a market maker and liquidity provider, unfettered by human emotions like fear and greed. Shortly after its inception in 2010, the "Robot" had helped the stock market see its largest average gains in more than a decade. In addition to the technology sector, nearly every asset class and commodity had gradually risen, lifting the U.S. and global economy out of recession and generating significant federal tax revenues, Adam had argued. Shutting down his "Robot" could potentially cause the stock market to plummet.

Donovan countered that high-speed trading had already caused more than one "flash crash," or a brief period when there was neither a buyer or nor a seller for a stock. This caused its temporary price to exponentially drop to zero, or at least well below its normal price.

Adam assured his former investment banking colleague that he would keep his influential hedge fund under wraps and asserted that everything his fund did was perfectly legal.

"Anything won by breaking the rules isn't worth having," he proclaimed.

"A lack of regulation doesn't mean something is legal; it just means there's no law to break," Donovan said as Adam escorted him to the elevator.

As Adam was walking back to his office, he reflected on the fact that he paid the U.S. government almost nothing in capital gains taxes, thanks to his decision to base his hedge fund's parent company in the Cayman Islands, a popular tax shelter among multi-national corporations and the ultra wealthy. He pulled up the fund's profile on one of his computer monitors.

"Techno Savvy Robot" was already up one percent for the morning, after just 15 minutes of trading. The Dow Jones Industrial Average was also up more than 100 points and was continuing to climb.

Adam leaned back in his office chair and placed his hands behind his smooth, bald head, admiring the genius of his creation. Thanks to the law of large numbers, even a small percentage of large number was still a large number. One percent of $20 billion was $200 million. *Not bad for 15 minutes of work,* he thought.

Chapter 19

NEW YORK CITY - 11 Wall Street, 6th floor, 9:50 a.m.

Six stories above the New York Stock Exchange, the twin supercomputers running "Techno Savvy Robot" quietly hummed inside a small, unmanned office behind a locked door marked 621. The "Robot" fund made its master huge sums of money by combining complicated algorithms with high-frequency trading and co-location. It scanned the markets for a buyer or seller of a stock, and just before the buyer and seller did business, the robot would use its lightning-quick reflexes to jump in between the sale.

In mere nanoseconds, the "Robot" program could buy or sell a stock or an exchange-traded fund for slightly more or less than it paid just moments before and turn a tiny profit. The program was ruthless at bargain hunting, a high-speed dealer in pricing arbitrage. Since the transactions occurred in private, unregulated dark pools of anonymous liquidity, neither the buyer nor the seller had any idea the robot had visited.

The real genius of the hedge fund was the co-location or close proximity to the exchange's own servers located in the room directly below. This allowed the robot to slip in between active trades thousands of times per second, exploiting small and fleeting price differences before human or other computerized traders could respond. An identical "robot" program located a few miles or even a few meters away would be slowed by the "ping," the amount of time required for light to reach its target and return.

Four years of steady, generous investment in technology companies had created a virtual tree of knowledge that was lush and filled with beautiful, enticing fruit. This fruit was ripe for the picking and just about to drop to the ground. It would all be rotten by tomorrow.

Six floors below, men in blue jackets were cheering the market's steady climb, while upstairs, surrounded by hallways decorated with antique drawings of sailing ships, the computers running "Techno Savvy Robot" continued to quietly hum and purr.

Chapter 20

On board the International Space Station, 14:00:00 UTC
TIME TO SOLAR IMPACT: 9 hours, 32 minutes

Aleksandr's wristwatch gave a quick beep. Six o'clock. He looked out a nearby window at the dark, Pacific Ocean. He was presently about 250 kilometers above Hawaii, where it was now 4 a.m. The space station had circled the earth twice in three hours.

For the past three hours, Aleks had been checking and running diagnostic tests on the International Global Navigation Satellite System, or GNSS for short. The GNSS is a federation of more than 200 worldwide agencies that share mapping and surveying data from orbiting satellites. This global navigational system is the backbone of both the Global Positioning System (GPS) and GLONASS, the Russian equivalent.

The satellite network normally provided users with updated navigational information several times a minute, but for some reason, the incoming data flow was gradually dropping. Aleks had been trying to locate some hard data that could help him generate a theory as to what was happening, but the only thing he had found so far was that the satellites were sending fewer signals. He ran a diagnostic test on all 950 satellites in the system and discovered than more than 50 satellites had not sent a single signal in the past three hours, including 10 Russian satellites and 30 American ones. The remaining 10 malfunctioning satellites were Chinese.

Two of the malfunctioning satellites were pointed at the sun and had indicated suspicious sunspot activity when he checked them earlier. Now they were not showing anything.

Aleks logged into his secure e-mail server and checked his messages. Nothing from command. Just then, an e-mail arrived, labeled as having been sent two hours earlier.

"Mishka says data inconclusive. If problem is widespread, seek assistance," read the message from Russian Space Command.

Aleks immediately rattled off another message.

"Just received last message at 14:05 UTC," he wrote. "Suspect solar weather may be disabling satellites. Seeking assistance from ISS crew."

He clicked "send," logged out of his secure e-mail and closed his laptop.

"Wilson!" Aleks called out as he floated through the porthole connecting the Zarya Control Module to the Unity Node. There was no response. He continued floating to the Destiny Laboratory where Chuck Wilson was usually stationed. Wilson was nowhere in sight. *How do you lose someone on a space station?* he thought as the sun quickly "rose" on the pod, flooding the room with bright sunlight.

"Wilson!" he shouted again from inside the Destiny Laboratory.

"Yeah, OK, just a minute!" a voice called out from inside one of the walls. A white panel slid open and Wilson floated out, his face bright red. "Sorry, I was checking on something. What's this all about?"

Aleks heard a small thump come from inside the closet out of which Chuck had just emerged. He peered inside and saw Japanese astronaut Mizuho Sakaguchi scrambling to zip up her blue jumpsuit over her naked body. Her face was also bright red.

Aleks smiled as he offered Mizuho a hand, helping her out of the closet. She smiled back bashfully, then looked at Chuck. Chuck looked from her to Aleks and all three laughed.

"We have a situation," Aleks said in English, his smile fading. "It is good I find you both, as this concerns all of us."

"What's up?" Chuck asked.

"We are losing satellites," Aleks said. "Fifty have gone offline in the past three hours, including 30 from America. I suspect space weather may be the cause. Earlier, I noticed dark spots on the sun from two Russian satellites, and now both of these satellites are down."

"A solar flare?" Mizuho asked, pulling her floating, shoulder-length black hair out of her face with both hands and sliding an elastic band off her left wrist to hold her hair back in a ponytail. Her face had returned to her normal, alabaster tone.

"That's what I was thinking," Chuck said, looking from Mizuho back to Aleks. "Actually, we are probably due for major solar flare this year. How much time do we have?"

"A few hours, perhaps," Aleks said. "Maybe less. Communications from both low-earth orbit and geosynchronous satellites seem to be vanishing."

"I will check on HINODE," Mizuho said, referring to the Japanese Aerospace Exploration Agency's new solar physics satellite. "Charles and Aleks, could you check on ACE, SOHO, SDO and STEREO?"

ACE, or Advanced Composition Explorer, measured solar wind; SOHO was NASA's solar and heliospheric observatory that collected data on coronal mass ejections; SDO was the agency's solar dynamics observatory, collecting data on sunspots, solar magnetic fields and solar corona; and STEREO was NASA's solar terrestrial relations observatory that utilized two separate but nearly identical satellites to create a stereoscopic image of the sun.

"Sounds good," Chuck said, opening up a nearby laptop and logging in.

"Da," Aleks agreed, floating back toward the Zarya.

"Good. Let's meet back here in one hour," Mizuho said, heading to the Kibo Module.

Chapter 21

LONDON - 260 Devonia Rd., Islington, 3:15 p.m.

Jacob Baker was bored with his video game and decided to take a break. He had been gaming for hours and had lost track of time, and now he was feeling a bit hungry. He checked his smartphone to see the status of his popular YouTube video.

"What the heck?" he said to himself as he did a double take on the video's hit count.

"How to Hypnotize Your Mom" had now been viewed 3,120,505 times, more than four times as often as it had been three hours earlier. The video also had approximately 200,000 "likes" and about 5,000 "dislikes".

He checked his messages to see if his mom had replied to his text from earlier. His mailbox had just over 1,000 new messages, with the most recent message from his phone's service provider sent about two hours earlier, informing him that his mailbox had exceeded its storage limit and was now blocked from sending or receiving new messages. The next seven messages were identical alerts from his provider, all stating that he was over his storage limit.

"Blimey," Jacob said as he did a search for messages from his mom. There was one.

"Gave my blessing to YouTube," the message read. "Can you pick up some milk? Don't spend the whole day inside. Loves, Mom."

Jacob walked to the kitchen and opened the refrigerator. He reached for the milk carton on the door and found it was completely empty. *That's stupid*, he thought, and then recalled that he drank the last of the milk that morning and it was he who had put the empty carton back in the fridge. He paused for a second to reflect on this, then put the empty carton back into the fridge.

He picked up his smartphone again and called his friend Hamish.

"Lo?" the young male on the other end answered.

"Hamish? It's Jake. Where you at?"

"Whoa, Jake! You're like famous, man! What are you doing?" Hamish asked.

"Been gaming all day, but I need a break," Jacob said. "Where you at?"

"I'm at the N1 with Lennon and Alfie," Hamish said. "You coming?"

"Yeah, I'm on my way. Where exactly are you?"

"Outside the French Connection," he said. "Seriously, you gotta get over here immediately! Everyone is talking about you."

"For reals? OK, I'm en-route. Peace," he said, pocketing his phone and heading to the front door.

Jacob stopped for a second to check his reflection in the hall mirror and brushed his hair with his hands to make it look extra shaggy. He was wearing a plain, white T-shirt, skinny designer blue jeans and white sneakers, but decided to put on a stylish, blue-and-black, horizontally stripped, hooded cardigan. He pulled out his smartphone and sent a short message to his Twitter followers, who now numbered more than 180,000.

"Famished, heading to French Connection at N1 for lunch. C u there?"

Chapter 22

TOLEDO, Wash. - 251 Layton Rd., 7:25 a.m.

After breakfast, Bob Layton spent a few minutes looking through his library for a book on animal behavior. He pulled out "Domestic Animal Behavior for Veterinarians and Animal Scientists," and looked at the cover. There was a white horse striking a peculiar pose. Bob took the book to the couch, sat down and began flipping through the pages. He got to the section on aberrant behavior and began reading.

"Whatcha lookin' at?" Maud asked, standing in the doorway to the kitchen.

"Some of the animals are acting strange today," Bob said, turning a page.

"Might be the heat," she said. "It's supposed to break another record today."

"It's the horses, goats and pigs," Bob said. Outside, the rooster crowed again. "And maybe the rooster," he added with a smile.

"Let's make sure they have plenty of food, water and shade," Maud said. "Besides that, there's not much we can do, other than call the vet. You want me to call her?"

"No, I'll keep an eye on them today," Bob said, closing the book and replacing it on the bookshelf. "If it gets worse, we might have to call the vet, but it might fix itself, too."

"OK," Maud said. "I'm going out to water the garden."

"Thanks again for breakfast," Bob said, giving his wife a smooch on the lips on his way to the extra bedroom.

The room had been their son's, but they had converted it into an office after he had moved out. Bob sat down at their six-year-old computer and scanned the news. The stock market was up 250 points that morning and continued to climb. *I don't know what I'm waiting for*, he thought as he logged into his retirement account's secure server.

The Laytons' account balance was just over $500,000, mostly due to the large loan they had received from their bank on Monday after refinancing the mortgage on their 40-acre farm.

Bob selected a basket of tech stocks and quickly scrolled through the online summary prospectus. The mutual fund was actually a fund of funds, with a substantial portion of its portfolio invested in large hedge funds, including "Techno Savvy Robot." In the last four years, the portfolio had risen an average of 15 percent a year, not including management fees. Bob pulled out a calculator from the desk drawer and quickly did some simple math.

Fifteen percent of $500,000 was $75,000 a year. That would be more than enough to pay the taxes on the land and house, and probably leave some left over for a new tractor, he reasoned.

He clicked a few buttons to add the basket of tech stocks to his account, as well as a broad-based market index fund. Before he clicked "confirm," he noticed a short sentence posted beneath the button. "Past performance is no guarantee of future results."

Bob clicked "confirm," and was directed to another screen informing him that since his trades were all regular mutual funds and not exchange-traded funds, they would take place at the end of the day at the market's closing price, not at the current market price. *I hope it doesn't go up too much before I get to buy,* Bob thought as he logged out of his account. As he turned in his chair, he saw Spike the dog sitting next to him, looking up into his eyes.

"We better go check on the animals," Bob said, pulling on his boots.

Chapter 23

NEW YORK CITY - The Chrysler Building, 65th floor, 10:32 a.m.
TIME TO SOLAR IMPACT: 9 hours, 0 minutes

Adam logged on to his hedge fund's secure server and checked the balance. The numbers were a continually changing blur of profits, delayed by approximately five seconds. He could immediately tell that "Techno Savvy Robot" was having another great day, but he wasn't sure how great. He did some quick math and determined that his hedge fund had grown by approximately $500 million in one hour.

That's insane, he thought for a moment, before checking to see how much of that money was actually his and not just the fund's. He knew that he charged his investors a standard management fee of two percent and a performance fee of 20 percent, but his brain began to swim in the numbers after a certain point. He realized he was starting to sweat and took off his jacket and rolled up his shirt sleeves. *Air conditioning must be off*, he thought.

Adam logged on to his private, numbered bank account in the Bahamas. Having his fund based in the Cayman Islands and his personal account based in the Bahamas made it a little easier to hide his money, but with everything automated these days, he could instantly access his money from anywhere in the world. A string of numbers flashed on the screen and Adam used his pencil again to help him count the decimal places.

As of that moment, Adam's personal net worth was listed as $10,128,403,996.77.

He couldn't believe it. Ten billion dollars! He was now among the richest men in the world. He briefly started to think about what $10 billion could buy, but the moment he did, he began to feel nauseous again. Other than art, he rarely bought anything. He logged out of his personal account and picked up his smartphone to check the latest news.

His smartphone had shut off again. He pressed the power button and a few moments later a message flashed across the screen informing him that his battery was dead. *Shoot, I forgot to charge my phone,* Adam thought as he plugged in a power cord connecting his smartphone with his desktop computer. The smartphone began charging and synchronizing its files and contacts with his other computer.

Adam opened up a web browser on his computer and began scanning the news.

> Markets Soar on China Solar IPO, updated 10 mins ago
> NEW YORK - International stock markets rallied this morning on the initial public offering of China's latest technological wonder, a magnificent solar array near the city of Zhangjiakou. The array comprises of an undisclosed number of large, photovoltaic solar panels spanning ...

Old news, Adam thought as he continued scanning the headlines.

> Congress Weighs $200 million NASA Request
>
> OPEC Votes to Maintain Quotas
>
> Arizona Wildfires Creep Toward Phoenix
>
> Viral Video Hypnotizes YouTube Followers

Adam clicked on this last headline and was directed to a story on Yahoo!News.

> Viral Video Hypnotizes YouTube Followers
> LONDON - Ever imagine you could hypnotize your parents? A 16-year-old Londoner is getting a dose of celebrity fame today after his video titled "How to Hypnotize your Mom" garnered more than 3 million

views in just a few hours. Click below to see the video.

Adam clicked the triangle "play" button over the video and turned up the sound on his computer.

A familiar-looking teenage boy with blue eyes, a wide smile, clean complexion and shaggy brown hair was grinning into the camera.

"Hey mates," the boy began, "has this ever happened to you? You want something from your mum or dad like some new shoes or a video game, and they just won't budge. 'Take out the garbage, do your homework, go outside and play,'" the boy said in a mock whining voice.

"It's enough to drive you bonkers. So what's a bloke to do? Try this one on for size," the boy said with a big, wide smile.

The picture cut to a slim-looking brunette sitting at a kitchen table with her back turned to the camera.

"Hey Mum? I was just thinking about my future and was wondering whether I should be a doctor or a lawyer," the boy said to the woman seated at the table. Upon mentioning the words doctor and lawyer, the woman turned around.

Adam's heart sank.

The woman in the video was about 40 years old and looked exactly like a woman he used to date. *What was her name?* Adam wondered. *Lisa? Lizzy? Lara? Lauren?* He thought for a moment as the mom and son continued to chat.

"That's wonderful, dear," the woman said. "Being a doctor or lawyer takes a lot of schooling and hard work. I know you can do it if you try, though."

"That's what I was thinking," the boy said. "And you know, it might be easier to get through all that schooling if I had some incentive, like some new shoes or a new video game. Once I finish my homework and chores, of course," he added.

The woman sitting at the table was speechless.

"You know, I think I'll get back to work on that homework," the boy said. "I just wanted to let you know that I'm proud of you, and that you're my inspiration for everything I do."

The woman smiled with a wide, broad grin. "Thank you, dear. That's wonderful. I'm proud of you, too. What kind of shoes were you wanting?"

Leah! Adam thought suddenly. *Leah Baker! Oh my god, how long ago was that? About 16 years ago?*

The boy smiled into the camera. "Future doctor/lawyer shoes? You're the best, mom. I love you."

"I love you too, sweetheart," the woman said.

The video cut to a shot of the boy walking down the street in his new shoes, in rhythm to the Bee Gees' "Stayin' Alive." He did a little dance, a quick spin and then winked as he smiled at the camera one last time. As the video ended, it flashed a brief ad for Sketchers sneakers.

Adam looked at the play count at the bottom of the video. "How to Hypnotize Your Mom" had been viewed more than five million times. He scrolled back through the video and paused on a picture of the hot mom. *Leah Baker. Man, she's still beautiful. Why did we ever break up?*

Adam scrolled forward a few frames to a shot of the boy. *And who is that?*

Suddenly it dawned on him. *Oh no!*

A wave of stomach bile made it halfway up his throat before he stopped himself, covered his mouth and swallowed again. *Crap, crap, crap*, he thought, unbuttoning his collar and loosening his tie.

Adam logged into his hedge fund's secure account. Down in the bottom right corner of the screen were two large buttons: a green button labeled "buy" and a red button labeled "sell." Adam clicked the red button.

The account directed him to a new screen, titled "Amount of assets to sell." Adam entered a two followed by 10 zeros and clicked "sell." The screen loaded for a moment, then displayed one last warning. "Are you sure you want to liquidate this fund?"

Adam considered his two choices, yes or no. His stomach heaved again briefly as he reached for a wastebasket. Nothing. He spun around in his office chair and looked out the window at the

Empire State Building and the Manhattan skyline. He thought for a moment before spinning his chair around and moving back to his desk.

The screen was still waiting for an answer. Adam quickly logged into his personal account with his smartphone and created a new transaction. In a few seconds, he had dedicated most of his $10 billion personal fortune to purchasing an enormous amount of triple-inverse exchange traded funds, with the bulk of the ETFs assigned to shorting tech stocks. The computers running "Techno Savvy Robot" could still spare some extra bandwidth, so Adam used them, routing his trades through a dark pool to cover his tracks. He clicked "confirm transfer" and logged out again. He turned back to his computer and looked at the choice before him.

A rumbling sound came from his stomach and he immediately felt sick again. Adam clicked "yes" and ran out of his office all the way to the men's room.

Chapter 24

LONDON - 2 Parkfield Street, Islington, 3:40 p.m.

Jacob Baker noticed something was different as he approached the N1 shopping center. Normally on a Wednesday afternoon, there weren't tens of thousands of teenage girls and boys milling about in the street, completely blocking traffic. Today it looked more like a crowded street fair without vendors or a summer concert without a band. It was actually the first of several flash mobs Jacob would create around the city this afternoon.

"What's going on?" Jacob asked a cute 15-year-old girl who was busily punching buttons on her smartphone. She had short, reddish-brown hair and was wearing a light-pink summer Chanel dress, Deichmann sneakers and a small, white leather jacket by Zara. Her fingernails were short and painted black. When she didn't look up from her phone, Jacob repeated his question in almost a yell in order to be heard over the buzzing noise of the crowd.

"Everyone's waiting for the Internet video guy," she yelled back, looking up from her phone for the first time. "Hey, you kind of look like him. Are you that guy?"

"I'm Jake," he replied with a wide grin. "What's your name?"

The color immediately disappeared from the girl's face the moment she recognized his smile.

"Oh my god," she whispered. "It's you. You're the guy, aren't you?"

Jacob extended his right hand in a friendly gesture. "And to whom do I have the pleasure of speaking, miss?"

The girl immediately broke into a wide smile. "I'm Kendra," she said, shaking his hand. "I'm one of your Twitter followers."

"Kendra? That's a beautiful name," he said, still holding on to her hand. "I love your jacket. It's totally cute. Listen,

Kendra, I think things are about to go Beatlemania here real quick. Wanna go somewhere quiet?"

Kendra smiled even wider. "Yeah! Let's jet!"

Still holding hands, the two began pushing their way to the edge of the crowd.

"Hey! That's him! That's the guy!" someone shouted, pointing at Jacob. A teenager standing next to them quickly took their picture with his cell phone. The camera app on the phone made a sound mimicking an antique camera shutter as it took the digital photo.

Jacob and Kendra stopped for a moment as the crowd hushed and 10,000 faces turned toward them. For a moment, no one spoke. Then Jacob had an idea.

"Thanks for coming, everyone!" he shouted. "Tell your friends they can get almost anything with a smile and a compliment!" But the crowd began to cheer after "friends" and they missed the rest. The mass of teenagers began to slowly lurch toward them as the cheering turned into a deafening roar.

Jacob looked at Kendra and squeezed her hand. She smiled and squeezed back. Still holding hands, the two kids turned and ran south on Liverpool Road, followed by a mob of starstruck teens.

Chapter 25

MECCA - Ibrahim Al Khaleel Street, 5:45 p.m.

Standing near the top of a 16-foot step ladder in the middle of a large, extremely crowded room, surrounded by thousands of people moving in every direction, a dark-skinned technician wearing green coveralls carefully adjusted the fastening of a ceiling mounting bracket and secured a high-resolution video camera in place with a final twist of his screwdriver. The ceiling was six meters or about 20 feet from the floor and was decorated in an ornate, geometric pattern of hand-carved, blue-and-white mosaic tiles.

The man's smartphone rang inside one of his breast pockets and he briefly looked down to check the caller ID, pulled the device out of his pocket and then returned it to the same pocket. He touched the wireless earpiece clipped around his left ear, activating a blue light.

"Hello Dear. Can I call you back?" he asked out loud in Arabic, trying to speak over the clamor of the room. "It's really not a very good time to talk."

"I'll send you a text," the woman said. "Love you!"

The call ended and Ibn Shaja'at Ali touched the glowing blue earpiece again, causing it to switch off. He finished replacing a triangular black glass panel, completing an inverted, four-sided pyramid that was suspended from the ceiling. *Actually there are five sides, if you count the bottom,* he thought. The camera he had just installed had a wide-angle lens pointed in each direction of the hallway and recorded the faces of everyone who walked by, which could be as many as a million people a day.

Ibn could see people of all ages and races everywhere he looked. He could see Egyptian, Iraqi, Iranian, Turkish, Indonesian, Palestinian, Lebanese, Syrian, Tunisian and Moroccan, among others. Nearly every male over the age of 16 including Ibn was bearded, and most were wearing the traditional pilgrim's tunic and cap, either black or white. The effect of so many people wearing black or white created a salt-and-pepper effect when viewed from above.

The corridor he was perched above reminded him of several touristy places in Cairo, only less noisy and with more Islamic art. He scanned for faces as he looked into the crowd, and for an instant he thought he recognized someone he knew, but he couldn't quite place the name or context. He saw another familiar face, but couldn't place it before it was gone. *That was the trouble with enormous crowds,* he thought. *The human brain has a tendency to overload when it becomes overwhelmed with too much new information, whereas a camera does not. And a camera does not blink.* All the cameras were interlinked to a database in the main complex, and Ibn was headed there next.

As Ibn carefully descended the step ladder into the crowd, he thought about how he was familiar with seeing cultural diversity around him and had learned to embrace it for the treasure it was. He and his family were Saudi Arabian but lived in a high-rise in Dubai, overlooking the magnificent Persian Gulf coastline and the city's futuristic skyscrapers. The most notable skyscraper was the world-renowned Burj Khalifa, currently the tallest manmade structure in the world. Towering 828 meters or more than 2,700 feet above ground, the 163-story building's jagged, silver spire cut through the sky like a shard of broken glass, confusing and confounding the senses as it seemed to stretch impossibly upward.

"Thank you, Ishmael," Ibn said to the man holding the ladder steady as he stepped off onto the floor. "Please take the ladder back to the depot and take the rest of the day off. I will call you tomorrow if I need you."

"Thank you, sir," the man said with a smile and a nod. Ibn's smartphone chirped, indicating he had a new text message. It was from his wife.

"Are we OK?" the text read. "US tech sector just crashed."

Ibn looked up for Ishmael but he had disappeared, with the ladder, into the sea of moving bodies. Ibn tried to find an opening in the crowd so he could get to one of the walls, but people kept stepping in front of and around him in their rush to get somewhere else. After a few moments, he gave up and simply stepped forward into the crowd and walked directly towards the nearest wall. He bumped into a few people and said "excuse me," but somehow the crowd found a way to move around him and accommodate his irregular path.

When he got to the wall, he pressed his back to it and checked his smartphone again. The U.S. stock markets were in a complete free-fall. He checked the stock price for his international technology company and was shocked to see its value was down by 50 percent. Ibn and his family had a significant portion of their life savings invested in his company and it appeared that their net worth had just been cut in half. He dialed his wife on his smartphone and activated his wireless earpiece.

"Is this a better time?" she answered, speaking in Arabic.

"Yes, I was standing on top of a ladder in a crowded hallway," he replied, scanning the news services on his smartphone for stories about the financial crash. There were none yet. "I don't see any news yet on the American market crash, but I'll keep looking and let you know. I don't think there's anything we can do at this point but wait and see."

While his wife was relaying his messages from home, more than 1,600 km or 1,000 miles away, Ibn bent down and unzipped his coveralls from the cuff of his pants, pulling up to his knees. He straightened out and unzipped the main zipper from his neck down to his waist. With a shrug, he slipped out of the one-piece outfit, revealing the professional, black business suit he had been wearing underneath. He folded up the green coveralls and stashed it in his bag.

There was a commotion ahead further down the hallway and Ibn turned to look. He was a little above average height and could see over most of the crowd, but he couldn't tell what had happened. He started to walk in the direction of the Abraj Al-Bait Towers.

"Are you still there?" his wife asked.

"Yes, Dear. I'm walking back to the clock tower. Was there something else?"

"Shahrazad wants to go out to a movie with her friends tonight."

"Well that's all right, isn't it?" Ibn asked out loud. "She's an honor student and she's 16 already. We told her she could if she kept her grades up. Tell her to keep her cell phone on."

"She says she doesn't want to wear a head scarf," his wife said. "None of her friends wear head scarves except for prayer and special occasions."

"How do you feel about it?" Ibn asked as he stepped out onto the sidewalk of Ibrahim Al Khaleel Street, which was somehow even more crowded than the hallway. Mecca's pervasive construction smells of fresh cement and machine oil filled his nose as his eyes moved upward, scanning the front of the building directly across the street. Ibn found himself looking nearly straight up before he could see the top of the building amid the blue sky. There was a huge clock at the top that said it was a quarter to six. The downtown sounds of traffic, construction work and the occasional music from a nearby street performer or car stereo made it difficult for Ibn to hear anything through his wireless earpiece, but he stuck a finger in his open, right ear and found he could hear his wife much clearer.

"My parents would never have let me out of the house without a scarf or a headdress when I was her age," his wife started. "But we live in a pretty progressive city. That sort of thing is much more common these days. It's not acceptable everywhere, but a lot of people are OK with it. What do you think?"

As he looked around, Ibn could see nearly 100,000 people standing outside and he didn't spot a single woman with an uncovered head. All of the men wore hats or headdresses of some kind, most of them black or white. Ibn was wearing a short black cap called a taqiyah.

"I agree with you that Mecca and Dubai are very different places," he said. "I don't see anyone out here with an uncovered head. I suppose it depends on the situation. Some places it's acceptable, while others it's not. I think we should let her use her own judgment."

In the distance he could hear a familiar rhythmic chanting coming from the nearby minaret, signaling the start of the afternoon prayer. Things were already begging to fall silent.

"I think we're getting ready to pray again," he said. "I'll let you know when I know more about the company. Take care and I love you."

"I love you too."

Ibn pressed the wireless earpiece to end the call, pulled off the device and put it in one of his suit pockets. He found himself a little personal space, unrolled his prayer rug and watched as the entire city quickly fell silent, almost all at once. All music in the city immediately ceased playing, trucks and other vehicle traffic came to a quick stop, construction cranes and jackhammers halted their work and all two million residents or visitors within the city, without exception, stopped moving and stood silently in parallel rows, hands to their sides, facing the city center.

As soon as the prayer song began, more than two million people began to move in a slow, rocking rhythm, kneeling, bowing and praying in unison towards the Kaaba.

Chapter 26

NEW YORK CITY - The Chrysler Building, 65th floor, 10:50 a.m.

Adam flushed the toilet in the men's room, walked to the sink and stared at his reflection in the mirror. His whole head was sweaty and blotchy. He splashed some cold water in his face, took a few deep breaths and dried his hands, face and head with a few paper towels. He realized that he hadn't eaten all day and suddenly felt hungry.

As Adam opened the door to the men's room and stepped back into the business world, he was hit with a wall of sound. The entire floor, nearly silent three hours earlier, was a cacophony of noise. Phones were ringing off the hook, people were running around shouting and papers were literally flying through the air. Adam checked his pocket for his smartphone and realized he had left it in his office.

When Adam got to the door of his corner office, he noticed that his assistant Karen was sitting at her desk with headphones on, watching a YouTube video. He stepped inside his office, closed the door quietly and sat down at his desk to check the stock market. The Dow Jones Industrial Average was now deep in the red. *How was that possible?*

Adam scanned the news on his computer.

> Markets Rally On Promising Outlook, updated 10 mins ago
> NEW YORK - Stock markets continued their vigorous rally Wednesday morning with the Dow Jones Industrial Average up nearly three percent on hopes of a new future of clean energy production worldwide. China Solar led...

That's not helpful at all. Adam looked back at the real-time market report. Instead of being up nearly 300 points, the Dow was down almost 500 points. *How could this happen? I was only in the bathroom for a few minutes,* Adam thought. Then it dawned on him. He checked the account for "Techno Savvy Robot," only to find that the account had been closed. *Oh, yeah.*

Adam quickly grabbed his smartphone and logged into his personal account. The triple-inverse ETFs he had purchased just minutes earlier were soaring as the stock markets tanked. He immediately turned off the ETFs and sat back in his chair. After a few moments, he checked the Dow and saw that the free-fall was beginning to level off after losing nearly 800 points in less than 20 minutes. The NASDAQ was down even further, but the drop was less than the 10 percent necessary to trigger the market's protective "circuit breaker" device that would temporarily halt trading.

He checked the website for *The Wall Street Journal*. "Breaking News: Stocks in Free-fall," the headline read. There was no story yet.

Adam looked at his personal account balance. He saw the number six in front of a whole bunch of numbers and thought for a moment that he had just lost $4 billion, but then he began counting the zeroes with his pencil. No, it wasn't $6 billion in his personal account; he was now worth $60 billion. He had liquidated his fund to an unknown buyer in China for cash in U.S. dollars, which was now being wired to his personal account in Grand Cayman.

He pressed the intercom button on his desk.

"Karen? Could you come in here please?" he asked.

Karen came in a few moments later to find Adam standing by his floor-to-ceiling window, staring out at the city. His blue and gray striped suspenders formed an "X" on his back.

"Yes?" she asked.

"I need you to cancel all my appointments for the rest of the day," he said, continuing to look out the window. "It's too nice to be inside," he added.

"Yes, sir," she said. "Is everything OK?"

"Could you please close the door?" he asked after a moment. Karen complied.

"I'm not sure if you've checked the markets in the last few minutes, but it's not looking good," he said, turning around to face his assistant. "What I'm about to tell you is not to leave this room.

'Techno Savvy Robot' is closed. Its assets have been liquidated and all its investors redeemed. I'm going to take some time off for a few days and get out of the city. I recommend you do the same. Before you go, can you get me the number of that trader with the sailboat?"

"Sir?" Karen asked.

"Um, last weekend, Natasha and I attended a party on a private yacht in the New York Harbor."

"The Fourth of July party?" Karen asked. Adam nodded.

"That was Niles Jones' boat," Karen said. "The *Reciprocity,* if I'm not mistaken. You need his number?"

"That's the fellow," Adam said. "Can you get me his number before I leave?"

"Not a problem," Karen said. "Will there be anything else?"

"Yes, there's one more thing, but I'll tell you as I'm leaving."

Karen smiled as she zipped out the door and sat back at her desk. Adam looked through his desk drawers and pulled out a checkbook, quickly scribbling down a few numbers. He grabbed his jacket, smartphone and other belongings and stepped out of his office.

"Here's Mr. Jones' number," Karen said, handing him a small piece of paper.

"Thanks," Adam said, "and here's a little something for your hard work." He handed her a check, folded in half.

"Oh, you didn't have to do that," she said with a smile as she unfolded the check and read the amount. The smile dropped from her face.

"You might want to cash that soon," Adam said, turning to walk toward the elevators.

"Adam! Wait!" Karen said, quickly standing up and running over to catch her boss, who wasn't slowing down. "What am I supposed to do with this? I can't cash this. It's too much."

"Consider it a bonus," he said as he reached the elevator bay and pressed the down button. "And keep your phone on today. I might need you again."

"Thanks, I will," she said. "Are you sure you want to take the elevator?"

The elevator door opened, but Adam just stood there, staring. After a few moments, the doors closed again. He turned to look at his assistant.

"One more thing," he said, handing her a laminated security badge and a brass-colored key. "Before you quit for the day, could you swing by the Stock Exchange and collect the computers in room 621? We won't be needing them again anytime soon."

Karen stared at Adam for a moment before reaching out and taking the badge and key.

"You got it, boss," she said as Adam opened the door to a stairwell and began walking down the 65 flights to the bottom.

After a few flights, Adam got into the routine of the fire escape. Eight steps down to a small landing, a 180-degree turn, eight more steps to the next floor. He pulled out his smartphone and dialed the number on the scrap of paper.

Chapter 27

NEW YORK CITY - Sheepshead Bay, Brooklyn, 10:58 a.m.

Frank checked the temperature outside. Ninety-eight degrees. *Way too hot to be outside,* he thought, cracking open another bottle of cold water and reclining on the leather sofa inside the *Reciprocity*, where it was a cool 75 degrees.

Frank resumed flipping through the latest issue of *Fortune* magazine. On the front cover was a photo of some middle-aged, bald, white man, with the headline "How Tech Stocks Can Save the World." On the back cover was an advertisement for Royal Caribbean International featuring a stunningly beautiful woman with fluffy, brown hair, pouty lips and thick, dark brown eyebrows, reclining on a deck chair aboard *MS Allure of the Seas*, the world's largest cruise ship.

Frank was not aware of it, but this particular issue of *Fortune* was the second time this month that the Morgans had made both the front and back covers of a magazine. The first time their places had been reversed.

Frank was about halfway finished reading the cover story:

> ... but Morgan's "Techno Savvy Robot" is more than a high-tech index fund; it's a high-class mixture of wealth, power, style and back-room dealings.
> "There's nothing dangerous about boosting the economy and profiting from the gains," Morgan told *Fortune* recently from his island paradise in the Bahamas. "Technology makes everything possible. When you mix rapidly advancing technologies with nearly unlimited capital, progress and innovation can quickly eclipse the status quo and anything can happen."

Frank turned the page and was about to continue reading when his cell phone rang. The caller ID said the caller had an unlisted number. Frank's number was also unlisted.

"Frank Rosario," he answered.

"Captain Rosario?" asked a man's voice on the other line. The voice sounded hollow and metallic, as if the man was calling from a small room or hallway.

"This is he. How may I help you?"

"Captain, I'm in need of your services. My name is Adam Morgan," the man said, sounding a little out of breath. "I'm a friend of Niles Jones and I'm looking to charter the *Reciprocity* and her captain for a few days."

"Aren't you the 'Techno Savvy Robot' guy?" Frank asked.

"Yeah, that's right! Do you remember me from last weekend?"

"Yeah, I know you. This might sound a little strange, but I was just reading an article about you in a magazine when you called."

"Well, you're kind of a hard man to reach," Adam said. "I did a search for you online and I couldn't find anything. I got your number from Niles Jones."

"I'm not really into the social network scene," Frank replied. "I don't have a website, e-mail, Facebook, Twitter or anything like that. This is my private cell phone you're calling, which is probably the best way to reach me."

"Do you have a minute to talk?"

"Absolutely," Frank said with a grin.

Chapter 28

On board the International Space Station, 15:02:00 UTC
TIME TO SOLAR IMPACT: 8 hours, 30 minutes

Aleksandr was floating upside down in a seated position with his legs crossed, busily scribbling numbers and equations with a pencil onto his paper notebook, when astronauts Chuck Wilson and Mizuho Sakaguchi floated into the Destiny Laboratory from opposite ends.

Aleks looked up from his calculations at his two shipmates and was momentarily disoriented to find his whole world turned on its head. He reached out his left arm to touch a nearby wall, and with a quick flick of the wrist, sent his body in a counter-clockwise spin. Once he had realigned with his crew mates and the decor of the space laboratory, Aleks steadied himself and stopped rotating.

"It still looks like solar flare," he said in English. "The more I look, the more I see a solar flare."

"HINODE confirms we have an inbound coronal mass ejection," Mizuho said, turning to look at Wilson.

"SOHO, STEREO, ACE and SDO all confirm," Chuck said. "Our sensors show a bright halo of material surrounding the sun, headed right for us. It looks like we have an estimated impact scenario in about eight or nine hours."

"Or less," Mizuho added.

"I calculate eight hours, 30 minutes," Aleks said, turning over his his notebook to show his shipmates his calculations. "The flare's speed appears to be steady at about 3,000 km/hour."

"Where does that put us?" Chuck asked.

"It puts us right here," Aleks said after a moment. "Cooked like beans in a tin can."

"We need to tell the Earth," Mizuho said. "This flare could do a lot more than disrupt some satellites. Anything electrical is potentially at risk, not to mention air travel, telecommunications, military systems, GPS, you name it."

"Is there any possibility this might be another false alarm?" Chuck asked, referring to the solar flare fiasco about a year earlier that put the modern world on high alert, shut down air travel and brought the power industry to a brief and grinding halt. After a big build-up by the media, the flare turned out to be aimed in a slightly different direction, missing Earth altogether.

Last year's false alarm had also tarnished the reputation of hundreds of scientists, delayed millions of travelers and reportedly cost businesses hundreds of millions of dollars in lost production.

"They say we cry wolf," Aleks said. "Maybe they do not pay attention this time."

"Another false alarm would be the best-case scenario," Mizuho said gloomily. "This time it feels different. Raising the alarm now might cost a lot of money and inconvenience, but it could save millions of lives."

"What do we do next?" Chuck asked.

Aleks and Chuck both turned to look at Mizuho.

"We tell everybody," she said.

Chapter 29

NEW YORK CITY - The Chrysler Building's lobby, 11:15 a.m.

Adam emerged from the stairwell into the main lobby, his shirt soaked with sweat. He paused a moment to catch his breath and to wait for the lobby's red walls and yellow marble floors to quit spinning, then put on his gray suit jacket and casually walked to the front door.

As he approached the revolving doorway, Adam was momentarily blinded by the daylight and reached into his jacket's inside pocket for his sunglasses. They were missing.

"Excuse me, Mr. Morgan?" called a dark-skinned man from across the room. The man had closely cropped black hair and was wearing a black suit, white shirt and black tie. He was quickly crossing the lobby to meet Adam, carrying a large, yellow envelope.

"Yes, can I help you?" Adam asked.

"Your secretary left this envelope for you," the security guard said, handing Adam the envelope.

"Thanks," Adam said, taking the envelope to an empty area of the lobby and inspecting its contents.

Inside was a pair of silver and blue Armani sunglasses, a laminated security badge, a key, a hand-written letter from his assistant and the folded check he had given her about 20 minutes earlier. He read the letter.

> Hi Adam,
> Thank you for the bonus and the vote of confidence, but this latest mission seems a little beyond my job description. I'm going to need your help on this one. I'm headed downtown to get things set up. Meet me at the NYSE ASAP! Call my cell if you have questions.
> Best,
> Karen

Karen had included her cell phone number at the bottom of the letter, even though Adam had it programmed into his smartphone.

He put on his sunglasses, straightened his collar and pushed through the revolving doors into the street.

The wave of heat hit him like a metro bus, momentarily knocking the wind out of him and causing him to start sweating profusely. He paused for a second to look around and saw the homeless man from that morning still sitting in a wheelchair on the corner, holding a cardboard sign that said "Need Help!"

"Got any spare change, mister?" the man asked Adam again. The man had obviously not showered or shaved in several days and his wretched clothes were in tattered rags.

Adam checked his pockets for change. Nothing. His stomach growled.

"Looks like I'm broke at the moment, but how about a bite to eat?" Adam asked. "I'm pretty hungry myself."

The homeless man's face lit up.

"That would be great, mister," the man said, his smile revealing several missing teeth.

"How about a ham and cheese sandwich?" Adam asked the man as he turned and continued walking down the sidewalk.

"I don't eat ham, but turkey is great!" the homeless man called out, still seated.

Don't get up, Adam thought as he stepped inside a corner deli. He ordered two turkey sandwiches with swiss cheese, a water bottle and an apple. The total came to $15, which he paid with his smartphone. Stepping back into the street, Adam retraced his steps to the lobby entrance and found the homeless man seated in exactly the same spot.

"Spare change?" the man asked as Adam approached.

"No, sorry, but how about a fresh turkey sandwich instead?" Adam said, handing the man one of the sandwiches, a water bottle and the apple.

"Gee, thank you mister," the homeless man said as he accepted the food. "God bless you," he added.

Adam attempted to hail a cab. Almost immediately, a cab driver saw the bald, white man in the expensive suit and pulled over.

Adam climbed into the air-conditioned back seat and looked back to see the homeless man slowly chewing his sandwich.

"Try to stay in the shade today!" Adam called out to the man as the cab sped away.

"Where to?" asked the driver, activating the cab's GPS navigational device.

"Wall Street," Adam said as he pulled out his smartphone and dialed Karen's number. The taxi sped south on Third Avenue. Karen's phone rang twice while his smartphone searched for a cellular tower, bounced the signal off an orbiting satellite, bounced to another cellular tower and finally located her phone.

"Karen Walters."

"Karen, it's Adam," he said. "I got your note; we can talk about that later. I'm headed to Wall Street right now in a cab and I should arrive in 20 to 30 minutes. I need you to pick up two portable hard drives and meet me at that place we discussed."

"What kind of hard drives?" Karen asked.

"I don't want to go into too many specifics over the phone," Adam said, looking at the rearview mirror and briefly making eye contact with the Arab cab driver before looking back out the window. "Get me something small and fast with a lot of storage space, like a flash drive."

Adam waited a moment, but heard no reply.

"Hello?" he asked.

"Yes, sorry," Karen said. "I was just checking my phone for the nearest Radio Shack. There are 17 stores between Grand Central and Wall Street. Driver, I need to make a quick stop at the Radio Shack at 781 Broadway. OK, boss, it's not a problem. Is there anything else?"

"Yes, can you call our destination ahead of time and tell them we're coming?" he asked. "It will speed things up later on."

"Call ahead," she repeated. "Got it. Anything else?"

"Thanks for grabbing my sunglasses," Adam said. "See you soon."

"You're welcome," Karen said. "See you in about 20."

Adam hung up the phone and bit into his turkey sandwich. *Kind of dry and bland for a six-dollar sandwich*, he thought, tossing the sandwich aside and immediately regretting that he gave away his bottled water.

Chapter 30

On board the International Space Station, 15:25:00 UTC
TIME TO SOLAR IMPACT: 8 hours, 7 minutes

Mizuho had been sending out a frenzy of e-mails from her work station inside the Japanese Kibo module, but had yet to receive a single reply. She looked up from her laptop out a small, circular window at the Earth below and saw a familiar shape racing past. At that moment, the space station was almost directly above Nippon, or Japan, a glowing archipelago of lights surrounded by an ocean of inky darkness. To the west, she could make out the eastern seaboard of China, Russia and South Korea in lights, but North Korea remained dark.

She checked her watch. It was 12:25 a.m. in Tokyo, which meant she had been up for about 17.5 hours. It also meant that most of her colleagues on the surface were probably asleep. Mizuho looked up the main number for the Tsukuba Space Center, the Japanese Aerospace Exploration Agency's operations facility. She put on a headset and dialed the number.

"Tsukuba Space Center," a man answered in Japanese.

"Hello, this is Astronaut Mizuho Sakaguchi calling from the International Space Station," she said in Japanese. "I have an emergency and I need to speak with someone at mission control."

"I see," said the man. "It's a bit late for jokes, don't you think?"

"This is not a joke," she said in a serious tone. "Please connect me with someone at mission control."

"Almost everyone here has gone home. What did you say your name was?"

"This is Astronaut Mizuho Sakaguchi calling from the International Space Station," she said again. "I am quite serious. I have an urgent matter than cannot wait. Please connect me at once."

"Just a moment," the man said. A few moments later, another man answered.

"Mission Control," the man said in Japanese. "Can I have your priority access code, please?"

"Sakura," Mizuho said.

"Thank you, Flight Engineer Sakaguchi, I am Assistant Director Yuki Fukuhara. How may I help you?"

"Sir, we are tracking an inbound coronal mass ejection projected to hit in approximately eight hours," she said. "We are classifying this as a possible extreme geomagnetic storm. I need you to contact the director immediately. Call him at home and wake him up if necessary. There isn't much time."

"Yes, ma'am," the man said. "Right away."

Across the space station in the Zarya Control Module, Aleksandr wasn't having much better luck contacting headquarters. He had sent out dozens of e-mails, but like Mizuho, had not received one reply. He sent a quick e-mail to his sister, Natasha.

> Tosh: Solar storm inbound. Suggest you leave the city very soon. Call me when you get this. Aleks

Aleks looked at his watch. 7:30 p.m. He put on a headset and dialed the direct number for his contact at the Russian Federal

Security Service, or FSB for short. The FSB was Russia's version of the American Federal Bureau of Investigation and was concerned with national security, surveillance, counter-intelligence and counter-terrorism.

"FSB, which division?" answered a female operator, speaking in Russian.

"This is Commander Aleksandr Manakova on board the International Space Station," Aleks replied in Russian. "I need to speak with Mishka right away."

"Is this a secure line?" asked the operator.

"Yes, it is."

"Please hold while I connect you," the operator said. After a short pause, a deep-voiced man answered the phone.

"Hello?" the man answered.

"Good evening, sir," Aleks said. "I am sorry to call so late, but we are having an emergency on board the International Space Station and I am having trouble contacting mission control."

"What seems to be the problem?" the man asked.

"Sir, we are detecting a large inbound geomagnetic storm," Aleks said. "It has already disabled several communication satellites and could cause significant damage to our electrical grid, pipelines, transportation systems and communications network."

There was a short pause. "How much time do we have?"

"Probably less than eight hours," Aleks said.

"When did you learn of this oncoming storm?"

"I have been tracking it for nearly four hours, sir," Aleks said.

"Four hours?!"

"Yes, sir. As I said, communications have been very spotty as a result of this storm's approach and I have not been able to go through the usual channels, although I did contact you first. My American and Japanese counterparts up here have helped me to verify this information. They are relaying this same information to civilian and governmental agencies around the world as we speak. Time is of the essence, sir."

"Who needs to be contacted?" Mishka asked.

"Everyone," Aleks said. "The president, the prime minister, the military, you name it. We could completely lose our ability to communicate through satellites and land lines in a matter of hours, and it is possible these systems could be down for several weeks or months following the storm. I recommend we power down our entire electrical grid and satellite network prior to the storm to protect them from permanent damage."

"This sounds very serious, indeed. I will get on this at once. You are to continue cooperating with the Americans and Japanese. Stand by for further instructions. That is all."

"Yes, sir," Aleks said, ending the call. "I'm not going anywhere," he said to himself.

A few meters away in the Destiny Laboratory, Commander Chuck Wilson was on the phone with the ISS Flight Control Room at the Johnson Space Center in Houston, Texas, where it was 10:35 a.m.

"That's affirmative, we copy your status," the male flight director said in a southern drawl. "Thanks for bringing this to our attention. I will tell NOAA to put out an alert."

"It looks like we still have some time before this thing hits, but I don't think I can stress enough the importance of advance preparation," Chuck said. "Anyone airborne or at high altitudes faces an increased radiation risk. Someone needs to contact the president, the Air Force and the Federal Aviation Administration. The ISS crew members and I have been sending out dozens of messages, but I don't think anyone has received them."

"This is the first I've heard of it," the flight director said.

"That's kind of what we thought," Chuck said. "Take a look at the data coming from the HINODE, SOHO, STEREO, ACE and SDO satellites. They all say the same thing: An extreme coronal mass ejection is headed our way in about eight hours."

"We'll get on this right away, commander. Thanks for the head's up and keep in touch. Over and out."

Chapter 31

LONDON - Covent Garden Piazza, 4:40 p.m.

Carrying a small paper plate of fresh pastries in each hand, Jacob Baker stepped through the crowded sidewalk area outside Covent Garden, careful not to step on the scores of seated children scattered everywhere. *Most of these kids haven't seen the video yet,* he thought. *We should be safe here.* Jacob paused to look for his new friend. *She has red hair.* He spotted Kendra sitting in the crowd, recording a video with her phone and sat down to join in the fun.

A few meters away in a small, make-shift theater, a puppet jester named Punch with a long nose and pointy chin was attempting to teach his baby puppet to walk. Quickly giving up, Punch sat on top of the baby, eliciting a cry of disapproval from the children in the audience. Another puppet wearing a dress and cap came over and asked Punch what he was doing.

"Babysitting," Punch squeaked.

Judy began clubbing her husband over the head with a stick, but Punch took away the stick and clubbed Judy over the head. A policeman puppet came over to investigate and Punch hid from him for a bit before eventually clubbing the policeman over the head as well. Throughout the performance, the children were yelling at the stage, shouting things like "look behind you!"

As Jacob ate his pastry, he reflected on his mad dash from the shopping center with Kendra through some of London's famous winding streets.

The two teenagers had run together, hand-in-hand, most of the way to the magnificent King's Cross Station, constructed in 1852 as the London terminus to the Great Northern Railway. From King's Cross, they hopped on the London Underground's blue Piccadilly line to Covent Garden, but not before taking their pictures in front of the station's sign for the imaginary Platform 9 and 3/4 from the Harry Potter series. Jacob posted the picture online and tweeted "Taking the Hogwart's Express. Feeling a tad magical today."

Jacob finished eating his pastry just as the show was ending. He looked at Kendra and saw her completely absorbed in her smartphone, busily typing something.

"I just made a video of the puppet show and put it on my webpage," she said, pulling herself away from her phone to make eye contact. "It's really cute, if you'd like to repost it."

Jacob noticed her lips were covered in powdered sugar. He looked at her lips and pointed to his own. Kendra cocked her head to the side curiously.

"I think you've got something on your lips," Jacob whispered.

"What?" Kendra asked in a whisper.

"Your lips," he said louder. "They have ..."

He lost his train of thought. Kendra was looking at him intently with sparkling green eyes. He licked his lips. She licked hers. They quickly kissed, sending a tiny spark of electricity between them.

An electronic shutter noise clattered from a nearby camera phone. Jacob turned to look for the cameraman, but saw only children. He looked back at Kendra, who was blushing.

"You want to go steady?" he asked. Kendra grinned and nodded. "Great! We should probably keep moving," he said, pulling out his smartphone and taking a quick snapshot of the puppet show. As he stood up, he posted the picture and sent another tweet. "Puppet shows make great first dates," he typed, adding a link to Kendra's newest video of the show.

Jacob tossed a five-pound note into the puppeteer's tip jar and turned to look back at Kendra, who was concentrating on her smartphone again. She was sending a text to someone named Charles.

"We shud c other ppl," she texted to Charles, then turned back to focus on Jacob. "That was my ex-boyfriend. Don't worry, I'm all yours," she said with a grin.

"Well that's good news," he said, standing up and taking her small hand in his. "Let's go see what's happening in Leicester Square," he said, pronouncing it "Lester."

A 14-year-old boy riding past on a bicycle in the opposite direction recognized them, pulled out his smartphone and snapped their picture, then attempted to post it online. The boy did not see a pothole ahead in the road and crashed his bike, landing on the hard pavement. Fortunately the boy was wearing a helmet and was not seriously injured, but he did break his smartphone, bicycle and his right arm. He began to cry in pain and confusion.

Jacob and Kendra did not see the accident and were oblivious to the boy's cries as they continued their walk westward, sharing a set of earbuds and listening to the same song together.

Chapter 32

NEW YORK CITY - 74 Trinity Place, 11:45 a.m.

Adam swiped his credit card through the card reader in the back seat of the yellow cab as it pulled to a stop in front of Trinity Church at the corner of Broadway and Wall Street. He punched a few buttons on the reader, leaving the driver a $10 tip.

Adam felt a sharp pang in his legs as he stepped out of the cab. *That would be the 65 flights of stairs,* he thought. He adjusted his sunglasses and straightened his tie before checking his smartphone for new messages. Finding none, he recalled that he had spent the past 20 minutes reading through all his e-mails, checking the latest news stories, giving directions to the taxi driver and checking current stock and commodity prices.

Adam turned east and started walking down the narrow, pedestrian-only street as he dialed Karen's number on his smartphone. The towering buildings on either side of the street created the sensation of walking through a dimly lit canyon, and the simple-looking, cobblestone streets belied their high-tech, subterranean secrets.

"Karen Walters," she answered.

"Hi, Karen, it's Adam. I just arrived at Wall Street and I'm headed to the exchange. Where are you?"

"Hi, Adam. I'm outside the exchange's main entrance. I've told them you're on your way. We should both be on the list."

"Did you get that thing I requested?"

"Have it on me," Karen said.

"I think I see you," Adam said. "Talk to you soon," he said, hanging up and waving at his assistant standing several meters away. As he approached the American flag-covered marble pillars outside the New York Stock Exchange, Adam reflected that nearly all of the trading these days was done electronically, yet big-time Wall Street traders like Niles Jones still paid upwards of $4 million for the privilege of working on the trading floor.

"There you are," Karen said as Adam approached. "You gave me quite a start earlier at the office. Right after you left, I checked the stock market and thought I might be walking into a bad situation. Actually, I didn't know what to expect."

"That's understandable," Adam said. "Sorry if I seemed a little cryptic at the office, but it's probably better if you don't know all the details. Do you have those drives?"

"That's not real reassuring," Karen said, handing him two four-terabyte USB flash drives.

Two heavily armed security guards standing on a corner near the exchange entrance turned to look at Adam as Karen handed him the small, white plastic bag. The guards were dressed head to toe in black, including black helmets with dark visors, black body armor and black M4 carbine rifles. They continued to stare at Adam and Karen without talking or moving.

"Oh, it's not as bad as all that," Adam said with a smile, casually touching Karen's left arm with his right hand and leading her a few paces away from the two guards towards the large statue of George Washington in front of Federal Hall. Adam did not take the plastic bag.

"Try to think of it more as technical support, less as cloak and dagger," he said in a quieter voice. "You want a little training? Come with me. All we're doing is replacing the old hard drives with newer ones. We're going to be in and out in a flash, hopefully before noon. Let's keep talking to a minimum and try not to attract attention to ourselves. Are you ready?"

Karen looked at the giant, marble columns and triangular pediment atop the massive building at 11 Wall Street that housed the trading floor, then back at Adam, who was smiling. She felt a little more reassured.

"OK, let's do it," she said, putting her smartphone into silent mode.

The two walked in silence to the gated entrance at 11 Wall Street, right past the two armed guards. As they approached the gate, another security guard wearing a black cap, black cargo shirt, cargo pants and black boots held up a clipboard.

"Are you on the list?" the gruff-voiced, mustached man asked. "You must be on the list."

"Yes, I am Adam Morgan and this is my executive assistant Miss Karen Walters," Adam said, showing the guard his passport and laminated NYSE security badge. "We need to check on our servers upstairs."

The guard found Adam's name on the clipboard, looked at the passport and security badge and handed them both back to Adam.

"I'll need to see a photo ID, ma'am," the guard said to Karen. She handed him her identification. The guard looked at the ID, then handed it back to her. "Please sign in and remember to sign out before you go," he grumbled as Adam and Karen stepped through the ornate brass doorway beneath a granite arch. After signing in with the receptionist, they entered a long hallway lined with large photos of various CEOs ringing the NYSE's opening bell.

One photo in particular caught Karen's eye, a 1992 picture of former Soviet Union President Mikhail Gorbachev and former U.S. President Ronald Reagan standing together on the trading floor. Karen didn't recognize the third man in the photo, but saw from the caption that he was a former chairman and CEO of the New York Stock Exchange and later became chairman of the U.S. Securities and Exchange Commission.

At the end of the hallway, they reached a row of elevators. Adam was reluctant to get in another elevator, but Karen gently nudged him inside. The elevator was older in design, with polished brass plating and numbered brass buttons. He pressed the button for the sixth floor and the doors closed.

"There's no 13th floor," Adam said quietly as the elevator ascended.

Karen looked at the buttons and noticed they skipped right over floor 13. This elevator accessed two basement floors all the way up to floor 17, but there were 23 floors above ground and five below in this particular building. The NYSE complex contained several interconnected buildings of varying height and architecture, and sometimes a corridor beginning on the eighth floor of one building could connect to the 12th floor of an adjacent building.

The elevator doors opened on the sixth floor and the two stepped out into a wide room with hardwood floors, beige and mahogany-covered walls and vaulted ceilings. Most of the walls were covered with antique drawings of sailing ships and large oil paintings of past stock exchange presidents. Karen noticed that all the presidents were middle-aged or older white men, and the only observable difference between them was the changing style of their neckties and facial hair. They continued walking through the room to a hallway of smaller rooms, filled with elegant, antique, hand-made furniture that no one ever sat upon. Approaching room 621, Adam tried the door handle. It was locked. He looked at Karen and pulled out a key from his pocket, unlocking the door.

Inside, the computers hummed quietly. Adam turned on all four monitors and sat down in front of the screen on the left. He turned to look at Karen.

"May I have one of the drives?"

Karen opened one of the four-terabyte flash drives and handed it to Adam, who inserted it into the computer's USB port. He typed a few commands and a moment later, the computer began copying itself to the portable drive.

"I'll need the other one next," Adam said as the downloading neared completion.

"Backup complete," an alert informed them. Adam ejected the flash drive and inserted the second blank drive into the empty port, repeating the process. When the files had been successfully backed up onto both flash drives, Adam deleted all the files on the computer related to "Techno Savvy Robot" and made sure to erase the computer's trash file. He quickly activated a new hedge fund called Occidental Industries Limited and listed himself as portfolio manager.

"That's it," Adam said, putting both jump drives in his jacket pocket. "I should be able to do everything else remotely. Let's make a quiet exit, shall we?"

Adam turned off the monitors and locked the door behind him. In the hallway, an exquisite grandfather clock chimed noon as Adam and Karen stepped into the elevator. After signing out at the reception desk, the two stepped back outside into the 105-degree heat.

"I could use a cool drink," Adam said. "Join me for lunch?"

"That sounds nice," Karen said as they walked south along Broad Street past the luxury clothing boutique Hermes of Paris, pronounced air-MEZ.

"Hold on a sec, I want to get something for Natasha," Adam said, stepping inside the store's elegant lobby.

A few minutes later, they found a nearby steakhouse pub and went upstairs.

Chapter 33

TOLEDO, Wash. - 251 Layton Rd., 9:07 a.m.

Bob Layton came back into the farm house after checking on his animals. The horses, goats and pigs were continuing to act skittish, refusing to eat and hiding in their pens. He took off his boots, sat down at his computer with a sigh and checked the stock market.

He could hardly believe what he saw. In the last two hours, the stock markets had taken a nose dive, erasing all of their gains for the entire year. Everything seemed to be dropping.

Bob logged into his retirement account's secure server to check his balance.

"Account balance unavailable at this time," a message read. "Please check back after 4 p.m. Eastern." His account also said he was prohibited from making any more changes today.

"WHAT THE HELL IS THIS?!!" Bob exploded. "This is investing? What absolute HORSE SHIT!" He pounded his fist on the desk in frustration.

Maud came over and asked what was wrong.

"Wrong?" Bob repeated. "The damn stock market is down almost 10 percent. In two hours, we lost about $50,000. They're crooks, I tell you. Goddam CROOKS!"

"Take it easy, dear," Maud said in a soothing voice, standing behind Bob's chair and massaging his shoulders. "It seems to me that the markets go up and down all the time. We even talked about this the other day. If you don't like the game, you don't have to play, but if you are going to play, there's no sense getting another ulcer over it. Why don't you turn that thing off and do something else? For all we know, the markets could completely rebound tomorrow."

Bob considered this for a moment, then logged off the computer, put his boots back on and followed Maud back outside.

Chapter 34

NEW YORK CITY - 25 Broad Street, 12:15 p.m.

"You were great back there, by the way," Adam said after he and Karen had ordered their lunch in the high-end steakhouse. "It wasn't so bad, was it? We didn't even get interrogated."

"No, I guess not," Karen said. "I actually feel kind of silly, now. I don't know if I thought I would get locked in a dungeon somewhere or be water-boarded at Guantanamo Bay, but I was pretty worried all the same. Especially once you gave me that check. All kinds of alarm bells went off in my head."

As Karen looked around the second floor of the steakhouse, she noticed that it looked eerily similar to the sixth floor of the New York Stock Exchange with its cream-colored walls and dark wood panelling. The first floor also bore an uncanny resemblance to a bank vault and in fact once belonged to J.P. Morgan, the famous banker and industrialist who used his vast wealth and influence to create monopolies like General Electric and the United States Steel Corporation. Morgan was also credited with saving the U.S. economy during the panic of 1907.

"Sorry, I forgot you aren't used to big bonuses yet," Adam said, taking a sip of beer. "It's pretty common in this business to reward the winners when big bets pay off."

He reached into his jacket pocket and pulled out the folded check, setting it down on the table between them.

"We had a pretty big day today," he said, taking another sip of beer. "That's your bonus; you've earned it."

Karen picked up the folded check and looked at it again. It said to pay to the order of Karen Walters, in the amount of ten thousand dollars.

"What am I supposed to do with this, Adam?" she asked in a lowered voice. "This is a lot of money, like two or three month's pay. It's probably going to bump me up into a higher tax bracket. I really don't want to get audited by the IRS."

"Cash it," Adam said. "You can cash a check for up to $10,000 with no questions asked. Take it into one of the bank's main branches and look for an experienced teller. You can get a stack of hundreds. Just pretend that you're rich, you've done this a hundred times before and it's no big deal. And stop worrying about taxes. You probably pay more in taxes than I do."

Adam was absent-mindedly scrolling through the news headlines on his smartphone as he was talking to Karen, but he turned his full focus to his phone when he read the following news:

> NOAA Issues CME Warning, 2 mins ago
> WASHINGTON - Officials at the National Oceanic and Atmospheric Administration have issued a high-priority alert for a possible coronal mass ejection (CME) event in less than eight hours. Officials say the solar flare could create a geomagnetic storm ...

He closed the news feed and checked the stock markets. The Dow was down almost 10 percent, not counting the morning gains, and crude oil trading on the FOREX foreign exchange was also down about as much, trading at $75 a barrel. Adam used his smartphone to activate the servers of Occidental Industries Limited, formerly known as Techno Savvy Robot.

When their food arrived, Karen began eating her salad, but Adam was too absorbed in his smartphone to talk with anyone, let alone eat his lunch. Instead, his new hedge fund began devouring stocks of major petroleum companies and energy-related exchange traded funds. He purchased 20 million barrels of West Texas Intermediate crude oil reserves at a fixed price of $100 a barrel, causing the price of crude oil to rebound almost immediately. His stock in petroleum companies began to rebound as well, slowing the Dow's decline and preventing the SEC's protective "circuit breaker" function from temporarily halting trading.

Adam set down his smartphone and took a bite of his 12-ounce gourmet cheeseburger. His smartphone made a small chime indicating he had a new text message. He wiped his hands on a cloth napkin and checked his messages. It was from his wife.

> Done with work, headed back home. Aleks says there's some kind of storm coming. Can u get off early? Call me.

Adam sent out a quick text in reply.

> Heard about the storm. I have a surprise for you. Can you be ready to leave in a few hours?

A few moments after he sent the text, his smartphone rang. The caller ID said it was Natasha. Adam took a quick sip of beer to wash down the cheeseburger.

"Hello, my dear," Adam said sweetly as he answered the phone. He looked up at Karen, who was absorbed in her own smartphone. The restaurant was beginning to fill up with customers, predominately white businessmen. "How was your morning?"

"I'm so tired of clothes," she said. "I just want to go naked for the rest of the week."

Adam's ears perked up. "Really?" he asked. Natasha giggled.

"Ha! You're funny," she said. "Hey, you should have seen this. Right after I said that, about a dozen guys turned to look at me."

"Where are you?"

"Right now, I'm in Times Square, headed back home," Natasha said. "I don't remember if I told you or not, but I'm having a small party this afternoon. Are you still at work?"

"No, I left early. Right now I'm in a crowded restaurant downtown with Karen, my assistant," Adam said, using his free hand to plug his other ear. "Do you think you could be ready to leave the city in a couple of hours?"

"Where are we going?" Natasha asked.

"That's a surprise," Adam said playfully. "But probably somewhere tropical," he added.

"OK, but you have to come by my party first. Ask your assistant to come and tell her I said 'hi.'"

"You got it," Adam said. "See you soon."

"I love you!"

"I love you, too," Adam said, ending the call. He turned back to Karen, who had finished her salad. The steakhouse was packed with traders, bank executives and other businessmen on their lunch hour, and everyone seemed to be talking about the market's volatility.

"Natasha says 'hi.' She's throwing a party at our Midtown place and asked me to invite you. Are you interested?" Adam asked, holding up his corporate credit card and briefly making eye contact with their waiter.

A businessman sitting nearby saw Adam motion to the waiter and recognized him. He waved at Adam, made eye contact and then stood up and walked over to their table. He was five-foot, five-inches tall, a little below average height. He compensated for this by being a ruthless trading shark, and he could always smell the other sharks in the pool.

"Adam Morgan, it's Niles Jones," the businessman said, introducing himself. "We spoke about an hour ago about the *Reciprocity*. Are you still interested?"

Niles had short black hair, pale white skin and soulless black eyes that were all pupil and no iris. He had switched out of his bright blue New York Stock Exchange jacket with the American flag patches into a lower profile, tailored navy blue sports jacket just before leaving the trading floor. Niles extended his right hand to Adam, revealing his fabulous gold Omega wristwatch. Adam glanced at the watch and recognized it. He wiped his hands on his napkin.

"I am," Adam said, shaking Niles' offered hand. Jones' grip was limp, like a rubber glove filled with warm mustard. Adam quickly released his grip. "I spoke with the captain a few minutes ago," he continued. "He seems like a good chap. How are you?"

"I've had better days," Niles said. "I took quite a beating this morning when the markets went haywire. Nothing makes any sense today. Say, would you be interested in buying her?"

"Who's that?" Adam asked, nonchalantly checking the time on his own wristwatch.

"The yacht *Reciprocity*," Niles said, suddenly captivated by Adam's stunning blue-and-white gold timepiece. "I'm looking to upgrade again."

"What are you asking?"

"Oh, around one-fifty or so," Niles said. "Is that a Blancpain Fifty Fathoms? That's a beautiful timepiece. Elegant, reliable and self-winding. Jacques Cousteau wore that watch."

Niles Jones' obsession with rare, hand-crafted timepieces seemed to mirror Adam's. Niles had eight wristwatches or pocket watches that each exceeded $50,000 in value. He had enough money, investments, real estate and expensive toys to satisfy most people for the rest of their lives, but for Niles, it was never enough. Luxury wristwatches were a status symbol among many affluent and powerful males, and Niles suddenly felt out-classed by the new alpha male. He envied Adam's life, his beautiful wife and most of all this glorious and masculine timepiece.

"Let me get back to you," Adam said as the waiter arrived with the check. "I still have your number. I'll call you this afternoon. It was good seeing you."

"You too," Niles said. "I'd better get back to the floor. Do you have any advice?"

"It might be considered insider trading if I told you any specifics, but oil always looks good," Adam said. "How about yourself? Are you bearish or bullish?"

"Bearish. Gold and cash are king," Niles said, handing Adam his business card. "This has my private cell on it. Let me know about the yacht. I'm sure we can work something out."

After Niles Jones had left, Adam handed a credit card to the waiter and turned his attention to Karen again. Since she had not been introduced, she decided it was acceptable to check her personal messages on her smartphone. Her youngest sister had a cute new boyfriend.

"So, would you like to come to our party this afternoon?" Adam asked again.

"Sure, I guess," Karen said, looking up from her smartphone. "Who's coming?"

"She had a photo shoot this morning, so I suspect it will be the usual models, agents and photographers," Adam said. "You know, the beautiful people."

The waiter brought back two receipts in a leather billfold. Adam wrote a $10 tip on the receipt, signed one copy and pocketed the other copy without looking at the total.

"I think I can swing by. Oh, and I need to stop by the bank while we're down here and pick up some cash," Karen said nonchalantly, putting her bonus check in her black Chanel purse.

"I'll come with you," Adam said as the two stood up to leave. "I'm completely out of cash myself."

Chapter 35

NEW YORK CITY - Sheepshead Bay, Brooklyn, 12:30 p.m.

Frank was going over his departure checklist when his cell phone rang.

"Frank Rosario," he answered.

"Hi Captain, this is Adam Morgan calling again," the caller said. "I just ran into Niles Jones and thought I'd check to see how everything is going."

"It's going great, Mr. Morgan," Frank said. "Mr. Jones said to take you anywhere you want to go. Where are we going, by the way?"

"To a little island in the Bahamas," Adam said.

"Great!" Frank said. "That's not a problem. I go down there all the time. Which island are you visiting?"

"Stingray Cay."

"I'm not familiar with that one," Frank said. "Is it in the Caribbean?"

"No, it's part of the Bahamas, but it's closer to Cuba than to Florida. It's pretty small, about 500 acres total. I have a couple of buildings, a marina and a 3,000-foot runway, but it's pretty deserted otherwise."

"I'm sure I have it on a map here somewhere," Frank said, flipping through his navigational charts. "Here it is. Kind of looks like a stingray, too. When are you looking to depart?"

"Ideally, I'd like to cast off by 4 p.m. today, if that's possible," Adam said.

"Not a problem. How many passengers?"

"Two?" Adam thought for a moment. "How much room do you have?"

"The *Reciprocity* has three rooms and can sleep up to five. I sleep aft by the stairs, but there's a master stateroom forward where you can have lots of privacy. The third room can be a single bed or extra storage, if you need it."

"What should we bring?"

"She's a 41-foot Hans Christian, so there's not a tremendous amount of storage space," Frank said. "I recommend you try to pack light, not much more than you would carry on an airplane. We have plenty of food and drinks on board, but you should let me know in advance if you have any special dietary restrictions."

"My wife eats like she's some kind of exotic bird," Adam joked. "I think she's a vegetarian. Is there room for extra luggage or cargo, like a painting, for instance?"

"I wouldn't advise bringing along any paintings, unless you've got them in water-tight containers. If you think you'll need it during the voyage, bring it. Otherwise, it's probably smarter to ship it separately. The Bahamas have high taxes on imported luxury items."

Adam thought for a moment.

"How long do you think it will take to travel from here to the Bahamas?"

"At least a week, if the weather's good," Frank said. "It can take up to three weeks if we go along the coastline and put in at port at night."

"One to three weeks? I was hoping you could get me there in a couple of days."

"*Reciprocity* was built for comfort, not speed," Frank said. "You can get there a lot faster by jet boat or jet airplane, for that matter. Forgive me for asking, but didn't you say you had your own airstrip?"

"That's OK," Adam said. "My jet has been having mechanical issues and I had to leave it on the island. It still might make more sense to fly there commercially. Actually, this trip is kind of a surprise for my wife, but I suppose I should ask her first. I'm assuming she would prefer sailing over flying. Can I call you back?"

"Yeah, that's no problem," Frank said. "Do you want me to still plan for a 4 p.m. departure?"

"Please," Adam said. "I've got a lot of errands to run before 4 o'clock."

112

"I like to do a quick boat safety class before we depart, so try to get here around 3 p.m."

"Three might be too close. I have to check on some things and I'll get back to you. In the mean time, please carry on."

"You can count on it," Frank said.

"Great," Adam said. "Talk to you soon."

"Bye," Frank said, hanging up the call. He looked back at his checklist. *We're going to need more food and vegetables,* he thought, peeking inside the crowded refrigerator.

Chapter 36

NEW YORK CITY - 1 Chase Manhattan Plaza, 12:35 p.m.

"Sorry about that," Adam said, slipping his smartphone into his jacket pocket.

"That's OK," Karen said. "I found that flight information you wanted. All the available flights to Oslo, Norway leave after 6 p.m. and arrive the next day. The flights to Nassau, Bahamas all have layovers in Miami, but will arrive tonight. OK, this is the place."

Adam looked up to see a peculiar sculpture in the middle of the outdoor plaza. "Group of Four Trees," designed and built by Jean Dubuffet in 1972, was a large, black and white sculpture consisting of irregular shapes and forms that contrasted the building's straight lines and evenly spaced windows. The building at 1 Chase Manhattan Plaza is 813 feet tall with 60 stories above ground and five below, making it the 11th tallest in New York City.

Adam reached into his Hermes shopping bag and pulled out the pink scarf he had purchased for Natasha. The beautiful, 36-inch square, silk-twill scarf was covered with a mosaic of red, pink, purple and white flowers, in the style of Indian fabrics from the late 16th century.

"You should wear this when you go in the bank," he said, handing her the scarf. "And you might want to let your hair down; it looks better that way."

Karen undid her bun, shaking out a cascade of shiny, shoulder-length red hair, then tied the scarf in a knot around her neck.

"Now you look like you have money," Adam said, holding open the glass door for her as she stepped inside and following behind her.

A few meters away, a large, white moving van pulled up to a stop outside the bank at the corner of William and Cedar Streets.

Karen was next in line and approached the large, middle-aged bank teller.

"Welcome to Chase. How may I help you this afternoon?" the teller asked.

"I need to cash a check for $10,000," Karen said calmly, handing the check to the teller.

"That's quite a large amount, ma'am," the dark-haired woman said. "I will need to see a photo ID. Do you bank with Chase?"

"Yes I do," Karen said, handing the teller her bank card and identification. "My boss just gave me a bonus. He's standing behind me in line if you want to verify it with him."

The teller looked past Karen at Adam, who smiled.

"Oh, that's OK, we know Mr. Morgan," the teller said. "I can give you a cashier's check instead, that way you don't have to carry around all that money. Or I can give you part of it as cash and part as a cashier's check."

"Oh, I don't mind," Karen said, playing with her pink scarf. "Cash is easier for me."

"How would you like this?" she asked. "Small bills, large bills or a mixture?"

"In large bills, if that's possible," Karen said. "Also, do you have a merchant money bag I could use? I don't think it will all fit in my purse."

"Certainly," the teller said, handing Karen an empty money bag. "I'll need to get the branch manager for such a large order. If you'll excuse me, it will just be a moment."

"That's fine," Karen said as the teller disappeared into a back room.

Karen thought for a moment about whether to try to stuff the cash into her small, cluttered purse or leave it in the larger money bag. She decided to empty the contents of her purse into the money bag, which included her passport and photo ID, smartphone, credit cards, checkbook, keys, make-up kit, two ball-point pens and various breath mints and chewing gum.

While she was waiting for the teller to return, Karen turned around to look at Adam just as he was being called to a different window. On the back wall, she noticed a framed photo of Adam next to photos of the bank's 11 other members of its board of directors.

"How may I help you today, sir?" asked the short, chubby male bank teller.

"I need a little spending money," Adam said, handing the teller his photo ID and swiping his bank card through a card reader. He punched his four-digit PIN into the keypad.

"And how much would you like today, Mr. Morgan?" the teller asked with a smile.

"I think a thousand should be fine," Adam said, adding, "in hundreds, if you have them."

The teller opened his drawer and quickly counted out ten $100 bills to Adam as Karen's teller returned, carrying a stack of one hundred $100 bills.

"Here we go. Sorry about the wait. One, two, three, four, five, six, seven, eight, nine, one thousand," Karen's teller counted, stacking the bills in piles of ten. "One, two, three ..."

"ALL RIGHT, EVERYBODY FREEZE!!" yelled a man in the lobby. Adam and Karen both turned around to see three heavily armed men dressed head-to-toe in black body armor.

Their leader was wearing a black ski mask and was waiving a black, Mossberg pump-action shotgun fitted with a pistol grip instead of a rifle stock.

He fired the gun once in the air, causing several people, including Karen's teller, to drop to the floor and cover their ears. A woman screamed.

Karen snatched the stack of hundreds sitting on the counter and shoved them into her empty Chanel purse, then discreetly tucked it underneath her skirt, between her thighs.

"All right now, everyone be quiet! This is a hold-up!" the gravel-voiced man yelled. "Nobody moves, everybody does exactly what I say and everybody lives. Got it?"

The room was silent. Several people nodded solemnly as the music from the satellite radio chirped happily in the background.

"Good! I want everyone to sit down on the floor right now!" the leader yelled, cocking his shotgun, spitting an empty shell onto the lobby floor and chambering another round. Everyone else in the lobby immediately sat down on the floor, including Adam and Karen.

"Spider, you get the cash from the tills. Hornet, check the customers for cash. Anybody moves without my saying and you won't get another warning shot!"

The other two robbers quickly began their search for cash as the leader stood guard.

"Boss, we've got a winner here," yelled the robber known as Spider when he came to Karen's counter. "Bank manager with keys to the vault."

"Sir, I need you to open the vault," the gravel-voiced leader ordered. "Hornet, you go with him. Spider, keep checking the tills. I'll search the customers."

The man known as Hornet led the bank manager into the vault, pointing an assault rifle at his back. The man known as Spider climbed behind the counter and began scooping the contents of the cash registers into a black duffel bag. When he got to Karen's counter, he grabbed the merchant money bag intended for her, shoved it into his bag and peered over the counter.

"Was this yours?" he asked Karen. "It's mine now. Say, that's a pretty scarf, rich bitch."

Karen sat frozen on the floor staring at her feet and said nothing. Spider watched her for a moment before continuing to empty the registers.

"Hello, sir. You look like a regular customer," the leader said, approaching Adam. "With a suit like that, you could probably run this bank. How about it? What you got?"

Adam calmly looked up at the leader.

"I came in here to get cash, but it looks like you beat me to it," Adam said. "I doubt I have anything you want."

"How about that shiny watch?" the leader asked, pointing his shotgun at Adam's blue-and-white gold Blancpain wristwatch. "That's beautiful," he added, gazing at the golden watch.

The bank robber's own digital wristwatch alarm chimed. He checked the time.

"That's sixty seconds! Time to go!" he yelled to his associates. He pointed his shotgun at Adam's face. "What's it gonna be, baldy?"

The man called Hornet ran out from the vault carrying four large, black duffel bags, dropping two by the door on his way outside. The man called Spider grabbed one of the bags and followed with his other duffel bag of cash.

"Looks like you already have a watch," Adam said calmly. "Better not be late for your get-away."

The robber looked at Adam for a second, then grabbed one of the black duffel bags full of cash and followed Spider and Hornet outside to the white moving van. Alarm bells immediately began to ring in the lobby as the van sped off southeast down Cedar Street toward the East River.

As soon as they were gone, Adam stood up and walked over to Karen, who was still sitting on the marble floor. He sat down next to her and put his arm around her shoulder.

"Are you OK?" he asked. Karen began to weep.

"I hate money," she said, pulling off the pink scarf. "It turns people into monsters."

Chapter 37

NEW YORK CITY - 6 East River Piers, 12:40 p.m.

After a high-speed run through lower Manhattan, the stolen white moving van screeched to a halt in front of Pier Six. Four heavily armed men, including the driver, hopped out of the van and ran down the dock. At the end, a family of four was climbing into a five-seat turbine helicopter, about to take a sightseeing tour of the New York Harbor.

"EVERYBODY OUT, NOW!!" yelled one of the masked men, pointing a shotgun at the passengers. The family quickly got out of the helicopter. "I SAID EVERYBODY!" the man shouted again, aiming his shotgun at the pilot. The pilot quickly took off his headset, unstrapped himself from his seat and got out.

"Down on the ground. Do it NOW!"

The pilot and passengers laid face down on the pier.

The van's driver climbed into the cockpit, put on the headset and started the engines as the other three men, dressed head-to-toe in black body armor, loaded five large, black duffel bags into the back of the helicopter before climbing inside and sliding the door closed.

The helicopter shot skywards, then banked slightly and headed southwest to New Jersey, passing between Ellis Island and the Statue of Liberty.

"We're headed to freedom, boys," the leader said, pulling off his black ski mask.

The other three men shouted as they removed their masks. Their faces were dripping with sweat from the heat as they removed their body armor and black clothes.

"Yeah!"

"Whoo-hoo!"

"Hell yes!"

Chapter 38

NEW YORK CITY - 1 Chase Manhattan Plaza, 12:45 p.m.

The robbers were already airborne by the time the police arrived at the bank.

"Is there anything you can tell me that might help us identify the perpetrators?" a police detective was asking Adam. The plain-clothes detective was wearing a dark suit and blue tie.

"They seemed to be very well organized," Adam said. "They were dressed all in black body armor, similar to the guards outside Wall Street, and they used code names to communicate. I have no idea how much money they took, but they filled four or five duffel bags full of cash and were out of here in just over a minute."

"Did you notice what kind of weapons they had?" the detective asked, taking notes with a pen and pad of paper.

"Two of them had M16-style assault rifles and their leader had a pump-action, tactical 12-gauge shotgun with a pistol grip," Adam said.

"That's pretty specific. You must have gotten a good look at it," the detective said.

"Yes I did. It was pointed at my face."

"I'm sorry to hear that," the detective said. "That must have been really upsetting."

"They left an empty shell over there," Adam said, pointing to the spent plastic shell.

The detective used his pen to pick up the shell casing and slipped it into a small plastic bag while Adam opened his billfold and pulled out one of his business cards.

"Did they take anything from you?" the detective asked.

"They took some money I had ordered, a thousand dollars, before I had a chance to sign for it, and their leader tried to take my wristwatch," Adam said, handing the detective his card. "That woman over there is a friend of mine and I believe she was quite shaken. Karen lost her phone and ID and everything, but I can vouch for her. You should definitely talk to her."

"I will, thank you," the detective said, looking at the card and quickly adding, "Mister Morgan. Sir, this was an extremely brazen robbery. Here's my card. Please call me if you remember anything that could help our investigation."

Adam thought for a moment.

"You might be able to track Karen's phone, if the robbers still have it," Adam said, taking the detective's card and pocketing it. "Are you aware that the Federal Reserve Bank of New York is directly across the street?" He pointed to the north.

The detective followed Adam's finger and looked at the colossal, irregular-shaped building located at 33 Liberty Street. The colorful, limestone bricks and wrought-iron decorations were considered priceless in their own right, but within their massive walls and vaulted ceilings, the fortress held more than 7,000 tons of gold inside, more than in Fort Knox or anywhere else on earth.

"*That* would be a brazen robbery," Adam said. He had a sudden thought.

As the detective was interviewing Karen, Adam checked the price of gold on his smartphone. Gold was selling at an all-time high. *Too expensive,* he thought. *This would be a good time to sell gold, not buy it. Still, I should keep an eye on the price in case it changes.*

He looked at the exquisite gold wristwatch that had nearly cost him his life and shook his head in disbelief. He picked up his smartphone, selected a business card from his wallet and dialed Niles Jones' number.

Chapter 39

EDISON, New Jersey - 3125 Woodbridge Ave., 12:56 p.m.

The stolen, five-seat Aerospatiale AS350 Squirrel helicopter touched down on a grassy field. Four men in civilian clothes jumped out, each carrying a large, black duffel bag filled with cash and a second bag filled with body armor and guns.

"OK, let's stick to the plan," the leader said, shouting over the noise of the helicopter's single-turbine engine as it powered down. "We'll split up here and rendezvous tomorrow morning in Philadelphia at that place we discussed. Remember to be smart and don't attract attention to yourselves. Good luck."

The men climbed inside four waiting vehicles and sped off in a caravan south on County Road 514 to the 440 interchange, where they parted in separate directions.

The man driving the white, 2012 Toyota Corolla turned south on Interstate 95, also known as the New Jersey Turnpike; the man driving a black, 2010 Ford F-150 truck headed west on Interstate 287 towards Metuchen before turning south on Highway 27 towards Princeton; the third vehicle, a red, 2013 Chevrolet Silverado truck headed southwest on Highway 1; and the driver of the green, 2014 Jeep Commander continued east on Highway 440 for a few miles before turning south onto the Garden State Parkway.

The robbers had chosen Edison for its central location and close proximity to alternate escape routes, but were unaware of the area's history. In the late 19th century, Thomas Alva Edison invented the phonograph and a commercially viable incandescent lightbulb just a few miles away at his home and research laboratory in nearby Menlo Park. The area was one of the first places in the world to use electric light for illumination and became the center of America's modern electrical grid. More than a century later, electricity was still a mystery to most people.

In the back seat of the green Jeep, buried inside one of the large duffel bags full of cash, Karen's smartphone was remotely activated and began relaying its position to the nearest cell phone tower, which bounced the signal off a nearby satellite to another cell tower in Manhattan and moments later to police headquarters.

Chapter 40

NEW YORK CITY - New York Times Building, 620 Eighth Ave., 1 p.m.

John Thompson's phone had been ringing off the hook all day. As a senior online editor for *The New York Times*, he was familiar with busy news days, but he hadn't seen activity like this in years. Something big was happening.

China had just activated a gigantic solar array that was unprecedented in size, and combined with the Three Gorges Dam, was capable of satisfying most of the country's energy needs. World markets had soared on the news. Then unexpectedly, stock markets around the world had crashed. Stock in the New York Times Company was deep in the red as well.

Now NASA and NOAA were warning about the approach of some kind of geomagnetic superstorm and indicated that several older satellites might be crashing to earth in the coming days. *That could explain why the television reception is steadily worsening*, he thought. John was currently reading about geomagnetic storms online and didn't like what he saw. He wondered whether there was any connection between the stock markets, China Solar, the brownouts in New York City and the coming solar storm.

"Where's my science editor?" John shouted over the din of the newsroom. "Where's my markets editor?" Dozens of telephones were ringing throughout the newsroom.

John's phone rang again.

"New York Times, this is John," he answered, scribbling notes on a yellow legal pad in shorthand. "Holy shit! Are you serious?" he asked after a few moments. "Sorry. When? Where? You're kidding. How much did they take? And where are they now? Thank you, sergeant. Please keep me posted."

He hung up the phone and stood up at his desk. The newsroom seemed eerily empty.

"We've got a bank robbery at Wall Street!" he shouted. "Next door to the Federal Reserve! Where's a cops reporter? Where the hell is everyone?!"

John looked over the top of the sea of cubicle walls for anyone who wasn't on the phone. At least half of the reporters in the newsroom were recent graduates of the Columbia School of Journalism and most had master's degrees but no experience. All of the cub reporters and interns were covering the upcoming midterm elections, even though November was still four months away. Outside the newsroom's third-floor windows, he saw a giant photo of a supermodel in a diamond-covered fantasy bra with large, white wings towering over Times Square.

John heard a familiar, rhythmic clacking sound and turned to see his editor, Anita Reinhardt, loudly walking towards him in her high heels and blue power suit. She could be quite intimidating at nearly six feet tall, and now she was headed straight for his desk.

Time to be managed, he thought as he sat back down in his squeaky chair.

"Hi John, do you have a minute?" Anita asked. She appeared to be having a lousy day.

"Sure, Boss," John said, following her down the hall to a conference room. "It's a little crazy here today, and I can't seem to find my staff. I've already written four stories today. What can I do for you?"

"I'm afraid we're going to have to let you go," Anita said after they both had sat down. "As you may know, our stock is in serious trouble and it's time to restructure and rebalance our resources. Corporate has informed me that we need to eliminate 100 positions in the newsroom by the end of this week."

"Are you serious?" John asked. "But why me? I've been here for 15 years and I'm a year away from retirement. I won a freaking Pulitzer Prize last year!"

"I know, and I'm really sorry about this," she said. "Due to your vast experience and expertise, we can offer you a buyout option that includes a generous severance package, but we need you to empty out your desk now and surrender your security badge."

"I don't believe this," John said. "This is one of the busiest news days in years and you're gutting our newsroom staff? Do you have any idea what's happening outside?"

"I've been told that other news agencies are making similar cutbacks as well," she said. "I'm sorry it had to be this way. You're one of our top editors and I wish you all the best of luck in your future endeavors. Jamal from Human Resources will escort you out."

John watched in disbelief as Anita stood up and walked away. When he got back to his desk, his phone was ringing again, but he just sat down in his chair and watched it. *Am I still a journalist?* The phone stopped after ringing four times. John untied his red and white, polka dotted bow-tie, loosened his collar and leaned back in his chair. *Well, they say it's a recession when someone you know loses their job, and it's a depression when you lose your job. This could be the start of another Great Depression. What do I do now? Should I retire early? Should I look for another job? Maybe I should start my own news website.*

John looked around the newsroom at all the young faces. He was one of the last of the old guard, a dying band of professional career journalists who had dedicated their lives to serving as the watchdogs of liberty and democracy, the fourth estate to the three branches of government. Most of his friends had left the business years ago, moving to the private side to work as public relations hacks, or to start entirely new careers. Not that he could blame them. Advertising and print circulation numbers had been steadily dropping for years, thanks to the ubiquitous presence of the Internet and 24-hour cable news. Readers no longer relied on morning newspapers once they realized they could find the latest information on their smartphones, instantly and for free.

In the last decade, John had watched as multi-national corporations bought up all the family-owned, independent newspapers across the country with leveraged debt, merged and consolidated editorial talent to increase productivity, slashed editorial budgets and resources, and laid off anyone with a salary that paid a living wage. They replaced veteran reporters with new college graduates and interns and assigned them to cover spot news or complicated beats they didn't understand. This rampant cost-cutting strategy provided temporary boosts to shareholder dividends and any losses were written off. The news industry was clearly in a downward spiral.

This collapse of quality was by no means limited to journalism and in fact mirrored the collapse of small businesses across the country. John had written or edited hundreds of stories about big-box discount retailers and fast-food franchises that swept into an area and undercut prices, forcing thousands of small businesses to go under. Multi-national corporations acquired thousands of trusted American brands, shut down production, laid off workers and outsourced everything overseas to wherever the workforce was cheapest. Local, hand-crafted merchandise and farm-grown food was replaced by low-cost, low-quality imports. Millions were out of work, the national debt continued to soar to record levels, and now John was jobless.

"Do you need any boxes?" asked a deep-voiced man from behind. John turned around to see Jamal towering over his desk. The enormous man worked nights as a bouncer at a nightclub.

"Yeah," John said, looking at his large Rolodex and the piles of newspapers, books and notes covering his desk and cubicle walls. "I think I'll need several."

Chapter 41

LONDON - Leicester Square, 6:10 p.m.
TIME TO SOLAR IMPACT: 6 hours, 22 minutes

Jacob and Kendra arrived in Leicester Square just in time for the evening rush. All around them, people were getting off work, trying to get home, looking for a place to eat or looking for entertainment. Leicester Square was home to several major cinemas including the Odeon, the Empire and the Vue; as well as notable West End theaters such as the Queen's Theatre, Her Majesty's Theatre, and the Prince of Wales Theatre, among others.

"Can we see a show?" Kendra asked, looking around at all the pedestrians, marquees and flashy advertisements. Jacob was scanning the news on his smartphone.

"We could; which show would you like?" Jacob asked, still looking at his phone.

His Twitter account now had 80,000 new messages and more than 400,000 followers, many of whom had reposted or shared his tweets, photos and videos. He shook his head in disbelief and looked the status of his YouTube video. "How to Hypnotize Your Mom" had gone viral and had already been viewed more than 10 million times in a couple of hours.

Jacob scanned the local entertainment news and saw that five of the top 10 stories were about himself and nearly 10 percent of all the traffic on Twitter was related to him. There were photos of him from the video, photos of him holding hands with Kendra, and several photos of him at the puppet show, including one of Kendra and him kissing, taken from a few feet away.

"How about Mary Poppins?" Kendra asked.

"That's a little creepy," he said. *Did Kendra take this one and post it?* he wondered.

"Who is? Mary Poppins?"

"Half the stories on the Internet right now are about me and you," Jacob said, showing Kendra the photo on his smartphone. "Did you take this one about an hour ago?"

"I put that on my private page," she said. "Please tell me that's where you found it."

"I saw it on a news story," Jacob said. "It's everywhere."

"That's stealing," Kendra protested. "What did they do, hack my Facebook page? I should sue them, or at least get photo credit for it."

She pulled out her smartphone and began rapidly pressing a bunch of buttons.

Jacob suddenly realized that he didn't know very much about Kendra. One of the gossip blogs called her a stuck-up self-promoter and an adolescent narcissist, noting that her Facebook page had more than 800 photos, mostly of herself. *That's not fair*, he thought. *Most of my friends have hundreds of photos of themselves online. They can't all be narcissists.*

"I'm a little confused as to what's going on," he said.

"You're famous," she said. "But better than that, you've got inertia. You're hot. You don't know it yet, but you have super powers, Jacob Baker. You can do anything you want. Wanna be on TV? MTV, E! London and Global Radio are all right here. Having hot people on their show makes them look hip. They'll promote you if you promote them. The more stories there are about you, the more people will hear about you and want to learn more. It's exponential, like in algebra."

"Wow, you're smart," he said, flashing her a smile. "Wanna be my manager?"

As they were talking, several pedestrians recognized the young couple and pointed. One of them took a photo of Jacob and Kendra with a smartphone and posted it online.

"Let's try to get you on the air," she said, taking his hand and leading him through the building's grand lobby to the studio reception desk.

The receptionist had been following the day's entertainment news and immediately recognized Jacob and Kendra. She dialed up one of her friends working upstairs — who was also a production assistant — and suggested she come down to the lobby immediately.

As they were waiting in the spacious, well-lit lobby to get a meeting with the assistant and later an actual producer, Jacob noticed a quotation written in large letters in the molding around the edge of the ceiling. He read the quotation out loud to Kendra.

"Some are born great, some achieve greatness, and some have greatness thrust upon them," he read. "That's so true."

"Shakespeare, Twelfth Night," Kendra said flatly, without consulting her phone.

Jacob watched Kendra for a moment as she flipped through a celebrity magazine and casually pulled out his smartphone. He typed in a few words of the quote he had just read into a web search engine and thousands of different online sources instantly confirmed the quote was from Shakespeare. He shook his head and wondered why he didn't know that.

Chapter 42

SOUTH AMBOY, New Jersey - On the Garden State Parkway, 1:15 p.m.

The driver of a green, 2014 Jeep Commander was cruising southbound on the Garden State Parkway, passing the town of South Amboy, when he noticed a police helicopter hovering overhead. The driver took the next exit, number 123, southbound onto Highway 9.

Immediately the vehicle's onboard navigational system began its stern reprimand of the driver in a feminine, mechanical voice with a hint of a British accent.

"You have deviated off course," the navigational system began. "Turn left in 0.2 miles onto County Road 615 Bordentown Avenue or turn around."

The driver maintained his course, rolled down the driver's side window and quickly stuck his head out the window, looking back to see if the helicopter was still following him. It was.

"Shit!" said the driver, who also went by the codename "Spider." He pulled out his smartphone and posted an update to his Twitter account, splitting his attention between driving and texting.

"They r on 2 me," he posted, then immediately switched off his smartphone.

"You have deviated off course," the female computer voice repeated. "Turn left in 0.8 miles onto Ernstrom Road or turn around."

The driver switched off the navigational system and increased his speed to 45 mph. He looked in his rearview mirror and noticed two police cars following behind him with their lights flashing. He increased his speed to 55 mph and blazed through the next intersection, despite the red traffic lights and hot police pursuit.

"You're gonna have to catch me first," Spider said with a chuckle.

He looked back out his window and saw that there were now two police helicopters following him, as well as a TV news helicopter. Spider increased his speed to 65 mph and began swerving around several slower-moving vehicles that were in his way. The two police cruisers behind him were joined by a third, also with red and blue lights flashing.

Up ahead, Spider could see that the highway was completely blocked by two additional police cruisers. He quickly scanned the surrounding terrain and saw what appeared to be a dirt road cutting through the woodlands to the west. Spider punched the brakes, swerved to the shoulder and steered his Jeep Commander off the highway, down an embankment and onto the dirt road. The rocky road was scattered with pot holes and graded bumps, but as soon as he put his vehicle into 4-wheel drive and sped up to approximately 50 mph, the Jeep skipped right over the bumpy surfaces and continued on without much trouble.

Spider looked back to see if the police cruisers had followed him, but saw only a large cloud of dirt and dusk in his wake. *Eat my dust,* he thought. The rough terrain was no match for the police cruisers, who called off their pursuit. The three helicopters continued to follow overhead as the Jeep tore through the wooded area.

***

Hundreds of miles away in Arlington, Virginia, a highly trained Homeland Security operative was sitting in a cubicle in a crowded, dimly lit room, waiting for her next assignment. Her computer gave a quick chime, indicating she had a new message.

Agent Stella Devine quickly scanned a few lines of her new orders and pulled open a live government satellite search program. She entered the cell phone number listed in the report into the tracking program and waited. After a few moments, one of her multiple computer monitors displayed a crystal-clear, top-down satellite image of a green Jeep speeding down a dirt road through a forested area. A red target symbol followed the Jeep, centered directly above it.

"Step one: Locate suspect. Check," Devine said. "Step two: Identify and assess containment options."

The 28-year-old security operative quickly typed in a few commands into one of the multiple keyboards at her workstation and activated an airborne Predator surveillance drone. The camera view on a second monitor showed a real-time high-definition video of the Jeep from a different angle, this time flying toward the vehicle instead of top-down. She zoomed in the drone's high-def camera and could clearly read the vehicle's front license plate. She typed in the seven-digit license and pulled up a profile of Javier Rico, alias "Spider."

The information on the vehicle indicated it was new, which meant that it had LoJack installed. The LoJack Stolen Vehicle Recovery System was originally designed to track stolen vehicles and was capable of remotely starting or stopping any stolen vehicle that had its hardware activated. LoJack had become so popular as a theft-deterrent in recent years that it was now a standard feature on all new automobiles. Car thefts were down 50 percent nationwide.

"Target vehicle has remote shutdown," she said into her headset microphone. "Checking for access code and ideal remote engine shutdown conditions."

A few keystrokes later, Devine located the remote shutdown code for the vehicle's engine. The drone's camera revealed the Jeep was headed for a sharp turn in the road. *Killing power to a vehicle traveling at high speeds just before a sharp turn could cause a dangerous crash*, she thought. *I'd rather not kill anyone today if I don't have to.* The Jeep tore around the tight corner at 35 mph and sped up. *I need to get the vehicle to slow down first,* she thought.

And then she saw it. Up ahead in the road, less than 200 feet from the speeding Jeep, a large fallen branch lay across the road. *If the Jeep doesn't slow down or can't slow down before it hits that branch, the driver could crash,* she thought. *This could be my chance.*

***

How am I going to get out of this? Spider wondered as he maneuvered his vehicle around a tight bend in the road, slowing down to about 35 mph and accelerating about halfway into the turn. The Jeep's tires kicked up a large cloud of dust as he sped up to 50 mph. Up ahead, Spider saw what looked like a log or a large branch blocking the road. He could drive over it, but not at fifty. He punched the brakes and slowed down to nearly a stop as he approached the obstacle.

Suddenly, his Jeep unexpectedly stalled out and the engine sputtered off, bringing the high-speed chase to an abrupt and anti-climactic end. The two police helicopters landed on the dirt road, one in front of the Jeep and one behind, and several heavily armed police jumped out with assault rifles raised. The TV helicopter remained airborne, filming the action.

***

"Step three: Neutralize," Agent Devine said. "Mission accomplished. Target vehicle has been safely neutralized and the suspect is in police custody. He's all yours."

She typed out a quick summary of what happened, electronically submitted the report to her superiors and closed the case. The Predator drone had already been assigned to a new target.

"That was easy. What's next?" the operator asked herself as she scrolled through a national database of active police incident reports. "Who needs a little Devine intervention?"

Chapter 43

MECCA, Saudi Arabia - Second floor of the Abraj Al-Bait Towers, 8:20 p.m.

Ibn Ali stepped inside the grand foyer of the hotel's restaurant and carefully untied and removed his black leather shoes. He was carrying two bulky leather bags and shifted one bag over his shoulder to free his left hand to carry his shoes. He was admiring the room's tall ceilings, sweeping arches and elegant geometric mosaic designs as he walked to the maitre d's podium. The delicious smell of the awaiting feast made his stomach growl.

"Good evening," the maitre d' said in Arabic. "Do you have a reservation?"

"Yes, I am Ibn Ali. I am attending a dinner party with Imam Hassan," Ibn said, setting his two bags on the floor. He noticed his reflection in a large mirror next to the podium.

Ibn was about six feet tall, 40 years old, dark-skinned and fairly handsome, with short, black hair and a neatly sculpted beard. He was wearing a dark two-piece suit and had on a matching short, rounded taqiyah cap.

"Certainly, please follow me," the man said.

"Do you have somewhere I could check my bags?" Ibn asked. He motioned to his luggage on the floor.

"Certainly, sir," The maitre d' said, pulling two numbered luggage tags from a bundle and tearing off the bottom half of each tag. He looked over at two servants standing nearby and loudly snapped his fingers. The two Lebanese immigrants saw the maitre d' and came over. The maitre d' handed half of each tag to the bellhops and the other halves of each tag to Ibn.

"Here are your tickets for your luggage, sir," the maitre d' said. "If you will please follow me, I can show you to your table."

Ibn followed the man through the crowded banquet hall to a long table filled with other male guests of the imam. There were no women present. Ibn found his name written in Arabic on a notecard by an empty plate and sat down for the feast.

The table was covered with baskets of whole wheat bread, large platters of grilled chicken, beef kabobs and several racks of lamb. There were also several mixed green salads and numerous bowls of humus, beans, rice, yogurt, cottage cheese and lentils. Once everyone had been seated, someone gave a quick prayer and the guests began to eat.

"How are you finding our great city?" the man seated to the right of Ibn asked in Arabic. He was dark-skinned with white hair, had a white beard and was wearing clean, white robes and the traditional Saudi red-and-white checked shmagh headdress. Ibn did not recognize him.

"Very well, thank you," Ibn replied. "It has changed much since I first visited as a boy. Most of the stone buildings have been replaced by concrete, glass and steel."

"You do not like technology and progress?" the man asked.

"Quite the contrary," Ibn said. "Technology and progress are my business. I believe that everything changes over time, and God willing, it changes for the better."

"God be praised," the man said.

"God be praised," Ibn repeated.

"Are you here on pilgrimage?"

"It is a pilgrimage every time I visit Mecca," Ibn said. "I am also here on business."

"May I ask what you do?"

"I am a telecommunications specialist," Ibn said. "I'm based in Dubai, but I grew up in Riyadh and still have Saudi citizenship."

"You are here doing telecommunications work?" the man asked. "What specifically?"

"I have just finished installing and testing a new security feature that uses facial-recognition technology to identify and track suspected terrorists before they act," Ibn said. "My name is Ibn Shaja'at Ali. And to whom do I have the pleasure of speaking?"

"You're the security expert. Why don't you tell me?" the man asked playfully.

"Would you mind if I took your picture with my phone?" Ibn asked.

"Not at all," the man replied in a friendly tone.

Ibn opened an app on his smartphone and took a quick photo of the man. His phone imitated the sound of a camera shutter, and an instant later the app had a positive identification. Ibn read the display on the small screen with surprise and repeated it out loud.

"It says you are Sheik Dr. Hassan bin Ali, president of the Saudi council of advisors and imam of the great Mecca mosque," he said. "Is this correct? Forgive me, I didn't recognize your holiness. This is your dinner party. Thank you for inviting me. It is quite an honor."

"You honor me by coming," the imam said. "I am interested to hear more about your business in our city and specifically your facial-recognition program. I am surprised by how quickly it identified me. How does it work?"

"The software uses a special facial-recognition pattern algorithm to create a positive identification of the individual or persons in a picture. It also scans digital photographs and videos uploaded to the Internet for comparison and can instantly identify everyone in the picture. I have found it works especially well with large groups. Mecca has thousands of video cameras, from traffic and mass transit cameras to ATMs and private security cameras. These photos and videos can then be tagged and cross-referenced with a database of known terrorists in real-time to effectively track the subject's movement virtually anywhere."

"I used to think that only God could see us everywhere," the imam said. "Is this system limited to search only for terrorists in Mecca?"

"Currently, yes," Ibn said. "But it could easily be expanded to identify and track the movement of suspected terrorists in and around every major city on earth. Next week I am traveling back to Las Vegas in the United States to install a similar system."

"Interesting," the imam said, stroking his white beard. "I would not give the devil that power. I have not been to Las Vegas, nor do I wish to. Mecca looks very peaceful from my room, but down here on the surface everything is so busy and crowded."

"Do you live up near the top, your holiness?" Ibn asked.

"My office and living quarters are on the 85th floor," the imam said. "You should come up tomorrow and see the view. Our elevators are very fast."

"Thank you, I would like that. Elevators make our skyscrapers possible."

"Technology is not always a blessing, you know, particularly if it is used in nefarious ways. For instance, is it possible your software program could be used to spy on or track the whereabouts of every person on earth?" the imam asked.

"It is possible, I suppose, but that is not for me to decide. I am just the messenger."

"We are all God's messengers," the imam said. "The challenge in life is to differentiate between God's message and man's message, between God's will and man's will."

"Amen," Ibn said.

Chapter 44

NEW YORK CITY - 110 Central Park South, 1:30 p.m.
TIME TO SOLAR IMPACT: 6 hours, 2 minutes

The doorbell rang inside the penthouse apartment's main gallery.

"Coming!" Natasha sang, briskly walking to the front door in three-inch high heels that made her stand just over six feet tall. She opened the door to find her husband standing next to a pretty, young woman with shiny, shoulder-length red hair. A wave of jealousy swept over her.

"There you are, darling," she said, putting her hands on Adam's shoulders and giving him a kiss on the lips as he stood in the doorway. Natasha was wearing the same white dress with black polka dots that she wore on the *Vogue* cover. "Thank you for making it. I hope you are feeling better than you were this morning." She looked at Karen and smiled, then back at Adam.

"I am, thank you," Adam said. "Natasha, you remember Karen Walters, my executive assistant? Karen, this my beautiful and lovely wife Natasha."

"Oh yes, Karen," Natasha said, giving her a friendly kiss on the cheek. "How good of you to come. Pretty slow day at the office?"

"Actually, no," Adam answered. "Today has been anything but slow. Karen and I were held up at gunpoint this afternoon."

"Really? That's terrible!"

"This was after the stock market crashed in the morning," Adam said. "We're fine now. Here, I brought you a gift," he said, handing her the Hermes bag with the pink scarf.

"What a nice babushka," Natasha said, inspecting the scarf and giving Adam a hug. "Please, come inside and mingle. Would you like to meet our guests?"

As they entered the Morgan's penthouse apartment, Karen did her best to avoid looking stunned. She was still disoriented from being robbed at gunpoint less than an hour earlier, only to be given another $10,000 in cash and an apology from the bank. She was carrying the merchant money bag and her black Chanel purse, clutched tightly in her hands.

Everywhere she looked, there was either million-dollar modern art or magnificent, two-story, floor-to-ceiling windows that revealed an astonishing view of Central Park to the north. A celebrity disc jockey was mixing together catchy beats.

"I wanted to have the party outside on our big terrace, but the weather is intolerable," Natasha said as she led them down a marble hallway covered with an exquisite Persian rug. "It's 110 degrees outside on the street, but up here, it's more like 120 degrees."

"Thanks to our art collection, we get to keep our apartment a cool 70 degrees year-round," Adam added, giving Karen a knowing wink. Natasha's face turned bright red.

"Can I talk to you for a minute?" Natasha asked in a firm, controlled tone.

Adam studied his new wife's body language for a moment, then quickly said, "Absolutely. I have important news. Let's go upstairs. Karen, help yourself to a drink at the bar and make yourself at home."

Natasha was already at the top of the spiral stairs, headed to their bedroom. Adam followed her inside and closed the door, tossing his grey suit jacket on the bed.

"What the fuck is that bitch doing in my house?!" Natasha seethed, her dark eyebrows and dark eyeliner intensely focusing her gaze, like a cobra about to strike its prey.

Adam took a nervous step backwards. This was the first time he had ever heard Natasha swear. She maintained eye contact as she crept forward, closing the distance between them.

"Um, that's Karen, my assistant," Adam said, carefully enunciating his words. "You've met her before. She's English."

"English? And how long have you two been together?"

Adam was backed up against the bedroom door. He planned his next words carefully.

"OK, listen for a second, please," Adam pleaded. "Karen has worked for me for about a year, but we're not together. We never have been. She's not my type at all. You are, baby. That's why I'm with you. What's this all about?"

Natasha's eyes began to tear up.

"Are you cheating on me?" she whimpered, sitting down on the bed.

"No! Are you crazy? Why would I do that?" Adam sat down next to his beautiful wife, who had recently been declared the sexiest woman alive. "Why would you even think that?"

She grabbed the Hermes bag she had set on the bed and produced the pink mosaic scarf. She inspected it closely for a moment before pulling off a long, red hair. Adam stared at the hair for a moment as he collected his thoughts. Natasha began to cry.

"I made Karen wear your scarf today and she got robbed," he said. "I'm sorry. It's a long story, and I'll try to be brief because it's already been a long, busy day. Number one: I am not cheating on you. Period. Number two: We have to leave the city. Soon. Number three: I crashed the stock market this morning and became incredibly, mind-blowingly rich. I'm talking like the *Count of Monte Cristo* rich. You thought we were rich before? Now we're crazy rich."

"You said you were held up at gunpoint," she said in a soft voice, staring at the floor.

"The whole bank got robbed," he said, sitting beside her on the bed. "Even I got robbed. I had a shotgun pointed at my face."

"You did? Were you scared?"

"Actually, no," he admitted. "I think I was pretty calm. The bank robber guy tried to take my Blancpain wristwatch but I wouldn't give it to him."

"You wouldn't? Why not? It's just a watch, Adam. Geez, he could have killed you!"

"It seemed worth it at the time. That's irrelevant now," he said, rolling up his shirt sleeves to reveal his bare arms. "I already got rid of it. It felt tainted, somehow."

"Like this babushka," she said, folding the scarf across her lap.

"Exactly," he said. "Look, I feel terrible about the scarf. I'm really sorry. I saw it at Hermes and thought of you. I made my assistant wear it when we went to the bank so she would look more affluent, and she got harassed by the robbers because of it. I offered to let her keep it after that, but she didn't want it. I completely understand if you don't want it either."

"It's a pretty scarf," she said quietly as Adam stroked her hair gently with his hand.

"But enough about me," he said. "How was your day?"

"Well, I *was* trying to have a fun, afternoon party," she said with a sniffle. Her tears had smeared her eye liner down her cheeks in dark, muddy stripes. She used the pink scarf to wipe the make-up off her face, smearing it further.

"You seem pretty stressed out," Adam said. "How was your photo shoot this morning?"

"Exhausting. I had to change clothes about 200 times in under four hours. They let me keep everything I tried on, but most of it's winter stuff."

"Remember me saying I had a surprise for you?" Adam asked. "The scarf wasn't the surprise; that was just spontaneous. The real surprise is that we're going on a trip."

"You said we need to get out of the city," she said.

"That's right. Have you heard from your brother lately?"

"He told me there was some kind of storm headed this way," she said, scrolling through her messages on her smartphone to find the one from Aleks. "Here it is. He said there is a solar storm coming and to get out of the city."

"I've been following this and I think it's related to that bright light I saw this morning," Adam said. "NOAA is calling it a geomagnetic superstorm. The FAA hasn't shut down air traffic yet, but if this is for real, they probably will in a couple of hours. If that happens, our options will dwindle rather quickly. Do you remember that yacht we were on last weekend?"

"Oh, yes. I *love* that boat."

"Well, I chartered it to take us to Stingray Cay. We leave this afternoon."

"Really?" Natasha wrapped her arms around Adam and gave him a big squeeze. "Thank you, thank you, thank you!"

"The captain said it could take a week or two, depending on the weather."

"Will the storm affect us?"

"I have a feeling this storm is going to affect everyone on Earth," Adam said. "The yacht has sails, so it might be OK. We should pack light and plan for a long trip. When we get to my island, we should have everything we need. I think the yacht is pretty well-equipped."

"What about my party?"

"We can probably stay here another hour or two, but we need to get moving to stay ahead of the crowds and traffic," he said, pausing to think for a moment. "You know, it might be fun to give away some of your new winter clothes as party favors. I find it liberating to give things away, especially stuff I don't really like or need any more. You can give away this scarf, too."

"That could be fun," she said, giving Adam another squeeze. "Oh, I love you, baby. I'm sorry I lashed out at you a few minutes ago. I think I could really use a vacation. Should we go join the party again?"

"I'll head down now, but you might want to freshen up a bit first," he suggested, giving her a quick kiss on the cheek. Just before he closed the door, he poked his head back in and added, "Don't tell anyone I crashed the stock market."

The music coming from the DJ's mixing tables filled the apartment as Adam went down the spiral staircase to the penthouse's lower level. There were probably 50 people in their house, mostly crowded in the kitchen and living room. Adam walked to the open bar by the kitchen and ordered a Tom Collins from the bartender, then went into the living room to mingle.

At least 20 of the guests were fashion models: young, tall, skinny and oddly beautiful. Adam walked over to an interesting-looking group and stepped in to join the conversation. A tall, extremely fit black man with neatly styled cornrows was talking loudly, waving his arms with great enthusiasm. He was wearing an orange mesh, see-through T-shirt bearing the image of Che Guevara, zebra-striped spandex pants, white leather high-tops and a purple feather boa.

"But what's the point of having money if you never spend it?" the man was asking in his squeaky voice. "For me, that's where fashion comes in. I say, wear whatever you want. People are going to judge you based on how you look, so who cares? Why not keep them guessing?"

"Is that why you wear that purple boa?" one of the guests asked.

"I wear this," he said, petting the long, thin stole of feathers with affection, "because I want people to judge me way before they meet me. You see, my fashion is my identity. My boa tells you that I'm colorful, flamboyant, fearless and hungry for attention."

And color-blind, Adam thought, looking about the room for anyone he knew.

He spotted Karen nearby, apparently trapped in a conversation with a short, rich widow. The elderly, white-haired woman was dressed in a cream-colored blouse with matching silk pants and she was wearing a large diamond necklace as well as multiple gold bracelets and rings. Adam recognized her as the little old lady who had lived in the apartment below them for the past 50 years. The woman had thick, black-framed glasses and long, red fingernails. She was explaining her longtime expense account at Tiffany & Co. that allowed her to purchase anything she wanted, anytime she wanted. Karen covered her mouth to stifle an involuntary yawn.

Adam was about to cross the room to save her when a waiter appeared carrying a tray of hors d'oeuvres and presented him with a small piece of white meat sitting on top of a thin piece of toasted bread, smothered with some kind of jelly.

"Smoked duck crostini with mint sauce," the waiter said.

Adam picked up one and popped it in his mouth. *Tastes like chicken*, he thought. He looked back at Karen and saw that Natasha had come downstairs and rescued her.

"Can I show you around, Karen?" Natasha asked, her make-up restored to its perfect, signature look.

"Yes, please," Karen said, admiring the artwork hanging around the apartment. "Is that a Picasso?" she asked, pointing to a large oil painting of three abstract figures.

"You have a good eye," Natasha said with a smile. "That's one of my favorites, the 'Three Musicians.' We also have a Picasso sculpture outside on the terrace, as well as one by Constantin Brancusi. Over here, we have a Van Gogh, a Jackson Pollock and a lovely piece by Cezanne. Upstairs, there are two paintings by the Russian abstract artist Wassily Kandinsky, and there is a Salvador Dali in our bedroom. Adam and I just love modern art."

"They're fantastic," Karen gushed. "I just love your taste. You seem to know a lot about modern art. Have you been to the Saatchi Gallery?"

"That's in London's Chelsea district, right? Some of the stuff in the Saatchi is a little too conceptual for me, but I think it's good to step outside my comfort zone once in a while. I prefer London's Tate Modern and the Serpentine Gallery to the Saatchi. Adam and I travel a lot and we usually try to check out the local art museums wherever we go. How about yourself?"

"I also love modern art, but I don't get around as much as I used to," Karen said. "Come to think of it, I don't think I've left New York City at all this year. The last time I was home was for Christmas. Fortunately, us New Yorkers have the Museum of Modern Art, the Guggenheim and the Metropolitan Museum of Art. The MoMA is my favorite, by far."

"Adam said you're from London?"

"Originally, yes. Bloomsbury. I still have family there. I went to school at Oxford and moved to the States about five years ago. You're from Russia?"

"Moscow," Natasha said.

"Wow, your English is very good. You must have had lessons."

"Thank you. I got into modeling when I was 17 and have been swept around the world ever since. I lived in Paris for three years before moving to New York."

"I *love* Paris," Karen said in French. "The Louvre is truly magnificent."

"There you are," exclaimed a short, raven-haired woman with olive-colored skin as she approached the two women. She was wearing a yellow and white polka-dotted sun dress and yellow designer high heels. "What do you think of the party?"

"It's good," Natasha said. "What do you think?" she asked Karen.

"I like the DJ," Karen said. "Sounds very American."

"He's from Brooklyn," the woman said. "Who's your new friend?" she asked Natasha.

"Kitty, meet Karen, Adam's executive assistant," Natasha said. "Karen, this is Kitty, my personal slave. She's the reason I'm still somewhat sane."

"Slavery was outlawed 150 years ago, dear," Kitty said. "I'm Katherine Johnson, publicist and supermodel manager extraordinaire. You can call me Kitty, of course."

"Nice to meet you, Kitty. I'm Karen Walters," she said, shaking hands with Kitty.

"Ah, I see your people have met my people," Adam said, joining the conversation. "You two might want to trade notes sometime. Sweetheart, may I steal you for a moment?"

"Certainly," Natasha said. "Please excuse us."

Adam led Natasha over to an arrangement of rare orchids by one of their floor-to-ceiling windows facing Central Park.

"Feeling better?" Adam asked.

"A little."

"You and Karen seem to be getting along. You two probably have a lot in common."

"She likes modern art," Natasha said. "How are you enjoying our party?"

"It could use a little more spice," he said. "This seems like a fun crowd. Why not crank up the music a few notches and get people dancing? Have you given any more thought to giving away some of your clothes? I've got some dress shirts and ties I could throw in for the guys."

"You know what? You're right. These people came to have some fun," she said. "Let's get this party started."

Chapter 45

LONDON - Leicester Square, 7:10 p.m.

"Wow, that was crazy," Jacob said as he and Kendra left the MTV recording studios and rode a long escalator down to the building's lobby, hand in hand. "I've gotta call my mum and head home before I get in trouble. You know how it is. Hey, what are you doing tomorrow?"

Kendra tried to remember, but with all the excitement, emotions and newfound celebrity, her mind was drawing a big blank. She pulled out her smartphone and checked her schedule.

"I have French lessons in the morning and piano lessons after that, but I'm free in the afternoon," she said. "I'm all yours."

"I suppose we should exchange numbers," Jacob said as they reached the bottom of the escalator. "My cell has been going nuts for hours, and I don't have any idea who most of these people are. Let me give you my home and cell numbers. Please try to keep them private."

Jacob texted her the information, instantly transferring it to Kendra's smartphone.

"That's a good idea," Kendra said. "Here's my home, cell, Twitter, e-mail and Facebook." She replied to Jacob's text with another text, which was then recorded in his phone. "If that doesn't work, you'll have to send me smoke signals or come find me," she joked.

As they reached the revolving glass door at the studio's main entrance, they were startled to find thousands of teenagers crowded around and blocking the entrance.

"There they are!" yelled a young girl near the door. Hundreds of people erupted into cheering and applause and suddenly the crowd became a sea of waving arms, camera flashes and homemade signs that said things like "We love you Jacob!" "Jacob + Kendra, London's sweethearts" and "You can hypnotize me any day."

"So much for privacy," Jacob said, looking at Kendra with a big grin. In front of all their adoring fans and to wild applause, the two teens kissed goodbye.

Chapter 46

NEW YORK CITY - 110 Central Park South, 2:22 p.m.
TIME TO SOLAR IMPACT: 5 hours, 10 minutes

The music in the penthouse was noticeably louder after the DJ was told to pick up the tempo. In the large living room, the 60-inch flat-screen TV was tuned in to *E!*, the entertainment channel, but the volume was turned off. Periodically, the images on the screen would momentarily freeze, then jump to a pixilated mess of multiple images before returning to normal.

A dozen or so people were dancing on the hardwood floor in the center of the living room and many of the guests were almost shouting to be heard over the music when Adam and Natasha came downstairs with two large cardboard boxes filled with designer clothes.

"Party favors!" Natasha shouted, flopping a large box down in one corner. Adam dropped his box next to Natasha's. Immediately about 20 people crowded around the boxes, grabbing designer dresses, halter tops, winter jackets and boots and various haute couture garments from all seasons. As the guests pulled out the clothes, they identified them by designer: Akris, Dior, Marc Jacobs, Donna Karan, Ralph Lauren, Oscar de la Renta, Vera Wang, Versace ...

One of the fashion models with short, blonde hair pulled off her own top and dropped her skirt right in the middle of the room before slipping into a bright red tube dress. A moment later, 10 other models followed suit, stripping down to their lingerie or less to try on the free clothes.

Karen and Adam were initially shocked at the lack of inhibitions on display, but they were the only ones who were. The lanky blonde in the red dress had returned to dancing and the other fashionistas seemed to be having a great time, laughing and shouting and dancing. Adam looked at Natasha and saw she was laughing and smiling as well. She saw him and beamed again. He gave her a thumbs up. More people were arriving and things were starting to get wild.

Adam was looking around the room at their successful afternoon party when an image on the TV caught his attention. He looked for the remote control to turn up the volume, but couldn't find it amongst all the party debris. There were clothes, drinks and appetizer plates scattered on nearly every horizontal surface. He quickly gave up and walked down the hallway to the kitchen, where it was much less crowded and noisy. He went over to the 27-inch TV set attached to the kitchen wall, changed the channel from a baseball game to *E!* and turned up the sound.

"Londoners were in a state of near hysteria today after a viral web video and its young star Jacob Baker made the rounds to some of the city's famous hot spots, including London's MTV and E! headquarters," said the television hostess, an attractive Latino woman with brown eyes and fluffy brown hair. She was wearing a tight-fitting yellow top with some kind of black vest or girdle around her waist. The video cut to a grainy home video of Jacob and his new redheaded girlfriend holding hands and kissing in Leicester Square in front of hundreds of cheering fans, then segued to a sound bite from an exclusive interview with the two teenagers.

"You can get just about anything with a good attitude, a smile and a compliment," Jacob said, turning to give his girlfriend a wide grin. She smiled back.

"Oh my god, that's my sister," said a woman standing behind Adam. He spun around to see his assistant standing next to him. "Her name's Kendra. I don't know how she got involved; she's not even in the video."

"Are you serious? That's really your sister?" he asked.

"I have two brothers and four sisters," Karen said. "She's the youngest. I'm the oldest."

"I guess the apple doesn't fall far from the tree," Adam said, turning back to the TV.

"Have you seen the video?" Karen asked. "It's been viewed like 10 million times."

"The viral YouTube video titled 'How to Hypnotize Your Mom' has already been viewed more than 20 million times today," the TV hostess said. "Pundits around the country are calling the 16-year-old boy's fresh face and wholesome attitude 'a breath of fresh air' that's badly needed during these sweltering summer doldrums. You can view the full video at youtube.com."

"Yes, I saw it this morning," Adam said calmly.

"You know, I don't get the media these days," Karen said as the channel cut to a pharmaceutical drug commercial. Adam turned the sound off. "I mean, there's some kind of huge solar storm about to hit, right, but there's not one word about it on TV. I haven't found one story about that bank robbery we were caught in today, even though those guys must have taken like a million dollars. The detective told me they escaped in a stolen helicopter. That's crazy."

"You think it's a conspiracy?" Adam asked.

"I don't think it's diabolical; I think it's stupid," Karen said. "It's like we get the world we deserve. They're not hiding the truth so much as selling us the truth. *A* truth. It's like they show us what we want to see, not what we need to see, so that we'll keep watching these commercials. I've never seen so many commercials for drugs as I have in the U.S. Is it any wonder all these prescription drugs are so expensive?"

"People see what they want to see," Adam said. "Did you see how those people in the other room went crazy when we started giving away free designer clothes? Some of those clothes retail for thousands of dollars, even though they cost like $2 to make. The real irony is that the top designers *beg* us to wear their clothes and they give us most of this stuff for free."

"In that case then, yes, I would say it is a conspiracy," Karen said, finishing her drink and ordering another from the bartender. "Gin and tonic, please. Thanks. Fashion, art, finance, pharmaceuticals, you name it. If someone's getting rich, it's probably a conspiracy. Because clearly, not everyone is getting rich."

"I see your point," Adam said. "So what's the solution?"

"I don't watch TV," Karen said, picking up the remote and changing the channel. CNN was showing a clip of a high-speed police pursuit of a green Jeep Commander just as the vehicle veered off the highway onto a dirt road. The news was interrupted by a special bulletin featuring a map of California with a graphic of an irregular, red star near San Francisco. The graphic said "BREAKING NEWS: SILICON VALLEY PLANE CRASH KILLS 300." The two news text feeds continued to scroll across the bottom of the screen, relaying unrelated information in 10 words or less.

"See? The 24-hour news cycle is a constant stream of crashes, murders and natural disasters," Karen said, changing the channel. "It creates the illusion of fear and chaos to keep you glued to the tube." The plane crash was also the top story on this other channel. She changed the channel. Again, the plane crash. "See?"

"Let me see that," Adam said, taking the remote and cycling through the channels. The Silicon Valley crash was on every channel. The DJ in the living room stopped playing. Adam turned up the TV's volume.

"We're just getting reports of a commuter plane crash in Palo Alto, California, approximately 34 miles southeast of San Francisco," a news anchor was saying. "Information is still coming in, but early reports indicate that the 300 passengers and crew on board the Boeing 787 Dreamliner were killed when the plane crashed into a Silicon Valley business district near Stanford University, setting offices, neighboring homes and parks on fire. There is no word yet whether anyone on the ground was injured or killed, but officials say the death toll could rise above 300 while emergency crews attempt to extinguish the blaze."

Adam set down the remote and went to the living room with Karen following close behind. Natasha and the guests, the band and the waiters were all standing in silence, staring at the TV. A few of the guests were wearing only their underwear. As Adam and Karen entered the room, the huge TV was showing live footage of a monstrous fire and an inky black smoke cloud.

Emergency response crews attempted in vain to douse the growing inferno with fire hoses.

It's begun, Adam thought. *It's a good thing I dumped all my airline stocks this morning.*

"Officials have not yet determined the cause of the crash," a news anchor was saying, "but an instrument malfunction or a terrorist attack has not been ruled out."

Adam's smartphone buzzed. He checked his messages and saw that he had received an alert regarding the FOREX trade he made two hours earlier. The message informed him that the foreign exchange markets had closed, and the price of West Texas Intermediate crude oil had topped off at just above $150 a barrel, twice the price it had been at lunch. He did a quick calculation on his smartphone and realized that he had just made another billion-dollar profit, and now he had access to 20 million barrels of oil, enough to fuel the entire United States for one day. His stocks in oil companies were skyrocketing on the new price and the plane crash.

Using an app on his smartphone, Adam checked his basket of oil stocks against his net worth, then cross-referenced this number with a list of the top five richest men in the world. Never before in history had so much wealth changed hands in one day, and some of his peers had taken steep losses. He was now at the top of the list.

Adam belted out an evil, maniacal laugh, causing everyone in the room to turn around and look at him. When he had finished, his face turned bright red at the unwanted attention.

"Oh, I'm sorry," he said, pocketing his smartphone. "I was laughing at something on my phone that was completely unrelated. Folks, this is a terrible tragedy. This day has already seen too many disasters, and this crash comes at a terrible time. In light of this, I think we should break up this party and send everyone home. Thank you so much for coming and a big thank you to our wonderful hostess, the lovely and generous Natasha. Safe travels."

The guests stood in awkward silence for a few moments before Natasha spoke up.

"I'm afraid we have to call it a day," she said. "Thank you all for coming and please remember to take your belongings with you. It's really wonderful to have so many friends, and I can't thank you enough for all you have done and continue to do, especially you, Kitty."

The guests began to gather their things and make their way to the apartment's main gallery, where they stood in line to take the elevator or the stairs to the lobby. Natasha hugged or kissed most of her friends and guests as they departed and she made a point to thank everyone again individually.

Their building had three elevators and only the oldest and smallest reached the penthouse floor. There was no way it could handle their 80 party guests in less than an hour without annoying the other building residents, but many guests had refused to take the stairs, such as their elderly neighbor who waited almost ten minutes to take the elevator down one flight. It was worth it, she had said, because she had avoided taking the stairs for years and unfortunately she no longer had the strength to manage them.

Instead of getting ready to leave, Adam flopped down on the couch in front of the giant, high-definition set and watched the news until nearly everyone had left.

Chapter 47

TOLEDO, Wash. - 251 Layton Rd., 11:45 a.m.

Bob Layton climbed into his 40-year-old, beat-up pickup truck, put his foot down on the clutch, put the key in the ignition and gave it a forceful turn. The starter cried a few times in its attempt to start the engine, but couldn't make the connection. Bob tried the key again, with the same result.

"Oh, come on!" he shouted as he climbed back out of the truck, walked to the front and opened the heavy metal hood.

His brown, 1974 Ford F-100 pickup was rusted out in several places and had a tendency to be temperamental, but with a little bit of maintenance and some tender loving care, Bob believed it could run for another 40 years. As he looked down at his truck's eight-cylinder engine, he reflected on the fact that it was made just before the Arab oil crisis began in October of 1973.

After 1974, most vehicles were equipped with computers and electric starters to make them more fuel efficient, but it also made them increasingly impossible to fix without advanced training. Bob usually preferred to fix things himself and didn't think it was necessary to call in a mechanic unless a problem completely stumped him. He wiggled the rubber caps on the spark plugs, checked the battery and hoses and shut the hood again. He got back in his truck, pumped the gas pedal once, pushed the clutch to the floor and cranked the ignition key. The starter cried for a moment before the engine sputtered to life. He pumped the gas pedal and revved the engine, sending out a blue cloud of dirty exhaust from the tailpipe.

"That's more like it," he said, putting the truck into reverse, easing off the clutch and backing out of his long driveway onto Layton Road with his right arm stretched across the back of the seat. On his way in to town, he drove past several of his tree farms on Layton Prairie, homesteaded by his ancestors more than 100 years earlier, before he turned onto State Route 505.

The tree farms were in varying stages of development, with some growing hundreds of perfect rows of young Grand and Noble Fir destined for Christmas trees, some growing Douglas Fir for paper, and others growing Western Red Cedar trees for home construction. Bob knew all the local species of timber and could readily identify them by sight, but he saw them so often he barely noticed. He thought for a moment about the game he and Maud enjoyed playing where they would spot and identify birds, plants and fungi by sight.

Bob was too modest to brag, but his cedars were truly his pride and joy. Some of the older trees towered more than 100 feet and created a number of diverse ecosystems on the ground and above. Most of the medium timber was also ready to be cut, but deciding when to harvest was a delicate balancing act of supply and demand. Most newspapers, magazines, books, financial statements and retail catalogs had recently switched to paperless, electronic delivery, causing demand for timber and prices to plummet. It made sense to let his trees grow a little bigger and taller until the demand changed.

Bob turned on the radio to listen to his favorite station, but National Public Radio was doing a test of the Emergency Alert System, so he switched the radio back off. The only signs or billboard advertisements along the road were religious in nature, with messages like "Believe on the Lord Jesus Christ and Thou Shall Be Saved." One double-wide trailer he passed simply had the word "Jesus" written on the wall next to the front porch in six-foot-tall red letters. *Probably works better than a 'No Trespassing' sign,* he thought with a chuckle.

Bob saw several people fishing in boats for trout and salmon as he crossed the bridge over the Cowlitz River into the sleepy community of 700. Most of the buildings were one or two stories tall. He pulled up to a pump at the local gas and service station and parked his truck.

"What the heck?" he muttered, looking at the price of gasoline. Gas was $5.09 a gallon. He got out of his truck and walked into the convenience store.

"Hey Rick, what's up with your prices?" Bob asked the cashier as he approached the counter. "Gas went up like 20 cents a gallon."

"Don't blame me," Rick said. "Oil prices are going crazy today. I'm probably gonna have to raise them again in a few minutes. Haven't you been watching the news?"

"I don't have time to watch the news," Bob said. "I heard the stock market was in the shitter again. What else did I miss?"

"Death, destruction, mayhem," Rick said, adding, "the usual. What'll it be?"

"Guess I better top off the gas tank while I can still afford to," he said, plopping two $20 bills on the counter. "Oh, and I'd better get some diesel as well. I brought my extra gas can. Do you think that'll be enough?" he said, pointing at the $40 Rick was holding.

"Diesel hasn't gone up at all, so maybe," Rick said. "I just got our main tank topped off this morning, so we should be good for a while. Go ahead and get what you need and we'll sort it out later."

"Thanks, Rick," Bob said, walking back out to the pump and filling up his truck with unleaded and his five-gallon gas can with diesel. A few minutes later he was back in the store.

"Let's see," Rick said, checking his computerized register. "You owe me another $19.97 for the diesel."

"Highway robbery," Bob said, pulling out his well-worn, brown leather wallet and tossed his last $20 onto the counter. "Keep the change."

"Thanks," Rick said.

"Hey, is the farmer's market this Saturday?" Bob asked, looking outside.

"Yep, from ten to four," he said. "Should be our biggest one yet. Cheese Days usually is, so come early if you want to reserve a spot."

Cheese Days was Toledo's busiest summer festival, attracting thousands of former residents and tourists for its parade, classic car show, frog jump, Reno night and other activities.

"Better put me down for a table," Bob said. "We've got eggs, milk, yogurt and some fresh greens from our garden."

"You got it," Rick said, scribbling down 'Bob Layton' on a clipboard.

"Oh, I should also get some spark plugs and a little fuel additive," he said. "This new ethanol fuel is hell on my carburetor. But first I'll need to get some more cash from the ATM."

"There's an ATM in the corner if you don't feel like walking to the bank," Rick said.

"Yeah, but yours charges a transaction fee," Bob said. "Plus, I could use the exercise."

Bob left his pickup parked at the pump and walked across Second Street to the post office to check his mail. The free, weekly newspaper he received in the mail was full of stories about Cheese Days and other summer activities in the surrounding communities.

"Hey Bob," said a man in a flannel shirt and shorts who was also checking his mail.

"Hey Tom," Bob replied, nodding his head.

Leaving the post office, he crossed the intersection at Cowlitz Street with its flashing yellow traffic light and walked up to the bank, kitty-cornered with the gas station.

The bank's Automatic Teller Machine was out of service. Bob walked in the entrance to a small lobby with rustic, wood paneling. There was a plastic Christmas tree in the corner.

"Hi Bob," said a teller.

"Think your ATM's busted," Bob said.

"It's been acting up all morning," the teller said. "I can do better than a machine. I can do anything it can do and I don't need batteries."

After getting some cash, Bob walked back across Second and waited by the crosswalk for traffic to stop on Cowlitz St., also called State Route 505. The first truck saw him and came to a stop at the flashing light, which also happened to be the town's only traffic signal. The driver gave Bob a friendly wave.

"Hi Bob," said the driver. "Happy birthday!"

Bob smiled and waved as he crossed the street back to the gas station.

Rick was outside on a step ladder changing the prices on the reader board. Gas had just gone up another ten cents a gallon to $5.19.

Bob walked to the base of the ladder and looked up.

"Hey Rick," Bob said. "Maybe I should sell this gas back to you and make a profit!"

"Funny. I put your spark plugs and fuel additive on the counter, next to the cash register," Rick said. "It came to $40. If you want to wait a minute, I can ring you up."

"That's alright," Bob said, walking in to the store. He came out a minute later carrying his supplies. "I left another $40 on the counter. Thanks a bunch."

After pouring the additive in his gas tank, Bob climbed back inside his pickup, sat down and pressed in the clutch. When he cranked the key, the starter cried for a few seconds before the engine sprang to life with a roar.

"That's more like it," Bob said to himself as he revved the engine and put on his seat belt. He put his truck in gear and began the five-mile trip back to his farm.

Chapter 48

NEW YORK CITY - 110 Central Park South, 3 p.m.
TIME TO SOLAR IMPACT: 4 hours, 32 minutes

Adam was still sitting on the beige, soft leather couch, mesmerized by the disaster news reports on every channel, when he heard two women laughing nearby. He looked over and saw his wife and his executive assistant talking and laughing. He fantasized for a moment about sitting in a bubble-filled jacuzzi with the two young, beautiful women, one in each arm.

"Honey, can we take Karen to the Bahamas with us?" Natasha asked. "It might be boring sitting on a boat for a week with no one to talk to but you."

"Oh, I wouldn't want to impose," Karen said.

"Oh, nonsense," Natasha said. "It'll be fun. I promise I won't let Adam boss you around. You'd be there as our guest, not our lackey. *Please*, honey? You won't regret it."

Adam thought for a moment. Karen was pretty useful to have around, she had a connection to his potential heir, and a happy wife was always a happy life.

"Of course she can come, if she wants to," he said. "The captain said there's an extra cabin on board, so there should be plenty of room. It's up to her, though."

Both the Morgans looked at Karen expectantly.

"Sure," she said. "Thanks!"

"Yay!" Natasha said with a squeal. "This will be so much fun! When are we leaving?"

"We cast off at 4 p.m., but the captain said to be there by 3 p.m.," Adam said. "What time is it now?" he asked, checking his wristwatch. He had replaced his blue-and-white gold, Blancpain Forty Fathoms watch with a similar blue-and-gold, Rolex Yacht-Master II. "Shoot, it's already three. I'd better call him and tell him we're on our way, with an extra passenger."

"We're leaving right now?" Karen asked.

"Is that OK with you?" Natasha asked.

"Well, I should probably swing by my apartment and pack some things."

"Where's home? We might be able to swing by on our way out," Natasha said.

"Spanish Harlem," Karen said. "It's not really on the way. And I don't have my keys."

"What do you need?" Natasha asked. "You can wear any of my clothes and we can pick up anything else we'll need on our way there. Adam and I are already packed, aren't we?"

"The captain said to pack light," Adam said. "Why don't you two go downstairs to Bergdorf Goodman and pick up some incidentals? They should have everything you need. I can meet you in about 20 minutes with a car and we can set off from there."

"Wow, you guys don't mess around, do you?" Karen asked. "Shouldn't we at least tidy up a bit before we go?"

Even though the apartment was a complete mess with cups and plates and clothes strewn everywhere, Adam and Natasha both looked at Karen as though she had said something odd.

"Darling, we have people to do that," Natasha said to Karen in French.

"Right, I forgot," Karen replied in French. "How silly of me. Perhaps you could send them to clean up my flat when they're done here."

Natasha and Adam both laughed at Karen's joke.

"Oh honey, don't forget to bring the you-know-what," Natasha said to Adam in English. He cocked his head to the side quizzically. "You know, the ..." she said, squeezing her breasts with both hands.

"Gotcha," Adam said. "You two have fun. Remember: 20 minutes."

The two women were all smiles as they linked arms and hurried to the floor's elevator.

A few minutes later, they had exited the air-conditioned lobby at 110 Central Park South into the sweltering summer afternoon heat, walked east to the corner and turned south, passing beneath the Plaza Hotel's waving flags and up the steps to the entrance of one of Manhattan's oldest luxury boutiques. Bergdorf Goodman owned two magnificent stone buildings located opposite each other on Fifth Avenue, one for women and one for men.

A doorman held open the ornate brass door as they stepped inside the cool, air-conditioned entrance. The pleasant aroma of fresh wildflowers filled the air. Karen was becoming increasingly accustomed to the lifestyle of the affluent and was noticing a pattern of beige walls, mahogany woodwork, antique furniture and exquisite artwork wherever she went.

Bergdorf Goodman's modern interior was a sharp contrast to the building's castle-like stone exterior. Inside, the furniture was made to intensify the effect of the clothes. Crisp edges and bold colors helped to make everything seem slightly futuristic. Notably absent were price tags or sale signs. *If you have to ask the price, you can't afford it*, Karen thought.

"May I help you ladies?" asked a well-dressed sales clerk in a friendly tone.

"Yes, we're in a bit of a hurry," Natasha said. "My friend and I are going on a weeklong sea voyage to the tropics and she doesn't have a thing to wear."

"May I inquire as to the kind of vessel you will be taking, your expected level of activity and any anticipated social events?" the clerk asked Karen. "This will help us to dress you for every occasion."

"I believe it is a small, private yacht," Karen said, admiring the spacious room, "with just three or four people, total. I need to pack sparingly, but I don't have anything with me."

"She'll probably need at least one evening dress, a few swimsuits and some day clothes," Natasha said. "Plus incidentals like sunblock, a vanity kit and such."

"Does the lady have any luggage, or will she need that as well?"

"She requires the full treatment," Natasha said. "And as I mentioned, we are on a tight schedule."

"How tight, may I ask?"

Karen and Natasha looked at each other.

"About 15 to 20 minutes," Natasha said.

"Very well," the clerk said. "It will be my pleasure to help you. Please come this way."

Over the course of the next 15 minutes, Karen tried on six outfits, four of which Natasha approved.

Karen chose to wear a lovely beige dress and bright red belt by Alexander McQueen that complimented her figure, and matching beige designer heels by Jimmy Choo. The new outfit transformed Karen's appearance from a professional-looking businesswoman to a head-turning, high-class knockout.

The sales clerk recruited three other sales associates who gathered the necessary items, including a fully stocked vanity case; several types of designer footwear, including some flip-flops; three swimsuits; a green silk one-piece teddy; three summer dresses; an elegant, black evening gown with an open back; high-quality foul-weather gear and a small first aid/survival kit. They folded and packed everything into a gorgeous, watertight Louis Vuitton suitcase.

"And how will you be paying today?" the head clerk asked Karen as they were finishing up their business.

"Um, credit?" she said, picking up her black Chanel purse. "What's the total?"

"The final bill comes to $11,205.74," the clerk said, handing Karen a leather folder with an itemized list of her purchases.

Karen was speechless. She stared at the bill for a moment in disbelief, then looked inside her purse for her credit card. Everything in her purse — including her ID, checkbook, credit cards, smartphone, keys and make-up — was gone, except for a fat stack of $100 bills. *That's right, I put everything in the money bag,* she recalled. She closed her purse and unzipped the merchant money bag she received from the bank. Inside were four bundles of cash, including a bundle of a hundred $50 bills, two bundles of $20 bills and a bundle of $10 bills, but nothing else. Confused, she turned to look at Natasha.

Natasha was trying on a large, black floppy sun hat and large, round sunglasses. In her black and white summer dress, she looked remarkably like Audrey Hepburn from the classic film *Breakfast at Tiffany's*. She turned to Karen and gave her a wide grin.

"My husband will get this," Natasha said. "There he is now," she added, pointing across the room and waving at Adam as he approached. His confident walk drew the attention of everyone in the room.

"Everybody ready?" Adam asked. "I love the look, darling. Karen, I'm impressed."

"Sweetheart, would you mind picking up the tab?" Natasha cooed.

"Not at all," Adam said, pulling out his leather billfold and selecting a credit card.

"Oh, and these too," Natasha said, picking up a white, floppy sun hat and putting it on Karen's head and handing her a similar pair of designer sunglasses.

"May I?" the clerk asked Karen, taking back the bill and adding a few numbers into the computer. Adam handed the clerk his credit card without checking the total. She presented him with an electronic touch-pad for security verification. He pressed his right thumb to the pad and a moment later the fingerprint reader confirmed his identification.

"Should I give her a tip?" Karen asked Natasha in a confidential tone.

"Gratuity has already been included," the clerk said. "It has been my pleasure to help you today. If there will be nothing else, may I say thank you, bon voyage and safe travels," she said with a smile as the three departed the store, arm in arm. A well-dressed male valet followed them outside with Karen's new luggage.

As they exited the store onto Fifth Avenue, Karen's eyes were drawn across the street to the Apple Store's iconic glass cube. Hundreds of customers were standing in line in the blazing heat, waiting to file down a glass spiral staircase into the futuristic basement to purchase the computer company's latest technological miracle. Every year the gadgets got faster and sleeker.

Karen's attention was diverted again to a white limousine parked directly in front of the Bergdorf Goodman entrance. The chauffeur pulled back the rear-hinged, passenger-side door, revealing a spacious inner sanctuary. When she stepped inside the 2014 Rolls-Royce Phantom EWB's white leather interior, Karen detected a faint odor of flowers, cigar smoke and leather cleaner. The luxury vehicle's elegant, bespoke craftsmanship both inside and out called to mind the Art Deco style of the previous century with its rich colors, clean geometric shapes, lavish ornamentation and embrace of technology. Adam opened a hidden panel to reveal a mini bar inside the wall and helped himself to a scotch on the rocks.

After putting the luggage in the trunk, the driver got back in the front seat, put on his seat belt and typed the Brooklyn address into the vehicle's GPS navigational system. The computer instantly plotted a course and a large blue directional arrow pointed straight forward.

He pressed a button to start the ignition and a few moments later, the white phantom shot south along Fifth Avenue.

Chapter 49

On board the International Space Station, 19:32:00 UTC
TIME TO SOLAR IMPACT: 4 hours, 0 minutes

The Tranquility was filled with artificial light as Aleks jogged in place, pulled to the COLBERT exercise treadmill with elastic belts. He was reading a news report on an American website about the California plane crash.

> Silicon Crisis: Palo Alto Fire Spreads North
> SAN FRANCISCO - Governor Cortez declared a state of emergency in Palo Alto on Wednesday, ordering the evacuation of surrounding areas after a tragic commuter plane crash set the city ablaze. Firefighters struggled in vain to control the inferno ...

He scrolled down to another news story.

> Earthquake Halts Construction on Kingdom Tower
> JEDDAH, Saudi Arabia - Construction was halted Wednesday on the 1 kilometer-tall super skyscraper known as Kingdom Tower after a 5.0-magnitude earthquake and several aftershocks shook the city. Engineers say the shutdown was a precautionary measure and that no structural damage has been ...

"Still working out?" Chuck Wilson asked, floating into the pod from the adjacent Unity Node. Outside, the space station was passing over a darkened Arabian peninsula. The desert sand glowed bright blue, accented by the glimmering lights of Cairo and the Nile River, Jerusalem and Tel Aviv-Jaffa, Riyadh, Jeddah, Abu Dhabi and Dubai.

Aleks checked the time on his wristwatch. It was half past eleven.

"Did you want to exercise?" Aleks asked, continuing to jog. "I will be done in two minutes. I did not follow my normal routine today."

"That's OK," Chuck said. "Take your time. We have about four hours left until the big showdown, so you might want to catch a few winks while you still can. Mizzy is sleeping right now, but I'm still wide awake."

"Have you thought about what will happen to us during this 'big showdown?'"

"Well, I don't really want to, but yes, I have," Chuck said. "I think the ISS will be bombarded with intense radiation, like the Mir was during the solar storm of 1989. Wearing our space suits will offer us additional protection, but we should all wear radiation badges to track our exposure. The CME will likely disrupt the Earth's magnetosphere, compressing the field on the sunlit side and extending it on the dark side. This'll give us a strong electrical surface charge as we pass around the Earth."

"We should switch the satellites and space station into safe mode before the storm hits to avoid problems," Aleks said. "They could be restarted later. What about the solar panels?"

"Our photovoltaic panels can crystalize during an extreme electromagnetic storm," Chuck said. "Our onboard batteries might lose their charge and we could become completely powerless. I think we should retract and stow the solar panels before it hits."

"Lower the sails before the storm," Aleks said, finishing his workout, unstrapping himself from the exercise machine and floating freely again. "One thing that concerns me is orbital decay. We must stay above 200 kilometers, but if the storm also warms the atmosphere, it may expand to higher altitudes. This will cause more drag, pulling us to Earth faster."

"That's a good point; I hadn't thought of that," Chuck said.

"Perhaps we should fire our thrusters to raise the station to a higher altitude while we still have the option."

"How high do you think we should go?"

"I would say at least 400 kilometers to be on the safe side," Aleks said, floating toward the Zarya Control Module, where the altitude regulator was. Chuck followed him through the circular hatch connecting the pods.

"I don't know if you're aware, but we've lost another 15 or 20 satellites," Chuck said.

"Lost?"

"Lost communication," Chuck said. "Some of the lower earth orbit satellites could start falling to Earth any time now. We may want to begin putting them into safe mode now while we still can. I'm reluctant to cripple communications networks before everyone has been warned, especially without orders from the higher ups, but shutting things down early could greatly improve recovery efforts later on, after the storm has passed."

"You may want to check with your Houston first," Aleks said, arriving at the Zarya's instrumentation panel, reaching for a handle bar and pulling himself to a stop.

"Your news is reporting a plane crash in California, but almost nothing else," Aleks continued. "Did you tell Houston about the coronal mass ejection? Airplanes also face a higher risk of radiation and communication interference. Moscow grounded air travel an hour ago."

Chuck's face turned white.

"Good God, you're right," he said, turning around and swimming through the air as fast as he could toward the Unity Node.

"You may want to hold onto something," Aleks shouted as he flipped several switches.

Aleks fired the space station's emergency thrusters, momentarily giving him the sensation of gravity. He quickly maneuvered himself and landed on his feet for an instant before floating back into midair.

In the Unity Node, Chuck cursed as he fell to the floor with a thud.

Chapter 50

LONDON - Trafalgar Square, 9 p.m.

The driver of a dirty white BMW sedan pulled up to a stop in front of Trafalgar Square's western end and looked around for a familiar figure.

The evening sun was setting, illuminating the statue of Admiral Lord Horatio Nelson, Britain's most famous naval captain, in a vivid, orange light atop its 50-meter-tall stone column. Four enormous sculptures of lions surrounded the monument, commemorating the victorious 1805 sea battle against Napoleon's navy that cost Nelson his life.

A young man tapped on the driver's side window, causing her to momentarily jump.

"Sorry I scared you, Mum," Jacob said, after he walked around to the vehicle's left side and climbed into the passenger seat. He set a liter carton of milk on the floor between his feet and put on his seatbelt. "Thanks for picking me up. You wouldn't believe what a day I've had."

Leah Baker shifted the BMW into gear and sped around the square before turning off on a narrow street. The car was as messy inside as it was on the outside, with empty plastic bottles strewn on the floor and back seat, crumpled up napkins and wrinkled magazines scattered everywhere.

"I know; I've heard about it," she said, shifting the car into a higher gear and navigating the city's winding streets. "You've been all over the news. I think I may need to start following your Twitter account so I can keep better tabs on you. So how was your day?"

Jacob recounted his adventures since leaving their Islington apartment, how he had met Kendra, their dash across the city to King's Cross Station, the puppet show in Covent Garden and his interview with MTV.

"When I saw the mob outside Leicester Square, I knew I had to change tactics," he said. "People went nuts over that video we made. The last time I checked, something like 40 million people had watched it today."

"I find that hard to believe," Leah said. "I mean, I thought it was cute, but it wasn't amazing. People must have been pretty bored to sit around watching YouTube videos all day."

"Yeah, I guess," he said. "I've been tweeting about it all day, and when I saw all those people following me, I started tweeting where I was and what I was doing. Suddenly it was like there was a mob following me everywhere. That part was unreal."

"You mean surreal?"

"Yeah. I'd tweet that I was at Covent Garden and post a picture as proof, and thousands of people would go to Covent Garden. I'd tweet that I was at Leicester Square and ten thousand people would be there, just waiting to see me. I couldn't even walk around without people following me or chasing me."

"Why didn't you stop tweeting?" she asked, as the car whipped around a corner.

"I dunno, it was kind of fun," he said, looking out the window. "After the mob at Leicester Square, I called you, then snuck over to Chinatown on Gerrard Street and picked up this disguise," he said, showing her a plastic animal mask in the shape of a cartoon dog and a crumpled up red windbreaker. "That worked pretty well. Great, actually."

Jacob recounted how he had taken several photos of Chinatown but delayed posting them until he had walked the 500 meters or so to Piccadilly Circus, where he continued donning the mask and windbreaker. He tweeted to his half a million Twitter followers to join him for some dim sum in Chinatown, then took a few pictures of the famous neon billboards and hoards of evening shoppers congregating around Piccadilly Circus, before heading back east to Trafalgar.

"When I was about halfway there, I started posting pictures of Piccadilly and I could literally track the crowd's movement on the news. It was crazy. I got to Trafalgar about a minute before you showed up. Luckily, nobody recognized me. That reminds me, I took some cool pictures of the sunset on Nelson's column that I want to post."

"Why don't you give Twitter a rest for the day?" Leah suggested. "In fact, why don't you just give me your phone or turn it off?"

"Aww, Mum. Why?" Jacob whined.

"Why? Because I don't want your mob hanging around our apartment all night, that's why. I think you've gotten into enough trouble for one day."

"Fine, I'll turn it off," Jacob said, holding down the power button. "See? It's off."

"Thank you," Leah said. "And thanks for picking up some milk. So, tell me about this Kendra. Are you guys a couple?"

"Mum, that's private," he said. "It's embarrassing to talk to your mum about girls."

"OK, we'll talk about something else," she said. "When are you going to learn how to drive? Girls like boys who can drive."

"Fine," Jacob said, slumping down in his seat. "Her name is Kendra, as you know, and she's really smart and fun. And she has good taste in boyfriends," he added.

"Obviously, if she's with you," she said. "Tell me more."

Chapter 51

NEW YORK CITY - Sheepshead Bay, Brooklyn, 4:15 p.m.

The white Rolls-Royce Phantom limousine rolled up to the front entrance of the marina and made a gentle stop. A few moments later, two tall, strikingly beautiful and well-dressed women stepped out, followed by a bald man in a well-tailored gray suit.

Frank Rosario rolled his eyes when he saw the trio walking down the causeway to the *Reciprocity*, followed by a chauffeur carrying several large suitcases. *This should be interesting,* he thought. *Ten bucks says none of these landlubbers know anything about sailing.*

As they approached the 41-foot yacht, Adam was struck by its meticulous appearance, tall masts and old-fashioned rigging. It certainly wasn't the largest boat in the marina or even the most expensive, but it had a sense of style and grace that no other could match. *This is perfect,* he thought, recalling that not 10 minutes earlier, during their limousine ride from Midtown, his smartphone had alerted him that the FAA had grounded all international and domestic flights.

His instinct to avoid air travel had been spot-on, and now he was about to leave the city. Tens of thousands of other travelers were not so lucky. The stock market had closed at 4 p.m., suffering one of its worst days ever. Adam briefly smirked as he reflected on his own enormous earnings. *Seventy billion and change*, he thought. *That's got to be a record.* Thanks to his shrewd financial prowess, he was now the richest man in the world.

Adam had also received an e-mail from the police detective investigating the earlier bank robbery. The detective said that Karen's smartphone, passport and other personal belongings had been recovered and would be released tomorrow morning. The detective had asked Adam to inform Karen that her items could be collected at police headquarters downtown, along with a reward for her assistance. Adam worried that this new development could further delay their departure and decided to wait until later to inform Karen.

Natasha had fallen in love with the yacht from the moment she had first laid eyes on it a few days earlier. *It's everything a sailboat should be,* she thought, studying the yacht's crisp, white lines, smooth sails, polished wooden finish and sleek form. Even the name *Reciprocity* was agreeable, referring to the exchange of items for mutual benefit. She knew she would have to sacrifice many of her creature comforts in order to live on a magnificent craft like this for a week, but it would definitely be worth it.

Karen's eyes were first drawn to the top of the mast, then down the smooth, white sails to the yacht's exquisitely polished exterior, like something out of a fairy tale. *All that's missing is a prince,* she thought, her eyes scanning the deck for the crew. And then she saw him: tall, dark-skinned and handsome. The boat's captain was wearing a red polo shirt with the logo of a yacht on the breast, cargo khaki pants and a black fedora. He hopped down from the boat to the floating causeway, landing with catlike grace, and confidently walked towards them in his white low-top sneakers.

"Welcome to the *Reciprocity*, ladies and gentleman. My name is Captain Frank Rosario and I will be your chief for the duration of the voyage. Before we get started, I need to ask if anyone has a medical condition or if you require special assistance of any kind. Once we depart, it will be very difficult to get supplies, so it's critical we address any concerns before we leave."

The three passengers said nothing. The chauffeur set down their luggage and returned to the limo to collect the rest of their gear.

"Good," Frank said. "I'd like to point out a few safety procedures before we go aboard to help you get oriented. Does anyone here have prior experience sailing on a vessel similar to this?"

Adam and Natasha raised their hands.

"Have either of you been on a sailboat in the open ocean?" he asked.

They both lowered their hands and shook their heads.

"Sailing on the open ocean can be a dangerous and challenging experience for even the most skilled sailor," Frank said. "There are a thousand different ways in which you could be seriously hurt or killed, often in the blink of an eye. You could be swept overboard and drowned. You could be crushed by the boom during a sudden change of wind. The boat could catch fire and you could be badly burned, or it could sink out at sea, hundreds of miles from shore in shark-infested waters. Safety is of paramount importance, and I cannot stress this point enough. Knowing and following proper safety procedures at all times could save your life and the lives of everyone on board during emergency situations, when people tend to panic, as well as during times of relaxation. Safety always comes first. Having said that, sailing can also be one of the most relaxing and enjoyable experiences of your life. The gentle, rhythmic rocking of the boat, the cool, salty breeze blowing through your hair and the freedom from the worries of life on land can transport you to an alternate reality that few experiences in this world can touch."

The chauffeur had returned with the rest of the luggage and was waiting politely for Frank to finish.

"That's everything, sir," the chauffeur said, motioning to the seven large Louis Vuitton suitcases sitting on the causeway.

"Thanks again for all your help," Adam said, slipping the chauffeur a $100 bill as he shook his hand. Adam directed his attention back to the captain.

"God bless you, sir," the chauffeur said with a big smile. "Safe travels!"

"It looks like we're ready to see the interior," Frank said, clasping his hands together. "Before we climb aboard, a quick word about footwear," he said, pointing at Karen's shoes. "High heels have no place aboard a yacht. They can cause you to slip, lose your balance and they can scratch my polished floors. Please take them off now, both of you."

Frank waited while the two women removed their designer heels.

"Now, if you'll carefully step along this gangway, we'll go see the top deck first, where I'll do a quick orientation and I'll show you where all the life preservers are located, then downstairs into the hull, where we'll locate all the fire extinguishers and life vests, the galley and the sleeping quarters. After you, ma'am," he said, helping Karen and Natasha aboard.

"Could you give me a hand with these bags?" Frank asked Adam, once the two women had gone aboard. Adam nodded and climbed halfway up the gangway.

Frank stood on the causeway and quickly handed up the seven suitcases to Adam one at a time. As Adam stacked the suitcases on the deck, the boat wobbled a bit as each new weight was added, then leveled out. Adam thought he heard Frank muffle a sneeze, but it was actually Frank's phone taking a photo of the inside of his pocket again.

"Bless you," Adam said automatically.

"Pardon?" Frank asked.

"Never mind," Adam said. "We're all set."

"Great," Frank said as he climbed aboard.

"Whenever we're on a ship, we always use nautical terms to avoid confusion," Frank addressed the group, once they were all on deck. "The front area of the boat is called the bow, the back is called the stern, also referred to as fore and aft. No matter which direction you're facing, the left side over here is always referred to as the port side, while the right is called the starboard side. This tall beam is called the mainmast and the lines running the length are referred to as the rigging. No one is allowed up the rigging without my permission, and then not without a proper harness. This horizontal beam is called the boom, and it swivels from side to side depending on the wind. Always be aware of the boom, as it can change directions suddenly and without warning. Please take note of the life preservers. Should any of us go overboard, clinging to a life preserver can help to keep your head above water and prevent you from drowning. We'll do a man-overboard drill later this evening, so you know'll what to do."

"Is this the steering wheel?" Karen asked, pointing to the large, wooden wheel near the stern. The wheel had six evenly spaced brass handles, polished to a shine.

"Yes, that's referred to as the helm, and it controls the rudder, which you can't see, that steers the craft underwater while we're moving," Frank said.

"Can this boat really run entirely on wind power?" Karen asked.

"Absolutely," Frank said, "provided there's wind. We have a 400-horsepower diesel engine that we can use to give us auxiliary power in case the wind isn't blowing in a favorable direction, to aid in docking and for giving us a little extra speed. If you'll follow me below, I can show you where the engine is located, but the engine room is strictly off-limits, for safety reasons."

"Aaah, I like it down here," Natasha said as she stepped downstairs into the main cabin area, where it was 20 degrees cooler. The aroma of linseed oil and fresh paint reminded her of her childhood, when her parents would take Natasha and her brother to St. Petersburg to see the old wooden ships and fishing vessels from a bygone era.

Over the course of the next half hour, Frank showed the three passengers the proper way to wear a life jacket, how to discharge a fire extinguisher and where all the fire extinguishers were located, the proper way of hauling a line end over end, how to use the toilet or head so it wouldn't flood the boat, where the ship's library was located and how the compass, charts and navigational equipment worked.

"This may seem a little overwhelming at first, but once you get used to your new surroundings, I think you will find living on a boat to be a really transformative experience," Frank said. "There's really nothing else like it. You'll work harder than you've ever worked before and sleep better than you ever have before. You'll get to see schools of dolphins and whales, fish that come right up to the surface, late-night bioluminescence, and you'll see stars like you've never seen in New York City. This will be the adventure of a lifetime."

"Um, captain?" Adam asked, raising his hand. "Where's the rest of the crew?"

"The four of us are the crew," Frank said. "Even on a small ship like the *Reciprocity*, it's just not possible to run things by myself 24/7, unless we put in anchor every night. If we have to do that, it'll take us at least a month to get to the Bahamas. I like to keep things pretty informal on my boat, so you don't have to address me as 'captain,' but you all need to respect my position and understand that on this ship, my word is law. We might come from different social circumstances, but on this boat, there is no difference between the haves and the have-nots. If there's an emergency, we're all going to have to trust and rely on each other. Your lives will depend on it. I'll take the first couple of watches until you get comfortable, but once we're at sea, we'll divide things into two or three watches. Everyone will pull their own weight. Are there any more questions before we set sail?"

Adam raised his hand again. Frank chuckled.

"Adam?"

"Thanks, Frank. The reason I asked about the crew was that when we were on board last weekend, there were waiters with cocktails and hors d'oeuvres, light music and fireworks. I guess I sort of expected something similar."

"Perfectly understandable," Frank said with a smile. "You can rest assured that we still have plenty of cocktails and hors d'oeuvres on board, but know that sailing across the Atlantic is entirely different from floating around New York Harbor. I can't promise you fireworks, but I think you'll soon find that this is a far richer, more fulfilling experience, one that you will come to cherish for the rest of your lives. By the time we reach the Bahamas, you might not be expert sailors, but you certainly won't be landlubbers anymore."

Karen was staring at Frank with a wide smile. Frank noticed and returned the smile. Natasha looked from Karen to Frank, then smiled herself. Adam checked his watch.

"If there's no other questions, I suggest we cast off," Frank said, loosening the lines connecting the yacht to the dock. "Let me be the first to wish you all good luck and bon voyage!"

Chapter 52

TOLEDO, Wash. - 251 Layton Rd., 2:00 p.m.

Maud was sitting inside on the couch reading a knitting magazine when the phone rang.

"Good afternoon," she answered.

"Hi, Mom," said a far-away voice.

"Tim!" she cheered. "I'm so glad you called. Wait just a second while I go get your dad."

Maud hurried over to the back door, opened it and stood out on the porch.

"BOB! TELEPHONE! IT'S TIMMY!" she shouted, leaving the door open as she hurried back to the phone. Bob had been working in the garden, but put down his tools and headed to the house when he heard his son was on the phone. It had been weeks since they had heard Tim's voice.

"How are you, honey?" Maud asked. "It's so good to hear your voice."

"I'm OK," Tim said flatly. "It's good to hear you, too. I missed your voice."

"Hello?" Bob said, picking up the phone in the kitchen.

"Hey, Dad."

"Hey, son," Bob said. "Where are you right now?"

"I'm still in Afghanistan, near Kandahar."

"Oh, wow. What time is it there?" he asked.

"It's about 1:30 in the morning," Tim said.

"What's the matter? Can't sleep?"

"No, not really," he said. "I have a lot on my mind. How are things on the farm?"

"They're pretty good," Bob said. "Your mother and I have been working in the garden all week, staying busy and getting things ready for Cheese Days."

"We're going to try selling some homemade yogurt at the farmer's market on Saturday," Maud said. "I figured out how to make it taste just like the Greek stuff you like."

A few seconds of silence passed before Tim spoke up again. "That's nice," he said. "I wish I could be there."

"Any idea when you might be coming home?" Bob asked.

"I wish I knew," Tim said. "All I know is it's not soon enough."

"Well everyone here has been asking about you," Maud said. "We're all so proud of you, Timmy."

"Don't say that, please," Tim said quietly.

"What's wrong, honey?" Maud asked.

Another few seconds of silence passed.

"I had a pretty rough day today," he said.

"Do you want to talk about it?" she asked.

"It's pretty upsetting," Tim said. "I can tell Dad, but I'd rather not upset you with it, Mom, if you can understand."

"Sure, honey," she said. "Do you want me to go?"

"Yeah, I think you'd better. It was good hearing your voice."

"I love you, sweetheart," Maud said.

"I love you, Mom."

"OK, I'll let you two talk. Bye, now. Be safe!"

Tim waited for the sound of the living room phone to hang up.

"Dad, are you still there?"

"I'm here, son. What's wrong?"

"Dad, you were in the service. Did you ever do something in a war zone that you weren't proud of?"

"Well, I was an aircraft mechanic and didn't see too much action," Bob said, aware that Maud could hear his end of the conversation from the other room. "I can think of a few times when I had to do certain things in order to survive that I would never have done, had it not been a life or death matter. Sometimes war is about survival, whether it's your own life or the lives of your friends and squad mates. I had to make a few hard choices, and I'm still here because of them, but I choose not to think about some of the things I had to do. Overall, I'm proud of my service, and I'm grateful that I was able to survive. I think I know what you're going through, if you need to talk about it."

Another few seconds of silence passed.

"I shot a kid today, Dad. I shot him in the head and killed him."

"That's awful, Tim. I'm sure you wouldn't have if you didn't have to."

"It was in self-defense. He shot me first, in the back. I was wearing my flak vest and fell down, playing opossum. He came up to me to finish me off and I got him before he got me. I didn't even know it was a kid until it was all over."

"It sounds like you did what you had to."

"Did I? Four members of my caravan didn't make it back at all. We were ambushed. I don't know what we're doing out here. It doesn't make any sense. I joined the National Guard to protect my country, not to shoot little kids. How can I come back home and teach sixth graders after this? What do I say to the kids on my baseball team?"

Tim's voice cracked at this last thought. He was silent again.

"I think you should talk to a chaplain or grief counselor," Bob said. "That's what they're there for. Somehow you need to find a way to leave what happened behind. Let it go. That's too much baggage for anyone to bring home."

"Thanks, Dad. I hope I can. Hey, I've got to go. It was good talking with you."

"I hope I helped," he said. "Remember what your mom said. We're all very proud of you for your service, for the things you wanted to do and the things you had to do. Take care of yourself and come home safe."

"Thanks, Dad. I love you."

"I love you too, son."

The call ended. Bob hung up the kitchen phone, walked in to the living room, sat down on the couch next to Maud and put his arm around her.

"We raised a good man," he said. "He had a bad day, but he's still a good man."

"I know," she said, sadly. "I know."

Chapter 53

On board the International Space Station, 21:30:00 UTC
TIME TO SOLAR IMPACT: 2 hours, 2 minutes

Chuck Wilson had traversed between the space station's different nodes more often in the past two hours than he did in a typical day, checking instruments, running diagnostic tests and looking up safety shutdown procedures.

He was currently strapped to the Tranquility's COLBERT treadmill exercise machine and was jogging in place. He was scribbling notes and calculations on a notebook with an elegantly designed, silver, zero-gravity ballpoint pen when the pen suddenly burst apart, sending pieces flying out of sight.

"What a complete piece of junk," he yelled, recalling that the U.S. space program had spent millions of dollars researching and developing new technology like weightless ink pens and powdered orange juice that didn't contain oranges, while the Russians had simply continued to use lead pencils and ate dried fruit. The design defect in this space pen was that it was made of metal and contained a tiny metal spring to hold the ink cartridge in place, but the heat from Chuck's hands had caused the metal to expand slightly, just enough to allow the spring to act and cause the over-designed writing utensil to self-destruct.

Chuck checked his jumpsuit's cargo pockets and found a felt-tipped pen. *This will work*, he thought, continuing his calculations. He was distracted again momentarily as Tranquility Node 3 was suddenly bathed in sunlight, illuminating several tiny spheres of liquid that were floating in front of his face. He wiped his brow with the back of his hand and inadvertently sent a trickle of sweat globules sailing through the air.

"Here, you might need this," Mizuho said, handing Chuck a moisture-absorbing, odor-absorbing, synthetic paper towel.

"Thanks," Chuck said, patting his face and hands with the towel and checking the time on his wristwatch as he continued jogging. "Oh, and good morning," he added.

Mizuho smiled and looked out the cupola at the spectacular view of the sunrise below. The cupola was attached to the earth-facing part of the Tranquility and functioned as a control tower and observation deck, offering panoramic views of Earth from six trapezoidal windows that surrounded a large, circular window. The space station was passing over Japan and eastern Asia as the sun's vast, sweeping arc pushed the fringe between night and day ever westward. Most of Asia remained in darkness, while to the east, the immense, glittering blue depths of the Pacific Ocean were already bathed in sunlight.

The land of the rising sun, she thought, reflecting on the literal translation of the word Nippon, before the gravity of her present situation shattered her momentary tranquility. *It seems smaller,* she thought, pulling herself away from the window and blinking her eyes a few times as they adjusted to the space station's interior.

"Are we getting higher?" she asked Chuck, floating alongside him.

Chuck looked up from his notes and seemed to study Mizuho's face for a moment before he understood the question.

"Yes, sorry," he said, looking a little flustered. "Aleks thought we should climb to a higher altitude in case the atmosphere expands. We fired our thrusters a few hours ago to gain a little elevation."

"Where is Aleks?"

"He's in the Zvezda trying to get a little sleep while he can. How was your nap?"

"I had a dream that I was falling towards Earth. I kept falling faster and faster, but I never seemed to get any closer. It was an endless, out-of-control free-fall."

"Weightlessness will do that to you," he said. "Messes with my dreams, too."

"What's the status on the solar storm?" she asked. "Where are we and what can I do to help?"

"We're about two hours from impact," he said. "I've been gathering all the schematics I can on various scientific, military and commercial satellites and I've already started putting some of them into safe mode, but it's really a race against time. We've already lost contact with about 60 or 70 satellites from countries around the globe, and we'll probably lose GPS worldwide in a matter of minutes. I practically begged the FAA to shut down air traffic a couple of hours ago, but those fools wanted to wait for the stock markets to close first. Can you believe that? There might not even be a stock market tomorrow."

"It's not so hard to believe," Mizuho said after a moment. "They don't see what we see from up here, Charles. We are like birds; they are like mice. We can warn the mice that the waters are rising, but there is little else we can do to help. I want to warn them to be prepared. I want to tell them to stay with their families, to comfort them and to tell them not to be afraid. I wish that the people below would stop and listen to the earth and the wind and the sea for just a moment. To really listen and feel their place amid it all. But more than anything, I wish that everyone at home could see the sunrise I just witnessed. I feel blessed to be alive."

Chuck stared at Mizuho in wonderment and admiration. *She's amazing,* he thought as he continued jogging in place. *It must be her Asian upbringing that makes her so selfless and kind. I wish I were more like her.*

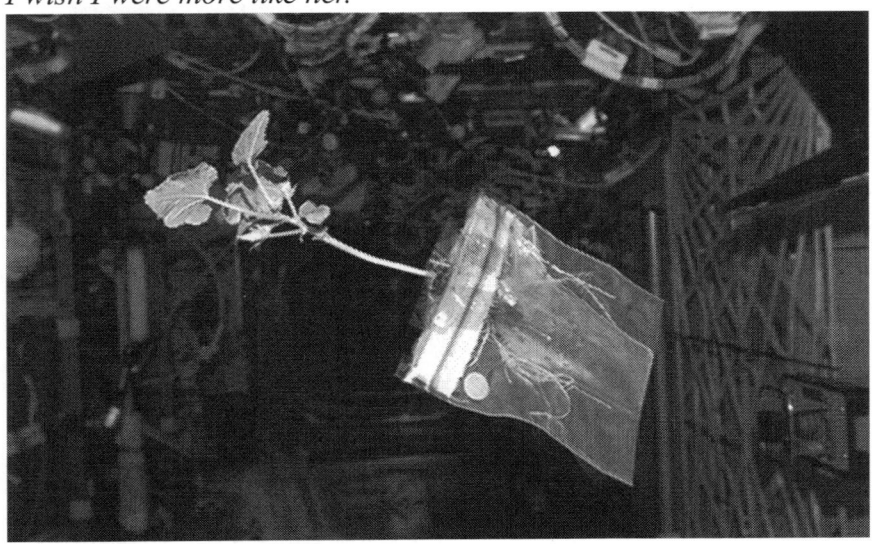

Chapter 54

ZHANGJIAKOU, China, China Solar Headquarters
200 kilometers northwest of Beijing, 6:30 a.m.
TIME TO SOLAR IMPACT: 1 hour, 2 minutes

Ming Chen peered out the venetian blinds covering his office windows at the sun creeping over the top of the Taihang Shan mountains. As president and chief executive officer of China Solar, he was frequently the first person to arrive in the morning. Today was no exception.

The headlines of the Chinese newspaper he was reading screamed of Wall Street's latest crash, with the editors and writers predicting a complete collapse of the West, crushed from within by its own limitless, capitalistic greed. *Possible but unlikely*, Ming thought, flipping through the paper to the financial section.

Ming's corner office became noticeably brighter as the first rays of sun began to hit the array's nearly two million solar panels stretching out over more than 15 square kilometers. The roof of his office building was covered with photovoltaic panels, but the vast majority of the array's power was generated by the less-expensive dish reflectors and parabolic troughs that concentrated the solar power and directed it to a number of receiving towers.

China Solar had gone public yesterday on markets around the world, with extremely mixed results. Trading had begun first in Tokyo, with the Japanese initially skeptical that solar power could ever be profitable in the short-term. When the markets in Shanghai and Hong Kong opened, Chinese optimism at this latest step toward complete energy independence had helped the stock price rocket upwards, causing Tokyo to reverse its course. European markets saw the enthusiasm of the Asian markets and added to the momentum, helping China Solar rise further. America's Wall Street seemed to love the idea and initially stoked the stock's valuation in a frenzy of early trading, but by mid-morning, the Americans had reversed course. U.S. stock markets had jumped off a cliff, pulling down China Solar along with practically everything else.

Why are we trading in America at all? he wondered. *They should be building their own solar power systems, not trading against ours. They'll never see any of this electricity anyway.*

An editorial in the jingoistic, state-run newspaper reiterated the need for China to be completely independent of foreign market forces and remain balanced in its onward, industrialized ascent. China Solar was another important step towards long-term energy independence, the paper wrote.

Ming put the newspaper aside and sat down at his computer to check his messages. Not one e-mail. *That's unusual*, he thought, opening up a spreadsheet with the latest energy figures.

The solar array at Zhangjiakou had been operational for almost a month and had provided a more or less steady output of electricity, particularly during the daytime demand peaks. The mountainous region had been experiencing a drought, but a recent, long stretch of clear, sunny days had been a blessing for the power plant. *Let's hope for good weather,* he thought.

Ming reflected that in a perfect world, China Solar would build its solar plants in the Gobi Desert or even as far west as the Taklimakan Desert near Pakistan, where the skies were reliably bright and clear for most of the year, but that future was still decades away. Electricity was needed most in large cities and near mining operations, few of which were located in the desert. Transporting the electricity from sun-baked deserts to population-rich areas like Beijing required high-voltage, long-distance transmission lines that could span hundreds of kilometers.

It would seem far more logical to build power plants in or next to large cities, but finding 15 square kilometers of available land near Beijing or Shanghai was not possible. The amount of electricity produced by the Zhangjiakou array was undoubtedly the largest of its kind anywhere on Earth, but its output was still significantly less than the electricity produced by a single modern nuclear power plant. Building the expansive array and long-distance power lines had cost billions of dollars and would likely take decades before it paid for itself, but its long-term benefits were substantial.

For one thing, the energy China Solar collected was 100 percent free and renewable. It created no air pollution or toxic waste. With minimal maintenance and cleaning, most of the panels would last for at least 25 years, producing their peak output midday, which also coincided with the peak demand. Back-up natural gas-fired plants were on hand to provide auxiliary electricity on cloudy days, but when conditions were optimal, electricity was essentially free.

The Chinese government seemed to appreciate this investment in the country's long-term future and was already in private negotiations with China Solar to develop a second and larger array farther south in the Sichuan Basin, near the Three Gorges Dam. Having two major, renewable energy producers would be a huge boon for the area, which also contained significant coal and natural gas reserves, abundant rice production and large urban areas like Chongqing.

Advances in solar power technology were also becoming increasingly cost-effective, thanks to the robust partnership between private investors and significant governmental subsidies for research and development.

Ming looked out his office window at the glassy terrain before him, stretching out to the horizon like a sea of mirrors.

There's no way the Americans could build something like this, he thought. *The capitalists would never take such a gamble.*

Chapter 55

NORTH ATLANTIC OCEAN, 10 miles off the coast of New York City, 7 p.m.
TIME TO SOLAR IMPACT: 32 minutes

The new crew of the *Reciprocity* had just finished running a successful drill simulating a passenger gone overboard. Natasha had pointed to an imaginary object in the water and yelled "Man overboard!" while Adam had tossed a life preserver out into the water. Frank and Karen turned on the engine, doused the sails and released the mainsail halyard, bringing the yacht to a halt. Being careful to avoid the swinging boom, they steered the yacht around to pick up the life preserver. When they had come within a few feet, Adam used an eight-foot gaff hook to grab the ring and pull the imaginary person out of the water. The whole ordeal took less than 10 minutes.

"That wasn't so hard," Adam said, returning the gaff hook and life preserver to their proper places on deck.

"You guys did a great job," Frank said from his place at the helm. "Excellent teamwork. It's much easier to do this in the daylight in warm, calm waters, especially when the procedure is fresh in your minds. We'll do this drill again sometime in the next few days, probably when you least expect it. Let's get the sails open and get back on course, and then we can start a little dinner, if you all are hungry."

Adam took the wheel as the other three went below deck to start dinner. Frank showed Karen and Natasha the galley, where the food was kept and how to work the stove and other kitchen equipment.

"I hope you don't mind me asking, but how much cooking experience do either of you have?" Frank asked.

"I can make a mean tossed salad," Natasha joked.

"I'm by no means a gourmet chef, but I think I know the basics," Karen admitted. "I've been cooking for myself for the past 10 years."

"What about Adam?" Frank asked.

"Adam never cooks," Natasha said. "We usually go out to eat or have the kitchen send something up."

"That's fine," he said. "If I'm cooking for myself, I usually don't do more than the standard rice or pasta, a sandwich and every once in a while I'll whip up an omelette or French toast. The reason I ask is that by now you've probably realized we don't have a gourmet chef on board. We all have to divide the work however we can, but traditionally the best cook becomes the ship's cook. We can talk about rotations tomorrow, but I'm getting the sense that Karen may be doing most of the meals while the rest of us take turns on watch, keeping the ship on course. Of course, we can still split up the chores however we want if that's not agreeable. I have a few cookbooks in the library with lots of easy recipes, as well as some more advanced dishes, if anyone wants to get creative or expand their culinary skills. We have a bunch of fancy hors d'oeuvres on board that were delivered this morning, before I knew we were going out on the ocean. Some of those are pretty easy to make; you're basically putting cheese on crackers and stuff like that."

"We can also look up recipes on the Internet," Natasha said, ducking into the master stateroom for a few moments to retrieve a sleek, gold-plated Personal Electronic Tablet.

"You have an iPET?" Karen asked. "Those just came out today. How did you get one?"

"I've had it for about three days," Natasha said. "I know a guy at Apple. He set me up with a deluxe version with all the extras, hence the custom plating. It has millions of books, movies and songs stored on its hard drive, and it has access to everything else."

"You have the world at your fingertips," Frank said.

"Can you look up a recipe for baby lamb lollipops?" Karen asked, looking at the boxes in the small freezer. "I've never had those before."

Natasha typed the word "lamb" into the search function and the tablet offered "Lamb of God" as the top result. There were no recipes for lamb the meat on the device, so she opened a web browser to search online. The iPET searched for a connection, but was unable to locate even the home page.

"We do have Wi-Fi out here, don't we?" Natasha asked Frank.

"I think so," he said. "I don't usually surf the web unless I'm at home, but you might have more luck getting a signal on deck."

Natasha stood up and carried her new iPET upstairs to the main deck.

"Do you think we have any lamb recipes in the library?" Karen asked Frank after Natasha had left.

"Yeah, probably. Let's look," Frank said, leading Karen to the ship's library. "Sailing on a yacht with a few other crew members can afford one plenty of leisure time, and I've found a great way to pass that time is by reading and expanding my mind. I've been working on this library for years and feel like I've got a pretty diverse collection."

Karen looked over the library and noticed that about half of the books were on yacht sailing and maintenance, but there were also books on bird watching, oceanography, geology, gardening and landscape design, cooking, astronomy, physics and quantum mechanics, Classical mythology, art and architecture, American history, woodworking and first aid.

"You're welcome to read anything that interests you, but I confess I don't have much in the way of fiction," Frank said as Karen read the titles on the book spines.

"Have you read all these?" she asked, skimming her hand over the hardback and paperback collection. There were dozens of paper scraps and other bookmarks protruding from the tops of the books, indicating they were well-used.

"Some more than others," Frank admitted. "I like to read whatever interests me at the moment, and I often jump around to different books, depending on my mood."

"What are you reading right now?"

"Right now, I'm reading this fantastic biography of John Adams. There's a great section where Adams sails across the Atlantic in the middle of winter, during the Revolutionary War. It's great if you're into American history."

"I confess I'm more inclined to root for the redcoats, being English myself."

"You're British?" he asked. "That's cool."

"I'm British, Natasha's Russian and Adam's a dual citizen of the U.S. and the Bahamas."

"This is really an international crew," Frank said. "I'm from the Dominican Republic."

"Really? I've always wanted to go there. Is that on our way?"

"It might be," Frank said, walking over to the navigation desk and pointing to a framed poster of a map of the Caribbean and Gulf of Mexico from 1715.

"First we're going to Bermuda, then south towards the Antilles or West Indies, also called the Bahamas. If we can catch a Westerly at the right time, we can bypass Puerto Rico and 'Hispaniola' and cut straight to the Bahamas through the Sargasso Sea and the Bermuda Triangle, but it might be safer and faster to go the long way, depending on the weather. That reminds me, I should probably go check on Adam and see how he's doing. Let's see ... lamb."

Frank pulled out a cookbook and flipped to the meat section, found the lamb area and handed the book to Karen.

"Here you go, have fun," he said, turning to go upstairs.

"Thanks!" Karen shouted as Frank hopped up the stairs, three at a time.

Up on deck, Adam and Natasha were standing on the starboard rail watching the sun slowly set over the bright lights of the New Jersey shore. No one was at the helm. Frank went to the wheel and slowly turned it counter-clockwise, steering the ship southeastward.

"Aren't we going south?" Adam asked, walking back to the helm.

"If we head due south, we'll get caught in the Gulf Stream, which comes up from the southwest this time of year, and that will easily add several days to our trip, if not weeks," Frank said as he made minor adjustments to the rigging. "I was just telling Karen that we'll stop over in Bermuda first, get more provisions and head south from there. We should get to Bermuda in about four to six days, if the wind cooperates. Then it's probably about another week or so to the Bahamas."

"Dammit, Frank. Seven hours ago you said you could get me there in a week and now it's turning into two or three weeks," Adam said, checking his smartphone. It was 7:27 p.m. He had no new messages and was having trouble getting the device's GPS or browser features to work. "You also said we could leave by four o'clock and it took another hour before we left. Now you say we're headed hundreds of miles out of our way because of the wind-stream or something. Can't we use our engines? I don't want to sound like a complainer, but I don't think you've been completely honest with me."

Frank studied Adam for a moment while he considered his response. The sky was beginning to get dark, gradually changing from blue to violet. To the east, the clouds reflected the setting sun in vivid, red colors, silhouetting the far-away skyscrapers.

"I recall telling you on the phone that it could take anywhere between a week to three weeks to get to the Bahamas, and I even suggested you consider other alternatives if this would be a problem," Frank said. "As for the departure time, I told you it would take about an hour to go over the safety procedures before we departed and I suggested you show up at three o'clock. Instead, you showed up after four."

"Screw your safety procedures," Adam said. "I'm not a sailor, I'm a money manager. How am I supposed to do my job if I'm stuck out in the middle of the ocean for a month without a signal?"

"I can see how you must be disappointed and a little disoriented by your new environment," Frank said calmly. "You're probably feeling a little stressed right now. I can assure you that I've made this trip many times before and that I know what I'm doing. Even the most skilled yachtsman is entirely at the mercy of the weather, but fortunately the weather appears to be on our side at the moment. That could all change in an instant. I'm sorry I can't give you a more precise E.T.A., but this is all part of the adventure. We have to sail where the wind is or we won't go where we want. I suggest you try to relax and unwind."

Adam stared at Frank for a moment as though he wanted to say something, but thought better of it and went down into his cabin instead, taking Natasha's iPET with him. Karen was in the galley looking through the cookbook for recipes and preparing dinner, while Natasha remained on deck, watching the sunset and making small talk with Frank.

Adam stowed the tablet device in the master cabin and returned to the galley where Karen was thawing the lamb. He looked through a few of the cabinets before finding the bottle of Johnny Walker Blue Label encased in its decorative blue box.

He located a glass tumbler and poured himself a shot, then sat down on the white leather sofa and took a sip. *This scotch is exquisite,* he thought, studying the liquor's slightly peaty flavor and malty aroma, and admiring the way its legs slowly slid down the sides of the glass as he twirled it around. He drained his drink, got up and grabbed the bottle, bringing it back to the couch. *This is more like it*, he thought, pouring himself another shot.

Back on deck, Frank held the ship on a steady, southeasterly course. He looked down at the ship's compass and noticed it had begun to swing erratically. The compass needle pointed north, then west, then north again. It swung around to point south, then north, then east. It held steady for a few moments, before spinning rapidly counter-clockwise. All the lights on the yacht went out at once, including the safety lights. Frank held the wheel steady and looked westward at the sunset over the New Jersey shore as the urban lights began to flicker off.

After a few moments, every electrical light in sight had gone out.

Part Two: Isolation

Chapter 1

NEW YORK CITY - Times Square, July 9, 2014, just before dark

The glittering lights of New York City's Times Square glowed and flashed and pulsated, bombarding anyone nearby with swarms of trivial information advertising everything imaginable, from designer clothes and soft drinks to financial service companies, cloud servers and banks. In every direction, giant billboards with video screens and holographic images sought to out-do the competition, but the effect of so much data on unaccustomed eyes was often temporary paralysis, or information overload. The advertisements seemed to glow brighter as daylight gradually faded into darkness, filling the starless night sky with an eerie, pink glow.

Tens of thousands of New Yorkers began to pour out of the tall, narrow office buildings onto Broadway, Seventh Avenue and the surrounding streets, most rushing to get to an underground subway terminal and begin the long commute home. The city had closed off several blocks to motorized vehicles in an effort to make the area more pedestrian friendly, but most pedestrians still kept to the sidewalks. Like waves against rocks, commuters flowed around and sometimes crashed into clusters of tourists and foreigners staring up at the thousands of billboards and marquees in their quest to find restaurants, movie theaters and Broadway shows.

Towering above Times Square on one of the many giant video screens, a familiar face began delivering a special broadcast. Hundreds of people stopped what they were doing and turned their attention to the screen to watch the president of the United States as he addressed the nation, while millions more watched from home. The crowd in Times Square quickly grew as passers-by began to stop and watch the flickering satellite broadcast. After a few moments, the president was on nearly every video screen. A hush fell over the square.

"My fellow Americans, today was a day of great tragedy and grief," the president said solemnly as the video transmission struggled to maintain a solid satellite connection. "From a deadly plane crash ... Francisco Bay area ... devastating crash on Wall Street, millions of Americans have been left stranded or jobless or ... My top advisors tell me that our sun is to blame, and the worst may still be to come. ... Fourteen hours ago, an extremely ... solar flare erupted from the surface of the sun, headed straight for ... don't know for certain how damaging this flare will be or how long ... will last, but I assure you your government is doing ... in its power to prepare for this global, natural disaster. Unfortunately, time has run out. Beginning at midnight tonight ... declaring a state of martial law. Wherever you are right now, go home."

The president's lips kept moving, but the transmission's audio had cut out, followed by the video a few moments later as the satellite feed was lost. Hundreds of thousands of people stood in a confused daze for a few seconds, before the entire city was plunged into darkness.

Chaos momentarily ensued as the city's mass transit systems went dark and ground to a halt, traffic lights switched off, cars smashed into each other, and the sounds of breaking glass and crunching metal reverberated off the walls of the towering buildings. Noticeably absent were the sounds of car horns, police sirens and car alarms. After a brief period of graceless entropy, the entire city fell into silence and nearly total darkness.

Almost in unison, seven million New Yorkers pulled out their smartphones to check the time, make an emergency phone call or simply use their device's display as a make-shift flashlight. Across the metropolis, millions of people cursed in hundreds of different languages as their smartphones failed to respond.

A few moments later, cigarette lighters began to flicker on one after the other, the tiny lights creating the hushed ambiance of a candlelight vigil. People turned to their neighbors and asked what had just happened, but most could only state the obvious: The power had gone out.

Several minutes after the blackout, the lights remained off. While some people panicked, most did not. Emergency workers, police officers and random good Samaritans directed strangers to exits and fire escapes, helped the young and old, and generally treated one another with civility and compassion. As there seemed to be no way to communicate with anyone who was not physically present, people acted on their own volition, and natural leaders stepped forward to help others.

"Can anyone tell me how to get to Brooklyn?" an elderly woman asked. In the darkness, no one could tell her age or race, nor guess at her economic situation by the quality of her clothes.

"I'm going to Brooklyn," said a young man's nearby voice. No one could tell in the dark, but the man was Eugene, Natasha's stylist. "You can come with me if you'd like. We need to go to the East River and cross the Brooklyn Bridge."

"Which way is east?"

"This way is east," said another man with a Middle Eastern accent. Earlier in the day, this man had taken Adam to Wall Street in a yellow cab. "Follow the sound of my voice. If we can find a way to read the street signs, we can find our way just about anywhere."

A few minutes later, the streets and bridges were filled from sidewalk to sidewalk with pedestrians, the massive crowd slowly moving together in the near darkness as millions of people tried to figure out how to get home.

Chapter 2

TOLEDO, Wash. - 251 Layton Rd., around suppertime Wednesday

    Bob Layton looked out across his fields at the snow-capped peaks of Mount Rainier and Mount St. Helens jutting upwards thousands of feet above the surrounding forests and foothills. The evening sun was creating a spectacular display as it dropped lower on the horizon. Bob watched as the clouds and the snow-capped mountains both reflected the oranges and reds of the sun, creating a striking contrast against the background of a darkening, violet sky. He thought he could almost see thin, green curtains of light beginning to form and quiver in the night sky. *We don't usually see the northern lights this far south,* he thought, *but maybe tonight.*

    Bob's stomach growled, indicating it was nearly time for supper. He left his barn and greenhouse and walked across the field to his two-story rectangular block farmhouse, built about 100 years ago in the style of the early homesteads.

    He and his wife Maud had retired a few years back and had hoped to do some traveling, but they hadn't actually left Washington state in years. The farm consumed all of their time, from sunrise to sunset, and there always seemed to be more work to do. They couldn't leave their animals and pets and plants unattended, and with their son serving overseas and their daughter living in Seattle with her family, they had no choice but to stay and work.

    "Hey honey, my radio's not working," Bob said as he entered the farmhouse, sat down and slipped off his boots in the dark. "N.P.R. was saying something about martial law when the radio just cut out. Is the power out in here, too?"

    "Been out since half past four," Maud said, pointing at the clock on the wall. The time was frozen in place at 4:32 p.m.

    "That clock's battery-powered," Bob said. "It should still be working. Maybe the batteries are dead."

    "You can try putting new batteries in, hon, but nothing seems to be working. The lights and appliances don't work, the computer won't start and the flashlights don't come on, even with fresh batteries. Heck, even the phones don't have a dial tone. Everything just quit all at once."

Bob picked up the phone receiver and listened for a dial tone. Nothing. He replaced the phone back in its cradle.

"You're right," he said. "That's pretty strange. Maybe the world finally exploded. Do we have any candles?"

"Oh, we've got boxes of candles," she said. "The venison in the big freezer probably won't last more than a few days without power, but we can eat that first. If you get me some firewood, I can cook up something on our wood stove."

"It might be too hot to fire up the stove tonight, but I bet the barbecue still works," Bob said. "It runs on propane, and I think the tank is full. Maybe we can have a campfire outside and look at the stars a little later on if you'd like. We may even be able to see the northern lights tonight, if we're lucky."

"That sounds romantic," Maud said.

"I'll go round up some firewood before it gets dark, just in case, but first I have to milk Betsy again. Do you think you could you fetch the candles?"

He sat back down by the door and pulled his boots on again.

"Sure thing, handsome," Maud said, giving him a smooch on the lips.

Chapter 3

ZHANGJIAKOU, China, shortly after dawn on Thursday
China Solar Headquarters

Ming Chen's desktop computer switched off just as he was about to send an e-mail. His office lights also went out. *Oh, this is just great,* he thought, checking the time on his digital watch. *I love it when the power goes out at the power plant. Real nice.* The CEO of China Solar rotated his wrist a few times in an attempt to read his watch's display, but the display was blank. *This really isn't my day. I guess that's what I get for buying cheap Japanese technology.*

He stood up at his desk and picked up the phone. There was no dial tone. He slammed the phone down again and walked to the window, yanking the cord on the venetian blinds and filling his office with sunlight. *At least the sun still seems to be working,* he thought, noting that the skies were crystal clear and the 15 square kilometers of solar reflectors were glimmering brightly, stretching far off into the horizon. He checked his smartphone, only to find it was turned off. He pressed the power button a few times to no effect. *Something's not right.*

Ming opened his glass door and stepped out into the office floor, a darkened sea of empty cubicles. There was no one in sight.

"Does anyone know what time it is?" he called out in Mandarin. There was no response. "We need to get the power back on immediately. Where is everybody? It's Thursday, not Saturday, people."

He winded his way through the building's labyrinth of shoulder-high, carpet-covered walls toward the employee break room, where he knew there was a large, analog clock on the wall. The clock read 7:32. *Most people don't show up until around 8 a.m.,* he thought. *There's not much I can do until then, anyway.* He returned to his office, sat down at his desk and resumed reading his newspaper with the natural light coming in through the window.

Ming tried to concentrate on the paper's financial section, but couldn't stop thinking about the power outage. He tossed his newspaper to the side and tried the phone again. *Still no dial tone. I'd better get to the bottom of this.* He grabbed a pair of sunglasses, a clipboard and a white plastic hardhat and set out to find some answers. He walked through the entire building, checking every room and making notes on his clipboard. After he had failed to find anyone inside, Ming stepped outside.

The sun seems unusually bright today, he thought, putting on his sunglasses. He looked up at the dozens of receiving towers protruding from the mirrored complex and noted that they were glowing white hot. He looked around but couldn't see signs of any workers or technicians. As he walked closer to one of the receivers, he began to feel noticeably warmer. *The mirrors appear to be working properly, concentrating the sunlight on the top of the receivers, but what happens if the heat isn't properly dispersed?* he wondered. He approached a locked metal gate surrounding the receiving tower and halted. The fence and tower were covered with signs warning of high voltage and extreme heat, and the door at the base of the tower was partly ajar.

"Is anyone here?" Ming shouted in Mandarin. "This is CEO Ming Chen. We are having a problem and we may need to shut off the solar receivers. I need someone to open this gate immediately. Can anyone hear me?"

Hearing no response, Ming grabbed the padlock but instantly jerked his hand back again. *Hot!* he thought a moment later, checking his fingers for signs of burns. His fingers were red. Ming held the clipboard over his eyes as a make-shift visor and scanned the area for signs of life. He was already beginning to sweat profusely when he noticed two twisted, charred figures lying on the ground next to the tower's open door. Ming turned and ran back to the main building.

As he opened the door to the facility and stepped inside, Ming was momentarily disoriented as he was plunged back into darkness. He pulled off his sunglasses and headed straight for the employee break room. *I need something cold*, he thought, putting a few coins into the Coca-Cola machine. The coins rattled inside, but failed to produce the promised beverage. *Oh yeah, the power's out.*

Ming grabbed an ice pack from the break room freezer and iced his burned fingers. The coldness stung as the ice pack contracted the capillaries in his blood vessels and began to reduce the swelling. He sat down in a chair to collect his thoughts and noticed the clock on the wall still read 7:32.

OK, what do I need to do? he asked himself. *I need to find a way to shut down those receivers before the molten salt burns through the towers, but if I get any closer to the heat source, I could be cooked alive. I need a heat suit.*

Ming put the icepack back in the freezer and quickly walked through the dark, empty building to the electrical room. It was locked. *I need some keys*, he thought, turning around and hurrying back to his office. Ming found a full set of keys to the entire facility in one of his filing cabinets, as well as a flashlight. *This is why I get paid the big bucks*, he thought, grabbing the keys and flashlight.

As he unlocked the electrical room, Ming tried the flashlight to no effect. In the darkness, he could tell that all the switches were still turned on, so he immediately switched everything off. Nothing happened. He noticed there was a large plastic binder on one of the shelves that said "EMERGENCY SHUTDOWN" in English and Chinese. Ming grabbed the binder and took it into the light.

"'To shut down a solar receiver in the event of an emergency, go to the electrical room, find the desired receiver and turn the switch to off,'" Ming read aloud. "I did that already. 'If the switch does not respond, you may need to manually turn off the solar receiver inside the receiving tower. Important: If the tower is experiencing an overload, the environment in and around the tower may reach temperatures exceeding 500 degrees Celsius. A protective heat suit is necessary in these extreme conditions.' Great. Where can I find a heat suit?" Ming asked himself, flipping through the pages.

"Here it is," he said. "'Emergency protective heat suits can be found in the office of the foreman, located in the maintenance facility.'"

Ming followed the map in the binder to the maintenance facility, located two suits and began to put on one of them. The heat suit bore a resemblance to modern firefighting gear and the spacesuits work by astronauts during spacewalks. It was extremely heavy, weighing more than 200 pounds, was uncomfortably hot inside and was cumbersome to use. *This is crazy*, he thought. *It will take me 20 minutes just to get outside.*

Ming removed the suit and loaded the top, pants and helmet onto a metal dolly that had a large handle, four wheels and a flat base, and rolled the suit to an exterior door. After getting it outside, he pushed the dolly all the way to the locked gate outside the receiving tower. He put on the suit, grabbed his clipboard and key ring and unlocked the gate with his heat-resistant gloves.

Carefully stepping inside the perimeter, Ming slowly approached the open door at the base of the tower. On the ground were the charred and smoldering remains of two unlucky employees, their blackened bodies unrecognizable, cooked like ants under a magnifying glass. As he stepped through the doorway and inside the small facility, he noticed a loud rumbling noise and began to sweat profusely inside his special suit. He found an electrical panel, located a large circuit breaker and switched it to off. There was no response.

Ming looked around the small room and quickly located the emergency shutdown valve. The non-electric valve was patented by a Japanese company and was powered by a compressed air cartridge. Ming released the emergency lever and heard the hissing sound of the compressed air as it manually closed a large valve. As he turned around, he noticed one of the large pipes was dripping what appeared to be molten lava. *That can't be good*, he thought. Suddenly his clipboard spontaneously burst into flames. He dropped it at once and exited through the door.

Ming quickly retreated to the fence surrounding the perimeter. *Only 29 more to go*, he thought, inspecting his suit for damages. The outer layer of the suit was charred and was beginning to peel off. The inside of his helmet was steaming up from the intense heat.

"This is absurd," he said to himself as he removed his helmet. "I don't think this suit can handle another heat blast like that."

As he looked back at the tower, he noticed the top of the structure was beginning to smoke. Ming put his helmet back on and walked back to the main building. Once inside, he removed the suit, left everything by the door and went back to the break room. He opened the refrigerator and found a few bottles of ice-cold water. He cracked the seal on one of the half-liter bottles and immediately drank its contents. *Thank God for water.*

He sat back down in one of the chairs and tried to collect his thoughts again. He looked up at the clock, which still said 7:32.

OK, Ming, what are you doing? he asked himself. *I was able to turn off one of the receivers, but it nearly destroyed my protective heat suit. There is an extra heat suit in the foreman's office, but I don't think it will last another 29 heat bursts like that first one.*

He thought back to the horrifying image of the blackened bodies still lying outside the receiving tower and gave an involuntary shudder. *I could be cooked alive,* he thought. *If I can't shut down all the receivers manually, they could catch fire or explode. That would be the end of China Solar.*

Just as he was thinking about it, a deafening explosion echoed through the building, followed a few moments later by a loud, sustained rumbling sound. The building's metal roof began to tremble.

Ming's face turned white as he sat frozen in fear. Another loud explosion boomed from outside. *It's over. Everything I've worked on for years has been destroyed. I'm ruined.*

Ming slowly stood up and staggered back to the outer door. He reached out and touched the metal door handle to check to see if it was hot. It wasn't. Ming pulled open the outer door and stared in disbelief at the landscape before him.

It was pouring rain. A massive thunder and lightening storm had finally broken the drought, and the darkened skies were dumping enormous amounts of precipitation on the area, turning the dry, cracked soil into mud and rendering the solar reflectors ineffective. The receiving towers that had been glowing white hot were now shooting clouds of steam into the air.

Ming fell to his knees in the doorway and began to weep. *I'm saved!*

Chapter 4

NORTH ATLANTIC OCEAN, about 20 miles off the coast of New York City, Wednesday night

Frank Rosario was a little worried about keeping the *Reciprocity* on its southeasterly course after the ship's power and GPS navigational system had suddenly gone out, and the ship's compass had unexpectedly begun to spin in circles. He had lost sight of land when the long, glowing band of lights along the eastern seaboard had flickered out, almost in unison. He looked up in the night sky for stars, but saw only an inky, black blanket above. *Pollution,* he thought.

"Do you have any flashlights on board?" Natasha asked in the darkness.

"Yes, I have some below, but it might be hard to describe where they are," he said. "Could you please take the wheel and try to keep it steady?"

With Natasha at the helm, Frank went below deck, briefly bumping into Karen on the stairway. She momentarily lost control of the basket of fresh fruit she was carrying, she but quickly pressed the basket to her chest, recovering the contents with poise.

"Sorry," he said. "Nice catch. I'm looking for a flashlight. Where's Adam?"

"Over here," called Adam from the sofa. "Don't worry about me; I don't need the light," he said, taking another loud slurp of scotch.

Frank found a flashlight but it wouldn't turn on. He rummaged around the galley's compartments for spare batteries and eventually found some, but those didn't work either. He found a box of matches and took them into his darkened cabin, where he located a set of candles.

As he lit the candle, his cabin was filled with a dim, flickering light. He took the candle back into the main compartment and placed it into a waterproof lantern, illuminating the galley. He had just lit a second candle in another waterproof lantern when a cry came from on deck.

"HELP! FIRE! FRANK, COME UP HERE NOW! THE SHIP'S ON FIRE!"

Frank grabbed one of the lanterns and ran upstairs. He was astonished by what he saw.

The crow's-nest at the top of the mainmast was engulfed in soaring blue flames, hissing and crackling like a wood fire. He stood in awe for a few moments, trying to comprehend what he was witnessing.

"What should we do, Frank?" Natasha pleaded. "How do we put it out?"

"We're not on fire," Frank said after a moment. "Or not in the customary sense. See how the flames are blue instead of yellow? They're not burning or damaging anything."

"I don't understand," Natasha said. "What is it?"

"It's called St. Elmo's fire," he said. "Saint Erasmus or St. Elmo is the patron saint of sailors, and this display is considered auspicious. I've never seen it before, myself."

"I still don't understand," Natasha said.

"It's a natural weather phenomenon, caused by ionized air molecules," he said. "It sometimes occurs during thunderstorms when the atmosphere is electrically charged."

"It's beautiful," Karen said, staring in wonder at the dazzling display.

Frank continued to gaze up at the glowing blue flames when he eventually noticed the clouds were rolling back, revealing the clear night sky, filled with sparkling stars. Just as the thought occurred to him to use the constellations to navigate the ship, he heard the sound of breaking glass below. *Now what?* he thought, racing back below deck.

Adam was sitting in the middle of the floor, slowly swaying from side to side, holding a bottle of scotch in one hand. The bottle was mostly empty and there was broken glass all over the floor.

"Could you fetch me another glass?" Adam slurred loudly. "Mine's busted."

"Did you drink all this scotch?" Frank asked, taking the blue-labeled bottle away from Adam, who was grinning. "This is like $250 a bottle. What's wrong with you?"

"The only thing's wrong is I can't get my feet with the ground jumping around all the time. Can you get me another gas? Glass? That's some damn fine scotch, I say. Damn fine."

"Do you know what we do with a drunken sailor?" Frank asked.

"Give him a blue ribbon?"

"You get to spend the night in your own private boat," Frank said cheerfully. "Come on, let's get you on your feet and get you up on deck."

"Oooh, that's a pretty light," Adam said, pointing at the crow's-nest after Frank had helped him up the stairs. "Fireworks!"

"Ladies, could you give me a hand?" Frank asked. "Adam's had a bit too much to drink and has ceased to be useful. In fact, he's become problematic. We're going to put him in the dory for the night to sleep it off."

Karen and Natasha each grabbed one of Adam's legs while Frank held him from under the arms. The three carried Adam to the stern and lowered him into the dory.

"OK, I'm sorry," Adam said without struggling. "Be gentle, my little angels."

Once they had set him into the boat, they removed the oars and tied a long line to its bow. Natasha removed Adam's suit jacket and replaced it with an orange life vest. On Frank's suggestion, they also removed Adam's shoes and placed two bottles of water inside the small craft. Adam was already sound asleep when they lowered the small, flat-bottomed rowboat into the water.

"Are you sure he's going to be OK?" Natasha asked Frank after they had secured the small craft about 20 meters behind the yacht.

"He just needs to sleep it off," Frank said. "I'm sorry we had to put him in the dory, but as I said earlier, there are a lot of small things that can happen on a boat that can quickly turn into big problems. A drunk can be a dangerous addition to any crew and can invariably sink the ship, set it on fire or both. We've just lost power and happen to be floating blindly in the dark, which is not a particularly good time for another disaster. That reminds me, there's broken glass all over the floor downstairs."

Natasha looked down at her bare feet.

"He's not usually like this," she said. "He's had a pretty stressful day today. We all have."

Karen came over to listen to the conversation.

"I was just telling Natasha that there are too many things that can go wrong on a boat, and having a selfish drunk on board is no help to anyone. Oh, and Adam broke a glass on the floor below."

"I can clean up the glass," Natasha offered.

"Thank you, I appreciate that," Frank said. "Look, I'm sorry I called Adam a selfish drunk just now. We all deal with stress in different ways. I guess I'm a little stressed out myself. He should be fine in the morning after he sobers up."

"That's OK," Natasha said, going below deck. "He *was* being a selfish drunk."

"I found some fresh fruit downstairs," Karen said after Natasha had left. "Sorry it's not very fancy, but it should do the trick. Is there anything you need before I go to bed?"

Frank thought for a moment. *Coffee?*

"You know, I think I'm good," he said. "I'm going to try to figure out our location and keep us sailing to Bermuda, which means I'll probably be up all night."

"Can I get you some coffee?"

"Coffee would be good," he said. "Hot coffee would be great."

"How do I boil water without power?" Karen asked. "Is the stove gas or electric?"

"It's propane, but I think the starter's electric," he said. "You could use a match to light it, but if you can't get it to work, you might try the solar water heater. That usually stays warm for a while."

"I'll see what I can do," Karen said with a smile as she went below deck.

***

Several hours later, Frank locked the helm in place and went down into the quiet galley. The candle he had put in the lantern had gone out, but the melted wax was still hot. As he lit another candle, he noticed that the emergency candle box advertised a no-drip, three-hour burn time. *So it's been about three hours*, he thought, *which would put it at about 10:30 or 11 p.m.*

Frank scooped two servings of instant coffee crystals into a tin cup and poured in some warm water, stirring the mixture in the dim candlelight. He gave an involuntary yawn and took a sip of coffee as he scanned around the room. *Bitter but strong*, he thought. *I'm not sure what she did, but that coffee Karen made was way better.*

He looked over at the curtain pulled across the doorway to Karen's cabin, located next to his quarters in the stern. *She smells terrific*, he thought as he quietly stepped inside his own cabin, lifted up the bed and retrieved a peculiar metal instrument from a wooden box. He set the glowing lantern next to a porthole window in the galley and went back on deck into the dark night.

As his eyes slowly readjusted to the dark, his other senses momentarily took over. He listened to the rhythmic creaking of the boat and the sails gently fluttering in the breeze. He could smell the warm, salty air and felt it blowing on the left side of his face. *That way's probably east*, he thought. He took another sip of coffee and tasted sea salt on his lips.

Once his pupils dilated, stars began to materialize out of the darkness. Like his ancestors thousands of years before him, Frank's mind began connecting the dots, and shapes quickly began to emerge from the chaos. *There's Ursa Major, Ursa Minor, and Polaris,* he thought. *That way's north. Over there is Orion, Taurus and Gemini. I can also see Perseus, Draco and Cassiopeia. What a beautiful night.*

Frank held up the sextant, an old-fashioned navigational instrument with a graduated arc that was used to measure the angular distance between objects. He had used the sextant several times before out of curiosity, but had always relied on the ship's global positioning system for navigation. Now that the GPS was out of service and the ship's compass had yet to pick a pole, Frank had no choice but to figure out the device. He attempted to point the sextant's sighting mechanism at Polaris, the North Star, but was having trouble keeping the instrument steady. *What I really need is a larger point of reference. I can't even see the horizon.*

From the corner of his eye, Frank detected a growing brightness. He pointed the sextant at the nearly full moon almost directly above and made a few quick calculations, scribbling notes on a pad of paper in the growing twilight. *And now I know where we are. We're headed south.* The *Reciprocity's* sails glowed white as its captain basked in the moonlight, observing the altered world around him. As he squinted his eyes, he noticed a curious shape ahead on the horizon.

A featureless, dark mass swallowed up the moonlight. Lifting a pair of binoculars to his eyes, he suddenly recognized the ghostly shape. It was a cruise ship, and it was apparently quite close. All the lights on the vessel were off, but in the moonlight he could still make out the name *MS Allure of the Seas* on the ship's stern, meaning it was pointed due south. Frank had heard of the *Allure*, widely known to be the largest cruise ship in the world, tied with its sister the *MS Oasis of the Seas*. Both were built by Royal Caribbean International.

Frank turned the wheel counterclockwise to the port, steering the yacht due east. The wind momentarily fell from the sails as the ship passed through the wind, but filled again from the other side when he steered northeast. *I'll have to tack for a while to get around her. There's no way I'm letting us get caught in its leeward shadow. We'd be dead in the water, just like her.*

He looked back at the cruise ship as it continued to grow larger and closer. Frank quietly steered the *Reciprocity* to the windward side of the cruise ship, passing within 50 meters of the gigantic luxury cruise liner without a sound. As he looked up at the massive, dark ship, it continued to grow impossibly larger. The *Allure* measured 361 meters long, 66 meters wide and 16 passenger decks high, nearly blocking out the night sky. While there were a few flickering lights on board, most of the ship's nearly 6,000 passengers and 2,400 crew members appeared to be completely stranded in the darkness.

They're probably all sleeping, Frank thought as he trimmed the sheets. *There's not much I can do for them now, but as soon as the radio comes back online, I can alert the Coast Guard to their position. The best thing I can do right now is to steer clear and stay out of the way.*

Adam awoke from his drunken slumber and found himself beneath a bright, full moon, surrounded by thousands of stars amid shimmering green curtains of light. He sat up and saw a sparkling, dark pool that stretched all around him. His head was still swimming in alcohol, but he was able to deduce that he was sitting in a small boat all by himself, and the boat was being towed behind a sailing yacht.

The yacht had recently changed course and was now sailing to the left of his bow, while his boat was continuing straight ahead. As he looked around, he noticed the night sky was getting considerably darker on his starboard side and seemed to be moving, while the sky on his port side appeared to be standing still. He looked straight up at an enormous black shape passing by, hundreds of feet tall and more than a thousand feet from bow to stern. *What is it?* he wondered. *A storm? A ship of death? A sign from God? Am I dead?*

Adam leaned closer to the starboard side of the small craft to get a better look just as the boat corrected its course, yawing to follow the yacht. The sudden movement through the ship's wake made Adam fall against the boat's port-side rail, causing the small craft to tip to that side. Reflexively he leaned forward, causing the boat to rock in the opposite direction. The rocking and wobbling sensation made him instantly seasick and he proceed to throw up his liquid dinner over the side of the craft. Gradually, the rocking subsided and Adam fell back into a deep sleep.

Once he had cleared the cruise ship, Frank returned the *Reciprocity* to its southeasterly course, headed for Bermuda. He checked to make sure the dory was still following behind him and saw Adam passed out in the longboat. *It's probably better he didn't see it,* Frank thought.

The dark shape of the cruise ship gradually shrank from sight as the *Reciprocity* continued on its course. A few minutes later, the *Allure* had disappeared altogether.

Chapter 5

EARTH'S ATMOSPHERE - On board the ISS

American astronaut Chuck Wilson, Japanese astronaut Mizuho Sakaguchi and Russian cosmonaut Aleksandr Manakova sat quietly in the Zvezda Node of the International Space Station, wearing their bulky space suits. The space station was currently passing directly above Canada and the snowcapped Rocky Mountains, some 400 kilometers or about 250 miles below. The 3,000-mile long mountain range split the continent in half. The western side remained bathed in a fading sunlight, while the larger eastern half, usually a glowing web of electric light, descended into a ghostly darkness.

Wilson was wearing NASA's Extravehicular Mobility Unit, a 280-pound personal space ship that contained 11 modular components, including seven advanced life support systems. His mostly white suit had multiple layers that protected him against the vacuum of space, extreme temperature differences and the possibility of damage from micrometeoriod debris, but he was already well-protected from these dangers inside the Zvezda Node.

The main reason he was wearing the enormous space suit that took 15 minutes to put on and 15 minutes to remove was to afford him additional protection against the sun's intense ultraviolet radiation. He had been wearing the EMU for about an hour and a half, but had not been able to communicate with his shipmates by radio ever since the coronal mass ejection had disabled all of the space station's electrical systems. The three-member crew had been reduced to communicating by hand signals and notes written on notepads.

Aleksandr and Mizuho were each wearing a Zvezda Orlan-MK space suit, the tan-colored Russian equivalent to the EMU. As the space station moved into the sun's shadow, the compartment quickly fell into darkness. Aleks motioned to Mizuho to unzip his suit's backpack, which she did. Less than five minutes later, he had slipped out backwards from the suit's simple hatchback entry and was now floating in the pod, wearing just his one-piece flight suit and socks.

He checked the time on his black and silver, B-42 Fortis Cosmonaut Chronograph wristwatch, which was still functioning perfectly. It was about 5 a.m. in Moscow. He turned to look at Chuck and Mizuho.

"We should be safe in the sun's shadow for about 40 minutes," Aleks shouted, pointing to his wristwatch and holding up four fingers.

Chuck couldn't make out what Aleks was saying. He slid open the ball-bearing fastener around his neck and removed his bulky helmet.

"What are you doing?" Chuck asked. He noticed there was still plenty of oxygen inside the compartment.

"This ship will not fix itself," Aleks said. "I cannot sit here and do nothing."

"You could be fried by solar radiation," Chuck warned. "It's too risky. We should wait until the storm passes."

Mizuho had removed her helmet in order to hear the conversation.

"If I am doomed, it has already happened," Aleks said. "We have about 40 minutes until we are in the path of the sun again. I will come back before it is light."

Aleks rummaged around through one of the built-in storage bins in the Zvezda Node and located a chemical glow stick. He folded it in half with a loud snap, then straightened it again. The stick glowed bright green as the diphenyl oxalate chemicals in the inner tube mixed and reacted with the hydrogen peroxide in the outer tube. The chemical reaction created a green, fluorescent light that did not rely on electricity or magnetic energy. Aleks rummaged through the storage bins a little more and found a clipboard with a pencil and paper.

"Dasvidania," he said as he turned toward the airlock.

Chuck and Mizuho watched in silence as Aleks made a corkscrew spin and floated away through the darkened space station, taking his halo of green light with him.

Aleks passed through the narrow, opened airlock portal into the connecting Zarya node and checked a few of the instrument panels. Everything was dead and unresponsive. He continued his quick and methodical diagnostic tests as he floated into the Unity node, then the Destiny Laboratory, the Columbus Laboratory and finally the Japanese Kibo experimental module, all with the same results.

Nearly every instrument and operation on board the International Space Station relied on electricity, and none of it was working. By the time Aleks got to the Kibo, he could already see the condensation from his breath in the air. The station's climate control systems and heaters were all electric, and the temperature was beginning to drop. Aleks also noticed that it was becoming more difficult to breathe as the oxygen supply quickly diminished. He made a few notes on the clipboard and headed back to the Unity node.

When he reached the Unity, Aleks checked his wristwatch and saw that he still had about 20 minutes before the space station was in the sunlight again. He turned the corner and floated through a different, narrow airlock into Node 3, also called Tranquility. The instruments and even the exercise treadmill were all unresponsive. He looked over at the cupola viewing node, but all the windows were shuttered.

Aleks carefully lifted one of the window's manual control levers and began to spin it clockwise, gradually raising the protective shade and revealing the view below. *My God, it's beautiful,* he thought. The curved surface of the Earth was coated in glowing bands of green and red auroras that twisted like ribbons or curtains of fluorescent, ionized energy. The space station was passing over an eerily darkened Europe.

Ancient Greeks and Romans believed Aurora was the goddess of dawn, he thought. *In the Middle Ages, Europeans thought they were a sign from God. They weren't wrong, just uninformed. Today we know they are caused by charged oxygen and nitrogen atoms, but that does not make them any less magical to behold. I wonder how they appear from below.*

Aleks gazed out the window in wonderment for a few minutes and soon recognized the upside-down shape of the Arabian peninsula approaching below. The aurora shifted in color from green and red to mostly red as the latitude and atmosphere changed. In the darkness below the red aurora, he could see several fires glowing in the middle of the desert. He checked his wristwatch and saw he had less than 10 minutes.

As Aleks was closing the window covering, he noticed a dark shape rapidly approaching. He watched as the space station narrowly missed colliding with a dead Chinese communications satellite, passing less than 10 meters below. *That would have hit us had our solar panels not been retracted,* he thought as he sealed the window and floated back into the Unity node, then into the Zarya and finally into the Zvezda module. He closed and sealed the airlock behind him and climbed back into his space suit through its hatchback entry.

Mizuho had just finished sealing him into his suit as the space station passed into the sunlight. With all the doors and windows sealed, the Zvezda remained in darkness, lit only by the glow from Aleks' green chemical light. He quickly wrote a note on the clipboard in English, using large, capital letters, and showed it to Chuck and Mizuho.

"ELECTRICAL COMPONENTS NOT WORKING," he wrote, holding the light over the top. "SHIP IS COLD, DARK AND RUNNING OUT OF AIR. NOT SAFE TO LEAVE ZVEZDA WITHOUT SUITS. AURORA OUTSIDE IS MAGNIFICENT."

Mizuho motioned that she wanted to see the clipboard and pencil. Aleks handed them to her and she began to write on a new page. After a few moments, she turned the clipboard over.

"WISH I COULD SEE IT," she wrote. "YOU ARE VERY BRAVE TO GO CHECK, BUT WE SHOULD STAY HERE UNTIL POWER IS RESTORED."

Chuck motioned for the clipboard, which Mizuho handed to him. He wrote a quick note and turned the clipboard around again. "AGREED," it said.

Aleks decided not to mention their near-collision with the satellite to Chuck or Mizuho and instead floated over to one of the storage bins that also served as a library. If they had to perform an emergency escape, it was possible they could re-enter the atmosphere in the Zvezda's spare Soyuz. But without electricity or any way to communicate with Earth, they would likely land in the middle of an ocean somewhere without hope of a rescue. *It is safer to stay inside.*

He looked at several Russian paperback classics by Fyodor Dostoyevsky and Nikolai Gogol before eventually selecting the novel, "A Hero of Our Time," written in the 19th century by Mikhail Lermontov. He carefully opened the book with his synthetic rubber spacesuit gloves and read the handwritten inscription on the cover page.

"Dearest Brother," the note began in Russian, "I hope you enjoy this classic as much as I have. You will always be my hero. Call me anytime. Love, Natasha."

Aleks thought about his sister's recent wedding as he carefully turned the page and attempted to read his book by the green glow of the chemical light. The story began slowly, with the narrator describing how he came to know of the hero. Aleks found it difficult to concentrate.

He was thinking about how he had somehow managed to cause quite a stir at Natasha and Adam's lavish wedding in the Bahamas, despite the fact that he was orbiting the earth on board the International Space Station at the time. Natasha had not answered her phone when he had called to congratulate her, so he pinpointed her position to within a few meters and called every smartphone in the vicinity, which turned out to be a few hundred wedding guests.

His timing was awkward too, as they were behind schedule and the priest had just asked the wedding party if anyone opposed the union. All of the guests' smartphones rang at once. Aleks realized his mistake when a few hundred people answered his call, and he used his quick wit to save the situation.

"I just wanted to wish this happy couple all the best," he had said in his best English. "I love you, little sister. And Adam, I am watching you."

Aleks reached the end of the first chapter, with the characters ready to begin telling the story. He enjoyed the steady, studied pace of the narrative and the detailed descriptions of driving an ox cart in a snowstorm before there was electricity or combustion engines. His sense of self and his own perilous situation seemed to dissolve as he devoted his full attention to the story. He carefully turned another page and continued reading.

Chapter 6

CAMP LEATHERNECK - Helmand Province, Afghanistan
Thursday, July 10, at dawn

The sound of reveille cut through the cool, desert air as the morning's first light flooded the large white tent. U.S. Marine Staff Sergeant Timothy Layton opened his eyes and sat up in his cot, but couldn't recall if he had been sleeping or if he had just lied awake in bed all night. He still felt exhausted.

The day before, Layton and his squad had been ambushed on patrol and were caught in an intense firefight that had resulted in four Marine casualties and at least as many enemy deaths. His superior officer had been among those killed and his replacement had said he would see about getting the men a few days off to recover their energy and spirits, but that was always subject to change in a war zone.

Layton checked his green Timex analog wristwatch. Four o'clock.

That's not right, he thought. *Dawn is at about 5 a.m.* He held the watch to his ear for a moment, but couldn't hear it ticking. His ears were still ringing a bit from yesterday's explosion, and now he couldn't feel the fingers on his right hand.

"Hey corporal, what time you got?" he asked one of his squad mates sitting nearby as he made a tight fist with his right hand. *Still no feeling.*

"I got 4 a.m., Sarge," Corporal Linfield said, checking his watch.

"That's what I have," Layton said. "Did the sun rise early today and nobody told me?"

"Nobody tells me nothing, Sarge," Linfield said.

Layton walked to the latrine with his razor and shaving kit. He pulled off his sweat-stained T-shirt and filled a small sink with water, splashing a little on his face and neck. He rubbed shaving cream on his 32-year-old caucasian face and made a few quick passes with a disposable razor blade. He emptied the sink, splashed a little water on his face and a little more around the sink to wash down his trimmings. He toweled himself off with his shirt and ran his hand over his short, crew-cut hair. His scalp felt prickly as usual, but his numb hand felt like a leather glove. He left the latrine and walked back to the large tent.

Layton couldn't believe that some Marines referred to Camp Leatherneck as "Camp Cupcake," as it was still a very remote and Spartan base. The cupcake moniker was typically used by older Marines who had been stationed at the base prior to the addition of amenities like running water and brick buildings for the officers, but living there wasn't easy by any stretch of the imagination. *Everything is easier now than it was as we remember it*, he thought as he put on his layers of body armor, *but it's only easier because we're better.*

"Sarge, the lieutenant wants to see you," Linfield said as Layton was buckling the strap on his kevlar helmet. Both men were fully dressed in their MultiCam combat outfits.

Layton walked across the sandy road to the officer's quarters, a long brick building with a metal roof. The building was draped in a tan, camouflage netting to obscure its appearance from above. The inside of the stone structure felt cool, particularly in the basement where his superior officer's office was located. The sign on the door read Lt. Mayberry. Layton knocked twice.

"Come in," a voice inside said.

"Morning sir, you wanted to see me?" Layton asked, standing at attention.

"At ease, sergeant," said the 21-year-old second lieutenant, sitting down in a chair behind his desk. Layton stood at parade rest with his feet apart and his hands together behind his back. All the lights in the small office were off, but a narrow window allowed sunlight into the room.

Lt. David Mayberry had graduated less than a month earlier from the United States Military Academy at West Point, specializing in Arabic, Pashto and Dari languages, as well as being well-versed in Middle Eastern history and culture. Mayberry had been stationed at Camp Leatherneck a week ago because of his skills, despite being in the Army not the Marines and despite his complete lack of combat experience, in order to provide logistical support to the Marine forces. Now he was commanding a sergeant 11 years his senior.

"Staff Sergeant, we've got a bit of a problem," Mayberry said. "I've just had word from higher up that all our communications networks are down. They said it was some kind of solar electromagnetic storm like an E.M.P. that has temporarily knocked out our ability to operate most of our arsenal, particularly anything electronic. This storm significantly reduces our tactical advantages and could make routine operations extremely vulnerable to attack. Fortunately for us, we're in the middle of Ramadan, Islam's holiest month, so violent attacks appear to remain diminished, with some obvious exceptions. I'm sorry to hear about your team's loss, and I hope, with your help, to be a good leader."

"I appreciate that, sir," Layton said. "What can we do about this storm?"

"Our first priority is to secure the base," the lieutenant said. "I volunteered our platoon to patrol the eastern gate before breakfast. If you have any trouble, send out a flare. We've planned for a number of contingencies that include the loss of electrical equipment, but most of our records and training manuals are electronic. We're trying to track down hard copies on base."

"Sir, Corporal Mullins in alpha company keeps a library of all the training manuals in hard copy," Layton said. "How long do you want us to guard the eastern gate?"

Mayberry wrote the words "Mullins" and "Alpha" in his notebook and checked his watch. The digital display was blank.

"I can't tell you exactly, but probably for a few hours at least," he said. "I have to give a briefing this morning, so stay there until you see me or until you're relieved by another platoon. That will be all, sergeant."

"Yes, sir," Layton said, snapping back to attention, saluting and exiting the barracks into the hot sun. *Looks like the best and the brightest are scratching their heads*, he thought.

Chapter 7

MECCA - Saudi Arabia, several hours before dawn

Ibn Ali was awakened by a deafening boom. He sat upright in his hotel bed, covered in a cold sweat. All around him, the hotel was erupting in noise. Men were shouting in Arabic in the hallway and pounding on hotel room doors. He shivered.

Ibn stood up and went to the window. Pulling back the drapes, the 40-year-old Saudi father of four looked down about 15 stories into a turbulent sea of human bodies throbbing in the darkness. Hundreds of thousands of men and women in white robes were chanting prayers and circling the Kaaba, a cube-shaped, dark-stone building thought to be the house of God. The glow of the robes in the moonlight were a sharp contrast to the darkness of the Kaaba and its ceremonial black silk and gold *kiswah* covering, but something still seemed different.

Everything is red, he thought, just as someone banged on his hotel room door.

"Hello, brother," Ibn said in Arabic as he answered the door.

"God is great," answered a dark-skinned stranger with black hair and a black beard.

"God is great," Ibn repeated. "What's all the commotion?"

"Today is the Day of Judgment," the man said. "God willing, we must all pray together. Join us outside at once. God is great!"

"God is great," Ibn repeated, closing the door. He walked back to the window and looked down on the crowd below. *Why is everything red?* he wondered, checking his analog wristwatch. It was half-past two. He tried switching on the lights, but they didn't respond. He checked the phone in his room, but there was no dial tone, and his cell phone refused to turn on.

Judgment Day, he thought. *What's another explanation? A terrorist attack?*

Ibn opened his laptop computer and attempted to turn it on, but there was no response. He retrieved a high-tech telecommunications kit from his luggage in the closet, but none of the devices were working, including his solar-powered satellite uplink. On a hunch, he pulled out a compass he kept in his travel bag and looked at the needle. It was swinging erratically, pointing in every which direction.

The magnetosphere must be disrupted, he thought. *That could explain the electronics.* He quickly looked through his dark closet at several custom-tailored suits, but opted instead to wear a traditional white pilgrim outfit as a sign of humility to God and solidarity to his fellow pilgrims, as well as to better blend in with the crowd. He grabbed his wallet and keys and stepped out into the hallway. Dozens of people were hurrying to the fire escapes. Ibn followed, descending flight after flight in darkness. Three floors from the bottom, the stairway was jammed with people and traffic was barely moving.

"Get these doors open!" a man yelled in Arabic from the floor above. "There may be another earthquake! We could be trapped! We must be outside!" The people on the stairway began to stir nervously.

Ibn considered himself a devout Sufi Muslim, but as a senior telecommunications specialist based in Dubai, he knew better than to blindly trust unverifiable advice. He had survived Saddam Hussein's scud missile attacks on Riyadh in 1991 as a teenager and had learned to pay close attention to details during periods of confusion and turmoil. Rare moments like these afforded opportunities both timely and unique.

"The doors are open," Ibn yelled in reply. "We are moving but it is extremely crowded. Please be patient." *An earthquake in Mecca would support the theory of Judgment Day*, he thought. *I remember reading about the earthquake yesterday in Jeddah, but it wasn't very large. Maybe we're due for an aftershock.* There was another faint boom from outside.

Every few seconds, the people in front of Ibn moved down another step. As he followed them step for step, the people in line behind him moved closer, filling in the spaces. By the time he reached the bottom of the staircase, Ibn could see what was causing the congestion. There were two sets of double doors at the stairway exit, but the doors on the left were shut and everyone was trying to squeeze through the doorway on the right, creating a bottleneck.

When Ibn got close enough, he stepped out of line and tried the doors on the left. They opened at once and Ibn exited into the over-crowded plaza of the Masjid al Haram mosque. Ibn had never seen so many people massed together. Thousands of people continued to pour out through the exits behind him, now utilizing both sets of doors. Ibn looked up and gasped.

The sky was an inky, smoky black with waves of shimmering curtains of blood-red light dancing mystically above their heads, stretching far off to the horizon. All the lights surrounding the normally well-lit mosque were turned off, as was every electric light in sight.

I remember reading about this yesterday, he thought, searching for a logical answer. *The news article said a large solar flare could cause electrical disturbances worldwide. That would explain the power outage and the magnetic interference, but I don't remember reading anything about red skies.* Ibn thought back to his astrophysics classes at Harvard University. *Red skies could be some kind of aurora. Aurora borealis is caused by electrical charges in the atmosphere. It fits,* he thought.

Ibn looked up at the enormous Mecca Clock that towered more than 500 meters above the ground. The giant face said it was still half-past two. He looked back at his wristwatch. *The clocks have stopped,* he thought. *What time is it really?* The four-faced clock tower and minaret were the uppermost parts of the Abraj Al-Bait Towers, the tallest building in Saudi Arabia at 601 meters, or about 1,972 feet, and the second tallest in the world. The building's large complex contained 1,500,000 square meters of floor area, more than any other structure in the world.

Another distant boom echoed through the night air, causing the crowd to lurch forward. Ibn was being pressed toward the

Kaaba by the mass of bodies and detected the pungent aroma of sweat and body odor. For a moment, he thought the silhouette of the dark building against the red sky bore a striking resemblance to the Empire State Building in New York City, with a crescent moon on top. At 95 floors, the Abraj Al-Bait seemed to stretch up into the heavens. There were so many floors, Ibn couldn't tell which room or even which floor was his. For the first time, he was glad his family hadn't accompanied him on this trip.

All the hotels in Mecca were currently filled to capacity for the holy month of Ramadan. The Abraj Al-Bait was the largest hotel in the world, capable of housing up to 100,000 people and it contained a four-story shopping mall with a parking garage that held 1,000 vehicles. Constructed by the Saudi Binladin Group for a price tag of nearly $800 million U.S. dollars, the five-star hotel, residence and convention center had required the complete demolition of the historic Ottoman Ajyad Fortress that had previously occupied the same space.

Out with the old, in with the new. Everywhere I look is scaffolding and skyscrapers, he thought, recalling his first visit to Mecca in the early '90s when oil prices were just beginning to rise again. *All our major cities are turning into Dubai.*

The swelling crowd stopped moving almost at once and a hush spread over the pilgrims.

If it is a solar flare, what is God trying to tell us? Are we really being judged? Is technology a blessing or a curse?

From high atop the minaret, the muezzin's *adhan* prayer song pierced the stillness of the night like an arrow, reverberating off the acoustic properties of the building's immense structure.

"God is great! God have mercy!" his voice called out from the tall minaret, his tones ringing clear as a summer song. Perhaps the electrically charged atmosphere had somehow amplified the muezzin's song or perhaps a higher power had intervened, but one thing was certain: His voice had never been louder.

Joining nearly a million people surrounding him, Ibn dropped to his knees, bowed forward and touched his forehead to the ground in prayer.

***

The red skies lasted for about an hour, before quickly turning green and dissipating. Shortly thereafter, the sun broke over the horizon, triggering the start of the day's ritual fasting.

Ibn Ali made his way back to the hotel and climbed the 15 flights of stairs back to his room. There still was no electricity, no dial tones, no anything.

My surveillance software is toast, he thought, looking down at the crowded plaza below. *Maybe the imam was right. Technology can be a blessing or a curse.* Ibn smelled under his arms and made a grimace. He reeked of sweat and body odor. He went into the bathroom, stripped off his pilgrim clothes and turned on the water in the shower, but the faucet was dry. He walked over to the small refrigerator in his room, opened the door and grabbed a bottle of water. As he cracked the seal on the water bottle, he briefly considered wetting his dry throat, but then he remembered the fast.

No eating or drinking during the day, he thought. He poured some water on a small wash cloth and wiped down his naked body in the early morning light.

When he had finished a few minutes later, he put on a clean, white dress shirt, a dark two-piece suit and comfortable black shoes. He capped the outfit by donning his round *taqiyah* hat, grabbed his two leather bags containing his laptop and communications equipment and stepped out into the hallway. He followed the signs to the main tower's elevator system and instinctively pressed the "up" button, but nothing happened.

Ibn looked around and located the fire escape. The emergency entrance to the fire escape had large signs written in Arabic and English warning that opening the door would trigger an alarm. No alarm sounded when Ibn pressed open the door and stepped into the darkened stairway. *The fire alarms aren't working,* he thought. He looked up a narrow slit between the stairs and thought he could make out faint traces of light from above. Strapping his leather bags diagonally across his chest, Ibn began to climb the stairs, one at a time.

Only 70 more flights to the imam's residence, he thought. *"Our elevators are very fast."*

Ibn sat down on the stairs on the 35th floor to rest and catch his breath. His throat was parched and he needed to use the bathroom. After a few moments, he stood up and checked the door to the 35th floor. It was locked from the inside for security. He sat down for a few more moments before standing and looking upwards. *Fifty more flights to go. You can do this.*

He took another break once he had reached the 50th floor, more than halfway to the top. He had made a point to breathe through his nose to conserve moisture, but he couldn't hold his bladder any longer and he really didn't want to pee on the stairs. Ibn tried the door to the 50th floor, but it too was locked. He took out his wallet, removed a credit card and gently slid it between the door frame and the lock near the door nob until he heard a click. He pulled open the door and stepped onto the floor.

I think I found another potential security breach, he thought, setting down his bags and walking along the deserted hallway to the men's room. After taking care of business, he returned to the fire escape and began climbing the stairs with ease. He made it about two flights before he realized why it was easier. He turned around and descended back to the 50th floor, jimmied the lock again and retrieved his luggage from the hallway. As he pulled his luggage straps over his head, he made a mental note that there were no security cameras in the fire escapes, but then realized this was irrelevant if there was no electricity. He began his ascent again.

After taking another rest on the 70th floor, Ibn finally made it to the locked door on the 85th floor, out of breath, thirsty and dizzy from the elevation and reduced oxygen environment. He knocked a few times, but hearing no answer, he had to use his credit card to force open the door. The hallway inside was filled with sunlight, causing Ibn to momentarily shield his eyes.

"May I help you?" asked an elderly man in Arabic. As Ibn's eyes adjusted to the light, he noticed the man had a gray and white beard and was wearing tan-colored robes and a white, rounded *taqiyah* cap, similar to his own. Ibn thought his voice sounded oddly familiar.

"Yes, I am here to see the imam," Ibn said, squinting his eyes.

"Is he expecting you?"

"We met last night at dinner," Ibn said, using his handkerchief to dab the sweat off his brow. "My name is Ibn Shaja'at Ali. His holiness invited me to come up and see the view."

"Please follow me," the old man said, walking down a wide hallway. Ibn followed the man for a few feet but began to feel increasingly lightheaded. His vision was filled with tiny shooting stars and growing black dots.

"I think I may need to sit down for a moment," Ibn said, setting his bags on the floor just before blacking out and falling face-first to the ground.

***

"God be praised," a white-bearded man said when Ibn awoke. He was wearing white robes and a red-and-white checked *shmagh* headdress. Ibn recognized the spiritual leader.

"God be praised," Ibn repeated, wearily. He was lying down on a sofa in the middle of a luxurious corner office with large, floor-to-ceiling windows. He had plastic tubes inserted into his nostrils that provided him with pure oxygen, and another plastic tube inserted into his left arm that fed him with an intravenous fluid drip.

"I was just thinking of you when you arrived," the imam said. "How did you manage to make it up here without the elevators?"

"I came the hard way, your holiness," Ibn croaked. His throat was still parched, but he knew that taking even one drink of water before sundown was a violation of the fast. As far as he could recall, IV drips and oxygen supplements were not considered forbidden, particularly during emergency situations. *If the imam approved it, it must be OK,* he thought as he concentrated on producing enough saliva to wet his tongue and restore his speech.

"You must be exhausted," the imam said. "I think you were unconscious for about an hour, but I can't be sure. All of our clocks stopped working last night. After you recover your strength, you should come see the view."

Ibn was still disoriented as he sat up and gazed out at the incredible view of Mecca and the surrounding terrain. They were just below the base of the giant, four-sided clock, and just above the tower's penthouse and five floors of royal suites. *It feels like I'm flying,* he thought, standing up and slowly walking toward one of the floor-to-ceiling windows. When he looked almost straight down at the plaza of the Masjid al Haram mosque, the building's walls appeared to narrow toward its base and it felt as though he was looking at the world upside down, with the crowded ground forming the sky. His head began to spin with vertigo again and he quickly turned around and sat back down on a couch next to the old man who had shown him in.

"What do you think?" the imam asked. "The city looks peaceful, does it not?"

"It is magnificent, your holiness," Ibn said, looking out the window again. He noticed several columns of black smoke rising far off. "Are those fires in the distance?"

The imam turned around to look at the dark clouds, but the other older man kept his gaze fixed on the floor.

"What is it, Hassan?" the old man asked.

"Dark smoke surrounds our city," Imam Hassan answered. "It draws closer."

"I would guess the pipelines have burst," Ibn said. "Sir, I don't believe we have been formally introduced," he added, extending his hand to the man seated next to him.

"Ali Ahmed Ribah," the man said, ignoring Ibn's proffered hand and continuing to stare at the floor. "I am pleased to meet you, Ibn Shaja'at Ali."

"Ahmed is our mosque's muezzin," the imam said. "He is blind, like many great muezzins before him."

"That was you this morning on the prayer call," Ibn said, retracting his hand. "I thought I recognized your voice. You were awe-inspiring."

"Thank you," the muezzin said. "So was your climb up here. I am interested to hear your opinion about these dark times. Tell me, do you believe that today is Judgment Day?"

"Yes and no," Ibn replied. "I think every day is Judgment Day. God is always watching us. He sees how we mortals treat each other and how we treat our world."

"God be praised," the imam said. "He is most compassionate and merciful. The Koran states that on the Day of Judgment, the skies will be rent asunder, the stars will fall down and the oceans will roll together. Every soul will stand alone and God will reign supreme. Earthquakes, giant fires, blood-red skies and the utter collapse of technology are surely signs of the end of times. Do you not agree? How else can these signs be explained?"

"God is great," Ibn said. "I believe that there are many ways to look at this question. For instance, I am also a man of science. There are many miracles and other mysteries of this world that can be explained through the scientific method, such as the way the perceived movement of the sun corresponds with our seasons, the way the moon affects the tides, the way gravity works, how plate tectonics cause earthquakes, and so on. Having this knowledge helps us to better understand our world and why things happen the way they do. I believe that God always follows the laws of nature and physics. He created physics as He created us. I believe that most or all of these signs of Judgment Day can also be explained through science."

"What is the scientific explanation for these signs?" the imam asked.

"Yesterday, our sun shot a large pulse of magnetic energy at the Earth called a coronal mass ejection. I believe this rare energy burst caused our red aurora this morning, is causing our electrical outages and could be the cause of the oil fires. When the pulse eventually fades in a matter of hours, I think it is likely that everything will be restored as it was."

"So you do not think that this is the end?" the muezzin asked.

"The end of what?" Ibn asked.

"The end of life, of the Earth, of everything," the muezzin said.

"I think that's rather unlikely, but I suppose we will find out soon enough," Ibn said. "I think it is more likely that this will be the end of one world and also the beginning of another."

"Do you believe God is trying to tell us something?" the imam asked.

"I can only guess at God's plan," Ibn said. "There are many different religions and faiths in this world, your holiness, and they all seem to have a slightly different answer to that question. What do you think?"

"I think God is testing us," he said. "He is using this event to reveal to us the one true religion."

"What makes you so sure God wants only one religion?" Ibn asked. "Billions of people — Muslims, Christians and Jews — all believe in and worship the same god. We differ on the details, but we all believe we have the truth. How can we all be right if we are so different?"

"They all believe in Judgment Day and the Revelation," the muezzin countered.

"Perhaps this Revelation refers to a personal one," Ibn offered. "I believe that the core of every religion is truth, love, compassion, nonviolence and following the Golden Rule, to treat others as you would want them to treat you. You asked if technology is a blessing or a curse. I think it is both. Technology can save us or condemn us, depending on how it is used and to what end. You pointed out last night that my terrorist-tracking technology could be used to spy on innocent people. That was never my intention when I created it, but if this technology fell into the wrong hands, its effects could be devastating. Now, thanks to the power outage, it no longer works. Whether that is a sign from God or merely a coincidence, I can never know for sure. The power outage also disabled our elevators, fire alarms, sprinkler systems, the Mecca clock, our hospitals, pipelines, automobiles and communications systems. Even our ability to spread God's message has been hampered. Surely not all forms of technology are evil, but they have all suffered the same fate."

"Perhaps God is trying to tell us that we are too connected," the muezzin suggested.

"Or that we are connected in the wrong ways," the imam added.

"We may all be correct," Ibn said, shifting in his seat. A sharp spasm of pain momentarily shot through his legs, reminding him of his physical and spiritual journey up 85 flights of stairs. "God is forcing us to change our ways and reevaluate the way we look at our world. I think that we should embrace this change and see where it leads. God willing, we will come through the other side with a new perspective on faith, on life and in ourselves."

"God be praised," the imam said.

"God be praised," the muezzin repeated. "You are a rare jewel, Ibn Shaja'at Ali."

"Thank you, sir," Ibn said. "Now if I am not mistaken, just above our heads is a lunar observatory and astronomy center. We should be able to determine the time of day without too much trouble. Let's try to get this clock working."

Chapter 8

LONDON - 260 Devonia Rd., Islington, England, sometime in the late morning, Thursday

Jacob Baker woke up and stared at the large, British flag hanging above his bed. He sat up and rubbed his eyes, stretched his arms and gave a loud yawn. He looked over at the novelty clock on his bedroom wall and noted the time. Big Ben said it was half past twelve.

"Blimey, that was a crazy day, yesterday," he said, standing up and shuffling his way through his messy room to the bathroom across the hallway. After relieving himself, the 16-year-old boy stood in front of the sink and looked at his reflection in the mirror. *World's most popular teenager*, he thought, running his hands through his slightly greasy hair and attempting to fashion it into a fake mohawk, or faux-hawk. Achieving this result, he chuckled in amusement.

Jacob walked into the kitchen and picked up his smartphone off the counter. He pressed the power button, but it didn't respond. He turned over the phone, opened the back cover and removed the battery. The battery looked normal and didn't appear to be defective, so he replaced it, replaced the back cover and attempted to turn on the phone again. Nothing happened.

He set his smartphone back down and opened the refrigerator. The light was off, but the air inside was still cold. He stood in front of the open door for about a minute before grabbing the milk and shutting the door. He found a clean bowl, poured himself some dry cereal and added the milk. As he was eating, he grabbed a remote control and tried turning on the small television set that sat on the kitchen counter. The TV didn't respond.

Jacob reached over and pressed the TV's power button, but that didn't work either. He stopped eating, got up and walked over to the light switch by the doorway. He clicked the switch on and off a few times, but the lights didn't respond. *Ah, the power is out,* he thought.

Jacob finished eating his cereal and set his empty bowl in the sink. He turned on the faucet, but nothing happened. He walked into the living room and flopped himself down on the couch. *I wonder what's going on today?* he thought, grabbing a remote control off the coffee table and attempting to turn on the living room TV. There was no response.

"No electricity, silly," he said to himself. *That means no video games, either,* he thought. He picked up a celebrity news magazine off the coffee table and flipped through it for a few minutes, but it just made him want to watch TV or surf the Internet. *No electricity means no Internet. This is pretty stupid. What am I supposed to do?*

He thought again about his wild day walking around the city with Kendra. *All those photos I took are on my phone, which isn't working. I could call Kendra, but all the contact info I have for her is also on my phone. I should probably call my mom.*

Jacob got up and grabbed the blue cordless phone hanging on the kitchen wall, but the receiver wouldn't turn on. He hung up the phone and walked down the hallway to his mom's bedroom, knocking lightly on the door three times. As he opened the door, he was momentarily startled by the mess. *Blimey! Her room is messier than mine,* he thought, noting the empty, unmade bed and piles of unfolded clothes and shoes scattered everywhere. *Do as I say, not as I do, right? If she were my kid, she'd be grounded.*

He found the old-fashioned telephone on the bed stand and lifted the receiver to his ear, extending the curly cord connecting it with the base. *What's her work number? I have it programmed in my phone, but that's no use.* Jacob noticed there was no dial tone and replaced the receiver.

It looks like there's nothing for it, he thought. *I might as well go outside.*

Jacob closed his mother's bedroom door and walked across the hall to his own bedroom. He put on a pair of skinny jeans, some black boots and a fake-vintage *Rolling Stones* T-shirt. He looked around through his closet and found a black leather vest, which he put on over the shirt, then checked himself out in the bathroom mirror again. *You look kind of bad-ass,* he thought, making a slight adjustment to his faux-hawk to make it stand more upright.

As he walked into the kitchen on his way outside, Jacob noticed the carton of milk still sitting on the counter. He thought of his mom as he grabbed the milk and put it back in the fridge, then decided to leave her a quick note.

"Mum, The power's out so I'm off to explore the city some more. Stay out of trouble, Jacob." His crooked penmanship was so terrible that the note was barely legible.

He chuckled at his cleverness of telling his mom to stay out of trouble, grabbed his house keys and wallet and stepped outside into the world.

It was another beautiful, sunny day outside. Jacob walked south along Devonia Road to a small newsstand at the intersection with Gerrard Road and browsed the daily tabloids.

"These are all yesterday's papers," he said to the East Indian-looking vendor. "Where are today's dailies?"

"The papers did not arrive this morning," the dark-skinned man replied. "Check back later. Yesterday's papers are half-off, but magazines are full-price."

Natasha's face was on the cover of several glamour magazines wearing heavy make-up and eye liner. Jacob picked up one of the magazines and began flipping through it.

"That one is four pounds," the vendor said. "No browsing, please."

Jacob pulled out his wallet and checked to see how much cash he had. He was broke.

"Pardon my intrusion, but are you not the boy from the web video?" the vendor asked.

"Yeah, did you see it?" Jacob asked.

"My daughter showed it to me yesterday," he said. "It was most amusing."

"Thanks," Jacob said. "Look, I'm out of cash right now. Do you think you could let me borrow this magazine for a while? I'll pay you back as soon as I get some cash."

"I will keep it safe for you until you return with payment," the vendor said, grabbing the magazine from Jacob and putting it behind the counter. "When you become a doctor, you may remember to carry more cash with you. Have a good day."

"Thanks, you too," Jacob said, turning away and continuing his walk along Gerrard Road. After a few meters, he stopped and wondered which direction he was headed, but realized he must be going west because he went this way all the time. *I should go back to the French Connection,* he thought. *Maybe my friends are there.*

Several random strangers spotted Jacob during his walk and pointed at him, but no one tried to chase him or take his picture. When he reached N1, he saw his friends Hamish, Lennon and Alfie sitting at a table. As soon as they saw Jacob, they stood up and clapped their hands.

"There he is!" Hamish cheered. "The legendary YouTube movie star in the flesh. How's it feel to be rich and famous?"

A group of teenage girls sitting at a nearby table pointed at Jacob, giggled and waved.

"It's not quite what I expected," Jacob said, sitting down in an empty chair. "I'm not sure how I can turn fame into fortune, but I'm open to ideas."

"Didn't YouTube pay you?" Alfie asked. "What about Sketchers?"

Jacob shrugged his shoulders. "Not yet."

"Even if you only got a half-pence for every play, that'd still be like a million pounds," Alfie said. "I think they owe you more than that, though. Did you see how they were pushing your video yesterday? It was bloomin' everywhere, mate, and ads everywhere, too."

"I think your math is a little off, unless his hypno video was played 200 million times," Lennon said. "Last I checked, it had about 80 million views."

"Well it still could be, right?" Alfie asked. "If more people watch it today."

"I dunno," Jacob said. "I couldn't check on it this morning. The power was out."

"I think it's still out, mates," Hamish said, clicking the power button on his smartphone. "I've got bleeding bollocks right now over this piece of crap. Won't even turn on."

"Mine either," Lennon said. "What do you reckon it is?"

"Maybe Jake broke the Internet," Alfie said. "He overloaded it with his schmooze."

The four friends had a good laugh.

"There's another matter even more pressing than the Internet," Jacob said gravely.

"Oh yeah!" Hamish grinned. "You've got a new girlfriend. What's her name?"

"Kendra," he said. "I really want to see her again, but I don't know how to reach her."

"Didn't you get her number?" Alfie asked.

"I did, and it's on my phone, which is comatose," Jacob said. "Even if I did remember her number, I can't call her if the phones aren't working. How do you find someone in a city of eight million people? I don't even know where she lives."

The four friends sat in silence for a few moments. Suddenly, Jacob got an idea and stood up. His friends watched as he walked over to the neighboring table of giggling teenage girls.

"Excuse me," he said politely. "Do any of you know a girl named Kendra Walters?"

Chapter 9

SOMEWHERE IN THE NORTH ATLANTIC OCEAN

Adam awoke to find himself all alone, floating in a small boat beneath an enormous canopy of blue sky. His head was throbbing and his stomach felt like it was full of battery acid.

He sat up and looked around. Directly in front of him was a 41-foot Hans Christian yacht. In every other direction he looked, Adam found himself surrounded by a vast expanse of salt water that seemed to stretch on forever. *I need to get back on that boat,* he thought, cupping a mouthful of warm sea water and drinking it, then immediately retching it up overboard. *Salty.*

He did a quick inventory of the items he had available. He was wearing a puffy orange life vest over the top of a light blue- and white-striped dress shirt he had put on the day before. He was also still wearing the tailored gray pants to his designer suit, but his jacket was missing, as were his shoes. *My jacket has my keys, smartphone, billfold and a flash drive,* he recalled. He suddenly felt helpless, even though those items would not have helped his current situation in the slightest bit. He also couldn't find his sunglasses, which would have been more useful.

Adam checked the time on his wristwatch. The elegant, blue and gold dial said it was half past seven. He looked around the small boat for anything else he could use and found two bottles of water. He immediately opened one of the bottles and drank the contents.

His head was still throbbing as he laid back down in the boat. *I really need to quit drinking,* he thought as he dozed off to sleep again.

***

About 20 meters away on board the *Reciprocity,* Frank was giving Karen and Natasha a lesson on tacking and jibing. He stood at the helm with Natasha at port and Karen starboard.

Karen and Natasha were both wearing stylish and provocative bikinis, Karen in red and Natasha in blue and white.

Neither woman was wearing makeup or footwear, but both were well-covered in sunblock. Frank was wearing a light green T-shirt, khaki shorts and his black fedora. He slipped on a pair of Ray Ban sunglasses, partly to reduce the glare, but also to allow him to discreetly observe his crew mates without embarrassment.

"If we head directly into the wind, our sails will go slack and we'll lose control," he said. "Conversely, if we go in the opposite direction with the wind at our backs, we can only sail as fast as the wind is blowing, which is currently around six to eight knots."

"What's a knot?" Karen asked.

"One nautical mile per hour," he said.

"So we're going about six to eight miles per hour?" Natasha asked.

"Nautical miles are a little longer than land miles, but yes, you are correct," he said. "Now by sailing diagonally to the wind, we can effectively harness its power. Just by steering the rudder and making a few minor corrections to the sheets and rigging, we can let the wind do all the hard work and take us anywhere we want to go."

"That's pretty cool," Karen said to Natasha. "How can you tell where we're going?"

"Normally we can use the GPS or the ship's compass to determine our heading, but for now we'll have to improvise," he said. "Presently the wind is blowing from the east. By keeping the wind on our port tack, or blowing on our port side, we can continue to head south or southeast with ease. Note the way the wind is filling the sails right now. Our port side is currently our windward side, meaning the wind is blowing from this side, while our starb'd is our leeward side, meaning the wind is not blowing on that side."

"I don't think I understand," Karen said.

"I don't either," Natasha said.

"You will soon enough," Frank said. "I'm trying to explain this as simply as I can, but it's important that the captain uses specific language to describe, but not necessarily show others what to do. We are currently sailing southeast. To change direction, we have to change both our course and our sails. You two can help with the sails. Those lines or ropes next to you on either side are called sheets, not to be confused with the sails. These sheets are attached on either side to the headsail, the sail in front of the mainsail, and they control our lateral movement. I'm going to steer us to the port side and I will give the order to haul the sheet on the port side. This means that Natasha will haul or pull in the sheet connected to the headsail. Once we start turning, the line will go slack and you can haul it in with ease. While she is doing this, Karen, you will need to slacken or loosen the starb'd sheets connected to the headsail, about the same amount that Natasha hauls in. When we have changed course, both of you will tie the sheets to a cleat. One sheet per cleat. Any questions?"

"The sheets are these ropes connected to the sails?" Natasha asked.

"Yes, and they will tighten or slacken as we change course," he said. "Now watch out for the boom as we turn due east, into the wind. Haul in the sheets port side!"

The headsail fell empty as Frank steered the vessel directly into the wind.

"We stopped moving," Karen said, tying the starboard sheet to the cleat. "How can we sail east if the wind is blowing from the east?"

"We can sail around it," Frank said. "I am continuing to steer us to the port side."

Frank turned the wheel again, steering the yacht northeast. The headsail filled again, but from the starboard side. Natasha hauled in the port sheet and tied it to a cleat, while Karen loosened the starboard sheet. Frank helped her tighten and tie the sheet to a cleat.

"Now the wind is blowing off our starb'd tack, meaning our port side is now the leeward side," he said. "That means we're headed northeast. If we stayed on this course, we would eventually reach Europe, in about a month or two. We're not going to Europe, however, so now we will return to our southeasterly course. Haul in the starb'd sheets!"

Frank turned the wheel to the starboard side. The wind fell from the sails once they were facing due east, but the sails filled again once they were facing southeast. With a little help from Frank, Natasha slackened and retied the port sheet while Karen hauled in and retied her sheet.

"We're back where we started," Karen said. "And my hands are really sore."

"Actually, we're a little farther east than we were before," Frank said. "So that's tacking in a nutshell. If you're trying to head in the direction the wind is blowing, you have to tack or go at the wind in alternating angles, like a zig-zag. If the wind is at your back, it's called jibing. Jibing is a little more difficult, but essentially it's the same idea in reverse."

"How do you know the wind is blowing from the east?" Karen asked. "Right now, the compass says we're headed northwest, not southeast."

"Intuition, mostly," he said. "The sun rises in the east. I watched the sun rise this morning and saw where it came up. The compass said it was west, but the compass was wrong. I also happen to know that the wind on the North Atlantic blows east and southeast in the spring and summer, and it blows west and northwest in the fall and winter. I also have a sextant we can use to find our bearings. As long as we keep the sheets tight, we can lay her course with ease."

"That sounds nice," Karen whispered to Natasha. The two women giggled.

"HELLO? AHOY!" a voice called out from somewhere aft of the ship.

Frank locked the helm's wheel in place and walked to the stern with Natasha and Karen. Adam was floating in the dory about 20 meters behind, sitting up on his knees and waving his arms.

"Permission to come aboard," Adam yelled.

"On one condition," Natasha called back. "No more drinking."

"DONE!" Adam replied.

Frank began hauling in the line connected to the dory. A minute or so later, Adam was back aboard the yacht. His face was slightly sunburned and covered with black and gray stubble.

"Man, I don't know what you guys were doing up here, but that little life boat began rocking like crazy," Adam said as he pulled off his life vest.

"Frank was teaching us how to tack and jibe by trimming the sheets," Natasha said.

"That sounds pretty nautical," he said. "Can you give me a lesson sometime, Frank?"

"I can show you," Natasha said, taking Adam's hand and leading him to the helm.

"I think I'll get started on lunch," Frank said, heading below deck.

"I'll help," Karen said, following him down the stairs.

"Which way is north?" Karen heard Adam ask, just before she went below.

Frank was bending over looking inside the refrigerator when Karen came into the galley. She pretended not to notice his tight shorts and muscular physique as she brushed past him and hopped up to sit on the counter. Frank stood up quickly and closed the door to the fridge.

"Sorry," she said with a smile, dangling her bare feet from the countertop. Her red bikini was covered with an intricate pattern of tiny beads that were arranged to look like flames. "This kitchen is pretty cozy. Can I help you with anything?"

"That's a pretty amazing swimsuit," Frank stated. "I mean, you look pretty in it. I mean, pretty hungry." He stopped himself. He looked down at the floor for a moment to help recover his composure and then looked back at Karen's face. She was grinning.

"You read my mind," she said. "I am pretty hungry."

Frank noticed that the yacht was changing directions. He considered going up to check, but figured it was just Natasha showing Adam how to tack. He thought for a moment for something he could say that wouldn't sound stupid or completely blow his chances with Karen.

"All the frozen food has probably thawed by now," he said. "We should probably eat it while it's still good, you know, before it spoils. How do you feel about stuffed mushrooms and duck tenders?"

"They'll do for now," she said. "Appetizers can quench the hunger, but eventually a girl's got to get a real meal."

Frank noticed the yacht was returning to its original course.

"I can appreciate a healthy appetite," he said. "Tell me, are you always this hungry?"

"Only when I see something I want," Karen said, coyly pointing one of her legs at Frank's knees. "Do you find it intimidating?"

"Appetizers don't intimidate me," he said with a nervous smile. "Beautiful women, on the other hand, scare me to death. Rich, beautiful women looking for playthings can be more dangerous than dynamite. And you, my dear, look like dynamite."

Karen gave a hearty laugh, causing Frank to admire his own wit. *Smooth,* he thought.

"Thank you for that, Frank," she said. "That might just be the best compliment I've ever received. You don't need to be intimidated. I'm not very explosive. I'm not rich or beautiful like Natasha. The truth is that I'm really Adam's assistant. I handle his calls, I take his messages and I run his errands. He has four assistants, but I just handle his New York offices, so I never get to travel. It's really not a very sexy job. I met Natasha yesterday at the Morgan's party and they sort of adopted me on the spot. They even bought me all these clothes so I wouldn't have to go home and delay their trip. I don't normally dress like this."

"Are you still working for him?" Frank asked as he began preparing the appetizers.

"You know, I have no idea," she said. "People like Adam and Natasha have assistants because they're incredibly busy all the time. I've been working for Adam for about a year and my social life has vanished. I've been so busy, I haven't had a boyfriend in a couple of years and I haven't seen my family since last Christmas."

No boyfriend, he thought. "Do you like your job?"

"That really depends on what day you ask me," she said. "Or what time of day. Sometimes I love it, sometimes I hate it. Do you like your job? Being master of the seas?"

Frank had finished arranging the appetizers on a metal baking tray so that the mushrooms formed a large outer circle with the duck tenders in the center. With the tray in his left hand, he extended his right hand to Karen. She took his hand and hopped down from the counter.

"You don't ever really master the seas," he said, guiding her up the stairs in front of him. "The wind and the sea are indifferent. They can turn on you in an instant, without warning or reason. No, the best you can do is master yourself and try to adapt to what comes your way."

"That sounds pretty wise," Adam said once everyone was on deck. "And those appetizers look great. I'm starving." He popped one of the duck tenders in his mouth and began chewing.

Frank and Karen also tried the duck. Natasha bit into a mushroom and spit it back out.

"Is this crab meat?" she asked.

"Yeah, I think so," Frank said. "The other ones are duck tenders, whatever those are."

"I'm a vegetarian," Natasha said.

"Oh I'm sorry," Frank said. "I forgot that. I think there's still plenty of fresh fruit in the galley. Do you want a peach?"

"Karen can get it," Adam offered, sampling one of the crab-filled mushrooms.

Frank turned to look at Karen. She was staring at Adam with a furrow in her brow but she said nothing and made no effort to comply.

"That's OK, I'll get it myself," Natasha said, going below deck for a few seconds before returning with a fresh peach.

"These are pretty good," Adam said, popping a duck tender and a stuffed mushroom into his mouth and chewing them together. He had devoured about half of the appetizers before he noticed that everyone was looking at him. "What?" he asked with a mouth full of food.

"Adam, I need to ask you to give me an extended vacation or a leave of absence, with pay, effective immediately," Karen said sternly. "If that's not OK, I'm sorry, but I quit. I'm not your executive assistant out here and you are not the boss of me."

Adam looked at Karen for a moment and swallowed his mouthful of food.

"Freedom granted," he said. "With pay. I have to admit I admire your moxie, girl. You go get 'em."

The four stood in awkward silence for a few moments before Natasha spoke up.

"Don't you have anything else to say?" she asked Adam.

"Like what?" Adam asked.

"I think you owe Karen an apology," Frank said.

"What is this, team up on Adam day?" he asked. "Look, Frank, I get that you guys like each other and I think that's fantastic. Knock yourselves out. But don't be getting the idea that you can throw me in a rowboat any time you want and have your way with my wife and her friend. I ought to sue you for leaving me out there all night."

"Adam," Natasha said, putting her hand on his shoulder. "You shouldn't talk to people like that. You're not on Wall Street anymore. Frank saved your life last night and he probably saved all our lives. He's never made a pass at me. In fact, everything I've seen him do or say has been to help all of us feel more comfortable and safe. I wish you could be more like that."

"Fine," Adam said, his voice dripping with sarcasm. "I'm sorry, Karen, Frank, Natasha. I'm sorry to everyone. It's not easy being the bad guy. Everybody is always trying to take what I have, because they all think they deserve it more than I do. Now you've got me outnumbered, so go ahead and take it. You want my stuff? Take it. Hell, take it all. I don't care."

Adam pulled off his elegant designer watch and held it out to Frank. "Take it," he said.

Frank stared at the blue-and-gold Rolex Yacht-Master II wristwatch for a few moments. He recognized the luxury timepiece from an advertisement in *Fortune* magazine.

"I don't want your stuff, Adam," Frank said. "I'm not upset or envious that you have a beautiful wife and a lot of money. Good for you. The thing that upsets me is when you act as though you are somehow above the rest of us, looking down. It's like you can see the problems of the world from up in your high tower, but you don't see how they apply to you. You think you're somehow removed from the problems of the world, but you're not. None of us are."

Adam stared at Frank but said nothing.

"I like to think of this ship as an ecosystem," Frank continued. "The four of us are central to this ecosystem, and everything each of us does has a direct impact on everything and everyone else on board. With just a little teamwork and cooperation, we can find a harmony in which everyone benefits. If one of us upsets the balance, the rest of us have to work a little harder to correct the problem and restore the balance. For example, take these appetizers you've been stuffing in your mouth or better yet, that $250 bottle of scotch you drank last night. Scotch is a rare luxury item on a small ecosystem like a yacht. There was more than enough for everyone to enjoy, but you got a hold of it and drank up most of the bottle in one setting. That was selfish and greedy, and you paid the consequences for it later."

"A night in the dog house," Adam said. "You all think I'm selfish and greedy?"

"Yes," the three replied in unison.

Adam walked to the bow of the ship and sat down by himself. He stared out at the horizon in silence for about an hour, watching the waves break against the yacht and feeling the warm, salty breeze against his face. He thought about Frank's concept of an ecosystem where everyone plays a role. *It sounds like Communism or Socialism,* he thought. *Or Marxism. What's the incentive to work hard or be innovative if everyone shares the same reward?*

He looked down at his watch. The dial still said it was half past seven. *This is bullshit,* he thought, slowly winding the watch's crown in a clockwise direction. *Everything I have has turned against me. Even my watch quit on me. I sure don't feel like the most powerful man in the world right now. I can't remember the last time I felt this alone. My wife might be the best thing that's ever happened to me and she just said I'm a selfish asshole. Maybe she's right.*

Adam thought he could hear his watch begin ticking again, but wasn't sure. It was set to 7:32 but he had no idea what time it really was. As he stared out at the vast, blue horizon, he noticed the rhythmic splashing sound had changed its pitch and tempo. He looked over the side and was surprised to see a school of flying fish enjoying the ship's company. Adam watched in wonder as the flying fish leapt out of the water and used their winglike pectoral fins to glide just above the surface before re-submerging. He considered telling the others, but when he looked behind him, he could see Frank, Natasha and Karen were already pointing at the flying fish.

Frank was at the helm when Adam stood up and rejoined his ship mates.

"You know, you guys are right," he said. "I have been selfish and greedy. But I wasn't always like this. Twenty years ago, I didn't care at all about money. It was just the means to an end. When I was young, that end was my art collection, but art costs money. I came to realize that money could buy beautiful things, and I naïvely thought that if I had enough money, I could save the world. Once I turned my focus to money, though, everything changed. Eventually I was forced to choose between love and money, but I had already made my decision."

"And you chose money," Frank said. "How's that going, saving the world?"

"Yesterday, Karen told me that money turns people into monsters. Do you remember saying that?" Adam asked. Karen nodded. "I knew there were a lot of monsters out there, but I thought that if I learned their ways I could outsmart them. Once I became rich and my influence and power began to grow, I considered giving my money away, but I realized that I would also be giving away my power and influence. The more powerful I became, the more interested I became in preserving and protecting the status quo, instead of changing it."

"You betrayed yourself by becoming your own worst enemy," Frank said flatly.

"I don't want to be hated!" Adam wailed. "I'm not evil. I don't want to poison the world around me or turn my friends into enemies. I wanted to make the world a better place, but I've tried and I've failed, and now I don't know if I can. How can I change the world without changing myself in the process?"

Adam took Natasha's hands in his and got down on his knees.

"Natasha, my love," he said, looking into her eyes, "I've been compromised by unseen forces and I've lost my sense of direction. I need you to be my compass and tell me what to do."

Natasha looked into her husband's desperate eyes and her own eyes began to water.

"I don't know if I can, baby," she said, her voice trembling. "It's hard to change some things, even if the will is there. But I promise I'll try, if you promise you'll try."

"I promise," Adam said. "I promise."

Adam put his arm around his wife and the two slowly walked below deck. They locked themselves in the master stateroom and began to plan their new empire.

"Great speech," Karen said after they had left.

"You too," Frank said, putting his arm around her. "I loved the whole 'You are not the boss of me' part. That was very sexy."

"He asked some good questions, though," she said, stepping closer and stroking her hand across Frank's tight abs.

"How can you change the world without changing yourself in the process?"

"You can't. Like Gandhi said, 'You must become the change you want to see in the world,' because the world changes with or without you."

"How about 'I'll promise to change you if you promise to change me?'" she asked, grabbing the bottom of Frank's shirt and slowly pulling it off over his head. She ran her fingers through his soft, black chest hair and looked up as his dark brown eyes met with her green eyes.

"That's one change I can believe in," he said with a smile as he bent down to kiss her lips for the first time. A tiny spark of static electricity shot between their lips as they met, sending a tingling sensation through both of their bodies.

Chapter 10

EARTH'S ATMOSPHERE - On board the ISS

With the electricity out all over the world, billions of people were passing the time by having parties, playing games and getting to know each other a lot better. That night, the hottest sex on Earth wasn't actually on the earth, but hundreds of miles above it.

Astronaut Chuck Wilson had been married twice before, but even his second honeymoon in the Caribbean with his former beauty queen ex-wife was no match for what he was now experiencing. Time and space had slipped away in the steamy embrace of his new lover, Japanese astronaut Mizuho Sakaguchi. He was completely lost in the moment and neither knew nor cared where he was, what time it was, or whether there even was a life beyond this seemingly endless, blissful hedonism.

The two lovers had attempted their first rendezvous the day before inside a large storage closet within the Destiny Laboratory, but their experience had been a bust. Their encounter had been spontaneous, clandestine and un-choreographed, but the physics involved with fornicating in zero gravity had caught them completely off-guard and left them both a little bruised.

In their passion, the two scientists had initially thrown their firm bodies at one another, but had collided in mid-air and separated just as quickly. The harder they pushed together, the harder they flew apart, often crashing against the opposite walls. Newton's three laws of motion dictated that objects in motion tended to stay in motion, that a change in the momentum of one moving body was proportional to the force acting to produce the change, and that for every action, there was an equal and opposite reaction.

Physics, and a total lack of privacy, had thwarted their efforts. Russian cosmonaut Aleksandr Manakova had accidentally barged in and caught them in the act before they could perfect their technique. Chuck and Mizuho were both left embarrassed, frustrated and hornier than ever. He never would have thought from looking at Mizuho that her quiet demeanor, petite figure and ordinary Asian face could conceal the inner sexual passion of a wild tiger.

Self-confidence is an enormous turn-on, he thought. *It's always the quiet ones that surprise you.*

There had been no time for a sequel once the solar flare had been spotted, but after the sun's coronal mass ejection had hit the space station, switched off the power and rendered the entire facility inoperable, there was little else to do and plenty of time to kill.

After checking to make sure the ship was completely adrift, Aleks had sealed the three astronauts inside the Zvezda Service Module to protect them from the sun's radiation, plunging the room into near total darkness. Closing the airlock had created a make-shift Faraday chamber that shielded everything inside from the sun's harmful rays, and it was far easier and more efficient to supply one chamber with oxygen, verses the more than 15 separate habitable chambers on the space station. They would rely on the ISS's momentum to stay in orbit.

Lit only by the glow of a chemical light, the astronauts soon found their bulky space suits cumbersome and frustrating, as most of the advanced features of the suits relied on electricity. Chuck, Aleks and Mizuho had helped each other out of their suits and retreated to separate sleeping closets inside the Zvezda. Each closet was its own metal-lined Faraday chamber for extra protection. They agreed to ration the oxygen supply to conserve as much as possible.

Soon after, Mizuho slipped over to Chuck's closet and tapped lightly on the door.

"Care to do a little scientific experiment?" Mizuho asked coyly. She was completely naked with wild, swirling black hair and had small but perfectly conical, weightless breasts.

"Actually, yes," Chuck said, unzipping his flight suit. "I have a hypothesis I would like to test regarding heat transference and microgravity. Please step inside my laboratory."

Hours later, the two lovers were still engaged in their slow, rhythmic rocking intercourse. Sometimes pressed against a wall, sometimes suspended in mid-air, the lovers held onto each other tightly and continuously and purposefully prolonged their climax. They were discovering a whole new form of Kama Sutra, a magical, weightless Tantric union the earthly world below had never known and could never know.

Thanks to the laws of attraction, as well as the laws of thermodynamics, their naked bodies were creating large amounts of heat and perspiration. The latter formed into tiny droplets that floated about the closet like multi-directional rain in slow-motion. Their miniature spheres of sweat mixed together and periodically splashed against their skin and the walls of their small suite, adding another challenge to their efforts.

She wrapped her arms and legs around his body as he ran his hands slowly down her slippery back and they both simultaneously pushed and pulled together as one. Deprived of light inside their small enclosure, the sensual lovers slipped in and out of consciousness, relinquishing the mind's need for order and logic, as well as their perceptions of self and linear time. Their initial, carnal feelings of desire for one another were eventually superseded by a new, intangible desire to maintain this sacred union in perpetuity.

***

In the fading green glow of the chemical light, Aleks finished reading his book, closed the cover and gave a deep sigh. *No one does melancholy like the Russians,* he thought. *It is true that men and women can allow their pride and vanity to destroy the things they cherish the most.*

In "A Hero of Our Time," Mikhail Lermontov's hero Pechorin had an uncommon ability to get whatever he desired, but once acquired, he quickly became bored with his new toys. His childish desire to seek the unattainable left him perpetually unhappy and unfulfilled, decreased the happiness of those around him and generally left his life devoid of any real purpose.

Aleks gave an involuntary shiver as he rubbed his hands on his arms and kicked his feet together inside his thermal sleeping bag. He checked the time on his cosmonaut chronograph wristwatch and saw that it was half past eleven. The self-winding watch had kept perfect time. *Could it really be that late?* he wondered. *I must have completely lost track of time.*

Aleks held the wristwatch up to his ear and could hear the faint movement of the instrument's tiny gears and self-winding mechanism. *At least something still works,* he thought. *I wonder where we are right now and whether it is safe to come out.*

Aleks pulled out his pencil and journal and began doing quick calculations by hand to determine the International Space Station's approximate position. After a few moments, he determined that the ISS was likely floating over the Middle East, where it was still nighttime. By his calculations, the coronal mass ejection was now entering its 20th hour, making it the largest and longest CME ever recorded. *It has to be almost over,* he thought, putting away his journal and floating out into the main Zvezda compartment.

The chamber was cold, dark and empty. Aleks located a new yellow chemical light and snapped it in half to activate it, filling the chamber with a warm glow. He looked around at the instrumentation and flipped a few switches controlling the compartment's lights, heating system and oxygen regulator. Finding no response, he switched off everything but one row of lights.

Aleks floated over to the sleeping closet that Chuck had chosen and tapped on the door.

"Hello? What is it, Aleks?" Chuck asked from inside.

"Sorry to bother you," Aleks said, "but it is time to get up."

"What time is it?" Chuck's voice asked from inside.

"It is late," he answered. He could hear a murmuring sound from inside the closet.

"Hey Aleks, could you get me a couple of clean towels?" Chuck asked. "I've got a lot of moisture in here."

Aleks found a roll of moisture-absorbent paper towels and tapped on the closet door again.

"Here are your towels," he said. "Did you have an accident?" The door opened a few inches and Chuck's wet hand reached out and grabbed the towels, pulling them inside.

"Thanks," Chuck said, shutting the door. "I'll be out in a minute."

Aleks floated over to the closet where Mizuho had gone and tapped on her door. There was no response. He tapped again a little louder.

"Mizuho?" he asked. "Are you OK? It is time to get up." There still was no response. "Chuck? Have you seen Mizuho?"

Chuck emerged from his closet and zipped up his one-piece blue flight suit, shutting the closet door behind him. He was rubbing a paper towel through his short, damp hair, causing it to spike straight up.

"She's fine," Chuck said. "She just needs a minute. Could you come over here for a moment? I need to ask you something." He floated over to the far end of the compartment, near the airlock, where he was joined by Aleks.

"What is this all about?" Aleks asked as he turned to face Chuck.

"You tell me," Chuck said. "You're the one who got me up."

Behind his back, Mizuho quietly emerged from Chuck's closet, still completely naked. She made eye contact with Chuck and smiled before turning around and quickly floating back to her own sleeping closet. Aleks turned around in time to see Mizuho's bare legs disappear inside the small room. He turned back to face Chuck, who was trying not to smile.

"You had a lot of moisture?" Aleks asked.

"I don't know how else to describe it. It was very hot and wet," Chuck said. "I've never experienced anything like it in all my life. Once we got into a rhythm, it was incredible."

"That sounds intense," Aleks said, checking over his shoulder.

258

Mizuho emerged from her sleeping closet wearing her blue, one-piece flight suit and floated over to Chuck and Aleks. She tied her long black hair back into a bun.

"What's the status?" she asked her two shipmates.

"The solar storm has lasted about 20 hours," Aleks said. "The power is still out, but I imagine it will be restored very soon. I have formulated a plan for how we can restart the space station and restore satellite communications. Here are my notes."

Aleks handed a few pages of his journal to Mizuho and Chuck, who looked them over.

"This looks really thorough," Mizuho said. "You obviously spent a lot of time thinking about this."

"It is sequential," Aleks said. "We have to manually open the Zvezda's solar panels before we can collect enough solar power to open the larger solar arrays. Once the large arrays start collecting power, we can begin turning on everything else."

"Should we get started right away?" Chuck asked.

"First we must wait for the storm to end," he said. "There is something I wish to show you while we wait. It should only take a few minutes."

Aleks reached into a cargo pocket on his flight suit and pulled out an ordinary-looking deck of playing cards and turned it over to show Chuck and Mizuho that it was a normal deck.

"When my sister was five years old, she was very curious about magic," Aleks began. "I was 13 at the time and was the right age for performing magic tricks. Natasha inspired me to learn everything I could about magic and I pushed myself to improve my presentation. I must admit I was quite good for my age, although five year olds are not that hard to fool."

Aleks held the deck perfectly still in front of him and with a playful flourish, he carefully let go, leaving the deck of cards suspended in mid-air.

"Look! It is floating!" he said, waving his hands around the motionless deck of cards. "My sister believed I had super powers when I would make something disappear or levitate, or even appear to levitate. The look on her face was without price. Priceless," he corrected.

He pulled out a black wand with a white tip and slowly moved it clockwise around the cards, being careful not to touch the deck. The cards began to spin in the same direction.

"The real lesson I learned was that all magic is an illusion, created by a magician."

He gently tapped a corner of the deck with his finger, causing it to tumble in mid-air. He slowly brought his wand toward the deck, and when he was within a few inches of it, the deck of cards leaped forward and attached itself to the end of his wand.

"Magic is the art of fooling the brain to make the impossible seem possible," he continued, waving the wand with the deck of cards still firmly attached to the end. "The magician pretends it is real and his spectators believe it, even if they cannot believe it."

Aleks detached the deck off the end of the wand and carefully turned it over again in one hand, showing his audience both sides. Suddenly the deck of cards disappeared. He showed his audience his empty hands.

"How did you do that?" Mizuho asked.

"And your spectators may beg or demand to know the secret, because the mystery is too much for the mind," Aleks continued, pulling out a red handkerchief from his pocket and straightening its corners in front of him to form a square. He quickly yanked the handkerchief away, revealing the deck of cards suspended in air again.

Mizuho smiled and clapped her hands. "How did you do that?" she asked again.

"Magic," he said. "The minute you tell your audience the trick is a loaded die, a stacked deck or box with a false bottom, they will cease to be amused. Once your spectators realize they have been tricked, they may resent you for fooling them so well. It is for this reason alone that a magician must never reveal his secrets," he said, returning the deck of cards to his breast pocket.

"They want to pretend it's real, but if they find out it's not, they blame you," Chuck said.

"All real magic works in this way," Aleks continued. "Once you discover the truth behind a mystery, you can use it to mystify others, but it will never be mysterious for you again."

"Knowledge is power but ignorance is bliss," Chuck said.

"The best audience for a magician is one that wants and chooses to believe the magic is real and does not question how the illusion was achieved," Aleks said, clapping his hands and revealing the deck of cards again. "With a large enough audience, a great magician could rule the world."

Just then, the florescent lights inside the Zvezda flickered on.

"Look! It's magic!" Mizuho cheered, clapping her hands. "Electricity!"

Aleks pressed the main power reset button for the Zvezda Node and turned on the space station's primary computer. After a few seconds, a small computer screen flickered to life, flashing its normal startup routine. Aleks waited patiently as the system attempted to configure itself and establish a connection with the network. This was not possible, because for the moment it was the only operating computer anywhere. There was no network to join.

A computer prompt flashed on the screen in Cyrillic text with Arabic numerals. The three crew members looked at the symbols and instantly recognized the message. It wanted to know the current UTC time — or Universal Time Coordinated — the standard international basis that all nations used to establish global chronological consistency. Neither Chuck nor Mizuho had even a guess as to what time it was at that moment.

Aleks looked down at his analog B-42 Fortis Cosmonaut Chronograph wristwatch and noted the local time in Moscow. It was a quarter to twelve, almost midnight. Aleks subtracted four hours for the Moscow difference and typed in 19:45 into the display and pressed the "enter" key. He set the date as 10 July 2014.

As he and his two comrades began turning on secondary computers and interlinking all of the onboard programs, opening additional solar panels for power and remotely restarting several high-priority military satellites, Aleks reflected that he had just reset modern civilizations's clock. Nearly every satellite, computer and cell phone on Earth and above would base its own clock on the time he had just entered. *That's relativity for you*, he thought.

A short time later, the International Space Station received its first satellite uplink request. The message was from Mecca.

Part Three: Illumination

Chapter 1

MECCA - Saudi Arabia, at the top the Mecca Clock Tower
Friday, July 11, 2014, before dawn

Dressed in his green work coveralls, a tool belt and wearing a black bag across his shoulders, Ibn Ali opened the Abraj Al-Bait Tower's highest service door, 575 meters above the ground. Moonlight spilled into the narrow room, illuminating the darkness with a disorienting glare. Ibn poked his head out into the cool night air and looked for a ladder or step of some kind. It took a moment for his eyes to adjust to the bright light from the full moon before Ibn saw the thin ledge and safety railing surrounding the great crescent. He clipped in his safety harness to one of the exterior fastenings, found his footing and stepped outside. Other than the slight breeze and any noise he made, it was completely silent outside.

Ibn gasped at the view before him and struggled to maintain control over his emotions. Black smoke clouds from dozens of nearby oil well fires had veiled the moon and night sky from below, but at the top of one of the tallest buildings on the planet, Ibn was standing a few meters above the clouds. The full moon lit the top of the clouds, creating a bright canopy of reflected moonlight that blanketed and obscured the view of the ground below. It also greatly diminished his vertigo, but he still didn't want to look down. Looking up instead, he saw the bright moon, surrounded by thousands of crisp, brilliant stars.

It looks like heaven, he thought, checking around to get his bearings. The cloud ceiling was blocking every available landmark below for hundreds of kilometers in every direction, making it difficult to tell which direction he was facing. He needed to point the portable uplink's photovoltaic solar panels at the sunrise. *Which way is east?* He looked up at the stars for answers but realized that he had never personally taken the time to learn the constellations. He had a great app on his smartphone that could identify any planets, stars and constellations just by pointing the device at it, but he hardly ever used it. Now his smartphone wouldn't turn on.

That's the problem with electronics, Ibn thought as he began moving counter-clockwise around the narrow viewing deck, the highest such platform in the world. *The faster they get, the more fuel or battery power they require. The more we use something, the more we come to need and depend on it.* He came back around to the service door and noticed for the first time an intricate, inlaid mosaic on the small circular floor of the platform. The mosaic was of a compass. The hair on his forearms and on the nape of his neck stood up as if electrified.

Ibn backtracked clockwise to a built-in metal rung ladder stretching up the last few meters of the spire to the enormous golden crescent on top. The ancient symbol looked tiny from the ground but was itself 23 meters tall and had the honor of being the world's largest golden minaret. He clipped his safety harness to the bottom of the ladder and took a deep breath. *It's just a few more steps. I've made it this far.* A soft breeze caressed his bearded cheek and he looked up to see the crescent silhouetted against the full moon. He felt calm and completely at peace as he began to climb the maintenance ladder, one rung at a time.

***

Ibn reflected on his amazing morning as he quickly ate an orange and drank the rest of the contents of his water bottle before the day's fasting began. He was back on the 85th floor in the luxurious office and personal apartment of the mosque's imam and the sun was about to rise. Dressed in his black business suit, he looked out a north-facing window of at the vast crowd of pilgrims gathered around the Grand Mosque hundreds of meters below. *There must be more than two million people down there,* he thought, realizing that the Friday morning prayer service during Ramadan was one of the most attended gatherings of the year.

As he looked out over the city, Ibn thought for a moment that the stormy, dark clouds just above were about to unleash a terrible rain on the city. But his rational mind quickly deduced that the black clouds were the smoke from dozens of burning oil wells that had spontaneously caught fire and exploded a day earlier, and had nothing to do with the solar storm. *Well, the storm could have changed the pressure in the pipelines, but all the pipelines should have been turned off by now*, he thought. *Most people don't know this. They are afraid and want guidance.*

Sheik Dr. Hassan bin Ali, president of the Saudi council of advisors and imam of the great Mecca mosque, walked over and stood beside him.

"It is almost time," the imam said in Arabic, looking at the crowd far below.

"We should be about ready to broadcast, your holiness," Ibn replied. "I was able to set up my satellite uplink kit on the crescent at the top of this building and as soon as the solar panels receive enough charge, I can try to establish a connection to a working satellite. Assuming everything works, in a few minutes, your voice will be broadcast to most of the Muslim world."

"Thank you, my son," the imam said. "Your technical prowess is far beyond my comprehension and borders on the miraculous. When I am finished giving the morning prayer, I would like you to say a few words."

"I am honored, your holiness," Ibn said. "Speechless, actually. What should I say?"

"Your knowledge of the Koran, modern science and your philosophy on life and history is a much-needed breath of fresh air," the imam said. "Speak from your mind and from your heart. Tell us what you believe, tell us how we can overcome these formidable challenges, and most of all, give us hope."

"I will do my best, your holiness," Ibn said.

"The sun has broken the horizon," the imam said to the blind muezzin, handing him a microphone. "It will be dawn on the surface in a few moments."

By the time the muezzin had finished singing his opening call to prayer, Ibn had contacted the International Space Station and established a live audio broadcast to the entire world. The imam gave a lengthly sermon in Arabic about hope and courage during times of adversity. Finally it was time for Ibn to take the microphone. The sun had risen high enough to be obscured above the dark clouds and the land below was cast back into a confusing, gloomy twilight.

"In the beginning, man and woman lived together in paradise," Ibn began. "Over time, the Earth pitched and turned, trembled and burned. Sea levels rose and receded. Tropical rain forests turned into swamps, then to seas, then to deserts. Paradise never disappeared; it simply became buried beneath the earth. We are living on top of this paradise, my brothers and sisters, and we always have been."

Two million pairs of ears below fixed themselves on Ibn's voice, and a hundred million more listened via radio.

"This ancient, carbon-rich paradise slowly changed into fossil fuels and is now our region's greatest export," he continued. "Oil has transformed the modern world, but I ask you, has it made the world better? This black gold has made a handful of us princes and a few of us kings, while the rest of us have been left with nothing but sand."

Several small protests erupted from the crowd.

"My friends and brothers, I believe God has sent us a message," Ibn continued.

The crowd began to quiet again.

"We have been fighting against a beast that threatens to consume us," he said. "Every day in a million different ways, this beast poisons our air, pollutes our water and corrupts our souls. We keep feeding the beast to keep it at bay, but it grows bigger and stronger because of our support. It preys upon our weak while the strongest of us do nothing. We shall not fear its attack once we realize that the beast would wither and die without us. Together, let us cut the head off the beast by cutting off our support, and we will watch as the beast consumes itself from within."

A wave of applause spread over the crowd.

"My brothers of Islam and my brothers and sisters of all faiths, we are faced with a very delicate situation," Ibn continued, raising his voice. "The world is changing. We must stand together in our resolve to fix the problems of the world, but most importantly, we must always take care not to replace the beast by becoming it."

Another wave of applause and cheering rippled through the crowd.

"Our greatest enemy has always been ourselves," Ibn shouted, his voice ringing melodiously in the crisp, morning air throughout Mecca and in Arab-speaking homes around the world. "Mohammed, peace be upon him, never told his followers to enslave and exploit the world in his or in God's name, nor did Jesus or Moses or Abraham. I believe that God wants us to love one another, to be happy and to celebrate our relatively short lives in peace and with humility. It has always been man who made himself king and changed 'obey God' into 'obey me.' Man, not God, starts wars for land and resources, and we all suffer the consequences. It is time for us to cast off these ancient shackles of power and control! We are free, and we demand our freedom!"

The vast crowd erupted in cheering. Some began chanting "Ali, Ali, Ali!"

"My brothers, today is our Judgment Day!" Ibn hollered over the crowd. "May God grant us hope and the courage to face our future without fear. God willing, we will give the world peace, balance and justice once more. Our time has come! God be praised!"

The entire city seemed to tremble at the deafening roar of the crowd below. A moment later, the minute hands on the giant Mecca clock's four faces simultaneously struck six o'clock. The deep booming of the clock bells further electrified the crowd.

All at once, the ominous, dark clouds blanketing the area vaporized into thin air, dropping a light mist of oil droplets and carbon dust on the pilgrims and surrounding lands. The pilgrims' white clothes turned instantly black and the skies transformed into a clear, vivid desert blue.

Ibn gasped and quickly switched off the microphone. The imam fell to his knees and began to weep. Ibn dropped to his knees beside him, bowed forward and began to pray, touching his forehead to the floor. The muezzin ran over to the two men, listened for a moment, then fell to his knees and joined in prayer.

When they had finished their prayers, Ibn and the imam both stood up and made eye contact, but neither man wanted to be the first to speak.

"What just happened?" the blind muezzin asked after a moment, still kneeling on the hardwood floor.

"A miracle," the two men said in unison.

Chapter 2

CAMP LEATHERNECK - Helmand Province, Afghanistan
Friday afternoon

Staff Sgt. Timothy Layton took one last look at the barren landscape of southern Afghanistan through his polarized sunglasses and slowly shook his head. *I can't believe it's over,* he thought. Camp Leatherneck was always meant to be a temporary outpost, not a permanent fortress, and now its complete deconstruction was being managed with surprising efficiency.

"Is everything OK, staff sergeant?" asked Lt. David Mayberry as he approached from behind. Both men were fully dressed in their combat gear and were sweating profusely in the 100-degree heat. They each carried a pistol and an M4 carbine assault rifle.

Behind them, thousands of soldiers were pulling down tents, loading crates of materials onto cargo planes and systematically destroying hundreds of tons of classified documents and equipment that couldn't be taken with them and couldn't be left behind.

"There's no green out here, sir," Layton said, turning around to face his superior officer. "Where I come from, we have fir and cedar trees that grow more than 100 feet tall. Everything is lush and green, even in the summer, but that's also because it rains a lot back home."

"Where is home?" Mayberry asked.

"Toledo, Washington," Layton said.

"You're from Ohio?"

"No, Washington."

"Oh, is that in D.C.?"

"No, it's this cute little town of about 700 people, located on a river in the southwestern part of Washington state, about 30 miles from Mount St. Helens. You can't get much smaller and still be a town. I was born and raised there, and now I'm hoping to raise my own family there."

"That sounds nice," Mayberry said. "I'm from West Texas, near Odessa. Actually this place kind of reminds me of home, but I haven't really lived there since I left for college."

"I heard you went to West Point," Layton said. "What was that like, sir?"

"West Point? It's hard to describe. It's sort of like some nineteenth century general's ideal version of the perfect military academy, mixed with futuristic equipment and training. It's extremely intense and fast paced. They crammed about 10 or 15 years of training into four years of college. I just graduated last month and I don't think I've stopped moving in all that time. Speaking of fast-paced settings, have you ever been to New York City?"

"No sir, I'm more of a small-town boy."

"Well, that's where we're headed," Mayberry said. "Get ready for the big city and huge crowds of people. West Point is about 50 miles from New York City and I used to go there quite a bit. You kind of have to see it to believe it. It's hard for me to picture it without electricity."

"Sir, is it true the president declared martial law?" Layton asked. "Are we really going to occupy Wall Street?"

"The U.S. is still under martial law, as are most countries right now," Mayberry said. "A lot has changed in the last two days. That solar flare really shook up our supply lines and removed most or all of our advantages. I was sent here to help with the drawdown of our troops by the end of this year, but things have sped up. The Afghans don't want us here any more and we don't want to be here, but it's much larger than that. The Chinese don't want us here, the Russians don't want us here, the Iranians don't want us here, and don't let me forget to mention our neighbors in Turkmenistan, Tajikistan, Uzbekistan, Kyrgyzstan and the entire Muslim world. I heard a broadcast in Arabic this morning that sounded almost revolutionary."

"Do you think we should be pulling out so soon?"

"I think we need to get out while we still can," Mayberry said frankly. "The people of New York need us a lot more than the Afghans do right now. Our work here is done."

"Sir, I wanted to thank you again for your help yesterday at the eastern gate," Layton said, slowly rubbing his hands together. He still had no feeling in his right hand.

"I'm just glad I could help, sergeant," Mayberry said. "Sometimes we must be warriors, while other times we must be diplomats and interpreters. It can be very difficult to separate logic from emotion, especially following a tragedy like the attack on your convoy the other day. How are you and your men handling it?"

"I know some of the men are still quite shaken, sir. We were on a peacekeeping mission when we were hit and had no choice but to defend ourselves and fight back. The whole concept of fighting against insurgents is very confusing. You don't know if someone is a friend or enemy until they try to kill you. How can we keep the peace and be diplomatic when the people we're protecting can turn on us at any minute?"

"That's a very good question," Mayberry said. "Trust can take years to build and only seconds to destroy. I think the key element to building and maintaining trust is to keep things on a human level. We're all human beings here, and we should always respect that fact. It's easy for the Afghans to think of us as Martian invaders when we dress up in identical camouflage and body armor, don't speak their language and seem to shoot anything that moves. When I found you at the eastern gate yesterday, it looked like that mob was just about ready to shoot them some Martians. Once I started speaking to them in their native tongue and treated them with sympathy and respect, the mood quickly changed."

"That was pretty amazing, sir," Layton said. "I've never seen anything like that. You disarmed an angry mob using nothing but kind words."

"And promises to leave when peace is restored, which is what we're doing now," he said.

"Sir, did you already know that we were going to leave when you promised that boy's mother that we would pack up our camp and go?" Layton asked.

"It wouldn't be much of a promise if I didn't know whether I could keep it. That's part of the trust I was telling you about. As long as the people you're trying to protect trust you and believe that you will protect them, they will support you. If they think you're trying to manipulate and control them, they will rebel against your authority. Our next assignment is similar in nature. We will be helping the New York Police Department keep eight million people safe, fed and protected from the few bad apples that will inevitably try to shake things up. We will stay there for as long as we're needed and hopefully not a minute longer. Martial law is not a natural part of democracy. Our own countrymen could turn on us just as quickly as the Afghans if we overstay our welcome."

Behind them, the mechanics working on the engine of a Lockheed C-130 Hercules transport plane yanked on a make-shift belt, causing the engine to cough and sputter to life. Corporal Linfield jogged over from the plane to the two men and snapped to attention.

"Corporal?" Layton yelled as the transport plane's engines began to grow louder.

"We're ready to roll, sergeant," Linfield shouted over the noise of the engines.

"Sir, we're ready to roll," Layton shouted, snapping to attention and saluting Mayberry.

"Let's roll," Mayberry shouted, returning the salute and following his men into the back of the large plane. The inside was filled with hundreds of Marines sitting in rows on the floor. Mayberry continued walking to the front of the plane.

"Hey, do y'all know if anybody on the plane speaks Russian?" Mayberry asked as he buckled himself into a seat near the cockpit. "That's gonna come in handy real soon."

A few minutes later, the enormous airplane sped down the runway, tilted its flaps and lifted itself into the sky. Once airborne, the Hercules turned north, in route to the United States via the north pole, flying over Turkmenistan, Kazakhstan and Russian airspace.

Chapter 3

TOLEDO, Wash. - 251 Layton Rd.
Saturday morning, "Cheese Day"

"OK, try it now!" the 68-year-old man shouted as he ran behind the rolling, rusted-out pickup truck he was pushing down his driveway. In the driver's seat, Maud Layton pushed in the clutch and shifted the transmission from neutral to second gear, then let out or "popped" the clutch, forcing the engine to start by compression.

Bob watched as his brown, 1974 Ford F-100 pickup coughed and sputtered down the driveway with his wife at the wheel.

"That's more like it," Bob said to himself as he slowed to a stop and caught his breath.

When she reached the end of the driveway, Maud turned the truck around and brought it back to collect Bob, their vegetables and other farm produce for sale at the Saturday market. Maud left the engine running as she got out of the cab and helped Bob load their supplies, then got in the passenger side so Bob could drive. Bob put his diesel generator in the bed of the truck.

"Nice job popping the clutch," Bob said as he climbed in the driver's seat. "This truck might be a piece of crap, but we still got it running without a battery. That's saying something."

Maud looked over at Bob and smiled but didn't say anything. The truck was Bob's pampered pet and she knew he was feeling pretty vindicated about his stubborn preference for older technology. She preferred to drive their much more fuel-efficient hybrid vehicle, but like everything else electric, it had failed to turn on after the solar storm.

Bob and Maud drove into town a few minutes later, passing dozens of cars and trucks stalled on the side of the road and abandoned by their owners. They did not pass another moving vehicle until they got to town. Bob turned on the truck's radio.

"This is a special message of the Emergency Alert System," a recorded message began. "Please tune your radio to 103.1 FM to hear an updated alert message." The message repeated.

Maud adjusted the radio dial to 103.1, twisting the nob through rising and falling waves of static. There was no music. She reached the emergency broadcast message mid-sentence.

"... cyber attack or terrorist attack. Emergency crews are currently updating and repairing critical infrastructure, but caution that repairs must be done locally and could take weeks or months to complete. Martial law remains in effect in most areas, although the midnight curfew has been lifted in many rural areas. Air travel remains restricted nationwide. Thank you for your cooperation. This message will now repeat from the beginning. This is a special message of the Emergency Alert System. United States government officials are attributing this week's widespread power outages to severe space weather. On Wednesday morning, our sun released a massive burst of electrically charged plasma known as a coronal mass ejection. When this burst of ionized energy reached the earth at approximately 4:32 p.m. Pacific time, it disrupted and temporarily disabled our planet's electro-magnetic field. The solar storm has ended and electrical and communications systems are already in the process of being restored. Government officials would like to emphasize that this week's geomagnetic super storm was a natural disaster affecting every country on earth and is not the result of a cyber attack or terrorist attack. Emergency crews are currently updating and repairing critical infrastructure ..."

Bob parked the truck in the shade near City Hall, turned off the radio and walked over to the middle school, passing by dozens of runners lined up in front of the fire station for the start of the annual "Cheddar Challenge" morning run. Maud went next door to the senior center to offer her considerable cooking skills for the large breakfast the community provided every year.

As he approached the football field next to the Toledo Middle School, Bob was surprised to see dozens of classic cars already waiting in line to register for the annual Toledo Cheese Days classic car show. The whole area was still without electricity, telephone, Internet or cell phone service since the solar storm a few days earlier, but that didn't seem to stop the old timers from showing off their toys.

Bob walked past the cars on his way to the registration desk and recognized the make and model of nearly every vehicle. There was a yellow, 1939 Ford Roadster; a red, 1958 Ford Fairlane 500 Skyliner; a bright red, 1967 Pontiac GTO; a white, 1959 Chevy Corvette; a black and flame-licked, 1928 Ford 'A' Tudor sedan; a green and gold, 1966 Ford Mustang fastback; a light-blue, 1955 Ford Thunderbird; a maroon and silver, 1935 Chevrolet coupe; a white, 1957 Pontiac Star Chief two-door; a jet black, 1941 Cadillac; a burgundy-colored, 1933 DeSoto four-door sedan; a classic black 1923 Ford Model T and a red and white, 1955 Chevrolet Bel Air soft-top convertible, all in pristine condition.

"Did you have trouble with your alarm clock this morning?" teased Steve Drake, one of Bob's longtime friends and a fellow Lions Club member, as Bob approached. Bob and Steve were wearing nearly identical white T-shirts that said Toledo Cheese Days 2014 on the back and had their first names written in red capital letters on the left breast. Hundreds of other Toledo locals were wearing matching shirts, making it very easy to remember everyone's name.

"Nope," Bob said. "The rooster woke me up at dawn, same time as always. I haven't seen too many cars on the road and wasn't sure the car show was still on."

"I heard on the radio that this week's solar storm disrupted or disabled just about every computer or electronic device, including most cars made after 1974," Steve said.

"That include emergency vehicles?" Bob asked, looking up at the clear blue sky. He heard a distant, growing rumble and tried to locate its source. And then he saw them.

Dozens of military transport planes and helicopters were approaching the town from the north in a "V" formation, filled with thousands of soldiers and reservists. It was a frightening display of force, and Bob's first thought was that Toledo was being attacked.

As the aircraft rumbled loudly overhead, Bob recognized the outline of several of the planes and helicopters, including a Boeing C-17 Globemaster III; several twin-engine, tandem rotor, heavy-lift Boeing CH-47D Chinook helicopters; a Lockheed C-130 Hercules; several Bell Boeing V-22 Osprey tilt-rotor aircraft and several AH-64 Apache attack helicopters serving as escorts. He quickly deduced that it was far more likely the aircraft were headed south to California, where they could provide emergency support to local law enforcement and emergency response teams.

"Yeah, I think so," Steve said, after the airplanes and helicopters had flown over and it was quiet again. "Come to think of it, I haven't seen a cop since Wednesday. Most machines that have computer components need electricity to run, although some can be forced to start without it. I'm assuming since you're here that you got your truck started."

"We did," Bob said. "Maud and I pushed her down the driveway and popped the clutch, which worked like a charm. We're parked over by City Hall."

Steve handed a registration form to the gray-haired driver of a green and gold, 1966 Ford Mustang fastback and directed the driver to park in one of the spots painted on the grassy football field.

"Well, I guess Cheese Day is officially on, even without electricity," Bob said. "I brought along my diesel generator just in case we need it."

"You should see if Rick or Dave need to use it," Steve said, handing a registration form to the driver of a maroon and silver, 1935 Chevrolet coupe.

"I passed by Rick's on the way here and I think he's got his own generator going to power the gas pumps," Bob said.

"Someone has gas for sale?" asked the driver of the three-window coupe.

"Rick's gas station downtown, just before you get to the bridge," Steve said.

"I hope you brought plenty of cash," Bob said. "Gas is up more than a dollar a gallon and probably won't come down again till this fall. I'm glad I filled up a few days ago."

"Here's my form and entry fee," the driver of the coupe said, handing the paper and cash back to Steve. "I'm going to go fill up while I still can. Save my place for me, will you?"

"Sure thing, buddy," Steve said as the the classic coupe turned around and headed out of the parking lot and down the hill. He noticed the coupe had Oregon license plates.

"Can you think of anyone who might need electricity this morning?" Bob asked.

Steve thought for a moment as he continued to hand out registration fliers to the cars in line. Up next was the yellow, 1939 Ford Roadster.

"There's a pancake breakfast at the senior center," Steve said. "You could pop by City Hall and the firehouse while you're there. I should be fine here if you want to scope things out."

"That's a good idea," Bob said. "I'll be back."

Bob walked back over to the senior center and saw more than 50 people in line for fresh pancakes, sausage and biscuits and gravy. Unfortunately, the kitchen ran on electricity, like almost everything else. Bob fired up his generator and provided power to the center, and his reward was one of the first plates of Maud's famous pancakes, delicious and hot off the grill.

***

Toledo's annual Cheese Day parade began at 11 a.m., led by a green and yellow, 1914 John Deere tractor. More than 2,000 people attended the parade, including hundreds of candy-catching children lining the sidewalks on either side of the parade route. The crowd cheered as wave after wave of tractors, classic cars, antique fire trucks, log trucks and horse-drawn floats meandered down Augustus Street, followed by the high school marching band.

After the parade, thousands of tourists gathered at the middle school to check out the classic cars, visit with old friends and classmates, and bask in the splendor and nostalgia of small-town life. Most of the tourists were former Toledo residents and their families who had traded their quiet lives working on farms for exciting lives in big cities like Seattle and Portland.

Several former residents said they wished they could move back to Toledo, but it seemed like all the jobs were in big cities, along with the traffic, criminals, fast-food franchises and shopping malls. Other than Cheese Day weekend, there wasn't much happening in Toledo.

***

That evening, after the car show had finished, Steve and Bob sat back in a couple of lawn chairs in the shade of a large commercial tent and watched as the various families walked past. Dozens of children and teenagers rode around on bicycles, skateboards and in-line roller skates. Bob noticed that for the first time in years, no one was playing with an electronic gadget.

"Turns out we didn't need power after all," Steve said, handing a can of beer to Bob. "Not sure how long this will last before chaos erupts, though. This is the last case of beer from the store."

"They're out of beer?" Bob asked, cracking open his beer and taking a long swig.

"They're out of everything," Steve said. "The Cheese Day crowd cleaned them out."

"We sold out at the farmer's market today, too," Bob said. "It always surprises me how much money some people will pay for organic food, when it's so easy to grow. The problem is that most people don't appreciate the amount time and skill it takes to make a delicious meal from food they grow themselves. People want fast food and instant gratification. You make things too easy and suddenly people get lazy. They take things for granted. Nobody wants to get their hands dirty putting in the time and effort to grow their own food or make their own clothes from scratch because it's too easy and convenient to simply let someone else do it for them."

"Right," Steve said. "Why not let China and Wal-Mart do all the dirty work?"

"I don't blame people for bargain-hunting, but big-box stores like Wal-Mart, Target or the dollar stores have run just about every small business around here out of business," Bob said. "Most of the stuff they sell is junk, but we still can't compete with their prices. What'll we do if China cuts us off one day and the Wal-Marts across America are suddenly empty?"

Bob waved at an enormous, tall, muscular man who was pushing a baby stroller and walking by with his wife and three other children in tow. The man waved back.

"Good to see you again," Bob said.

"Likewise, sir," the man said. "Think I need to follow your lead and take it easy."

"Oh, we're just getting started," Steve said, taking a sip of beer.

After the young man and his family had walked out of earshot, Bob and Steve started gossiping about him.

"That boy was a powerhouse in high school," Bob said. "You remember when he played linebacker? He was such a force of nature, the other teams' coaches said they would plan their offense around him 'cause he could stop just about any play that came his way."

"I heard he hurt his knees in college," Steve said. "That was it for his career."

"Where did he go to college?"

"Somewhere in California, I think. I'm not sure where he's living now. Did you see his kids? I bet his boys will play ball someday like their dad. How's your boy, by the way?"

Bob finished his beer and crushed the empty can in his hands.

"We talked with Tim on Wednesday and he was still in Afghanistan," Bob said.

"How long is his tour?"

"Six months, I think. Hopefully he'll be back for the fall school year. He missed the entire baseball season this year."

Steve finished his beer, crushed the can and grabbed two more, handing one to Bob. The two men sat in silence for a few minutes, enjoying Toledo's best weekend for people-watching.

"You know, there may be a lot you can't do without electricity, but there are some things you can *only* do without electricity," Bob said after a while.

"You mean like rob a bank?" Steve asked.

"Maybe if we were bank robbers," Bob said. "Too many people know us in town. We'd never get away with it. I was thinking of something that's a little less risky and complicated."

"What did you have in mind?" Steve asked.

"How about a drag race?" Bob suggested. "Who do you think has the fastest ride here?"

"Shoot, there are several hot rods here that are screaming fast," Steve said. "I'd probably put my money on one of the muscle cars from the '60s and '70s, like a Corvette, or a Cobra, Camaro or Chevelle. Maybe a Mustang. Where would they race?"

"The Toledo airport is still closed, right? I haven't seen any civilian air traffic for days. The airport has a pretty long runway and it's not too far from town."

"Let me ask around," Steve said, standing up. "Let's try to keep this on the down-low."

***

An hour later, Steve, Bob and about five other guys were standing at one end of the Ed Carlson Memorial Field, looking down the 4,479-foot runway. Next to them were several older muscle cars, including a metallic blue, 1966 Cobra and a bright-red, 1966 Corvette that were slated to race first. Both muscle cars had massive 427 cubic centimeter engines, each producing a staggering 425-horsepower force.

The evening skies were clear of clouds and air traffic as two middle-aged, pony-tailed drivers started their engines. Bob had $10 on the Corvette to win, while Steve was rooting for the Cobra. Steve walked out in front between the two cars and raised a make-shift starting flag. The two drivers revved their engines.

Steve quickly lowered the flag and the two muscle cars roared as they tore off down the runway, neck and neck, leaving behind a substantial cloud of blue smoke and exhaust.

Bob couldn't tell which car had won until they reached the end of the runway and turned around a few seconds later. The red Corvette turned around first, followed by the Cobra.

"That's what pure beauty looks like, my friend," Bob said as Steve slapped a $10 bill into his hand. "Best two out of three?" he asked as he added the ten to a fat wad of cash he had made from the farmer's market.

Chapter 4

LONDON - 260 Devonia Rd., Islington, England
Sunday morning

Jacob Baker was playing goalie for Manchester United, fending off an assault by a rival team, when he was awoken from his dream.

"Jacob, sweetie, it's time to get up," his mom called.

The 16-year-old boy rolled over in his bed and groaned, but didn't get up.

"Come on, Jacob, let's get up," his mom said a minute later.

"It's Sunday and it's summer. Everything's closed," Jacob mumbled.

"We're going to church this morning," Leah Baker said. "Get up and get dressed."

"Church?" Jacob asked. "We never go to church."

"Well, we're going today. Let's get up. And wear something nice."

He thought for a moment about his dream and looked over at the large poster of the Manchester United football team hanging on one of his bedroom walls. He looked back at the Big Ben clock on the opposite wall. It still said it was half past twelve.

Jacob sat up in bed and ran his fingers through his greasy hair. *I would bet the power is still off,* he thought. *I should shower, but there's probably no water pressure if there's no electricity.* He got up and walked to the bathroom. The light switch did not respond, nor did the sink faucet. After relieving himself into the sink, Jacob checked out his reflection in the mirror. He grabbed a comb and some hair gel and sculpted his messy hair back away from his face into a fashionable pompadour. *Not bad,* he thought.

Crossing back to his bedroom, Jacob put on a pair of khakis, a white dress shirt, a blue and red, diagonally striped tie and his navy-blue sports jacket with the crest of his school on the breast pocket.

"You look nice," Leah said as Jacob emerged from his bedroom a few minutes later. She was wearing a very cute, light green summer dress with a yellow and white flower pattern.

"Thanks, Mum. So do you. So what's the occasion again?"

"We're going out and I want us to look nice," she said. "I know we don't usually go to church, but this has been a crazy week. I think we should be thankful that we're still here. We're going all the way to St. Paul's, so make sure you wear comfortable shoes."

Finding food and drinking water had been challenging. Leah had gone to a local farmer's market on Friday morning only to find all the food gone. One of the first people to arrive had purchased everything at double the usual prices. Leah searched everywhere for available food and ended up raiding the vending machines in her office building in the financial district. On Saturday, thousands of people arrived early at the same farmer's market and found the same situation as the previous morning. One wealthy person had purchased all the available food and supplies and was having it sent somewhere else. The crowd of hungry Londoners nearly rioted as they commandeered the food and redistributed it among themselves, but there still wasn't enough for everyone. Luckily Leah and Jacob still had some food leftover from Friday.

After a quick breakfast of potato chips and candy bars, Jacob and his mom headed south along Duncan Terrace in the bright, morning sunshine. Jacob put on sunglasses and Leah wore a floppy, cream-colored hat. As they approached the nearest London Underground tube station, they noticed the stairway to the subway was shut and locked with a metal gate. A sign informed them that all the city's mass transit systems were still offline until further notice. They checked out a large street map of the area that was hanging by the terminal and looked around to get their bearings. Once they determined which direction was north and south, they plotted their course. Goswell Road would take them almost directly to St. Paul's Cathedral in the City district. As they continued walking, Leah and Jacob began to talk.

"If you don't mind me asking, how's Kendra doing?" Leah asked. "Were you able to find her the other day?"

"I was," Jacob said. "I had to be Sherlock Holmes for a bit and collect clues, but eventually I was able to track her down with a little help from my friends. I found out that Kendra lives in Bloomsbury, near London University. Her parents are both professors there, which is probably why she's so smart."

"That's fortunate. And Bloomsbury is close to Islington. Are you seeing her again?"

"We're supposed to meet tomorrow at the British Museum," he said.

"Ah, a proper date. Sounds like she has culture. I didn't think you liked museums."

As Jacob and Leah crossed Old Street, Goswell Road turned into Aldersgate Street. Most of the shops along the way were either shuttered or looted and they had yet to see a moving vehicle anywhere. Large piles of garbage were beginning to pile up in the middle of the streets where they would ripen and cook in the morning sun.

"That's what I told her, but she insisted that the British Museum was her favorite place in the whole city. She said she would show me all the best stuff."

"You don't sound that excited."

"I'm excited to see her again; I'm just not that keen on looking at a bunch of statues and paintings of old, dead people."

"There's more than that, trust me. It's history," Leah said. "Our history."

"History is boring. Why should I care about what happened to some dead guy a thousand years ago or some old building that doesn't exist anymore? It's all a jumble of dates and names that don't mean anything to me."

As they approached the Museum of London at the intersection of Aldersgate Street and London Wall, Jacob could see the glowing white dome of St. Paul's Cathedral poking above the

City's financial district. Leah stopped for a moment next to an historical marker.

"Jake, honey, take a look at this for a moment," she said. "This street was once an enormous stone wall that surrounded the Roman city of Londinium about 2,000 years ago."

"Londinium?"

"Ancient London, built by the Romans during the time of Julius Caesar. Part of the original wall is still here. You have heard of Caesar, haven't you?"

"Everybody's heard of Julius Caesar, Mum," Jacob said. "It looks like an old brick wall."

"A very old brick wall," she said, taking a flier and checking the Museum of London's schedule. The museum didn't open for another hour, so Leah and Jacob kept walking south, crossing into the City district. The brochure said the vast majority of the area's buildings were classical stone-covered banks, financial institutions, governmental buildings and churches. The district had no major residential areas, making it a deserted ghost town on the weekends.

"London's position on the Thames River has made it a very busy port since its foundation," Leah read from the leaflet. "Like other early European cities, as London expanded, it eventually outgrew its protective walls. But even today, a few pieces of the old city remain."

"Whoa, look at all those people!" Jacob said when they got to the churchyard.

There were at least 50,000 people on the grounds surrounding the cathedral. Many were sitting on chairs or colorful blankets spread out over the lawn, talking and watching people and children playing in the morning sun. Church volunteers were handing out free bread and water to parishioners at a long table on the lawn. As they worked their way through the bread line, dozens of strangers recognized Leah and Jacob from their viral video that no longer existed and tried to make small talk. Afterwards, they found a separate line to get into the cathedral and joined the queue. After the 8 a.m. sermon finished, thousands of churchgoers poured out and Jacob and his mom followed the line inside through the main entrance at the West Porch.

Jacob was astonished by the cool, bright, orderly and spacious interior. Every surface was either cream-colored polished stone, clear glass or some form of intricately carved Baroque ornamentation. He picked up an historical brochure and read a few facts about the cathedral as they followed the procession to their seats to wait for the 10:15 services to begin. As he crossed the threshold directly beneath the inner dome, Jacob saw an epitaph for someone named Wren.

"Mum, who was Chris Wren?" Jacob whispered once he and Leah had taken their seats next to a pair of talkative, well-dressed English ladies wearing elaborate hats. Leah was surprised by her son's question and thought for a moment before answering.

"Christopher Wren was the engineer and architect of this cathedral, as well as about 50 other churches in the area," she whispered. "He redesigned and rebuilt St. Paul's after the Great Fire of 1666."

"The Great Fire?" Jacob whispered. He looked back at the historical brochure. It said an enormous fire swept through the City of London in September of 1666. The fire demolished most of the city's buildings, including the old St. Paul's, which had been in existence in some form since the year 604. The brochure had an excerpt from an eyewitness account at the time.

"The stones of St. Paul's flew like grenades, the lead melting down the streets in a stream ... God grant mine eyes may never behold the like ... Above 10,000 homes all in one flame, the noise and crackling and thunder of the impetuous flames, the shrieking of women and children, the hurry of the people, and the fall of the towers, houses and churches was like an hideous storm."

The brochure said the City was eventually rebuilt and prospered for centuries, but it was destroyed again, most recently in 1940, during the German bombing raids of World War II. Miraculously, St. Paul's survived the Blitz with minimal damages.

Jacob thought about the damages caused by the recent solar storm and realized that a loss of electricity paled in comparison to a Nazi bombing raid, the huge fire that incinerated the city in 1666 or the bubonic plague that killed nearly 100,000 Londoners the previous year, in 1665. As he waited for the services to begin, Jacob turned over the brochure and read the back.

St. Paul's had several famous persons buried in its crypt, most notably the poet John Donne, T.E. Lawrence of Arabia, Florence Nightingale and the aforementioned Mr. Wren. Jacob read the short biography on each and was surprised to find he vaguely recognized their names.

The Anglican preacher spoke for nearly an hour about faith, hope and humility, quoting passages from Romans, Proverbs, Matthew, Luke and Revelation, among others. When he had finished, they passed around a collection plate, the congregation sang a few hymns and everyone quietly exited the cathedral. Once outside, the churchgoers burst into conversation as they walked past the long line waiting to come inside.

"Do you think that helped?" Jacob asked his mother after they had exited the church.

"What do you mean?" she asked. "Do I think attending church helped to save London and restore electricity? Probably not, but it made me feel a little better about things. How did it make you feel?"

"It felt irrelevant, or rather, it made me feel irrelevant," he said. "I wasn't really sure what the priest was talking about half the time, whether it was literal or allegorical, and almost nothing he said seemed to apply to my daily life or experiences. It seemed like a lot of the people knew each other, but I didn't know anyone there. Also, I didn't understand the purpose of all the rituals. I did enjoy reading the brochure about Christopher Wren and the Great Fire."

"That's probably my fault for not taking you to church more often," she said. "If you go often, the community and rituals can be comforting and the stories become timeless, but I think some of the values need updating, like the parts about unwed mothers being stoned to death."

"Is that why we don't go every Sunday?"

"You can go to church any time you want, honey," Leah said. "I go whenever I want, which isn't too often. Where would you like to go next? The Museum of London or the Tower of London?"

"Whichever one has the best architecture, weapons and dirty history."

"The Tower it is," Leah said with a wide smile.

Chapter 5

HAMILTON, Bermuda - Fifteen miles west of the island in the Atlantic Ocean, Monday morning

"Good morning, sleepy," a young woman's voice called out, rousing Adam Morgan from his slumber.

"What time is it?" he asked, keeping his eyes closed. "I was having a good dream."

He tried to remember the dream he had been in a moment before. *There was gold,* he recalled. *I was sitting on a golden throne in a golden hall, wearing a golden crown.*

"It's time to wake up," the woman's familiar voice cooed sweetly. "I want to show you something."

Adam opened his eyes. He was lying on a soft bed in a small, comfortable room. The curved walls and ceiling were polished teak, and he could see blue sky through an elliptical porthole window nearby. The room was gently rocking as little spots of light danced about the cabin like a disco ball. He could hear a faint, rhythmic splashing sound coming from nearby.

Adam turned to his wife. Natasha was resting on her knees next to him on the bed, gazing at him expectantly. She was wearing the famous diamond-covered fantasy bra that towered over Times Square, and nothing else. Her fluffy, brown hair had turned blonde in the summer sun, and her skin was darker and a little sunburned on her nose, lips, shoulders and arms. She was not wearing any make up, yet she was still undeniably sexy. Adam gazed into his wife's blue eyes and smiled. She returned his smile, revealing her naturally large, white teeth.

"I've got a surprise for you, Mr. Morgan," she said, arching her back so that her diamond brassiere caught the sunlight coming through the porthole, sending a rainbow of tiny lights dancing around the cabin. "This will be better than your dream, I promise."

"It feels like I'm still dreaming," Adam said, sitting up in bed. "What day is it?"

"Does it matter?" Natasha asked, pushing Adam back down on the bed and pulling away the dark green sheets to expose his lean, muscular body. She leaned in and kissed his lips, then moved down his body, gently kissing his reddened cheeks, shoulders, collarbone and chest.

Adam had also gotten quite sunburned a few days earlier, but Natasha's kisses felt cool on his skin. The pain from the burn was mostly gone and his skin was already beginning to turn into a nice tan. His face and head were covered with salt-and-pepper whiskers, giving him a darker and more mysterious appearance. The limited diet on the *Reciprocity* and the abundance of physical activity had sculpted the bodies of the crew members better than any personal trainer could have. At his wife's insistence, Adam had also quit drinking alcohol and was now in the best physical shape he had been in years.

"This is your reward for good behavior," she said. "Keep up the good work."

This sure beats a hangover, he thought as Natasha climbed on top of him. Adam slid his hands along his wife's back and was about to unclasp and remove the custom-made fantasy bra, but thought better of it. *So far, this is the perfect morning,* he thought as he gently slid his hands further down her back and across her thin, muscular thighs. *Why mess with the perfect fantasy?*

***

After their morning workout, Adam and Natasha got dressed and climbed the stairs to the main deck, where it was warm and sunny.

Frank was standing at the helm, monitoring the colorful, nylon spinnaker sail as it pulled the craft forward with additional speed, bringing the *Reciprocity* up to about 12 knots. Karen was lounging on deck, flipping through an illustrated field guide to the birds of North America.

Adam checked the time on his wristwatch. It said it was half past seven.

"Morning, everyone," Adam said as he stood on deck and squinted his eyes at the clear, blue sky above. "What's new?"

"Karen made fresh coffee and I made landfall about an hour ago," Frank said, pointing to the bow.

Beneath the spinnaker and just to the right of the rising sun, Adam and Natasha saw a small nub of land poking upwards from an endless expanse of clear, blue water.

"Is that Bermuda?" Natasha asked.

Frank looked at Natasha for a moment then yawned, stretching his arms outward.

"Bermuda's the only thing out here, right?" Adam asked. Frank nodded his head.

"We should arrive in about an hour," Frank said, yawning again. "Excuse me," he said after he had finished yawning. "I think I might need another cup of your coffee, Karen."

"I'm happy to take the wheel for a bit while you get a little rest," Adam offered.

"Thanks, Adam," Frank said, stepping aside and allowing Adam to approach the helm. "Just keep her pointed at the island. I have a few things to take care of before we reach land. Would either of you care for some coffee?"

"I would love a cup, thanks," Adam said.

"Water, please," Natasha said, walking over and sitting down next to Karen. "Whatcha reading?" she asked, looking over Karen's shoulder as she flipped through pages of illustrations of birds. Both women were within earshot of Adam's position at the bridge.

Karen looked up from her field guide. Natasha's habit of asking the obvious could get tiring at times, but Karen was beginning to realize that Natasha was smarter than she looked. Her approach of asking obvious questions could make her seem a little dim, but it was also disarming and reassuring, particularly on men who liked to feel smart, and it often opened the door to a more in-depth conversation. Karen assumed Natasha was just trying to be friendly.

"Birds," Karen said, turning the book so Natasha could see the pictures better.

"There's so many of them," Natasha said. "How do you tell them apart?"

"It's a little overwhelming at first when you're trying to identify a particular species and you don't know where to start. All the birds sort of look the same to the untrained eye. You have to go 'it's not that one,' turn the page, go 'it's not that one' again, turn the page and so on."

"That sounds really slow and frustrating," Natasha said.

"It is at first, but Frank says it's like learning anything — whether it's identifying plants, birds, mushrooms, sailing yachts or designer shoes — it helps to pay close attention to subtle details like color, shape, size, family and habitat. The more attention I pay to details, the easier it becomes for me to eliminate the wrong birds and narrow down my search."

"I have an app on my iPET that can do all that in an instant," Natasha said. "I just point my tablet at the bird or car or plant, take a picture, and within seconds, the program tells me exactly what I'm looking at. It's way easier than having to memorize a huge book."

"How's your iPET working out?" Karen asked. "I don't see you using it."

"The battery's still dead," she said.

"That's too bad," Karen said, turning a page to reveal a large illustration filled with different types of gulls in various life stages. "We'll probably see some of these today."

Frank came up the stairs from the galley with a mug of hot coffee and two water bottles.

"Here you go, sir," Frank said as he handed the coffee to Adam, then turned and walked toward Natasha and Karen.

"Ladies? May I interest you in some water?" Frank asked as he held out the two bottles.

"Oh, thank you, Franklin," Karen said playfully. "You're such a gentleman. I was just telling Natasha what you said about how an astute attention to detail and a simple process of elimination can help one to identify just about anything. Then

Natasha said she had an app that can do all that in an instant, after she finds a way to recharge her battery."

"Ah, the old dead battery problem," Frank said, handing the other water bottle to Natasha. "A contemporary concern, it is. I think we should be able to fix you up today. Just before dawn, I saw lights on the horizon, coming from Bermuda."

"Electricity?" Natasha asked.

"Bingo. Bermuda's an island," Frank said. "They have to produce their own power. They get hit by storms all the time and are probably accustomed to power outages. After we clear customs, we can look for somewhere to hook up and literally recharge our batteries."

Frank paused for another big yawn.

"Excuse me, I think I need to recharge my batteries," Frank continued. "You are all welcome to peruse my library. I don't have every book ever written, but I do have a pretty good collection. Having said that, a library's not much use unless you actually use it. I think that's the main difference between having access to knowledge and having actual, personal knowledge. True knowledge plus experience equals wisdom, but a library alone can't give wisdom to the uninterested mind. The more I learn about the world, the more I realize how much I don't know. I only know what I know, but I can also learn and adapt as I go along.

"It's humbling, really," Frank continued, stifling another yawn. "I think technology can be extremely useful and convenient, provided that everything is working properly, as designed. When it's not, it's a huge hassle. If it doesn't work when you need it to, that convenience is matched by the inconvenience of figuring out a backup plan. When you live and work in a harsh environment like a sailing vessel, where things are breaking down all the time, it's extremely useful to know how to do things manually. GPS is a perfect example. As long as it's working, you can never get lost, but if you don't know how to get to where you're going without it, you really are lost without it. A surprisingly large number of people can't even read a map."

"I'm impressed you were still able to get us here in a couple of days without GPS, a compass or modern navigational aides," Adam said. "I wouldn't have had a clue what to do."

"I think you would if you were a sailor," Frank said. "You're just out of your element. I have nearly a decade of experience sailing in a wide range of environments and situations. My knowledge and experiences inform my intuition, so that when the GPS fails and the compass fails, I still have a sense of direction. I really think electricity is the Achilles heel of modern civilization. Now if you'll excuse me, I could really use a quick cat nap before we arrive. I don't want to bore you with any more speeches, but the key take-away is that too much reliance on technology can be a serious crutch."

"Thanks, Frank," Adam said. "Enjoy your nap. We'll wake you before we arrive."

"Bye, Frank!" Karen cheered as Frank walked below deck.

"Thanks for the water bottle," Natasha said as an afterthought. "He sure does like to give speeches, doesn't he?"

"I admit I kind of enjoy listening to his perspective on things," Adam said. "Has he told you girls the story of the banker and the fisherman?"

Natasha and Karen looked at each other and shook their heads.

"Tell us," Natasha said. "We love stories."

"It's a pretty inspiring tale," Adam began. "Frank told me this a few days ago, and it goes something like this: There was a young man. He could be from anywhere. Since he was a boy, this man always dreamed of being a fisherman and one day owning his own boat. The young man went down to his local marina and saw that all the boats for sale cost much more than he could afford. In order to raise enough money to buy his dream boat, the young man took a job in the city as a banker and spent the next 30 years of his life working in an office, never setting foot in the sea. As often happens in life, he met a girl, got married, had a family, bought a house and car, etc. As hard as the man worked, there never seemed to be enough money to buy a boat or time to go sailing because something always came up. The man finally retired, but his wife thought she had married a banker and didn't share his dream of spending their life savings and retirement puttering around on a fishing boat. When she eventually died a decade later, the now older man sold his house, bought his dream boat and began to fish."

"So his persistence paid off," Karen said.

"It did," Adam continued. "One day in the harbor, the man met another fisherman his same age. They got to talking and it turned out this other man also dreamed of someday owning a boat and being a fisherman, but as a young man, he decided to start right away, bought a boat on credit and paid it off over several decades, using the income from the fish he caught to pay off his loans. Along the way, he met a girl who loved the sea, they got married and had a family. This second man and his family lived by the harbor and he spent every day of his life fishing."

"Same outcome, different approach," Karen said.

"Who was wiser and happier?" Adam asked. "The banker who waited his whole life to fulfill his dream, or the man who got right to it and spent his whole life living his dream?"

"The one who followed his passion," Natasha said. "The fisherman."

"That's a pretty obvious story," Adam said, "but it made me think about how my own life has changed course several times and it made me wonder whether I really enjoy what I'm doing. If I spend my whole life waiting to be happier someday in the future, I may miss my chance when it comes."

"John Lennon once said, 'Life is what happens while you're busy making other plans,'" Karen said. "This is your life right now, this moment. It's never too late to change."

But Adam wasn't really listening anymore. He was thinking of his own youth and the happiness he had squandered during his ambitious pursuit of fame and fortune. *She never told me she was pregnant,* he reflected. *I'm not sure what I would have done differently had I known at the time, but things could certainly have gone in a different direction. I can't go back and change the past, but I can do things differently going forward. So what should I change?*

Adam thought in silence for almost an hour, watching as the island of Bermuda slowly grew closer on the horizon and the sun crept higher in the sky.

Natasha and Karen chatted about their previous jobs, gossiped about their current situations and speculated about the future. Karen's early stint as a barista in Oxford had refined her coffee-making skills, but the free coffee wasn't enough of a perk to make up for the low pay, unpredictable schedule and uncertain advancement opportunities. She'd wanted a 9-to-5 job.

Natasha had excelled at textiles and fashion design from an early age, frequently winning awards for her hand-stitched clothes and stuffed animal toys, but as she matured into a young woman, her uncommon physical beauty promised a far more exciting career in modeling. Now that her modeling career was booming, she could use her celebrity to start her own clothing line.

Frank eventually came back on deck, clean-shaven and wearing a white, button-up shirt, khaki shorts and his signature black fedora. He was carrying a yellow flag.

"Got to look the part," he said, attaching and hoisting the flag up the main mast.

"What's that for?" Natasha asked, pointing at the flag.

"This is the quarantine flag or Q flag for short," Frank said. "We have to fly it when we enter a foreign port to signal we're healthy and request clearance or 'pratique' to the port."

"Which port?" Natasha asked. "I'd like to do some shopping and go to a spa."

"We'll sail in to Hamilton, which is also the capital," Frank said. "We can lay anchor just about anywhere, but I think we'll want to dock at the Royal Bermuda Yacht Club. I've been there before and they really take good care of you. And there are plenty of nice shops nearby."

"What's the procedure for customs?" Adam asked.

"Once we arrive, a customs official will come aboard and inspect the ship and crew," Frank said. "He or she will want to check our passports and make sure we're not bringing fruits, vegetables or illegal contraband onto the island. I'll tell them we're on vacation to the Bahamas and we're only stopping to restock our supplies. If you have cash or valuables worth more than $10,000 per person, you'll have to declare them and you'll probably have to pay a duty."

"What should I do about my passport?" Karen asked.

"That's right, you said you lost your passport," Frank said. "Without a passport, you'll probably have to stay on board the whole time we're in port, which shouldn't be very long. Personally, I think we should restock the ship and continue south as soon as possible, but it's possible we could stay a day or two and take in the local sights, if that's what everybody wants."

"I have to stay on the boat the whole time?" Karen asked. "I want to see Bermuda."

"Now that I think about it, Bermuda is technically a British Overseas Territory," Frank said, taking control of the helm from Adam. "Since you're a British citizen, you might be able to get a replacement passport here. They can usually turn those around in 24 hours if there's a rush, but that's under normal circumstances. You can ask the customs official when he gets here."

"Do you need money for supplies?" Adam asked. "I don't think we've talked about money this whole time. How much do you need from us? Do you want a deposit?"

"I'm glad you brought that up, Adam," Frank said. "It took us five days to get here from New York and it will probably take another week or so to get to the Bahamas. Normally I charge about $1,000 per person per day, plus fuel, food and other expenses, but in the spirit of reciprocity, we can make other arrangements that are mutually agreeable."

Karen stood up, excused herself and walked down to her cabin. Adam and Natasha whispered a few words to each other in confidence. When Karen returned, Adam spoke again.

"Do you take Visa?" he joked. "I'm afraid I'm a little short on cash at the moment. I can give you $500 now and more after we find a bank, or I can write you a check. You can hold my wristwatch as collateral until we settle things."

"I can give you $5,000 now and another $5,000 when we arrive in the Bahamas," Karen said, pulling several bundles of cash out of the zippered money bag she received from the bank.

The wind caught the corner of one of the bundles she was holding and the cash began fluttering loudly, but no bills blew away. She quickly stuffed the cash back in the money bag.

"Maybe I better give it to you downstairs," Karen said with a sheepish grin.

"Jesus, Karen, I thought we were the ones who got robbed," Adam cried. "How much cash do you have?"

"More than ten grand," she said casually. "Is there a stiff duty or something?"

"There's usually a tariff," Frank said. "It varies depending on the item, but it can be 25 or 35 percent on some items. If you forget to declare something and the inspectors find it, the government can seize your property."

"Karen, would you consider giving us a short-term loan?" Adam asked. "I know you're not a bank, but if you lent us some of your excess cash, you wouldn't have too much for customs and we could have a little spending paper for supplies and incidentals. Assuming the banks are open, we can pay you back this afternoon."

Karen looked at Adam, then at Natasha.

"Please, Karen?" Natasha asked. "I don't even carry cash anymore."

"Sure, I can loan you some money," she said. "I'm sure you would do the same for me."

***

The Bermuda customs official who came on board was wearing the customary suit jacket, tie, knee-length Bermuda shorts and knee-high black socks typical of professional islanders. The first question he asked was whether they had arrived for the big cricket cup. He explained that the island had regained electricity that morning after a few days without and things were still getting up to speed. But the weekend's cricket tournament was still on, he added.

Frank explained that they were stopping en route to the Bahamas and needed to restock their provisions, but that they were open to suggestions. The official took a quick tour of the vessel, checked all the cabins and then inspected and stamped their passports.

When the official got to Natasha's passport, he flipped through pages and pages of foreign entry stamps before he suddenly recognized her as a famous fashion model and proceeded to gush over her beauty, celebrity and the handsome ship and crew traveling with her. Natasha held herself with poise and grace, thanking the official for his kind words and hospitality. She was radiating beauty and confidence, partly due to secretly having a $3 million diamond brassier concealed beneath her clothes.

Karen had to explain why she was traveling without a passport or identification of any kind, recounting how she and her boss, Adam, had been held up at gunpoint at a major bank. The oncoming solar storm had necessitated a speedy exit, and she had had to rely on the generosity of her friends and shipmates to get to where she was now. The customs official invited her to come back with him to City Hall and the main governmental offices, where they could try to confirm her identity and see about issuing her a replacement passport.

Since he was already a member of a prestigious yacht club, Frank was invited to dock the *Reciprocity* at the Royal Bermuda Yacht Club. The club gave the 41-foot Hans Christian a prime berth right in front of the main entrance so that other boaters and passersby could admire her beauty. After carefully docking using only the sails and rudder, Frank connected his ship to the marina's power system and proceeded to recharge the ship's batteries. He took advantage of this break to take a nice, long nap in his cabin.

Adam and Natasha went ashore to shop and explore the island's wonders. Most of the historic buildings in the capital city had formal Victorian facades painted in bright pastel colors. Adam purchased a polyester/straw Bermuda hat and khaki Bermuda shorts that covered his knees, while Natasha bought a coral pink-colored dress and a matching sun hat.

After several failed attempts to use his credit cards, Adam went into the Bank of Bermuda to access his accounts, but discovered problems there as well. All of his accounts had somehow been locked, blocked or were simply inaccessible. The bank manager came out and apologized to Adam for the inconvenience, explaining that widespread power outages on the island and elsewhere had caused unprecedented problems and delays that were still being sorted out.

The Morgans found a local farmer's market and used some of their cash to restock the list of supplies and provisions Frank had made for the rest of their journey. As they were returning to the marina, they ran into Karen, who was on her way back from City Hall, accompanied by an official escort. Karen looked shaken, like she had just been told some upsetting news.

"What's wrong?" Natasha asked. "Didn't you get a replacement?"

Karen stared at Natasha for a moment in silence while she considered how to respond.

"They can't find my records," Karen answered. "I told them I e-mailed a copy of my passport to myself in case something like this happened, but that didn't help."

"They wouldn't let you look online?" Adam asked.

"I tried," Karen said. "Haven't you heard what happened?"

"What happened?" Natasha asked.

"It's not there," Karen said simply.

"What's not there?" Adam asked.

"The Internet," Karen said. "It's gone."

"What do you mean, 'it's gone'?" Adam asked. "You mean the website's down?"

"Yes," she said. "Everything is down. They said something happened during that storm last week that erased the Internet. When I say it's gone, I mean everything has been wiped clean, without a trace. This nice man is escorting me back to our ship, since I won't be able to get a new passport today.

"There's more," Karen said as she handed Adam a copy of the *Bermuda Royal Gazette*, Hamilton's daily newspaper. The paper she had was dated July 14, 2014. It was still warm from being freshly printed a few hours earlier. "You remember what I said about the media? You may want to sit down before you read this."

Adam took one look at the front page and gasped. It was crammed full of tragedy.

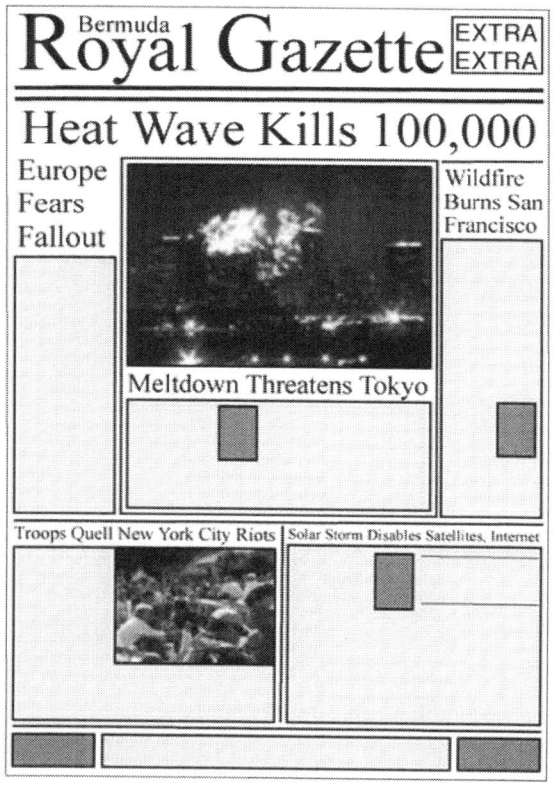

Bermuda Royal Gazette EXTRA EXTRA

Heat Wave Kills 100,000

Europe Fears Fallout

Wildfire Burns San Francisco

Meltdown Threatens Tokyo

Troops Quell New York City Riots | Solar Storm Disables Satellites, Internet

"No! No! No!" he yelled as he flipped through the newspaper.

> Heat Wave Kills 100,000, Europe Fears Fallout
> PARIS - Nearly 100,000 Europeans are feared dead following an oppressive heat wave last week that left millions of people without food, water or electricity.

Officials say the death toll could rise as relief efforts ...

Wildfire Burns San Francisco
SAN FRANCISCO - A deadly plane crash and wildfire swept through Silicon Valley and the San Francisco Bay area, destroying homes and businesses in Palo Alto, Cupertino and Mountain View. Millions of displaced residents were stupefied ...

Meltdown Threatens Tokyo
TOKYO - Major urban areas were evacuated last weekend, following a critical meltdown of one of Japan's largest nuclear reactors. Officials say the radiation has been contained, but long-term damages ...

Troops Quell New York City Riots
NEW YORK - The National Guard was called in to Manhattan last week to quash rioting, vandalism and widespread criminal activity, following last week's solar storm and stock-market crash. Initial reports of 100 deaths and damages exceeding $1 billion ...

Solar Storm Disables Satellites, Internet
HOUSTON - NASA scientists say recent worldwide power outages were caused by a solar superstorm that disrupted the Earth's electromagnetic field and severed international communication networks, including the world wide web. Astronauts aboard the International Space Station were exposed to dangerously ...

Adam had read all the news on the front page and turned to the inside.
"Wait!" Natasha cried. "What does it say about Aleks? Is he OK?"

Adam flipped back to the front, found the jump for the NASA story and followed it to the corresponding inside page, where he continued reading.

> ... high levels of cosmic radiation. With the United States still unable to execute a rescue mission in space, officials are relying on their Russian counterparts to orchestrate an emergency evacuation of the space station. When pressed for a rescue timeline, Russian officials declined to offer specifics, emphasizing the difficult and unique nature of the situation. Meanwhile, the astronauts aboard the space station report they are in good health and are making excellent progress restoring international satellites and global communication networks. Many international cities were still without power on Monday due to widespread disruptions in electrical transmission infrastructures ...
>
> Massive Bermuda-Bound Cruise Ship Missing
> HAMILTON - The MS Allure of the Seas has not been seen or heard from since last week's solar storm, U.S. Coast Guard officials said Sunday. The massive luxury cruise liner and its nearly 8,400 passengers and crew were last seen in the vicinity of the Bermuda Triangle on Wednesday after departing from New York City. Coast Guard officials say an international rescue mission is being planned, but unexpected complications from the power outage ..."

Adam turned the paper over to the sports page on the back and began to read.

> Bermuda Prepares For Cricket Cup Match Saturday
> HAMILTON - Global crises notwithstanding, Bermuda's die-hard cricket fans are eagerly awaiting this weekend's annual Cup Match, pitting the East End against the West End team. Thousands of spectators, live music, gambling ...

Adam closed the newspaper and sat down on the ground. His head was spinning from the news. There had been so much death and destruction throughout the world, yet he and his crew mates had managed to steer clear of all of it. *Where will we go now?* he wondered.

"Sir? Are you OK?" asked Karen's escort, a tall, dark-skinned, muscular local with strong arms and broad shoulders. Adam looked up at the enormous man and stood to face him.

"Pardon me, I've just had quite a shock," Adam said to the man. "Thank you for your concern. We can see Karen back to our ship if you'd like to head back."

"Sorry, sir. I've got orders to see her back onto the ship," the man said.

A nearby musician with a steel drum began playing a sweet, tropical melody on his large metal instrument. Adam turned to address Natasha and Karen.

"Let's get back to the boat and talk to Frank," he said. "He'll probably want to know what's happened."

"Maybe we shouldn't tell him," Karen suggested. "He might not want to know."

"I kind of wish I didn't know," Natasha said. "It feels like a loss of innocence. I hope Aleksandr is OK. Now I'm really worried about things."

"You both think so?" Adam asked. "OK, how about we give him the basics but we don't go into the details unless he asks. Does that sound fair?"

"Yes," the two young women said in unison.

***

When they climbed back aboard the *Reciprocity*, they woke Frank from his siesta and told him that they had all the necessary supplies and provisions. Due to widespread power outages and data retrieval problems, they were unable to get any money or a replacement passport for Karen, and it could be several days before circumstances changed.

"Should we wait here a few days or keep heading to the Bahamas?" Frank asked.

"There's nothing going on here other than rum swizzles, pink sand beaches and a cricket tournament this weekend," Adam said. "I think we should leave now."

"I'm ready to go, too," Karen said. "I don't think I can stand a week of island time."

"Me three," Natasha said.

"So I take it you're not going to be able to pay me today," Frank said.

"I said you can hold my watch as a deposit," Adam said, slipping off his gold wristwatch and offering it again.

"What time is it?" Frank asked.

Adam checked the dial on the luxury timepiece and noticed it was still stopped at 7:32.

"It just needs a new battery," he said sheepishly.

"That's a very nice watch, Adam, but it's not my style," Frank said. "I'm afraid I would break it, lose it or someone would try to kill me for it. Thanks, but no thanks."

"What do you want?" Adam asked.

Frank gave careful thought to his answer. *This is it. Ask and you shall receive.*

"Reciprocity," Frank replied.

"You mean the ship? Great! It's yours, after you take us to Stingray Cay," Adam said.

"What do you mean? You'll buy it for me?"

"I already bought it, before we left," Adam said, producing a paper with the receipt.

Frank studied the bill of sale and saw Niles Jones' signature transferring ownership of the *Reciprocity* to Adam Morgan.

"And you'll sign this over to me when we reach Stingray Cay?" Frank asked.

"Absolutely," Adam said, offering his right hand. "Consider it a gesture of goodwill."

"You've got a deal," Frank said, shaking Adam's hand. "Let me just tell the harbor master and we can depart with the next wind."

As he was making the necessary preparations for departure, Frank noticed a series of puffy, white cumulus clouds beginning to form on the horizon. *As long as those don't turn into cumulonimbus formations, we may be fine,* he thought as he located his departure checklist. *I wish I had a better weather forecast.*

Chapter 6

EARTH'S ATMOSPHERE - On board the ISS
Tuesday at 11:00:00 UTC

Aleksandr Manakova was halfway through his afternoon exercise routine on the Tranquility node's COLBERT treadmill when his B-42 Fortis Cosmonaut Chronograph wristwatch chimed the hour. He noted that it was now three o'clock in the afternoon in Moscow, yet it was still totally dark outside. *Fifteen minutes until they call,* he thought as he continued jogging.

American astronaut Chuck Wilson and Japanese astronaut Mizuho Sakaguchi floated into the Tranquility from the adjacent Unity node and positioned themselves in front of the node's large cupola window, taking care not to block Aleks' view.

"We thought we'd all watch the sunrise together," Mizuho said, adjusting the cupola's windows to make sure the shutters were fully extended. Chuck switched off the electric lights to the node, plunging the room into near darkness. Aleks continued jogging.

Outside the window, the Earth was without form and void. Darkness was upon the face of the deep waters of the South Pacific Ocean. A few moments later, an almost imperceptible blue glow began to form in the firmament, just above the dark horizon.

The three crew members watched as the thin, blue band of twilight began to widen and arch, revealing the curvature of the earth. Moments later, a bright orange pinpoint of light popped above the horizon as the International Space Station soared northeast over the surface of the earth at approximately 17,500 miles per hour or 28,000 kilometers per hour.

The warm, orange sunrise lasted for a few seconds as the light penetrated the Earth's troposphere — the layer of atmosphere that contained most of the planet's water vapor, clouds and precipitation — then quickly changed into a brilliant white glare once the astronauts' view of the star was no longer obstructed by moisture and gas.

As the sun continued its relative ascent, its radiance bathed the ocean with warmth and light, sending its rays far beneath the surface and changing the darkness into a glimmering blue stripe that widened with every passing moment. The space station's full acre of photovoltaic solar panels began to tilt and rotate to maximize the incoming sunlight.

"You know, the sun doesn't ever really rise or set," Chuck said. "It's all a matter of perspective. We're orbiting the earth and the earth is orbiting the sun, spinning on its axis. But from the ground, it appears the opposite: That the sun is orbiting the earth. You have to remove yourself from the earth to actually see it as it truly is."

"Or use your imagination," Aleks said. "Watching a sunrise from space is a rare and beautiful sight, but for me, the novelty has worn off. I am glad it continues to delight you."

"I think it's beautiful," Mizuho said as the Tranquility was bathed with natural light. "Even if we see it every 90 minutes, it's still magical to me. Just look at this view."

As they looked down at the earth, they saw a narrow isthmus of land connecting the two American continents and recognized the country of Panama. Dawn was just breaking in the Caribbean, hundreds of miles below, though most of the rest of the world's land masses were already basking in daylight.

For the first time in nearly a week, clouds were beginning to form again.

"See those clouds? It appears the Forbush decrease is over," Mizuho said.

"The what decrease?" Chuck asked.

"The Forbush decrease is a rapid decrease in cosmic ray intensity," Mizuho said. "I did my dissertation on it last year. It was discovered in the late 1930's by an American astronomer, physicist and geophysicist named Scott Forbush, who noticed a peculiar inverse relationship between cosmic ray intensity and coronal mass ejections during solar maximum. Basically, he found that the large coils of magnetic force fields released by coronal mass ejections push aside other galactic cosmic rays for a number of days, giving the earth an extra blanket of protection."

"And you said that had something to do with the clouds?" Chuck asked.

"Yes, the CME also released a proton storm that vaporized the aerosol molecules in our atmosphere, causing clouds everywhere to vanish," she said. "The CME didn't stop the normal evaporation cycle, though, so now we have a large build-up of humidity and precipitation forming, which could result in some pretty severe weather below."

"What about radiation?" Aleks asked. "My dosimeter reads a lower than average exposure. Did you say this Forbush decrease gave us extra protection?"

"It's possible," Chuck said. "Still, we should monitor each other for signs of acute radiation poisoning. Symptoms include nausea, fatigue, vomiting, low blood count ..."

A sudden wave of nausea swept over Mizuho and a second later she vomited. She was quick to cover her mouth, but a small amount escaped, floating about the cabin in several small spheres. The air inside the Tranquility instantly smelled like sour milk. Mizuho found a plastic bag and quickly captured her weightless puke, which she discreetly stowed.

"Are you OK?" Chuck asked. "What happened?"

"I don't know," she said. "Suddenly I felt extremely sick. But I feel better now."

Aleks stopped jogging and disconnected himself from the machine, floating freely again.

"Oh, I'm really sorry, Aleks," she said. "I didn't mean to barf where you're exercising."

"Do not be sorry," Aleks said, floating over to Mizuho and Chuck. "I am concerned. Perhaps we should all do a blood test to check for signs of radiation poisoning."

"I think that's a great idea," Chuck said, "... just to be on the safe side. I'm not sure what kind of treatment options we have available, but obviously our options are limited. Have you heard any word on a possible rescue mission?"

"I will check with Moscow again," Aleks said. "If we did emergency escape right now, we could land somewhere unexpected, most likely in the middle of the ocean. From there, a rescue could be very difficult. It is better to wait. While I have you both here, what is the status of our solar monitoring satellites? Are they operational yet?"

"HINODE, STEREO, ACE, SOHO, and SDO are all back online and are transmitting incredible scientific data. This will greatly improve our understanding of future coronal mass ejections and their aftereffects," Mizuho said as she spritzed the room with a lemon-scented air freshener. The sour smell in the room changed into a pleasant, citrus aroma.

"That's nice," Chuck said a few moments later. "It smells like pink lemonade."

"Japanese engineering," Mizuho said with a proud smile.

"Look at that!" Aleks shouted, pointing out the window.

The space station was passing almost directly over Bermuda, where it appeared a large tropical storm was beginning to form.

"I have to take a call from Moscow, but you should send out an alert on that storm as soon as possible," Aleks said to Chuck. "We should keep an eye on hurricane and typhoon formations everywhere and try to warn the people in advance."

"I was just about to do that," Chuck said as Aleks grinned and pushed off the wall with his feet, spinning out the porthole in an elegant corkscrew maneuver.

"Dasvidania," Aleks said as he passed out of sight into the Destiny Laboratory.

When he had left, Chuck turned to Mizuho.

"Are you feeling better?" he asked.

"I am now, but when you were describing the symptoms of radiation poisoning, I thought about the reactor meltdown in Tokyo and a sudden wave of nausea swept over me," she said.

"I'm really sorry about that," he said. "Have you heard from your headquarters yet?"

"Things are pretty chaotic and probably will be for weeks," she said. "The official statement is that everything was contained and minimal radiation was released. I am a little worried that I have not been able to contact my family yet. I'm going to go find the blood tests and other radiological equipment and begin some tests."

"OK, sayonara," Chuck said with a grin and pushed off the wall with his feet, just as Aleks had a few moments earlier. He attempted to swim in a spiral but lost his balance and bumped into the wall. "Needs practice," he quickly added before slipping out through the portal.

***

Aleksandr's head was still swimming several minutes after his briefing with Mishka.

Check up on your sister, Mishka had said in his deep voice. *Make sure she's OK.*

Mishka had told of many new developments in the world. Peace and international cooperation were being tested by suspicion, superstition and xenophobia. Moscow was unable to communicate with many areas of Siberia and widespread damage to the nation's electrical grid, oil pipelines and transportation infrastructure had shattered the country's confidence in their government. Shortages were reported everywhere and there were rumors of American war planes flying over parts of the country.

We need to show the people we are still in control, Mishka had said.

An emergency rescue mission was underway, he had said. A Soyuz rocket had lifted off from Kazakhstan several hours earlier and was due to arrive at the ISS in about two days with a replacement crew, replacement parts and equipment. The current ISS crew was to remain on board and continue repairing satellite communication systems until their relief arrived. Due to the short notice, the three crew members would all be Russian cosmonauts. It had also been decided that there would be minimal media coverage of the rescue mission until after Aleks and his crew members were safely back on earth. The official message would celebrate the merits of international cooperation, but the real glory would go to Mother Russia, he said.

Aleks was told that a total of 15 satellites had been spotted re-entering earth's atmosphere. A Russian weather satellite had crashed in the Kashmir region near the border between Pakistan, India and China, igniting old tensions and suspicions. The lack of trust and communication from all sides put the three nuclear powers on high alert for nuclear war. A Chinese military satellite had crashed in southern Canada near Calgary, Alberta. Two U.S. satellites had crashed on land, a scientific satellite in the Gobi Desert in northern China and a military satellite in the deserts of Saudi Arabia. The remaining 11 satellites that had been spotted streaking through the sky landed in an ocean or sea. Miraculously, there had been no reported injuries or deaths in any of the crashes.

Mishka told Aleks to refrain from discussing certain details with Chuck or Mizuho until they had been briefed by their respective countries, after which the three could confer.

There were other political developments in the world that Aleks should know, Mishka had said. A new power was rising in the Middle East. A commoner had stood atop the Saudi kingdom's mightiest minaret and claimed his freedom before the king, as well as the freedom of the kingdom itself to reject the status quo. Middle Eastern leaders had gloriously proclaimed Ibn Ali the new emperor of the Second Ottoman Empire, a massive territory that included all of the Middle East, Northern Africa, Central Asia and several large Southeast Asian countries.

Ibn Ali had humbly declined the honor, insisting on creating a democratic nation with elected representatives and a constitution that guaranteed free elections, freedom of speech, universal suffrage, universal health care and complete religious freedom. He was unanimously named president-elect of the new United Nations of Islam, and his first order was to halt all petroleum exports while the new nation's infrastructure was constructed.

They will probably give him the Nobel Peace Prize, even if it means the collapse of the modern world, Aleks thought as he pulled up an advanced missing persons search program on his laptop inside the Zvezda Service Module. *If he lives that long. If any of us live that long.*

Aleks though about Mishka's final orders. *Check up on your sister. Make sure she's OK.* He was attempting to perform a trace on Natasha's cell phone number, but he was having trouble remembering it. Her number had been saved in his computer, but all the hard drives in the space station — along with almost all the hard drives elsewhere on earth — had been erased during the storm and had been reset to their original factory settings. *Her phone's unique signature would still be valid, and as long as her phone was charged and turned on, it should be able to send and receive calls,* he thought. *Except I don't have the number. Did I write it down anywhere?*

He had an idea. He checked his personal locker and found the book he had just finished reading, Mikhail Lermontov's nineteenth-century classic "A Hero of Our Time." Natasha had written an inscription on the cover page and had included her phone number. *That's it!*

Aleks went back to his laptop, opened the missing persons search application and entered Natasha's cell phone number. The tracking program indicated her phone was in the middle of the Sargasso Sea in the North Atlantic. He couldn't find an available Russian satellite, so Aleks commandeered an international navigational satellite that was directly above her signal. He pulled up the live satellite image and zoomed in. He thought he saw a glimpse of a sailing yacht briefly passing beneath the clouds, but a storm was obscuring most of the picture. Aleks dialed the number and a few seconds later the digital call timer began counting.

"Hello?" answered a woman's voice. Aleks recognized his sister.

"Tosh! What are you doing in the middle of the ocean?" he asked in Russian.

"Mostly throwing up," she replied in Russian. "How do you know I'm in the ocean?"

"I am looking at a live satellite feed of your position," he said. "There is a huge storm forming all around you."

"Tell me something I don't know," she replied. "It's Aleks," she said to someone who was in the room, continuing in English. The phone's signal was beginning to fade. "He says we ... middle of a storm. Yeah, that's what ... said. Aleks, we're sailing ... Bahamas. Should be ... bout a week. Adam ..."

"Tosh, I am losing your signal," Aleks interrupted in Russian. "You are headed directly into the Bermuda Triangle. You need to ..."

The call ended abruptly and displayed the message "Call faded. Signal was lost." The timer stopped its count at 59 seconds.

Aleks looked out a nearby window at the view of the world spinning below. The ISS was currently somewhere above Iran or the Arabian Peninsula, but the geographical view was completely obscured by clouds. He could see flashes of lightening coming from the hundreds of storms that were spontaneously forming all over the earth. *Nature is adjusting to the changing conditions,* he thought. *It appears the political world is changing as well.*

***

Chuck finished talking on the phone with an administration official at the Johnson Space Center in Houston, Texas. The official said they were back online, but it was 6:30 in Houston and the morning shift didn't start until 8 a.m. He said he would personally notify NOAA about the tropical storm forming on the eastern seaboard, and said he would schedule a conference call to begin in two hours.

As soon as the call ended, Mizuho floated in to join him in the Destiny Laboratory.

"Hey you," Chuck said affectionately. "How'd your tests go? Find anything?"

"Well, I decided to do a complete blood count to check everything — red and white blood cell levels, platelets, you name it — and I discovered a trace of the hormone called human chorionic gonadotropin, or hCG for short."

"I'm not a biologist," Chuck said. "Is that good or bad?"

"hCG only occurs in pregnant women," Mizuho said. Her cheeks were flushed.

"Oh my gosh!" Chuck said, straightening out his arms and legs. "Congratulations, I think. I guess this complicates things a little. How are you feeling?"

"Scared. Tired. Nauseous. Confused. Mostly tired," she said. "Worried."

"Well, don't worry too much," he said. "Worrying is wasted energy. Things are going to be OK. Whenever something totally unexpected happens in life, I just think of the serenity prayer I learned a few years ago at a retreat. It goes something like this: 'God grant me the serenity to accept the things I cannot change, the courage to change the things I can, and the wisdom to tell the difference.' That's pretty good advice for just about anything."

"Thank you, and thanks for trying to cheer me up," Mizuho said, floating over to Chuck and giving him a peck on the cheek. "I'm really tired and think I'll go to bed. Good night."

"Goodnight," he replied, checking the time again. *My day's just beginning,* he thought.

As Mizuho was getting ready to climb into her sleeping bag inside the Kibo experimental module, she looked westward out one of the large, circular portholes at the rapidly setting sun over the archipelago of island nations that included Indonesia, Malaysia and Singapore.

Just above the darkening, curved horizontal limb of the Earth, a thin band of orange and yellow light channeled the sun's last rays as they filtered through the troposphere. Above the orange band, a thinner, pink region of atmosphere called the stratosphere glowed almost white, followed by a wider, blue region that contained the planet's middle and upper atmospheres. Above the blue band, there was nothing but the dark, empty void of space.

Mizuho watched the swift sunset with childlike innocence and wonder as the evening's colors blended and then were reduced to a fading, blue light. A few seconds later, it was gone.

About the Author

Jake Blake has been an avid fan of science fiction for decades and has eagerly awaited making his debut into this popular and classic genre. His frequent travels around the world and his lifelong fascination with learning and mastering new skills continue to inspire his work and adventures.

"Sunburned" was created using a laptop with an Internet connection, a library card and a little imagination.

Jake lives in the United States on a quiet farm in Toledo, Washington with his family and pets. This is his first novel.

Publisher's note: "Sunburned" is the first of a series of science-fiction adventure novels by Jake Blake. To find out what happens to Adam and the other characters from "Sunburned," look for the next book in the series. Coming soon, "Collapse" follows the characters and events from the first book as they face terrible storms and enormous competition for supplies and resources.

Copyright © 2012 Morgan Online Media. All rights reserved.

Made in the USA
Charleston, SC
03 December 2012